"Jennifer, please stop! My beautiful . . . dearest girl . . . I cannot bear to see you cry."

At this, her eyes opened very wide. "You—you're weeping, too . . ." she gulped.

"I know," he said. And lost to everything but her grief, added with a tender smile, "You hit me in the eye."

"Oh." One hand lifted to caress his cheek. "My . . . poor dear . . ."

He could no more have stopped from turning his head than have stopped the sun in its journey; no more have refrained from kissing that soft white hand than have ceased to love her.

Gazing into his eyes, reading the adoration for her, Jennifer was as enchanted as he. She lifted her face.

The village idiot bowed his head and kissed the lady of Castle Triad, and, for a heavenly stolen moment, the world and its problems ceased to be. . . .

Also by Patricia Veryan:

Published by Fawcett Books

A SHADOW'S BLISS

Patricia Veryan

FAWCETT CREST • NEW YORK

A Fawcett Crest Book
Published by Ballantine Books
Copyright © 1994 by Patricia Veryan

Library of Congress Catalog Card Number: 93-44038

ISBN 0-449-22343-4

This edition published by arrangement with St. Martin's Press, Inc.

Manufactured in the United States of America

First Ballantine Books Edition: April 1995

10 9 8 7 6 5 4 3 2 1

Some there be that shadows kiss
Such have but a shadow's bliss.
—Shakespeare
The Merchant of Venice

❧ *Author's Note* ❧

Cornwall, the southwestern "claw" of England, was for centuries rather astonishingly isolated from the rest of the British Isles. She was not entirely cut off from the world, however. Despite her sometimes inhospitable coasts, shipping reached her. As time passed, there arrived conquerors from Rome, immigrants from Iberia, Celts from France, Mediterranean merchants, Irish voyagers, sailors from Spain. Some came by choice, some were cast up on Cornish beaches by the violence of wind and waves. All brought with them their gods, their spells and incantations, and as Cornwall remained remote and overland travel difficult, the superstitions became ever more a part of the way of life.

Two miles from Veryan Bay lies the charming village of Veryan, where are five cottages, each circular, and each surmounted by a cross, the idea having been to provide no corners in which Satan might hide. I knew of this, but although I am British born and lived in London until after World War II, I had not realised when I started researching this story just how deeply entrenched were the myths and legends and superstitions of the county. I was, in fact, intrigued to discover that many beliefs and rituals I had assumed to have vanished with the eighteenth century, actually persisted even into the 1940s.

If, therefore, kind reader, you should feel inclined to raise an eyebrow at some of the episodes in this book, I beg you to believe they are not entirely the products of my imagination.

I also assure you that I have left out a great deal more than I have included!

❧ *Chapter* 1 ❧

England, Spring, 1746

Earlier in the day the advent of spring had brought sunshine to warm the modest stone church on the cliffs, but clouds had come in to chase away that warmth, and with the approach of evening the small room behind the sanctuary was chill.

The wind was rising, and from the beach came the measured booming that told of Atlantic breakers pitting their might against this southernmost toe of England. These were the only sounds to break the silence as one of the men in the room struggled with his thoughts, and the other waited tensely for him to speak.

The light was fading, and although the only window faced east, away from the gales, a cold draught stirred the faded curtains. Father Mason rose from the bedside. A short, sturdy man with a mane of white hair, his strong face was troubled as he crossed to a chest against the wall and took up a tinder box. He lit one of the two candles, drew the curtains, and carried the candlestick back to the bed. Standing there, he looked down at the man who watched him so desperately. A young face, the light brown hair tumbled and untidy against the pillows, the grey eyes sunken into dark hollows, and the cheekbones high and gaunt above cheeks that were also sunken and marked by lines of suffering.

The priest asked gently, "How old are you, Jonathan?"

"I think . . . perhaps five and twenty, Father." The words

came haltingly, and with a timidity oddly at variance with the strong lines of nose and jaw, and the resolute chin.

Father Mason shook his head, stifled a sigh, and set the candlestick on a table near the bed. He sat down again, and muttered, "So young, to carry such a weight of responsibility. You must have been very good at your chosen profession."

"Not ... good enough." The words were spoken painfully, and the sick man closed his eyes and jerked his head away, as if seeking to escape an unendurable memory.

"Do you truly wish to atone?" asked the priest.

The thin face turned to him again. There was the glitter of tears in Jonathan's shadowed eyes, and he said with faint but passionate intensity, "If only I could! I ... lack the ability to turn time ... backwards, alas."

"You have the future, my son."

"Do you mean a—a penance, sir?"

The priest did not at once reply. His lips pursed, he stared at the flickering flame of the candle, and when he spoke it was to ask another question. "Have you decided where to go when you leave me?"

"Only that it must be far inland. I cannot—I cannot bear the sounds of the sea."

"Not surprising."

The sick man recoiled slightly, but said nothing through another pause.

"Where—inland?" asked the priest. "Do you mean to try and find your family? You said you recall a lady, I believe? Wife? Sister? Mother?"

"I don't ... know. My life before we sailed is ... a jumble. Bits and pieces with no seeming connection. Besides, if there was anyone they would not want me. Not ... now." A long thin hand was stretched out; the tormented eyes fastened to the priest's stern countenance imploringly. "Father, I beg you. What must I do? Only tell me."

"I am an unimportant, and not very learned man." The priest took that outstretched hand and then released it as though the contact was distasteful to him. "I am not omniscient."

"You are a man of God."

"Say rather that I am His most humble servant. I cannot grant you absolution, Jonathan. Even were I to point you the way that—were I in your shoes—I would take, my judgment might well prove faulted."

"Point, sir! I cannot live with ... with my conscience and not try to make amends."

"So be it. First, then, you will not go inland." Father Mason heard the hiss of indrawn breath, and acknowledged, "It will be hard for you, I know. But the sounds you so dread will be a reminder of your guilt, and your vow."

"Dear God! Better I had died!"

'Much better,' thought the priest, but he said inexorably, "Will you swear to this? That until you believe with all your heart that you have made atonement you will stay on this coast? Within sight and sound of the ocean?"

"That must mean for ... all my life!" Wretchedly, Jonathan muttered, "Father, how can I *ever* hope to atone?"

With rather brutal candour the priest said, "Probably never. You can only try. Well? Shall you take the vow?"

"Is there—more?"

"You must forget your former station in life, and neither seek nor accept aid from family or friends, if they should chance to find you. You will live here, among the poor, abandoning all pride and showing always a gentle humility."

The thin fingers tightened. In a flare of indignation, Jonathan exclaimed, "But I would be a misfit! They'd never accept me!"

"Your cultured way of speech, certainly, would cause most simple folk to look upon you with suspicion. But they are suspicious of anyone not born in Cornwall."

"And for a man of my size to behave as you suggest must earn only contempt!"

"Which you do not deserve ..."

Jonathan tensed, then acknowledged wearily, "Which I deserve. But—Father, I may defend myself if—if the need should arise?"

"Do you say you still feel you have a right to raise your

hand 'gainst another human being?" The priest sounded shocked.

After a moment, barely audible, came the response. "No. No, I have no such . . . right."

"A greater Man than you or I said, 'whosoever shall smite thee on thy right cheek, turn to him the other also.' "

"I—I don't know if I can be that humble, Father. Am I . . . would I be allowed to work?"

"For your food, or lodging. But not for money—unless it is taken to help others. Any kind deed you can perform, any kind word spoken, may ease the weight of your guilt. And in this manner alone may you use these." Father Mason touched the fist that was so tightly clenched on the blanket. "To the defence of those who are abused or brutalised. But never—no matter what the provocation—*never* in your own defence!"

He drew back, and there was silence again, while the shadows deepened in the corners and the room became ever more chill.

At length, Jonathan said, low voiced, "You have been very good, sir. To take me in, and—and care for me. The men who found me would do nothing."

"Cornish folk are a fierce and proud lot, I'll own. But they've been betrayed often down through the centuries. They have no love for strangers. Which will not smooth your path, I fear."

Jonathan asked hesitantly, "Do you think I shall ever be . . ."

"Forgiven?"

"No. I don't ask that much. But—if I could just be granted . . . some peace of mind."

"Conscience is a merciless taskmaster, but perhaps, with time, you will be, my son. Certainly, your physical health improves. You may like to wait until you are fully recovered before you take such a solemn oath. It would be—"

"No, Father. I'll take it now."

The priest stood. "As you wish."

He left the small room where the sexton had lived, when he'd been able to afford a sexton, and walked in his digni-

4

fied way into the sanctuary to get the beautiful old Bible that was used only for the various services and on such occasions as this one. Taking it reverently from the lectern, he paused, his thoughts on the man he had just left. Such a tragedy, that so fine a young fellow, who had certainly enjoyed all the advantages of birth and breeding, should have made such a shambles of his life. And ended so many others!

"Some peace of mind," he muttered.

And, shaking his head, he carried the Bible back into the cold little bedchamber.

Summer, 1748

August had been blown in on a great gale which lashed the southeast coast from The Naze to Selsey Bill, and created havoc as far inland as London and Reading. Trees were uprooted, roads flooded, bridges washed away, and countless buildings stripped of roofs and chimneys. Within a week the weather did an about-face and became more normal. Temperatures soared and the southland sweltered. London was stifling, and all who could manage to do so abandoned the Metropolis in favour of country estates or the seaside.

After its fashion, the far west country followed a different pattern. Devonshire basked in springlike warmth and gentle breezes. In Cornwall the wind blew strong off the Atlantic, but the sun shone benevolently on the great breakers as they exploded in clouds of white spray against Penwith's rugged rocks and cliffs.

Perched atop those cliffs was Roselley Village. Actually, it was more a hamlet than a village; a widespread scattering of gaunt granite cottages, a small tavern, and a few stunted trees twisted into grotesque shapes by the constant storms that the ocean sent to batter the land. Atop a hill a mile to the north loomed the mighty tower of Castle Triad. Across the moors to the east a tall and crumbling chimney was all that could be seen of the once prosperous Blue Rose Tin Mine, now silent and abandoned.

On this bright morning the Widow Newlyn was making her way along the wide dirt path that served Roselley as a road. She hummed merrily to herself, seemingly unperturbed by the flapping of her voluminous skirts, or the crinkly dark hair that escaped her cap to be whipped about her round face. There were few people to be seen. Many of the tinners who had been put out of work when the mine closed down had left the Hundred, others eked out a living at the Castle, or hung about the Morris estates, a dozen miles to the south, hoping for a few hours' labour.

A tabby cat sat on the doorstep of the Lawney cottage, its eyes closed as it cleaned one front paw industriously. The widow paused, watching the little creature. "Over the ear!" she murmured, nodding. "Rain. That's no surprise, puss."

Three boys darted, squealing, from behind a cottage, confronted the cheerful little woman, and with guilty gasps stopped so abruptly they all but fell over themselves.

" 'Tis the Widow Newlyn!" piped the smallest among them.

His voice appeared to restore the use of their legs. They averted their eyes and fled.

"Rascals! You should be in the school," Mrs. Newlyn called, in the pleasant singsong that is the way of Cornish folk.

The boys had come up from the left, but each had taken pains to pass on her right, and she shook her head rather ruefully. One must, she knew, always pass a witch on the right.

The sound of hammering hung loud on the air, and she followed it, halting briefly outside Mr. Gundred's cottage to steady herself against the sturdy post from which hung a sign proclaiming simply SHOP. There were no windows on this side, of course, but the gust that had rocked the widow also blew the front door open. Several men gathered about the hearth looked up. The proprietor hurried to shut the door, and greeted the widow genially. In the spring she had relieved his little daughter of terrible nightmares, and he was grateful.

"Put the sign back up, has ye?" she said redundantly.

"Aye."

"I wonder you don't just paint it on your wall."

"I'll not bow to the wind," he declared. "Besides, what'd me mates have to bet on if I gave in?"

"A penny says it'll be down by Friday."

He nodded. "A penny you've bet," he said, and bade her good day.

Noah Holsworth's was the northern-most cottage of the village, and quite a distance from Gundred's shop, its nearest neighbour. It was to Noah's that Mrs. Newlyn was bound, but reaching the cottage, she changed her mind and went on past to where the inward curve of the cliffs marked the start of Bridget Bay. A small stream flowed busily from the high moors to hurl itself over the edge in a tiny waterfall, known locally as Devil's Ladder. From here to far past Castle Triad the cliffs were too sheer to be scaled unless a man had climbing equipment, but at this point the stream had worn a slight depression in the face of the rock, and a few reckless young men had struggled to the top, though more had fallen in the attempt. An ascent could only be tried in dry weather when the stream was reduced to a trickle, and even then it was treacherous, as the winds could blow up very suddenly and with devastating force.

The widow paused at the very edge of the cliff, but her intent was far removed from climbing. She sought about for a leaf, discarding several until a large yellow one pleased her. She held it to her lips between both hands, muttering in the ancient tongue now all but forgotten, and at length placed the leaf carefully in the stream. It was gone in a flash, and in her eagerness to see what became of it, she lost her balance and had to hop frantically to regain it.

"Phew!" she exclaimed. "Thank you, wind from the west! Now—where did my Informer go?" She peered again, but this time took the precaution of doing so on hands and knees. She had expected to see the leaf in one of the tidal pools on the sands. Her eyes were keen, but although she narrowed them and sought about painstakingly, there was no sign of the "Informer." "You are most disobliging," she grumbled. "You know very well this is the only day this side of the next full moon that I can cast you off! You are yellow enough, goodness knows, which is why you were chosen, since yellow can be seen for a greater distance than any other— Good gracious!" About to give up her search, she checked, inspecting a clump of dandelions on a small outcropping. "Is that you? Oh, well then, you are a silly!" She stood, brushing off her skirts, then peered downward once more, and admonished sternly, " 'Tis no use hiding yourself in those dandelions. I see you, and you are quite mistaken! Were there any strangers about, I should know. Especially *that* many strangers! Stuff and nonsense!"

She was still disgruntled when she returned to Holsworth's cottage, and made her way around to the leeward side. Two men toiled busily here. One she knew to be her own age, which was five and forty. The other was younger, but his age she did not know, since Jonathan—or Jack, as most folks named him—couldn't recall exactly what it was.

". . . and even if they do hear, they don't listen, so what good is it?" Noah Holsworth's mighty voice matched his mighty frame. He was not as tall as his companion, but his breadth of chest and shoulders and a pair of muscular legs conveyed an impression of power, only slightly mitigated by the fact that a mining accident had taken his left hand and wrist.

"Hold it steady, Jack," he roared, "so I can whack it square." He raised his hammer, only to emit a howl of frustration as his helper was staggered by the wind, and lost his grip on the board. "Curse and confound it," raged Holsworth, his deep-set pale blue eyes glinting. "I said *steady*! Can you not even—" He broke off as the younger man drew back, his head ducking as though in anticipation of a blow.

The Widow Newlyn clicked her tongue impatiently, and hurried along the path between the neatly kept rows of flowers and vegetables that struggled to survive in the shelter offered by the cottage. "Might have known I'd find you bellering, Noah Holsworth," she scolded. "Great brute that ye be! And Jack half your size."

Holsworth reddened, and snatched off his wool cap, sub-jecting his thick greying hair to the mischief of the wind. He said uneasily, "Half my size he may be, Widder, but he's taller'n me, and nigh half my age I'll warrant, *and* has both arms, ye'll mind. 'Sides"—he raised the steel hook that served him in lieu of a left hand and rapped it gently on the other man's broad but thin shoulders—"he do know as I mean him no harm, does ye not, Jack?"

The wind-blown fair head lifted again. A pair of grey eyes met the widow's and a deep but diffident voice said, "My fault, Mistress Newlyn. Mr. Noah's kind. I'm just—I'm clumsy, is all."

"Then kind Mr. Noah won't mind me taking you off, will he?" she said, with a warm smile for the man she called Jack, and a toss of the head for Holsworth.

"Taking him off?" echoed the big man with considerable indignation. "Ye did but now lend him to me! And full well you know how hard it be for me to work without no helper."

"Fiddle," said the widow. "You've got your hook, which is worth two helpers!"

"Even so, I'd be main glad to hear why you need him so desperate urgent."

"You've had him slaving on your silly boat for a week, and—"

Holsworth, who had just replaced his cap, now tore it off, threw it on the ground and jumped on it. "*Silly boat* she calls it!" An impassioned wave of his hammer took in the low, wheeled platform behind him, on which was braced a rather odd partially completed structure that re-sembled a very large and high-sided longboat. "Silly boat! By the pyx! And did not Mr. John Wesley himself inspire me to build it? Is it the great holy man she'll be mocking with her 'silly boats'?"

Jonathan intervened at this, his voice a little surer. "Mrs. Newlyn meant no offence, Mr. Noah. I'm bound to—"

"Aye! Bound to her because she took ye in. And so you

9

should be. But there's no reason it must make you her slave forever! You were promised to help me with my great task. 'Tis not fair you should be lured away when I most need you!"

The widow gave a deprecatory snort but wandered closer to the object under construction, and, peering at it curiously, spoke as though she addressed it. "He heard little Mr. Reverend John Wesley tell the tale of the Ark, and because his name chances to be Noah, he must think himself called to build another one! A fine piece of foolishness, when there's so much else a big strong man might do with his days. Has he not heard of the rainbow? And of the promise made to us by the Lord never to send another such flood?"

Holsworth crossed his arms, and growled, "Not *such* another, maybe. But there's enough evil right here in Roselley to make the Lord take a fancy to send a *small* flood. Noah my name be, right enough. And when I heard Mr. Wesley, I knowed what I was called to do. Let them mock as will."

Despite his shabby clothing and extremely dramatic stance, there was a dignity about the big man. The widow's eyes softened, and she said in a kinder tone that she was bound to admit Mr. Holsworth was making his "ark" good and strong, and that she had intended no mockery. "Besides, it looks to me like you're nigh to finishing. The outside, at least."

Holsworth groaned something having to do with women and boat building, and added that he was nowhere near to finishing.

"Well, I'm sorry for you," said the widow. "But I promised Miss Jennifer last week that Jack could help with her schoolhouse. Very likely Charlie Jones or some others not digging now can lend you a hand here."

Jonathan had been waiting patiently, but at this his head jerked up and his eyes lost their meekness and became very bright. He asked eagerly, "Shall I go now, ma'am?"

The widow nodded. "Hurry along. And—no more trouble, mind!"

Watching him stride off, Holsworth grumbled, "There's reluctance for ye! I wonder he don't run!" Mrs. Newlyn, who had formed her own opinions, smiled faintly but said nothing, and he went on, "Nor I don't see why Charlie Jones couldn't go to Miss Jennifer, and Jack stay with me."

"I'll tell you why. 'Tis because Miss Jennifer pays me more for his work than you do. And she asked for him. Pointed. Which isn't to be wondered at, seeing as he's got a far better gift for carpentering than has Charlie."

"I won't argue that. But his head's full of worms, and for Miss Jennifer to look on him kindly don't help him none with the other men."

"Miss Jennifer has a kind heart. Which is more than you could say for the rest of the Britewells. And Jack's head is *not* full of worms. He may be a mite forgetful at times, but—"

"A sight more'n a mite! And a sight more'n forgetful! They don't call him Crazy Jack for nought. I wonder Sir Vinson or her brothers allow a lovely young woman to have a man working down at the schoolhouse who does strange things and then can't recollect ever doing of 'em! Or who can't even recall his own name, nor where he comes from! He's thin now, 'count of he was so ill. But he's tall, and a sight stronger'n he seems. Oh, don't look so curdled! I like him well enough. And when he knows what he's about he's a good worker. Besides, if he should run amok with me, I could handle him. But Miss Jennifer shouldn't take such chances." He tapped his temple significantly. "You can't never tell, with his kind."

Flushed and angry, the widow snapped, "What ugly things to say about such a fine young chap who was likely ill-wished by—"

At these dread words the rugged might of Noah Holsworth seemed to quail. He cast an apprehensive glance over his shoulder and interrupted urgently, "Softly, woman! Softly! If that suspicion gets about, folks might start looking for the witch that ill-wished him!"

"And settle on the Newlyn witch, eh?"

"I ain't one with them as thinks you're a witch, and ye know it. You've cures and knowings as other folks hasn't, but you're a good woman, for all your silly tongue. Have some sense do, and don't set folks to whispering more'n they are already!"

She sniffed and said defensively, "It wasn't me who shouted that the lad's likely to run amok! I might have known I'd be abused for coming here! A lady can no more rely upon a man who builds arks, than on a yellow leaf!"

Noah Holsworth set his jaw and girded up for battle.

He was to be near her again! Wonder of wonders, she had asked that he come to help her! There were other men she might have called on. Bigger, stronger men, who were her own people. Tinners, who'd laboured long hours in the mine and now found time hanging heavily on their hands. Lawney, or Worden, or even Ben Blary, who never had a kind word for anyone—all of them would jump at the chance to work for her. Everybody loved her. Who could fail to love so gentle and beautiful and gracious and alto- gether adorable a lady?

Such the thoughts of a man crushed under a heavy bur- den; a man without hope, yet who now strode purposefully towards the abandoned old cottage that perched on the very edge of the cliffs at the south end of Roselley. Miss Jennifer Britewell had appropriated the cottage for a school, and three days a week she came and gave of her time to in- struct the village children. She would be there now, patient and gentle with her pupils. He could picture her, tall and slender, standing by the desk he had built for her, the sun- light awaking golden gleams among the thick brown curls that clustered below her dainty cap, her tender mouth grave, but a smile lurking in the eyes that were as blue as the skies over Suez.

There had been a smile in those eyes the first time he saw her, five months ago. She had come to the Widow Newlyn's cottage, bringing soups and jellies for the beaten and half-starved wreck of a man who'd managed to crawl into the widow's garden to die. When he'd seen her lovely face hovering over him, he'd thought for a moment that he really had died. And then she'd said in that dear and com- passionate voice, "No, pray do not try to speak yet. You must lie quietly and get better, and then you can tell us who you are, and from whence you have come." He had lost his heart in that moment. Completely, and forever. Scarcely an hour had passed since but that he thought of her. Never a night that she was not in his prayers. And always he knew that he daren't betray by the slightest sign how he worshipped her. She was the daughter of a proud and powerful nobleman. He was—what he was.

He'd stayed in Roselley, knowing he would seldom be granted the sight of her. But when he'd recovered to the point that he was able to make some repairs to the Widow Newlyn's cottage, Miss Britewell had admired his work. After she decided to start the little school, he'd been commissioned to build her desk, and later had made the student desks. Thus, he was able to see her far more often than he'd hoped. Sometimes she had come to watch him work. Always on those joyous occasions, she spoke to him kindly. At times she questioned him about his past, which threw him into a panic, but when she saw that he was distressed, she would unfailingly turn the subject. His devotion grew ever deeper, and like all lovers, he had his dreams. Even when he indulged such folly, however, he did not allow himself to go so far as to envision some rosy future in which he could declare his love. But there was the hope that he might be of real use to her someday ... Perhaps, come between her and some terrible peril, like one of the knights of old who had ridden along these very cliffs, and—

His reverie was interrupted by squeals and giggles of boyish glee. He checked, and turned aside, walking between two cottages where a group of boys were apparently thrusting something into a sack. There was a deal of shrill squawking and movement from their victim, and whoops of triumphant laughter as the top of the sack was tied.

Jonathan asked, "What have you got there?"

Quietly as he had spoken, the result was consternation. Four scared faces whipped around to him. The sack was thrust behind the back of the biggest boy, whom he recognised as Isaac, Ben Blary's husky thirteen-year-old.

"Aw, it's only Crazy Jack," said Isaac contemptuously. "Stay back, looney, or I'll tell me Pa, and you know what his boot feels like. You oughter."

"I also know he wants you to learn to read and write. You should all be in school."

One of the smaller boys uttered a yelp and made a dash for safety. Jonathan caught him with a quick movement, but kept his eyes on Isaac whom he'd found in the past to have an unerring aim with stones. "What is in the sack, Young Porter?"

Young Porter, so named to distinguish him from his elder brother, whined, "It's just a silly bird."

Albert Pughill, a miniature version of his belligerent father, said, "Me mum paid a sailor man a penny for it, but it don't sing and it don't talk, like he promised."

"It's got a withered foot," put in Isaac. "It's not good for nothing, 'cept maybe a feather duster."

"You'd as well let it go, then," said Jonathan.

"Well, we ain't," jeered Albert. "We're going to put it to the cliff. All no-good things gets put to the cliff." His dark eyes challenged Jonathan's grey ones, and he added, "Or they should."

The thought of anything being trapped alive in a sack and tossed from the cliffs into the relentless sea sent a chill down Jonathan's spine.

Young Porter gave a kick and a wriggle and broke free. Whooping, they all made off.

Jonathan called, "I'll buy him from you."

Those magic words stopped them, but they snatched up stones before turning back.

Isaac shouted, "How much?"

"A penny."

A hushed silence.

Willie Worden, who was eight, with hair like a flame and a thousand freckles, said an awed, "Ye never would! Why would he, Isaac?"

"He don't know why," declared Isaac. "Likely, he don't know where he is this very minute!"

14

Strategically positioned behind Isaac, Young Porter agreed, "He don't know *nuthink*!"

"He don't know how to fight like a man," put in Willie Worden.

Albert said, "Me Pa says any man what won't stand up fer hisself ain't a man. He's nothing but the shadow of a man. Let's see your money, Shadow Man."

Jonathan dug out one of the two pennies he'd intended to give to Mrs. Newlyn.

"Throw it here," demanded Isaac.

"Give me the sack first. Then you'll get your money."

Isaac muttered to his cronies, and four grubby hands held four good-sized stones ready. Stepping forward, Isaac held out the sack cautiously. Jonathan offered the penny on the palm of his hand. Isaac snatched the coin, then jumped away, but Jonathan moved faster, and seized the sack.

For once frightened of this despised individual, Isaac let out a screech, retreated a few paces, and he and his cohorts hurled their rocks.

Jonathan ducked, but attempting also to protect the hapless captive in the sack, he was not altogether successful.

❧ *Chapter 2* ❧

Jennifer Britewell watched her ten students file politely from the cottage and metamorphose on the steps into ten bundles of unrestrained exuberance. Amused, she gathered pencils and papers from the desks Jack had fashioned with his skilled hands. He should be here at any minute, unless he was already waiting outside. The shouting took on a different note. A small frown chased the smile from her eyes as she hurried to the door.

Jack was coming, one hand clutching a sack in front of him, and the other flung up against the shower of stones that a group of hooting boys hurled at him.

Jennifer ran onto the steps. "Stop that at once!"

The children scattered.

Jonathan lowered his arm. There was blood on his face near the old scar that angled across his right temple. Jennifer called, "Isaac! Willie! Albert! Young Porter! Come here!"

Instead, they ran faster, silent now, knowing they would be punished.

She said angrily, "Those wretched boys! Oh, what a nasty cut! Can you walk up the steps?" She took Jonathan's arm. "Lean on me."

His head hurt, but he was quite capable of walking. One did not turn away a taste of paradise however, and, enraptured, he leaned on her.

She guided him to her own chair, then wet her handkerchief from the water pitcher and set to work. The cut was jagged and had bled profusely, but she was accustomed to tending the hurts of her father and her three brothers, and was not squeamish.

Her hands were very gentle. Enveloped in a sweet fragrance, Jonathan could not resist watching her from under his lashes. She was bending over him, engrossed in her task, her lips slightly parted. The sweet swell of her bosom was just under his chin. A wave of longing swept him. She was so close; so tender and delicate and beloved. His arms ached with the need to hold her. He clenched his hands tightly, and fought against betraying himself, knowing that such behavior would not only be dishonourable, but would put an end to any chance of seeing her in the future.

Vaguely aware that she had said something, he smiled up at her.

"Hold the handkerchief," she repeated gently. "Can you?"

He murmured a dreamy, "Thank you. But I must keep the sack."

Compassion came into her eyes. She took up his left hand, pressed the rag into it, and guided it to the injury. "Hold it there."

"Oh. Yes—of course." He flushed in embarrassment. "How stupid I am."

"A trifle confused, perhaps," she said kindly, and never dreamed how narrowly she escaped being swept into two yearning arms, and kissed and sighed over.

Yet knowing none of this, as always, the mystery of him intrigued her. She drew up one of the children's benches and sat on it, watching him. The boys had been shouting the same abuse: "Looby!" "What's yer name?" "D'you know where ye are, Crazy Jack?" And Isaac Blary had yowled something about a shadow of a man and a feather duster making a good pair. She was sorry for this tall shy man, but she could not judge him the village idiot, as her brother Howland named him. Admittedly, he was unable to recall much of his past, and several times he had apparently suffered a complete loss of awareness. Once, while working on the schoolroom desks, he had suddenly rushed outside and climbed to the roof; and on another occasion he'd called Noah Holsworth "Bobby" and ordered him to "be more careful with the lady's portmanteaux!" Afterwards he'd seemed exhausted, and had denied all knowledge of the incidents. Blary and Pughill and a few other villagers had wanted to have him driven away, but she had interceded with her father in his behalf. Despite those odd lapses, and the humble manner that had made him a joke and a pariah, she found intelligence in the well-cut features, integrity in the clear grey eyes, and strength in the firm line of the jaw.

He darted a glance at her, then his eyes fell away with the familiar bashful humility, and he started to untie the string from the sack he held. At once, the cut started to bleed again.

"Let me." Jennifer untied the string, then drew back with a gasp as a small pale blue bird flew out with a great flapping of wings, only to drop onto Jonathan's hand.

"Poor little fellow." He stroked the tiny chest with one long finger. "You're safe now."

"Is that the bird Mrs. Pughill bought from the sailor man?" Jennifer peered at it curiously. "Why, how very pretty it is. I never saw such a creature."

"It's called a parakeet. They're numerous in—" He bit back the word *India*.

Accustomed to such amputated sentences, she said smoothly, "Pughill was very angry because his wife bought it and didn't notice it was faulted. How come you to have it?"

"Ow!" said Jonathan. "Why the ungrateful rascal! It pecked me!"

"Should it be grateful to you? Why?"

His amused grin faded. He said in a low voice, "The boys meant to put it to the cliff."

"Those cruel little savages! Oh dear. I should not say such things. They're only children."

"I think," he murmured shyly, "we're all born savages. We have to be taught honour, compassion, integrity. And—

and if we're not taught those things, we continue to be savages."

She was seldom able to get so much from him, and, pleased, she said, "Yet many men who *are* properly bred up still are cruel and abuse the helpless. How do you account for that?"

"Perchance Old Nick is stronger in some." He smiled. "I don't say that teaching banishes the violent side of our nature. Only that it shows us how to control it. It's always there, just below the civilised exterior we show the—the—" Startled by his own volubility, he broke off, and stared at her shoe.

The blow on the head must have weakened his defences somewhat, she thought, and she said mildly, "You certainly control your own impulse to violence. Sometimes ... too well, perhaps."

His gaze lifted to her face. She said, "I only meant that—well, for example, you helped Mrs. Blary when her husband made her carry that great load of driftwood from the beach, even when he warned you 'gainst interfering. But when he turned on you, you didn't raise a hand to defend yourself. You are taller than he is, Jack. If you would only stand up to bullies like him and Wally Pughill, people would have more respect for you."

So she judged him a coward. It was logical enough. He said helplessly, "I—I cannot."

The moment was gone, and he had retreated once more. "Well now," she said cheerfully, "what about your small friend here? Do you mean to keep him? I feel sure Mrs. Newlyn would permit another lodger. She has such a kind heart."

"Be sure I—I know it, ma'am. Lord knows, I've dwelt on her charity these past months."

"What nonsense! She has told me that she dreads the day you leave Roselley, for you wait on her hand and foot and are never done working about the house. Besides, you pay for your keep."

His smile was rather pathetically grateful, and she thought it very sad that a young and comely man should be so afflicted. She stood and began to look about for a container for the bird. "I fancy you will be moving on before winter sets in."

"You think I should—go away?"

She was taking a small covered basket from the cupboard, and didn't see his aghast expression. "I think your talents are wasted here," she said. "Will this serve to carry him?"

He thanked her, and she watched as he put the bird into the basket and closed the top quickly. "You will want to try and find your home and your people," she went on. "If you could come into your own district, you might remember more of your past."

Jonathan held the lid of the basket closed, and stared down at it blankly.

"My papa thinks you may have been a soldier," said Jennifer, handing him a ball of string. "Or one of the officers on the transport ship that was wrecked off Lizard Point. So very many poor souls drowned. I shall ask my brother Royce to make enquiries when he rides down to—"

"No! I am not—I—I wasn't—I was in C-Cornwall long before that—that wreck!"

The hunted look was in his eyes with a vengeance, and he seemed so distraught that she said at once, "Well, then that was a silly notion, and we shall have done with it and turn our eyes elsewhere. To London, perhaps, for certainly you speak as an educated man. 'Twould not surprise me . . ."

She went on with her conjecturing, but he scarcely heard her soft voice as he wound the string around the basket. 'London . . . !' He started to sweat.

"Jack?" She was laughing at him. "T'faith, but you must think you've a roaring lion in there!"

He had wrapped almost the whole ball of string around the basket. Mortified, he stammered, "Jupiter! I—I must have been—"

"Wool gathering," she declared, in mock scolding. "That's what you were doing. And I think heard not one word I said!"

"Well, what d'you expect, Jennifer? I've told you before not to have the looby about you."

Irritated by that sardonic drawl, she turned to face her eldest brother.

Howland Britewell had the height and fine build that characterised all the Britewells. Seven years Jennifer's senior, he was a handsome man, but resembled her only in that his eyes were the same deep blue. His neatly tied-back hair was unpowdered, and several shades darker than hers. His features were well formed, but there was none of her warmth to be found in his hard eyes or about the rather thin-lipped mouth, and a ruthless set to the chin made him seem older than his thirty-two years. He came into the room with quick impatient strides, and before she could respond went on, "Gather your things, Madam School Teacher. We've company come, and Papa wants you home."

He reached for the basket. Jonathan picked it up, and Britewell gave him a hard shove and jerked it away. "Get out, half-wit! You've no business hanging about here."

"I sent for him," argued Jennifer, taking the basket and returning it to Jonathan. "I want him to repair the front door. And he is not a half-wit."

"Likely you're right. No wits at all, I'd wager." He snatched the basket again and holding it high said mockingly, "Only see how well he secures an empty basket."

"'Tis not empty! No—Howland! Give it back! It belongs to him."

He held the basket above his head, laughing at her attempts to reach it. "And what does it contain? His worldly goods? Riches beyond compare, eh? Very well, the clod may have it. If he asks for it politely."

With an inarticulate cry of anger, Jennifer again tried to snatch the basket from him. Fending her off, Howland pushed harder than he had intended, and she almost fell. Before he could steady her, his wrist was caught in fingers of steel. Astounded, he met a pair of narrowed eyes in which humility had been replaced by a murderous glare.

"Why you damned gallow's bird!" he gasped. "How *dare* you lay your filthy hands on me?"

His attempt to wrench free failed.

Jennifer saw his face, and cried desperately, "Jack! Do not!"

Howland whipped up his left fist. Jonathan let him go with a jerk that threw him off balance. Infuriated, Howland started for him again.

Running between them, Jennifer pleaded, "Don't! Howland, he thought you were hurting me! He meant no harm!"

"I'll harm the makebait!" he growled, pushing her away.

"No! I'll come now. Please, dear." She tugged at his arm, keeping always between him and Jonathan. "You said Papa was waiting. Come, then!"

Still livid with rage, he fumed, "By God, woman! D'you realise this loathesome yokel dared to—"

"Yes, yes. But—but you yourself said his wits are disordered. You are above soiling your hands on such. Come."

"He needs a lesson, I tell you!"

"No doubt, but I've had all the lessons *I* need today! Teach him another time, love."

She took his arm, smiling up at him and tugging him gently towards the door until, muttering dark threats about having the looby driven from the Hundred, he at length accompanied her.

Jonathan stared after them and took up the basket absently. He was relieved to hear squawking and flutterings about. "So you're still among the living are you," he murmured. "I've some work to do, and then I'll take you home."

The tools Mr. Holsworth had loaned him were still in the cupboard, and he carried them to the warped front door and set to work.

He'd not endeared himself to Howland Britewell, but having acknowledged that fact, he dismissed it from his mind. How sweetly she had tended his hurt, how bravely interceded for him. 'His wits are disordered . . . You are above soiling your hands on such.' He flinched, but she'd not meant it. She was too compassionate to have meant it. She'd merely been trying to distract her brother. She had guessed he was an educated man, bless her. And she'd spoken of London. The fond smile on his lips died. London. Long and long ago, in that misty other-life, he had lived there. There had been a big and happy house . . . the squeals of children . . . a kind gentleman . . . love, and laughter. His own family, perhaps. He may have been one of the children. But they could as well have been friends or acquaintances, who had forgotten him and no longer cared what had happened to him.

He bowed his head against the door and stifled a groan. There were others who would care, heaven help him! There were others . . . !

The craftsmen of the fourteenth century had built Castle Triad to last, and last it had, defying siege, bombardment, and the elements, through four hundred stormy years. It had been erected on the highest point of the cliffs and some distance inland, but year by year strong winds and hungry waters had made their inroads, and now the castle reared its defiant tower only a hundred yards from the cliff edge.

Triad lacked the massive size of such fortresses as Windsor, or East Anglia's Green Willow Castle, nor could it boast the majestic height that made Castle Tyndale in Ayrshire such a fairy-tale structure. In point of fact, Triad was more a keep than a castle. Its ten-foot-thick walls were of rough-hewn stone and thrust upward from bastion to battlements with no softening ornamentation to indicate that this was a dwelling as well as a fortress. The only variations in the outer walls were the occasional narrow and deeply inset windows of the upper storeys, and the rows of gun ports that encircled the ground floor, or bastion, and the first or "fighting" floor.

Roselley was only a mile south of the castle, but Howland Britewell had ordered out a coach and four to fetch his sister. Through the short ride home, he berated her for consorting with "dangerous lunatics," and for having opened the village school. "You demean yourself by overmuch mingling with the common herd," he declared. "It invites a familiarity they'd best not attempt with me."

She studied his handsome, arrogant face, and said dryly, "I feel sure they know what to expect from you, Howland."

"Good." He gave a short laugh. "They respect those who keep them in their place. The way you coddle 'em does but encourage impertinence. And be damned if I'll allow you to be subjected to that! Least of all from a filthy vagrant like Crazy Jack."

Indignant, she said, "He has *never* been in the slightest impertinent towards me! And he is neither filthy, nor a vagrant! I admit he suffers lapses of—of memory, but he's never shown the slightest inclination to harm anyone, and you must allow he has the speech and manners of a gentleman."

"Which is another reason to be rid of the fellow. Who can say where he came from, or what he may be hiding? For all we know, he might be a thief—or worse, and running from Bow Street."

"A thief would choose a better place to ply his trade, I think. The village folk have nothing, and there's little in the way of great works of art upon our walls, or gold in my father's store. Aside from the pieces Mama left me, I've not much jewellery."

"You could have. Grandmama left you enough lettuce to enable you to live like a queen."

Having wound its difficult way up the rutted road, the carriage was drawing to a halt before the side entrance to the bastion, rather than proceeding to the long flight of wind-whipped steps that climbed past the two lower floors to the impressive main entrance. Jennifer gathered her shawl closer about her shoulders, and pointed out coolly, "She left you more, only you gambled it away."

He scowled at this home truth. "At least I didn't hoard it like any miser."

"Grandmama wanted me to be able to provide for myself after Papa is gone, as you very well know."

The footman swung down and made to open the door, but Howland gestured to him to wait, and said with low-voiced intensity, "There would be no need for you to provide for yourself if you found a well-circumstanced husband. You're a pretty chit, Jennifer."

She looked at him steadily. "I thank you. But a gentleman needs heirs, wherefore I shall never marry. Now pray stop talking rubbish and let me go."

Grumbling, he nodded to the footman to open the door, then sent him off. "Damned servants!" he muttered. "Always having their ears on the stretch."

Jennifer started up the steps, her skirts billowing in the wind. "Why you went to the bother of calling out the coach, I cannot fathom. 'Tis a short walk to the village."

"A short walk! 'Tis more than a mile to Devil's Ladder alone, and deuce take me if I'll trudge up and down the hill in this wind, and with clouds blowing up for rain. Besides, a coach and four with servants on the box gives the yokels something to gawk at. They get little enough in the way of entertainment."

"I thought you didn't care about the opinions of the simple folk."

"No more I do." He opened the ponderous iron-bound door for her and they walked side by side across the gloom of the bastion. The cannon had long since been removed, and the gun ports were shuttered, but the candles in the occasional wall sconces flickered to the draughts. "An I had my way," muttered Howland, "I'd show my back to this accursed castle tomorrow and never set foot in it again!"

"I wonder you do not," she said equably. "Papa would likely be willing to set you up in London, for that's where you long to live—no?"

"Aye. I like Town life. And never pretend *you* enjoy this lonely desolation. I've seen how you look at the Morris ladies in their elegant gowns and their elegant mansion."

Jennifer's steps slowed. She said guiltily, "I hope I do not look at them with envy. Grandmama used to say that envy—"

"Consumes the soul. How well I remember her prosing on with her fusty moralising! 'Tis not a matter of envy—or if it is, surely it's natural enough, so do not be thinking yourself a sinner." He said in a kinder voice, "You think I don't know, but I do. It's blasted miserable for me to rusticate here, but a man can always search out entertainment, and my father ain't backward in keeping me busy. For a girl to be shut up in this grim old place, away from pretty gowns and parties and bazaars, is downright unfair."

Sometimes, she did feel rather hardly done by, and her smile was wistful. "I thank you for the thought. But you know that what I said is truth. After the accident, Dr. Fowey told Papa—"

"Pox on the old curmudgeon!"

"He's the finest surgeon in Plymouth, and—"

"And has never journeyed farther north than Devonshire since he finished his training. There are other surgeons in London. Up to the minute, and better a thousand times! Besides, even if you cannot ever bear children, not all men need 'em."

She halted as a fierce pang transfixed her, snatching her breath away. They all pitied her, but no one really knew how desperately she had wanted children of her own. Little ones to cherish; innocent minds to mold and prepare so that they might meet the world with gentleness and courage and integrity.

Misinterpreting her silence, Howland peered at her, and said bracingly, "I know you don't believe it, but there's plenty of fine gentlemen who judge you quite beautiful, and would be dashed eager to take you to wife if you'd not be so everlastingly touch-me-not-ish."

Jennifer regained her voice, and standing very still said, "Are there indeed? I wish I might know of one who is not in his dotage."

"I know of one." He looked at her from the corners of his eyes. "A good man. A man of great fortune. A man who fairly worships the ground you walk on."

"Goodness me! His worship must be very subdued, for I've heard no such declarations."

"He has not declared himself as yet. But he's here now, and means to speak to my father."

26

She turned to face him. "Do you say that this ardent suitor has come to Triad only to make me an offer?"

"Well—er, not that only." Howland's eyes slid away from her candid gaze. "He has business to discuss with Papa. But I am very sure he admires you, and would make you a dashed fine husband."

"I am all agog, for he sounds a paragon." They started up the flight that led to the fighting floor, and she said demurely, "What a relief! Do you know, I had feared for a moment you meant that disgusting creature who wants to buy the Blue Rose Mine."

"Disgusting creature?" He gave a scornful snort. "Here's a high flight! Lord Hibbard Green is a peer of the realm. A man of wealth and power who would be a splendid catch for any girl!"

"Always provided," she said, her eyes flashing, "she wants a great boorish brute, with the manners of a hog, and as much sensitivity as—"

"Sensitivity will not buy you beautiful gowns and jewels and several great houses. Have some sense, do! You should be flattered that a gentleman of his high station would so much as glance your way. No, never fly out at me. I'll own you're a little younger than he. But you're too tall to attract most men, you know you are. Lord Green is generous enough to forgive that flaw, in addition to—er, all else."

"Don't bother to wrap it up in clean linen," she said hotly. "What you mean is that he will forgive that I cannot provide him an heir. How noble of him! Seeing that he already has one who is older than me! You forget, I think, that I have met Rafe Green, who is as loathsome as his gross father, only perhaps a shade less honest of a rogue! I take leave to tell you, Howland Britewell, that you do not excel as a matchmaker!"

Seething, she walked rapidly across the echoing vastness of this area that had once teemed with fighting men and rung to the din of battle, but was now empty save for a few rusting suits of armour and a rather forlorn collection of swords, shields, pikes, and other impedimenta of war.

At the far flight of steps, Howland was before her and

blocked her way. "Little fool! You could get away from here! You could be a baroness, and able to indulge your wildest dreams!"

"How willing you are to sell me to your nasty friend, never caring that he is said to have driven his first wife to an early grave. All you see is his fortune. Well, I believe my dreams are not very wild, but they don't come *that* cheaply, I promise you!"

"I can guess what they are," he jeered. "That some tall and handsome young gallant will ride into your life and carry you away across his saddle bow. How long do you mean to wait, Miss Fanciful? How many handsome young aristocrats of gentle sensitivity and charming manners have trod these cliffs in a year? Or ten? The most dashing suitor you're ever like to find is that madman you coddle! And his only rank is that he's a rank coward and brainless to boot!"

She said through her teeth, "I had sooner wed an itinerant tinker than Hibbard Green, with his sly eyes and busy hands! Now stand aside and let me pass, or have you forgot, as he has, that you were born a gentleman?"

Stung, he let her pass, but called spitefully, "Has my father a modicum of sense he'll sign the marriage contract and be done with you! He has the right. Much good your hoity-toity notions will do you if he chooses to exercise it."

Jennifer ignored him and hurried up the stairs. She resisted the urge to run, and held her head high. But her nature was too gentle to enjoy a quarrel, and she was trembling.

The second floor was luxuriously appointed and immaculately maintained. Avoiding the great hall, Jennifer went through the dining room into a long corridor. Rugs from Persia and India were spread on the flagged floors and the air was spiced with the smells of luncheon. She paused outside the door of her father's study, but recoiled when she heard laughter and the raucous voice of Lord Hibbard Green. She went on quickly, and gave a sigh of relief when she at last came to the third floor and entered her small private parlour.

Tilly Mays sat by the single window, sewing the hem of a petticoat. She was a short somewhat scrawny woman, whose best feature was a pair of bright dark eyes that lit up her pinched face and saved her from being judged plain. At the age of nine she had been brought from the Foundling Home to be scullery maid. Despite Cook's kind attempts to broaden her mind, her outlook remained narrow, and her nature suspicious, but she had an innate shrewdness and had learned quickly how to benefit from the politics of the servants hall. By the time she was twenty, she had worked her way up to be an upstairs maid, and when Nurse had left and Miss Jennifer was to have an abigail, Tilly had begged for the chance to learn those duties. She was devoted to and fiercely protective of her young mistress, and when she discovered that gossip and her often acid criticisms of her co-workers were not appreciated, she was wise enough to guard her tongue.

She stood as Jennifer entered the parlour, but her welcoming smile died, and she said anxiously, "Oh, miss! Whatever is it? You're pale as any ghost!"

Short of breath, Jennifer said, "I expect I came up the stairs too quickly. Mr. Howland tells me we've company arrived."

"Aye. Lord Hibbard Green come back again, miss. Brought that ugly man of his, what looks like a vulture." After a long moment during which Jennifer gazed unseeingly at the window, Tilly added, "The master sent word up. He wants you to please hasten, and—er . . ."

"And welcome our charming guest. Yes. Of course." Jennifer thought, 'I'd as soon welcome a serpent!' But she knew she must proceed with caution, so she washed, and changed her dress quickly, and went downstairs wearing a pink silk gown with moderate hoops, and with her curls clustering prettily below her frilled cap.

The gentlemen had gathered in the great hall that served the Britewells as withdrawing room, morning room, and book room. The furnishings were massive and masculine, the wainscoting darkened by countless decades of smoke. Bookcases flanked the vast fireplaces on the north and south ends of the room, and there were several screens to circumvent draughts.

Jennifer was mildly surprised to find that Sir Vinson had contrived to pry her brother Fleming from his books, but she thought with pride that her menfolk presented a fine picture. Sir Vinson's frame was sturdy and his head more proudly carried than those of his three sons, but even he looked slight compared to the man whose harsh voice rang through the room.

With his great height and large frame, Lord Hibbard Green might have presented a commanding figure, but he had never checked an early tendency to gluttony. His tailor had probably done his best, but any counsel he might have offered had been ignored. My lord's vast bulk was accentuated by a purple coat lavishly trimmed with gold braid. His waistcoat was pink satin embroidered with scarlet hummingbirds, and lilac satin unmentionables did nothing to mitigate the size of his stomach. Scarlet ribands were knotted at his knees, and his chunky calves were encased in white stockings on the sides of which purple *fleurs de lis* flourished.

As Jennifer entered, he was sprawled in his chair booming an indictment of the "fools in Whitehall" and of the crippling taxes that had, he said, driven many an honest Briton into becoming a free-trader. "Not that I hold with smuggling, mind," he asserted, waving the hamlike hand that clutched his tankard. "But 'tis not so despicable, to my way of thinking, as the wreckers you people allow to prowl your coastline."

He had touched a nerve. Sir Vinson abominated wreckers, and his distinguished head tossed upward. With more than a touch of frost in his voice, he said, "Such practices are neither condoned by—nor, as you rather oddly phrase it, sir—*allowed*, by me! Of all things, I find it most contemptible. The man who would deliberately lure a ship onto the rocks, without a thought for loss of life, or the misery of those left bereaved—and only for his own gain, is truly a fiend. On this point alone, I am at one with the squire."

His lordship was suddenly breathlessly still. His voice very soft, he demanded, "Who?"

Royce Britewell, at three and twenty the youngest of the family, answered, "Lord Kenneth Morris. The local squire, sir. A jolly good man, for all he's a touch top-lofty."

"A harsh judgment from one of less than vast experience in the world," murmured Fleming, his thin intelligent face disdainful.

Royce, who had inherited his sire's light brown hair and fair complexion, flushed darkly and his hazel eyes slanted a resentful look at his scholarly brother.

"I don't hold with young men taking the measure of their elders," declared his lordship, completing Royce's mortification. "Bosom bow of this—er, squire, are you, Britewell?"

"I'd not use that term," answered Sir Vinson, irritated. "Lord Kenneth enjoys a more—ah, frivolous way of life than I prefer."

Green's black button eyes almost vanished into his heavy cheeks. "Plenty of lettuce, eh? I shall have to meet the gentleman. Er, to learn how he plans to handle these wreckers," he added hurriedly.

Noting his parent's increasingly frigid expression, Howland said, "My father employs strong measures 'gainst 'em, do you not, sir?"

Sir Vinson nodded. "A summary hearing on the spot, when they're caught, and then they are hanged. Which is a kinder end than the vermin deserve."

Lord Green uttered a bellow of laughter that rattled the glassware. "That's the barber! Let 'em kick out—"

Not bothering to conceal his disgust, Fleming interjected, "How pretty you are, Jennifer."

They all stood, and Sir Vinson came at once to usher her into the room. "You are indeed pretty, my dear," he said fondly. "You will remember Lord Green, I think?"

She murmured an acquiescence and made her curtsy.

A glow came into my lord's eyes as they travelled her from head to toe. He bowed over her hand. She caught the aroma of the unwashed, and her nose wrinkled involuntarily. Over his lordship's massive shoulder, she met Royce's amused eyes. He winked, quick to sense her reaction and to endorse it.

Green was expressing his admiration and his prodigious pleasure at being permitted to visit Triad again. Somehow, she managed to keep her countenance and to utter the polite commonplaces expected of her. She pulled her hand from his lingering warm and wet clutch, but he was their guest and she couldn't escape her obligation to take his arm as they went in to luncheon. En route, he stroked her fingers, and it was all she could do not to again jerk free.

Luckily, his lordship was not one to encourage conversation in a lady, and most of the meal was passed in a male discussion of the Blue Rose tin mine and Green's conviction that his engineers would be able to restore it to a paying proposition.

Since he indulged the unpleasant habit of talking with his mouth full, Jennifer avoided looking his way, but twice when she glanced up, he was watching her. There was a slyness in his expression; a suggestion of gloating that appalled her. She looked away at once, and encountered Howland's brooding gaze. It was clear that he was not pleased with her. Her eyes flashed to her father. Sir Vinson also watched her. He smiled, and his hazel eyes were fond. She thought, 'Bless him! He would never force me into such a dreadful marriage, no matter what Howland wished.'

But she could not dismiss the knowledge that he doted upon his heir. She must, she decided, have a private chat with dear Papa. Very soon!

❧ *Chapter 3* ❧

It was light by the time Jonathan finished the cage. He glanced to where the sun was starting its climb up the cloudless sky, and judged it to be near five o'clock. Time to get back to the widow's cottage and stoke up the kitchen stove. Noah had said he could take any left-over scraps of wood, and they'd be useful for the fire. He added the small pile to the cage and closed the door. It was a good cage, he thought as he passed Noah's quiet cottage and started down the road. Little Duster would be glad to be released from the crate the widow had loaned for a temporary home.

The morning was bright; brisk, but not cold, and he found the prospect beautiful in the proud, unyielding way so typical of this part of Cornwall. No gentle rolling hills or green valleys here; no spreading oaks or colourful gardens, or hedgerows ablaze with wildflowers. Here were soaring cliffs, the great lonely expanse of the moors; stark rocky upthrusts, and the strange granite monoliths left behind by those who had dwelt here long and long ago. Knowing the tide would be out at this hour, he looked downward. There were broad still pools on the sands, and rivulets wandering westward. He forced his eyes to follow them.

The sun sprinkled the ocean with diamonds. Far out, a sailing ship lay motionless, waiting for a breeze. Even now the sight was more than he could bear, and he jerked his gaze from the ship, only to find himself staring at the jagged rocks that were scattered like small islands about the wet sands. Behind each of those treacherous islands were the ghosts of ships sunk in the fierce storms that could come up so swiftly along this coast. Ships whose masters— 'Lord!' he thought, and turned his head to the east.

Inland, white vapours still wreathed the high moors in mystery. This whole country was rooted in mystery and legend: tales of the dreaded owls, and hares able to change their shape and appear human; witches and pixies sent by the Evil One to plague the unwanted inhabitants of this wild land. 'Superstitious nonsense,' he thought, but as he had discovered to his cost, woe betide the man who dared speak against it.

He glanced over his shoulder. Castle Triad rose in stern grandeur against the deepening blue of the sky. Somewhere in that great pile his lovely lady would be sleeping. A smile softened his mouth. She would be as beautiful in slumber as in wakefulness. More beautiful, with her glossy hair brushed out and spreading across the pillows; a dainty nightgown, all gossamer and lace, slightly rumpled perhaps, slipping from one creamy shoulder to—

"Outta my path, ye danged looby!"

A rough hand staggered him. 'Ben Blary,' he thought, and moved aside.

Accompanying his large and ill-tempered father, Isaac laughed. "What's that he got, Pa?"

"He's bin stealing wood, is what he done. You bin stealing, Crazy Jack, and here-along we don't like them as steals."

Another, harder shove.

Jonathan said coolly, "I stole nothing. Mr. Holsworth said I could have whatever was left from—"

"And what do a looby want with wood?"

He knew, of course. He only wanted an excuse to bully. Jonathan moved the cage behind him.

"It's a cage, Pa," said Isaac.

"For the rats what the witch uses in her spells? We don't need 'em! You'd oughter know that by now. But 'spite o' yer fancy talk, ye don't know much. So being as I got a kind heart, I'll try ter teach yer." Blary threw one of his dreaded right jabs. Jonathan was prepared and swayed aside, but Isaac came up from behind and seized the cage. Jonathan half-turned and retrieved it, and Blary seized his opportunity and lashed out again. Jonathan reeled and fell to one knee.

"I 'spect that there cage is for the stupid bird what Mrs. Pughill went and bought off the sailorman," contributed Isaac.

Breathing hard, Jonathan steadied himself and reached for the cage.

Blary laughed. "A ugly bird like that, and so big as a thimble? He don't need that great huge cage. Ye built it all wrong, maggot-wit." His boot stamped onto Jonathan's outstretched hand. "Now don't get above yerself. I hasn't give ye leave to stand up. Jest answer. Perlite, like." He bore down harder. "Why'd you make it so big for that flea-bite of a crooked bird?"

It never got any easier. "Because," Jonathan gasped painfully, "nothing should—should be shut up in a small space, and— No—don't!"

Blary had moved his boot, but it was now poised above the cage. Holding on to his son's shoulder for support, he said, "Say 'please,' Shadow Man."

Isaac shrieked with mirth.

Jonathan's undamaged hand clenched tight, and he had to concentrate on a deep voice that had decreed, "*. . . no matter what the provocation. . . .*" Through gritted teeth he managed to utter a low-voiced, "Please."

Grinning broadly, Blary stamped, and the carefully fashioned bars splintered. With a gleeful shout, Isaac jumped on the wreckage, flattening it.

Blinded with rage Jonathan started up. Blary's boot smashed into his ribs, sending him sprawling. Hilarious, Blary drew back his foot again.

His laugh became a howl. Clutching his elbow, he spun to face the man who had come up silent and unnoticed. "Wha' the hell . . . ?"

Jonathan dragged himself to one elbow, and scanned the

newcomer. He saw a tall slender individual, clad in ill-fitting and much worn garments. His face was heavily bearded, and jet black hair straggled from under an object that had once been a tricorne.

His white teeth gleaming in a savage grin, the stranger flourished a sturdy branch as though it had been a small sword. "Kick him again, my unlovely dirtiness," he invited, a laugh in the cultured voice. "I would purely enjoy bestowing some bruises on your smelly self."

This gent talked Quality talk, thought Blary. But he wore rags. And Quality gents didn't sport big shaggy beards, nor have eyes what was a shape no one ever see before. 'A foreign gent,' he decided, 'what's gone and ruined hisself.' Reassured, his bullet head lowered menacingly. "I'll bruise yer," he snarled, and rushed to show this interloper why no one in Roselley never dared stand up agin Ben Blary.

Holding his side painfully, Jonathan struggled to his feet. He was permitted to help if the stranger was endangered.

Mr. Blary was not able to explain, later, quite what went wrong. The foreign gent didn't seem to move about much, yet somehow, no matter how quick he himself dodged about, the stranger always managed to be behind him. The nasty branch slammed across his broad hips; whacked across the back of his other elbow, causing his arm to tingle to the fingertips; and cracked onto his head. Cursing loud and lustily, but for once hurt and scared, he backed away. Isaac, having attempted to attack the stranger from the rear, had caught a solid swipe across the middle, and stood to one side, gulping in air.

"Take yer wicked hands off my poor little boy," whined Blary, clutching his throbbing head. "Ye got no cause to attack honest folk."

"If I see any, I promise not to do so." The stranger made a lunge with his branch, and Blary and son retreated at speed.

"Ye do not live in this Hundred," accused Blary over his shoulder. "Where'd you come from so sudden, is what I'd like ter know."

"Begone, Mr. Raff and Mr. Scraff! Before I give you the thrashing you warrant!"

"You're a changeling!" shouted Blary. "Evil, is what ye be"—he pointed at Jonathan—"same as him!"

Branch whirling, the stranger leapt forward.

Isaac squealed and fled, his father quickly overtaking him.

Jonathan said, "Thank you, sir. That was a fine thrust in *tierce*."

The stranger turned his head sharply, and for the first time Jonathan noticed that his eyes, which he'd thought were near black, were instead the darkest blue he'd ever seen, and that they were of a slightly alien shape. 'He's part Chinese,' he thought, and there came a quick sense of familiarity, gone before it was fully comprehended, as of a dream tantalizingly just beyond recall.

"Damme!" His rescuer strode closer, eyeing him narrowly. "I thought you were—" He hesitated.

"The village idiot?"

"Yes. Else I'd have let you fight your own battles. Why the devil didn't you? I despise most men. Poltroons, especially."

Jonathan flushed, but said nothing.

The piercing eyes continued to scan him curiously. "Who are you?"

"I'm—they call me Crazy Jack."

"Do they. They call me September."

"But—this is—"

"August. So 'tis. Do you know me? I'd swear we've met."

"I—don't think so. I can't always tell."

"Hmm. How long have you been here?"

"Not long, sir."

"Where did you come from?"

Avoiding those keen eyes, and beginning to be alarmed, Jonathan said, "Garrison Pen."

"Convenient, since 'tis now buried under the sands. Where before that?"

"I—I don't know. I can't remember."

A lean white hand shot out. Jonathan's wrist was caught in a grip of iron. "Can't? Or won't? You're no lunatic. Did Underhill send you here? Or are you one of the Squire's hell-hounds?"

Bewildered, Jonathan stammered, "Sir, I am not acquainted with—with a Mr. Underhill. I have seen Lord Morris, but from a—a distance only. My—my hand, sir . . ."

September glanced down and his fingers were removed at once. "You'll have a fine bruise there. Our departed bully's boot, I take it." He scanned Jonathan's troubled face again. "Something of a chameleon, ain't you. If you really can't recall your past, you've my sympathy. Although not all pasts are worthy of recollection." The strange eyes were brooding and he was briefly silent. Then, he said abruptly, "You're no heavyweight, but you look capable of holding your own in a brawl. It does no good to bow to a bully. He'll kick the harder and the more often, till you give him back his own." His white teeth flashed in a grin. The hat was removed. With a grace that was at odds with his shabby appearance he bowed low. "You may count yourself blessed, Crazy Jack, for I never give advice."

He strolled a few steps, then turned back. "By the bye, do you know aught of a fellow called Hibbard Green?"

"He's not from this Hundred, sir," evaded Jonathan, not sure what to make of this man.

"Hundred? What the devil's that?"

"A district. Cornwall is divided into nine of them. You are in what is called the—the Penwith Hundred."

"Hum. No, the creature is not from this desolation. And you didn't answer my question. You've no cause to be afraid to speak out. I'm not a Trap, nor a Riding Officer after your free-trading friends."

'The creature . . .' Jonathan smiled. "A stranger came to the castle a few weeks back. He's here again. I heard he might—might buy the old mine."

"Now that's much better! And does this stranger resemble a great bloated toad, perhaps?"

Jonathan's laugh effected a transformation that astonished

Mr. September. " 'Twould be reckless in the extreme, sir, for a common man to endorse such a description of a peer of the realm."

"Then I'll not put you in harm's way." September strolled off.

"Again, I thank you, sir," called Jonathan.

Without turning, September waved his branch.

Jonathan looked after him thoughtfully. He had enquired for Lord Green, but he was walking toward the high moors rather than north to Triad. Perhaps he hoped to find his lordship out at the mine. Perhaps he had some message that would send the repulsive baron away.

He gathered up the remnants of the shattered cage, which would at least be of use for the stove, and walked on. A strange fellow, this "Mr. September," and unless he mistook it, a dangerous one. Whoever he was, 'twas unlikely that he'd given his true name. That he was a gentleman was past doubting—yet he went about bearded, and in rags. Why? And what did he want with Hibbard Green? He'd said something about "the squire's hell-hounds." Lord Kenneth Morris was the local squire, but there were no hounds at Breton Ridge. Only cats. And who a'plague was "Underhill" . . . ? The feeling that they'd met somewhere had evidently been mutual. As well, he thought wryly, that in that connection September's memory was as faulted as his own . . .

In return for the work he did for the widow, Jonathan had been allocated the shed at the foot of the garden. It was quite a spacious if not very weatherproof shed, and he'd improved it until most of the rain and draughts were shut out. Next, he'd added some shelves, a row of hooks for his clothing, two chairs, and a small folding table, and now he felt quite comfortable.

On this windy night, he was recklessly burning two of his precious tallow candles while he carved a perch for the crate in which Duster still resided. The little bird was allowed to escape his temporary quarters once the door was closed for the night, and he perched on the table, preening his feathers, but checking on Jonathan's progress from time to time, as though making sure the work was done to his liking.

After two years of loneliness, even so small a creature was a valued companion, and Jonathan had fallen into the habit of talking to him. "The thing is," he explained now, "that I am not doing very well." He sighed, and waved his knife at his small friend. "Of late—especially when I'm near . . . her . . . I have back-slid. And that could be disastrous. Can you credit, Duster, that so exquisite a lady is still unwed? The Widow says 'tis because she suffered an injury as a child and will never be able to bear children. But someday a gentleman of sense will see her, and he'll think of the many little children starving and abandoned who could be taken in and loved. And adoring her—though never as much as I adore her—he will offer for her and take away his precious prize, and I will . . . never see her again."

He paused, staring desolately at the knife in his hand until a chirp from Duster roused him. "Was that a comment upon selfishness, I wonder? You are perfectly correct, and I should be hoping she finds some . . . some fine gentleman to make her happy. Instead of which, I came perilous close to kissing her yesterday. Me!" He smiled bitterly. "You'd never guess, would you, that I was bred up to the Code of Honour?"

Duster used his withered claw to scratch behind his ear, but his bright eyes, fixed to the man's face, held a look of censure. Or so thought Jonathan.

"You're perfectly in the right of it," he admitted. "A kiss—even a touch from—from such as I, would be desecration. And there's my head, you see. Sometimes I suppose my brain sort of—stops."

Having attended to his ear, Duster puffed out all his feathers, and uttered a chirp.

Jonathan nodded. "Thank you. I know I restrained myself. But the thing is that— You see, I—I love her so very much. To be near her . . . to hear her dear voice—see her pretty lips curve into that so beautiful smile . . . is—heaven.

And—hell. I'm afraid, Duster. Afraid that I might—forget for a moment what—what I am." He put down his knife and drew a hand across his eyes distractedly.

Duster bobbed his bright shoulders up and down and squawked again.

Drawing a deep breath, Jonathan said, "Right again, friend. There are other areas where I'm weakening. There was my discussion with that animal, Blary, and— There I go! D'you see? I—who have done a far worse thing than ever that—that man has done—have the gall to name *him* 'animal'! And, far worse, Duster—I damned near forgot my vow. Oh, if you but knew how I yearned, absolutely *longed* to let him have a good right to the breadbasket!"

Despondent, he began to wind a length of wire around one end of the swing. "If I break my vow, I become even more—despicable. God help me, I know what I am, but— sometimes it's very hard."

Duster hopped a shade nearer, and cocked his head on one side.

"Yes, I know you'd help me if you—" Jonathan checked, staring at the bird. "By Jupiter," he exclaimed. "I think perhaps you can!"

He put down the swing and held one finger in front of the tiny blue chest. Duster eyed the finger with marked scepticism.

"Come now," said Jonathan. "You can trust me I hope." He nudged gently.

Duster gave him a warning peck, but then hopped aboard.

Cautiously, Jonathan lifted him. "I've heard some of your friends chatter away quite fluently," he said. "I'm going to teach you a name, Duster. So that you can remind me of—of why I took a solemn oath, and help me not to break it."

Duster's beady eyes scanned him unwinkingly.

But now Jonathan's courage failed. There were so many names from which to choose, and every one made him cringe. The cabin boy's bright impudence came into his mind's eye; little Bobby . . . but he was quite unable to make his lips form the name. There was Joe Taylor, the ship's carpenter, quick tempered, but loyal, and always ready to pull out his old fife and "whistle up a tune" as he'd been used to say, which would unfailingly set toes to tapping and lighten moods. And the pretty spinster lady, God rest her! ... but her name was mercifully lost somewhere in his clouded memory. Other faces came to him, until, the sweat standing out on his brow, and his voice hoarse and shaking, he forced himself to utter a name. And he made himself keep on saying it, over and over again. "Bobby ... Bobby ... Bobby."

Duster watched him for a while, turning his small head from one side to the other, as if striving to understand, but he made no sound and at length he hopped down and fluttered into his crate in search of sustenance.

For Jonathan, the self-imposed task had been as shattering as he'd feared. He said wearily, "Our first lesson, my small conscience. But not the last, for heaven knows I'm not likely to run out of ... names for you." He gazed at the bird dully, then gave a wry shrug. "And if truth be told, I'd be more honest did I give you no names at all. One word really is—is all that's needed ..." He sank his face into trembling hands and his voice was an agonised whisper as he spoke that dread word. "Murderer!"

"Whatever are you doing, Jack?"

He hadn't expected her to come to the school today, and her lilting voice set his heart leaping and so startled him that he dropped the paintbrush he'd been cleaning. With an inward moan for his clumsiness, he snatched it up quickly, and stammered, "I hoped—I mean—I thought I'd have it finished before you came, ma'am."

The smell of paint was strong, and Jennifer left the door wide open as she walked inside. She wore a riding habit of soft green, and a long green feather curled down from the turned-up brim of her hat. The brisk early morning air had painted roses onto her smooth cheeks, and her blue eyes sparkled. Awed, he gazed at her. How vibrantly alive she was; the joyous personification of pure and lovely femininity.

Jennifer had grown accustomed to admiring glances, and in her unassuming way she judged that many of the compliments she received were inspired by her father's position. But there was that in this man's gaze which caused her to be unaccountably flustered. To add to her folly, she was sure she was blushing, and there came a strange new confusion, to hide which she walked over to admire the doors of what had once been a china cabinet. "Why, how very much better this looks. So bright and clean. Wherever did you get the paint?"

"Your brother, Mr. Royce, bought it for me. I hope I did not—overstep my place, ma'am? If the colour is not to your liking . . . ?"

He looked so anxious. She smiled at him kindly, and assured him that she was most pleased. "But are you sure Mrs. Newlyn can spare you?"

"Mr. Holsworth took her up to the moors to gather herbs. I know she—"

The breeze from the open door fluttered Jennifer's habit. He dropped the paintbrush in the pot and sprang forward. "Have a care, ma'am! That's wet!"

In the nick of time he restrained the billowing skirts, then gave a gasp, and drew back, his face scarlet with embarrassment. "Oh, gad!" He drove a hand through his hair agitatedly. "I—I do beg your pardon, ma'am!"

It occurred to Jennifer that were one to look at him from an artist's perspective, as Mama might have done, one could not but admire the well-cut features, even with the long scar across his right temple and the smaller one beside his ear. He kept himself clean and neat always, and the thick light-brown hair that showed the hint of a crisp wave was sternly tied back. If he were set beside my lord Green, even wearing the much darned coat and patched breeches, there could be no doubt as to which was the better— Aghast, she caught herself up. Whatever was she thinking? This man was no more than a tramp, and an afflicted tramp besides; coming from he knew not where, bound only for a life of grinding poverty, eons removed from her world. That sensible acknowledgment disturbed her also, and she said with considerably less than her usual composure, "What? Oh, I—er, am only glad I have not a painted habit! Goodness! Whatever happened to your hand?"

He assured her that it was of no consequence. "Just a small, er—"

"Encounter?" she interposed, frowning in a way he thought unutterably delicious. "With Ben Blary, perchance?"

If she'd heard of that episode she must know that Blary had kicked him. He nodded wretchedly, and avoided her gaze by cleaning paint from the floorboards.

"He is a horrid bully," she said, looking down at his bowed head and taking note of the breadth of his shoulders. "I worry for his wife, and I've no doubt his son's life is full of hard knocks."

Jonathan straightened, and stirred the paintbrush around in the pot of turpentine. "I'd think some of the local men would . . . would have stood up to him."

"Oh, they're all afraid of him because he's so burly and quarrelsome. I'd hoped that someone as tall as he is—" She broke off. The paintbrush was suddenly quite still. He was very likely ashamed, she realised. And after all, what right had she to expect more of this troubled stranger, than of her own villagers? "I must not judge Blary too harshly," she amended in a lighter tone. "At least, he has allowed Isaac to come to school, which is more than I thought he would do."

"Why ever would he not? Surely, any parent must only be grateful to you."

"I think most of them are, and some of the children walk a long way so as to attend class. But Blary and one or two others grumbled that I would give the children ideas beyond their station."

"What nonsense!" he exclaimed, indignant. "If they learn no more than to read and write, how greatly their lives will be enriched!"

"So I think. Some of them have never left this Hundred,

not even for a day. They have no knowledge of the beauties of the rest of the British Isles. No conception of the wonders of the wide world. All the different cultures and climes and people."

Her enthusiasm was enchanting. Quite forgetting both paintbrush and his lowly state, he asked smilingly, "Have you travelled abroad, ma'am?"

"Alas—no. And there is so much I long to see. Paris. The great mountains of Switzerland. Italy, where the sun always shines. India, where lions and tigers are worshipped and roam the streets at will." She sighed, then the dreaming look faded and she said, "Now why do you laugh?"

He answered solemnly, "Never that, Miss Jennifer."

"You kept your countenance, to be sure, but your eyes laughed. I think I am provoked, and must demand to be told what I said to amuse you?"

He chuckled. "Only that I think someone has been hoaxing you, ma'am. Lions dwell in Africa, not India. And the Indian tiger is very fierce and a man-eater. You would see a crowded bazaar empty in a flash did a tiger come shopping."

It dawned on her that they had been chatting like equals, and she thought wonderingly that it was as if a curtain had been drawn aside to reveal, behind the shrinking wreckage she knew as Crazy Jack, another man. A man of poised self-confidence, with a whimsical twinkle in his fine eyes. And who was disconcertingly attractive.

She said, "Why . . . you have *been* there! Is my father in the right of it, then? Were you a sailor, or in the military?"

At once, the curtain was lowered. The poised gentleman vanished, and it was Crazy Jack who paled, and shrank away. Jennifer put a detaining hand on his arm and said in her gentlest voice, "No, please do not be afraid of me. I meant only to try and help. Won't you confide in me?"

"I—I have nothing— There is nothing to—" And slanting a glance at her concerned face, he added desperately, "You see, I cannot . . . recollect."

"Can you recollect what it was that Ben Blary took from you yesterday?"

He stared down at her gloved hand and breathed the sweet fragrance of her. A familiar fragrance. *"Caresse Translucide."* He saw astonishment in her face, and realised he must have spoken aloud. 'Fool!' he thought, and answered her question hurriedly. "It was a—a birdcage."

"Did Noah Holsworth make it for you?" She spoke lightly, but her eyes were watchful. "Blary said 'twas big enough for a great owl."

"Mr. Holsworth was so kind as to let me use some of his left-over scraps of wood. I suppose 'twas a—a good size for such a little bird, but I think that to be shut up . . . in a small space . . ."

The schoolroom shimmered and was gone. He was in the cabin. Trapped. He could smell the brandy . . . Feel the frenzy of terror . . . He was so cold—so dizzy . . .

"What a pity it was smashed."

Jennifer's calm voice came to him like a lifeline, and he clung to it gratefully.

"Perhaps," she went on, praying he wasn't going to drop at her feet, "you should seek your building materials on the beach. Driftwood is always washing up. But you'd have to get there early, before other people." She went on talking easily until he was breathing normally again and a tinge of colour had come back into his drawn face. Relieved, she said with a smile that she must not keep her brother waiting, and walked to the door.

Jonathan followed her into the sunshine, not daring to speak, dreading to think what she must have thought of this latest evidence of his ridiculous mental state.

Tommy Lawney was walking her mare. Jennifer waved to the boy, and belatedly remembered why she had come. She said idly, "Oh, by the bye, who was the man who came to help you? When Blary smashed your cage, I mean."

"I don't know, ma'am. That is—I never saw the gentleman before."

"What did he look like?"

"He was slender, and a young man, I think. Very dark, and bearded." His brows knit. He said hesitantly, "There

46

was something . . . I seemed to— But—" The words faded into silence.

Jennifer waited hopefully, then said, "Blary says he had strange eyes."

He nodded.

"Why did you name him a gentleman? He was poorly dressed, no?"

"His speech was cultured, and he seemed . . . very proud, very arrogant."

Amused, she asked, "Do you find all gentlemen proud and arrogant?"

"Some are, I think." Encouraged because she did not seem repulsed, he ventured to add, "Often, the ones with the least right to be so."

She shook her head, laughing at him. Tommy came up, leading the mare proudly and she paid him his groat.

Jonathan bent to receive her boot and toss her into the saddle, and she thanked him and rode off.

Distantly, she could see a horseman coming down from the castle. Royce, no doubt, ready to ride with her and air his grievances about Lord Green, whom he loathed, and who had, thank heaven, gone down to Breton Ridge with a letter of introduction from Papa. She held the mare to a slow pace, wanting to be alone with her thoughts for a little while.

So Crazy Jack may have served in the army, or been a seafaring man, perhaps. And their "village idiot" was no stranger to costly French colognes. It would appear also that Ben Blary's spiteful tongue had spoken truth, for once. There really had been a stranger; a mysterious stranger with a black beard and dark eyes of an alien shape. Eyes like none he'd ever seen on this earth, Blary had asserted. Add that to his tale of cages for evil owls, and the rumour mills would flourish.

She frowned uneasily. Despite her education and her cool common sense, she was Cornish born and bred, and could not entirely dismiss tales of witchcraft and magic spells. She had known people cured of crippling illnesses by bathing in the Madron Well. She had met Charmers, who could banish warts and other ailments. But that Jack would invoke spells and incantations, or "wish" people harm through the dreaded owls, she would not believe. Nor could she deny, however, that he was a mass of contradictions. She had caught a brief glimpse of another man today. Was it possible that he had erred and let a mask slip? Could he actually be an Exciseman? He would have to be a consummate actor. No, that was ridiculous! But ... if he *was* a Riding Officer sniffing out men engaged in the smuggling trade, then he was a real threat to many hereabouts. Perhaps, to her own family. And if the villagers found him out ... !

Royce shouted cheerfully, and she forced a smile and rode to meet him, dismissing such gloomy and doubtless unwarranted imaginings.

Although Jonathan had carved slots in the crate in which Duster was housed, it was not a comfortable home for the bird, and the swing had proven to be a mixed blessing. He had intended to build another cage days ago, but materials were scarce and he had no intention of following Miss Jennifer's suggestion that he go down to the beach and gather driftwood. However, waking before dawn one morning, as was his habit, he found the shed clammy and chill, and the smell of fog on the air. When he opened the door to look outside, a grey cloud billowed in. It was still too dark to see much, but he suspected it was one of the dense fogs that could sweep in very suddenly to blanket this coast. Which might, he reflected, be to his advantage. As he closed the door, a faint squawk came from the crate. He said, "Aye, aye, sir!" and removed the sack he flung over the impromptu cage at nighttime. Duster fluttered about, retreated to the farthest corner and regarded him with an unmistakable air of reproach.

"Were you a little wiser," he said, beginning to shiver through the business of rolling up his blankets then washing and shaving in the frigid water he had carried in last night, "you would look on me with gratitude, rather than fancying yourself hardly done by."

48

Duster muttered and scratched about the crate.

"Yes, I know you resent the sack, and I'll own it isn't the purple velvet cover you would prefer. But 'tis some protection 'gainst the cold for you, young fellow, and some protection for me 'gainst your midnight acrobatics."

A flurry of ruffling feathers and preening ensued. Jonathan threw an amused glance at the little bird, and applied razor to chin. "You want me to risk the beach in this fog, do you? Much you'd care if I broke my neck!"

He finished shaving, threw on his clothes, and provided the parakeet with fresh water and a small measure of the seeds he had bought from Mrs. Pughill. This procedure unfailingly threw Duster into a frenzy, but today the bird seemed slightly less alarmed, and was so bold as to peck his hand, though not very hard, as he withdrew it.

He repeated Duster's lesson several times, but as usual he was ignored, and having warned that this attitude was not likely to win a purple velvet cover, he put the tools he would need into his knapsack, blew out the candle, and left.

He stepped into a hushed, grey cloud and took several paces before the cottage loomed into sight through the cold wraith-like drifts. Sprat, the big tortoise-shell cat who divided his time between Mrs. Gundred and the widow, joined him on the back steps and wound around his ankles demanding admission. He darted inside when Jonathan opened the door, and finding his bowl empty embarked on a campaign calculated to prevent the human from overlooking his presence. The widow would not get up for another two hours or more, and despite Sprat's assistance, Jonathan hurried through his morning tasks, building up the fire in the stove, removing Sprat from the table, pumping water, removing Sprat from lying slavishly on his foot, setting the kettle on the idle-back hanger, bowing to outright flattery and feeding Sprat, and preparing the small table for Mrs. Newlyn's breakfast.

The mantelpiece clock indicated it to be ten minutes until six o'clock when he left again, taking with him a heel of dark bread and a piece of cheese for his own breakfast.

The fog had become glaringly white, but was just as

dense. Sprat accompanied him for a little way before re calling pressing business elsewhere and darting off. Lacking such a sense of direction, Jonathan had to grope his way and almost missed the crude path that wound down the cliff. It was a treacherous descent, but from this point northward the cliffs became ever more sheer and there was no other path until one reached the steps that had been cut into the rock below Castle Triad. Several times the drifts were so thick that he could see no more than a few yards ahead. Certainly, he had no need to fear catching sight of the ocean.

He ate his bread and cheese after he reached level ground and began to make his way through this strangely isolated world. The only sounds were the muffled cries of the seagulls. The tide was far out at this hour, but the sands were still wet, the smooth surface marked here and there by the fine precision of bird tracks. Occasional tidal pools appeared suddenly at his feet, glistening, and still as glass. Twice, he almost stumbled over gnarled and bleached tree limbs, but both were too large for his purpose, and he searched on. He came upon a shallow pool where tiny crabs scuttled about busily in their miniature world, and he paused to watch them, then took up a shell so perfect and so delicately hued that he put it carefully into his pocket thinking that someday, if he summoned the courage, he would give it to Miss Jennifer.

Minutes later, he was brought up short by something he had not expected to see: a broad swath of boot prints. Curious, he followed them along the beach and northward, toward Castle Triad. The tracks of at least twenty men, he judged. Obviously, they had passed this way since the tide went out. Perhaps Sir Vinson entertained a large party of friends, although it seemed an odd hour for company to have arrived. Then again, the boots may have belonged to free-traders. But free-traders would surely have been met by ponies to carry their tubs. Lost in speculation, he awoke to the realisation that time was passing and he was following a set of boot marks like a bewitched fool, instead of tending to his own business.

As luck would have it, almost immediately he found a large tree limb having many off-shoots that would serve his need admirably. It was short work to chop off a number of these, but took rather longer to saw some rounds from the main branch to be used for the top and bottom of the cage. Adding his collection to the knapsack, he slung it over his shoulders, then was stricken into immobility. Faint, but discernible, his shadow was on the sand. His head jerked up. The sun was breaking through, the fog almost dispersed. Before he could check the impulse, he had turned to the west.

How stealthily it had crept in. The long shining line that was the outstretched arm of the mighty Atlantic. Even as he watched, frozen, a clear green wave lapped toward his boots . . .

The great ship wallowed helplessly, tossed by mountainous waves and battered by the screaming gale. With all his strength he fought to stand, but his legs would not obey him. A deafening crash. A shocking impact that hurled him from the bunk and extinguished the lamp, plunging the cabin into darkness. The need to get out became a frenzy. She was going down . . . Somehow, he was crawling along the slanting quarter-deck. Then the freezing, tumultuous water had him in its relentless hold. He tried to swim, but his efforts were too feeble. He was drawn under . . . suffocating . . . tossed up again into the ravening night, choking, blinded, gulping air into his tortured lungs, only to be dragged down . . . down . . . He was cold . . . so terribly cold . . . He *must* get back up to . . .

Daylight. His cheek was pressed against the ground. He was panting, and bewildered because the beach was bent in a most odd fashion. He lifted his head, had the dizzy sensation of falling, and with a convulsive grab, steadied himself. He looked again at the beach. A shocked gasp was torn from him, and a cold sweat broke out on his skin. Once again his mind had blotted out an indeterminate interval, returning him to a here and now that was nightmarish. He was halfway up the cliff, with a sheer drop below, and an equally sheer rock face stretching above. His hands, clinging desperately to a clump of furze, were scratched and dirty. His head swam when another quick scan confirmed the fact that he was somewhere north of Castle Triad and far past the point at which the cliff could be climbed without rope and pickaxe. Whatever could have possessed him to do so insane a thing? Why must his mind continually force him to such pointless and humiliating acts? That he had clawed his way this far was well nigh incredible. Dreading to do so, he made himself look up. The rock wall soared above, high and stark and unconquerable. He closed his eyes, trying to get his breath. He had wished for death often in these past two years. Well, here it was, for he could not possibly climb up, and the sea was directly below now, the waves rushing in as though eager to receive him. The dread of falling again into that terrible embrace turned his bones to water, and in desperation he tightened his hold on the furze. Whatever happened, he must not let the sea take him!

And so he searched the rock face until he found a likely fissure. Bracing his boots against a slight outcropping, he made a wild grab with his left hand, and was able to take hold. Again, he sought about. A jagged outthrust above his head looked impossibly far, but he lunged at it. The edges crumbled under his fingers. Frantic, he gripped harder, feeling his nails splinter as his hand slipped, and breathing again when his clawing fingers closed around a firm surface. Displaced particles rained down into his face. He ducked his head against the cliff, blinking tears and dust from his eyes, then strove on, driven by the all-consuming need to escape the hungry tide that surged and waited far below.

His progress was torturously slow. Soon, each breath cut like a red hot knife through his chest, and his arms and shoulders ached fiercely. But he struggled on, never looking any farther than for his next hand-hold, fighting to survive for just another foot or two, often slipping, but somehow contriving to hang on. He was tiring and knew he couldn't last much longer. Despairing, he dared look up. His heart gave a wild leap. The top of the cliff was less than a yard above his hand! For an instant, he was so elated that his vigilance relaxed, and almost, at the moment of triumph, he lost his hold. But with a surge of strength, he clawed his way up until he could grasp the edge, and, Praise God! there was a root to be seized and clung to. Another minute, and he was sprawling on level ground at last.

Gradually, his thundering heartbeat eased and he was able to order his thoughts. He must present a fine sight, for his coat was torn, and the knees of his breeches hung in bloodstained rags. Inevitably, Jennifer's dear image came to mind. Suppose she had been on one of her early rides? Suppose she'd seen his stupid performance? She would believe then that he was well named: Crazy Jack, with a brain that played cruel tricks. Perhaps, one day he would no longer be permitted to return from his nightmarish lapses ... Perhaps his deepest dread was becoming a reality, and he was going mad.

He lay gazing up at the sky, and knew that he had no right to whine, or to sometimes, however briefly, allow himself to forget that truly he was, at best, only the shadow of a man.

❧ *Chapter 4* ❧

Howland Britewell held back his spirited black, and leaning toward his sister enquired teasingly, "Not too chilly for you this morning, I trust, Madam Professor?"

Jennifer gave him a laughing glance. The fog had burned off, unveiling one of those rare and brilliant days that sometimes arrive with late summer. The air was brisk and invigorating, the sea sparkling under the clear blue bowl of the heavens, and this proud and rugged coast at its most beautiful. "I am all a'shiver," she declared gaily. "We must gallop to warm me up."

"Of course. But first I'd like to chat a while, an you don't object."

He smiled still, but she felt a twinge of apprehension. Howland could be such a dear person when he chose, and this past week he had been at his charming best, full of fun and good humour, neither goading Fleming into defending his obsession with the world's great religions, nor mocking Royce's "revolutionary notions." Not once, since Lord Green's departure, had he spoken of the baron's admiration for her. She had hoped, in fact, that he had decided to respect her feelings in the matter. Heaven knows, she'd made them sufficiently clear. Without comment, she drew her mare to a walk, and waited.

"I met Miss Caroline Morris yesterday," he said idly.

"When you were in St. Ives? Oh, I wish I had gone with

you! Is she well? It seems an age since any of them came to see us."

"So it is. His lordship doesn't really approve of us, you know. And for my part I've no admiration of his high-in-the-instep condescension. The lovely Caroline is another matter, however."

Jennifer smiled. "That comes as no great surprise, dear. Had she a message for me?"

"Indeed, yes. And some news that *will* surprise you. Caro sends you her affectionate regards, and . . ." He watched her quizzically.

"What? What? Oh, Howland, *pray* do not be such a tease!"

"And I am instructed to tell you that you are to be invited down to Breton Ridge for a few days, when her second- or third- or some such cousin arrives."

"A party?" Jennifer gave a squeal of delight. "How lovely! Which cousin, do you know? They have family everywhere. Oh, I hope 'tis the Bath Morrises. Do you recall when they came two years ago? Miss Eliza Morris was such a merry—"

"It is not Miss Eliza. Nor any sort of Miss at all, but some fellow from Surrey—or is it Sussex?—who will likely turn out to be fat as a flounder and a dead bore, with a squint and a wooden leg, so do not be indulging any romantical flights of fancy, when— By Jove! Only look who has come back."

Jennifer looked. The colours in her cheeks heightened as rapidly as the sparkle in her eyes faded. In low-voiced vexation she said, "You arranged this! Oh, how could you be so sly? I *thought* it remarkable that you should offer to ride with me, when you so seldom—"

"Tally ho!" Hibbard Green rode to meet them. Resplendent in a puce coat over-burdened with silver braid, and a cravat whose laces bore mute testimony to several meals, he waved exuberantly. He had an atrocious seat, and the exertion of riding had left him puffing and red faced, but he declared disjointedly that Miss Britewell put the sun to shame, damme if she didn't. "And how are . . . you,

Britewell? Here's the bad penny . . . turned up on your . . . doorstep again, eh?"

Jennifer smiled with good manners, if not warmth.

Howland clasped his lordship's hand and said, beaming, "Welcome, sir! May we count on your making a longer stay at Triad this time?"

"Be my very great pleasure." Manoeuvring his mount between them, Green eyed Jennifer with exaggerated roguishness. "Any man worthy of the name delights in the chase, especially when the quarry is so enticingly curvesome, no?"

Even Howland looked taken aback by this gaucherie, and Jennifer's astonished stare caused his lordship to add a rather too hearty, "And never be so formal, Howland. No need to 'sir' me. There ain't many years between us, y'know."

Blinking, Jennifer said, "Really? When I met your son Rafe, I was sure he was at least—"

"At all events, you're well met," inserted Howland quickly. "I recollect that I promised my father to go over the deeds to the mine with him and our man of business. My apologies, Jennifer, but perhaps Lord Green will oblige me by taking you for that gallop."

"I could not be more willing," remarked his lordship, with a sly wink at the deus ex machina.

Pale with anger, Jennifer said, "Thank you, but—"

"No 'buts,' sister mine," said Howland. "Poor Hibbard will think you have taken him in dislike if you refuse his escort."

Lord Green looked crushed. "Jove, but have I offended, then? In truth, I've the greatest admiration for you, Miss Jennifer, but if you find me repulsive, I shall take myself off."

She did indeed find him repulsive, but to admit that would be both unkind and an unthinkable breach of manners. From the corner of her eye she saw Howland regarding her grimly. Why he should be so set on this creature purchasing the mine was beyond her, but there was no doubt that she was properly trapped. Bowing to that fact, she said that his lordship had given no offence and that she would be glad of his company "for a short gallop."

Green brightened, and with a satisfied grin Howland rode away.

Determined to give the odious baron no least encouragement to flirt with her, Jennifer led off across the high moor at a steady trot. His lordship accompanied her eagerly, but he was very soon panting and dishevelled, his unlovely countenance ever more heated as he bounced all over the saddle. Almost, Jennifer pitied him, but she was sure he meant to make her an offer she had no wish to hear, and when he gasped out a request that they stop and have "a friendly cose" she replied, "Oh, but you promised me a gallop, sir," and touched home her spurs.

Her mare was full of spirit, and needed no urging. An excellent horsewoman, Jennifer leaned forward, thoroughly enjoying the rush of wind against her face as they raced along the cliffs. She glanced over her shoulder, sure that Green had been left far behind. She had reckoned without the man's implacable determination. That his temper was exacerbated was evident, but he was closing fast. He was mounted on one of Papa's favourite horses, and unaccustomed to flailing whip and goring spurs, the big bay was clearly frightened.

With a pang of conscience for the sake of the animal, Jennifer slowed and as his lordship thundered up, protested, "Lud, sir, but you are mighty free with your whip!"

"Sometimes," he jerked out, "one must be cruel . . . to be kind." He guided the snorting bay very close. "I think you must not have heard, ma'am. I desired you to stop."

Disliking the small space between them, Jennifer reined Chanteuse to the left. "As my brother informed you, I came out for a gallop, my lord. There is not the least need for you to feel obliged to accompany me."

"There is every need, my dear," he argued, again pulling closer. "I've something to offer you which will, I am assured, bring joy and pride to your pretty self."

A confident smirk overspread the coarse features. It was incredible, she thought, that he did not sense her aversion.

More incredible that a man more than twice her age, and with neither looks, physique, nor a pleasant demeanour to recommend him, should believe himself so splendid a catch. She said coolly, "Since our acquaintance is of such brief duration, sir, 'twould be improper for me to accept a gift from you."

"A gift!" He slapped his thigh and gave a roar of laughter. "That's rich! But perchance you're in the right of it, for in a sense 'tis the greatest gift a man may offer a maid."

"Then I most certainly could not accept, my lord." He was so near to her now that his knee was brushing Chanteuse's side. Jennifer could only be grateful that he had not come up on the left, in which case his knee would be making contact with her own, and once more she drew the mare away. "Furthermore," she said, "I do not care to—"

His bay lunged at her. Before she could react, his great fist had closed on her bridle. "You're a coy puss," he grinned. "But do not over-play your hand, sweeting, else—"

"I am not your sweeting," she declared angrily. "And you crowd me, Lord Green. It does not do to ride so close to the edge. Pray let go!"

"So I will, when you have heard me out." He forced Chanteuse to a prancing halt, and without releasing Jennifer's rein said, "There's no call to play the demure schoolroom miss with me, m'dear. I am already caught in your toils. Aye, I'll own it. There were obstacles my sire would have balked at, I grant, but there's no call for you to worry. I know you're barren, and it don't weigh with me. I've got myself an heir. I'll own I'd like it better were your father of higher rank, but my own lineage will counterbalance that. As for your fortune, y'r brother tells me 'tis not large. Mine is. I'm a warm man, love." He chuckled appallingly, and bent towards her. "In more ways than one . . . So you need not fear I'll be unable to satisfy you in the bedchamber. There now, I'll wager you never dreamed of winning such a splendid offer, eh?"

Momentarily rendered speechless with disgust, she thought, 'Not in my worse nightmare!' It was clear that the dense peer believed he had paid her a great compliment however, and keeping a tight hold on her temper she managed to say more or less evenly, "I assume you have asked my father's permission to pay your addresses."

"No need for that, my duck. Sir Vinson will be overjoyed that you've made such a catch. Come now," he released her bridle and reached out a massive arm. "A kiss or two ... to seal our bargain."

The thought of allowing those thick loose lips to touch her mouth was revolting. Incensed, she drove home her spurs.

Chanteuse gave a surprised snort and bounded forward.

"Hey!" roared Green.

"You forget your manners, sir," cried Jennifer leaning forward in the saddle.

His angry curse was not muffled. His spurs raked the bay's sides and the terrified animal leapt into a full gallop, very soon coming up with the mare.

"I like a lass with spirit, burn me if I don't," said Green tersely. "But do not push me too far, puss."

Alarmed, as he crowded her dangerously near to the edge, Jennifer cried, "Let be! You leave me no room!"

"Then stop your playing, and—"

The ground here was fractured and uneven. Panicked, Chanteuse reared. Only her superb horsemanship kept Jennifer from being thrown. His lordship wrenched the bay around. The horse cavorted, neighing his terror. One back leg slipped over the edge. With a wild plunge, he managed to scramble up.

My lord Green was less fortunate. Uttering a deafening screech, he hurtled from sight.

With his scream ringing in her ears, Jennifer flung herself from the saddle and ran to the edge of the cliff. Much as she disliked the man, she would never have wished him harm, and she peered downward, dreading to see his lifeless body far below. His lordship was still clinging to life, however. Literally. His great hands were gripped around a jutting rock, his legs flailing as he sought in vain for a foothold.

"Thank heaven!" she gasped. "Hold tight, sir. I'll fetch help."

"No!" he shouted. "Help me now!"

Even if she could reach his hand, she knew she'd be unable to pull him up. But she might contrive to steady him until he could gain a foothold. She lay flat and reached down, but although she leaned as far as she dared, she was far short of touching him. Distracted, she called, "It is no use! I must get help. Try to—"

"Stupid girl! I *am* trying! Find a—a rope. Or *something* to throw down. I can't last—much longer!"

His face was almost grey with fear, his eyes bulging and frantic. In desperation, Jennifer looked about for some way to help before he plummeted to his death.

"Miss Jennifer!"

The shout came like the answer to a prayer. She gave a cry of gratitude as Crazy Jack sprinted to her. A corner of her mind registered the fact that he looked dreadfully tattered and untidy, but then he was holding her outstretched hands, and she half-sobbed, "Thank God you have come! Poor Lord Green has fallen over the cliff. Help him, I beg you!"

He went at once to the brink. Green was clinging to an outcropping and had managed to brace one foot against the side, but terror made his voice hoarse as he wheezed, "Help! I'll—I'll make it worth your while!"

It was now high tide, and hypnotised by the sight of the waves far below, Jonathan scarcely heard him.

A small hand touched his arm. He started and looked into Jennifer's pleading eyes, and all that mattered was that he was here, when she needed him.

He patted her hand and looked about for something to use. Except for some clumps of furze, and Green's riding crop, which was too short, there was nothing. But the knapsack was still on his back, and he had the small axe. He shrugged out of the harness.

Green gobbled something incoherent.

Watching Jack empty driftwood and tools from the knapsack, Jennifer tried to keep her voice from trembling. "What can I do?"

"Bring up the horses. Gently." He flashed her a quick smile. "Don't scare them."

She was enormously relieved by his unexpectedly assured manner, and obeyed at once. The big bay was grazing, but he was still nervous and flighty and each time she tried to catch the trailing reins he tossed his head and danced away. She turned to Chanteuse and led the mare to Jack.

He used the axe blade to cut the reins off close, while Jennifer again attempted to catch the bay. The big horse shied at her approach, then moved off again. Her heart sank and she ran back to report failure.

"For the love . . . of *God*!" howled his lordship.

"Coming, sir," called Jonathan.

Jennifer watched him knot the reins with swift and practiced ease. One end was tied securely to the mare's stirrup, and the other attached to a shoulder strap of his knapsack.

He led Chanteuse to the top of the cliff. He was far from sure the improvised rope would be long enough, and was elated when the free-hanging strap of the knapsack dangled only a foot or so above the baron's head. "There's a loop within your reach," he called. "Take hold, and we'll have you up in no time."

Green's terrified eyes glared at him. "How can I—take hold, damn you?" he screeched. "I can't let go! Come down for me!"

Jonathan stood very still. He had just fought his way up that terrible rock face and he was still shaken. It was asking too much to expect him to endure such an ordeal again.

"No!" Jennifer caught his arm. "You cannot!"

"Come *down* I—tell you!" howled Green. "I'll—I'll pay you! A hundred pounds! Come down!"

"The rope won't hold you both," called Jennifer. "The loop is well within your reach! Won't you please *try*!"

But Green would not relinquish his hold, and repeated his demands that she send "the looby" after him, a sob in his voice, and curses alternating with his frantic pleas.

On his previous visit to Castle Triad, Green had come to see the school-house. He had laughed at Jack's carpentry and thoroughly enjoyed himself by taunting the "village idiot" in front of Jennifer. How disgraceful it was, she thought, that even in this terrible moment he would villify the man he commanded to risk his life to save him.

Jonathan fought to conceal his own terror, but his hands trembled as he pulled the leathers up again. "He's properly panicked. I'll have to go down, Miss Jennifer."

He twisted the free shoulder loop twice about his left arm, then with the same hand took a firm grip on the knapsack above it.

Jennifer's face was chalk white, her eyes dark with anxiety as he sat on the edge of the cliff. She whispered through dry lips, "But—the leathers . . . they surely cannot . . ."

"With luck, they'll only have to hold us both for a few minutes. Hold the mare steady until I have him, then back her, and pull us up."

He spoke lightly and made it sound easy, but she knew better. "God bless you," she faltered.

He smiled at her with a calm he was extremely far from feeling, then swung over the edge and began to lower himself. For as long as was possible, he clung to the top of the cliff with his right hand. His foot located a firm toe-hold, and he called hopefully, "Green! Can you reach my ankle?"

"The—the hell with your blasted . . . ankle! My *hand*, curse you! Take my hand!"

Confound the fellow! Steadying himself against the granite, Jonathan abandoned his hold on the top. The makeshift rope lurched and the loop of the knapsack tightened, biting into his upper arm. To an extent he was able to brace his feet against the side, but most of his weight was on that loop now. The wind was rising, the breakers coming in faster and harder. Above those sounds he could hear the sobbing rasps of Green's breathing. His lordship's convulsed face was just below. He steadied his boot against the cliff and stretched down his right hand. "Take hold, sir!"

Green hunched his great shoulders, then howled, "Too

far! Come nearer, you block! Quickly, damn your eyes! *Quickly!*"

Jonathan glanced up and caught a glimpse of Jennifer's gown fluttering in the breeze. "I can't come much lower. Brace your feet, and grab. *Try!*"

"No! It's—it's too far! *Closer*, I tell you!"

Jonathan shouted, "Can you come just a step nearer, Miss Jennifer?"

Chanteuse was balking, her eyes rolling with fear. Stroking her sweating neck, Jennifer said soothingly, "It's all right, girl. Just a little way. Just one pace. Good girl ... easy now ..." And she thought, 'Pray God she doesn't rear up! Please, Lord—let her not sidle.'

Another jolt on that terribly thin line, and Jonathan leaned down again. "Come," he urged breathlessly. "Take my hand."

Tears streaked his lordship's pale face as his staring eyes fixed on Jonathan's outstretched hand. He gabbled, "I—I cannot! I daren't let go! I *daren't*! The leather is—is too *thin*. It won't hold us!"

There was hysteria in the voice. Jonathan said sharply, "It's the only chance you have. The leather will hold if you brace your feet as we go up. If you don't, we'll likely both fall."

The fingers of his lordship's right hand fluttered, only to clamp down harder. "Damn you! I *can't!*"

"Good Lord! Do you *want* to die? I promise you I do not! My arm is getting numb. I'll count to three, then you must climb up alone. One ..."

"No! Do not *dare* to leave me, you worthless—clod!"

"Two ..."

"Very well! Very well!" The words were a sobbing wail. "But—if you let me fall ..."

"Grab my wrist if you can. *Now!*"

With a mighty effort, his lordship snatched for and caught Jonathan's wrist. The added weight caused the makeshift rope to jerk madly, and Jonathan held his breath, and wondered if his life ended here. Green lunged again, missed, let out a piercing shriek, and, kicking madly at the cliff face propelled himself upward and seized Jonathan's forearm.

Feeling that he was being torn in half, and convinced the leather must snap at any second, Jonathan shouted gaspingly, "Back . . . Jennifer! Back!"

Chanteuse was snorting and tossing her head about in terror. Guiding her away from the edge, Jennifer scarcely dared glance at the thin, taut leather, and she talked to the mare gently, trying not to betray her own fear. One step . . . two . . . Was it her imagination, or was the saddle slipping . . . On the thought, the saddle jerked to the side. The mare whinnied shrilly and tried to tear free. Clinging to the bridle with all her strength, Jennifer cried aloud, "Dear Father in Heaven—don't let them fall . . ."

It was a prayer Jonathan echoed. His right arm felt as if it was being dragged from the socket, and the strap had bitten so deeply into his left arm that he could no longer feel the fingers that gripped the knapsack, so that he dreaded lest he should unwittingly relax his hold. With both hands immobilised he was unable to guide their ascent except with his feet, and Green's bulk hampered those efforts.

"Try to . . . brace yourself," he gasped.

Green responded hoarsely, "If you . . . let me fall . . . you'll pay, I promise you! Can't you . . . move faster?"

Jonathan did not dignify such nonsense with an answer. They scarcely seemed to move. The blood began to roar in his ears, and his eyes were blurring. There was a sudden sharp crack and the pressure on his left arm was released. He thought in anguish, 'The leather snapped!' and tensed, waiting for the terrible plunge into the sea.

Strong hands tugged at him. Jennifer was saying breathlessly, "Let go! Lord Green—you are safe now, you can let his wrist go."

He was lying on the turf! Jonathan thought, 'Halleluiah! We're up!'

The pack was being unwound from his arm. Jennifer was peering into his face, rolling back his sleeve. "Oh, but you will have some horrid bruises! Does it pain you very badly?"

He tried to tell her that his arm was numb, but his words were drowned by a wrathful howl.

"Never mind *him*! Spare a moment's compassion for . . . for your guest!"

Jennifer turned to the baron. Her first irreverent thought was that he looked like a beached whale. Ashamed of such unkindness, she saw that his face was brick red. Dreading lest he suffer a seizure she knelt beside him and took his hand. "Poor soul. Thank heaven Jack was able to pull you up."

His sense of ill-usage exacerbated by the uneasy suspicion that he had been made to appear ridiculous, Green gulped chokingly, "Had it not been . . . for your . . . missish airs, I'd not have . . . been thrown."

Her nerves were in shreds, but she managed to refrain from pointing out that it was his own deplorable conduct that had plunged him into such peril. She was unable, however, to infuse any warmth into her voice when she enquired, "Can you stand? Or shall I ride for a carriage?"

He did not at once reply. Then, he growled, "You may help me up."

She helped as best she could, and he leaned on her heavily as he struggled to his feet. He was still puffing, but his physical strength, together with a complete lack of imagination, was already enabling him to feel more the thing. He kept his arm about her, murmuring, "Well, now. This is better. Be damned if you ain't a choice armful."

"I see you are recovered," said Jennifer dryly. "Let me go, if you please. I must help poor Jack. He has—"

Green spared a glance at his rescuer. "The looby don't need you. He's— Hey!" He pushed Jennifer aside. "What the devil have you got there?"

Jonathan had managed to get to his knees, and was looking at a small glittering object he had found lying in the grass. It was a piece of quartz, no more than three inches in height, about half an inch thick, and shaped rather like a gravestone with a rounded top. The primitive outline of a large head, with stubby legs beneath, was carved into the front, and two fine opals formed the eyes. He thought inconsequently that it must be very old; probably quite valuable ... Vaguely comprehending that Green had bellowed something, he glanced up in time to see his lordship's heavy riding crop whizzing down at him. Instinctively, he jerked his head aside, but the crop slammed against his temple, and sent him sprawling again.

Green wrenched the small figurine from his lax hand, and, apparently in the grip of an uncontrollable fury, rained blows at him, while Jonathan tried dazedly to get to his feet, and threw up an arm to protect his head. "Filthy scum!" snarled his lordship. "Thought you could slip it in ... your pocket, did you? ... I'll teach you some respect for—"

Jennifer, who had been momentarily frozen with outrage, ran to seize his arm. "Are you gone demented? Stop that at once!"

His countenance almost purple, his lordship thrust her away. "If there's one breed of vermin I cannot abide, 'tis a sly ... worthless ... thief!"

His whip cracked down to emphasise each accusation.

A blinding wrath seared Jonathan.

Jennifer saw his eyes narrow to slits of steel, and the long hands clench into fists. Horrified, she thought, 'Do not hit back! For pity's sake, do not! They'll hang you!'

Jonathan's hand flashed out and caught the flying thong of the whip.

His lordship gave a startled growl.

Trying to come between them, Jennifer demanded, "Have you no gratitude? This man just saved your life!"

Green swore blisteringly and jerked at the whip. Jonathan hung on and pulled himself to his feet, eager to deal with this carrion that called itself a man.

'Never, whatever the provocation ...'

He thought prayerfully, 'God, *please*! Just this once ...?' But he had sworn on what was left of his honour, and honour must be obeyed. And thus, though it took every ounce of his willpower and left him trembling with frustrated rage, he mastered his temper, and relinquished his hold.

"Did you see the swine?" bellowed Green, swinging the whip high. "Tried to attack his betters, be damned if he didn't!"

"He tried to stop you only," countered Jennifer, tugging at his upraised arm. "You know very well he dare not defend himself 'gainst you!"

"Did you hear how the scum called me? 'Green!' he said! *Green*, damme! As though he were my equal! Stand aside, madam!"

"Did you expect him to bother with titles when every second counted? How can you be so *foolish*? He did not steal your silly jewel!"

Green saw that Jennifer's lovely face was flushed with fury. "Well, well," he sneered. "Here's a heat. Taken a fancy to the half-wit, have you?"

Her head tossed upward. She said haughtily, "I think you forget yourself, my lord! But I'll not deny I admire courage. And your own behaviour leaves much to be desired!"

Briefly, an ugly expression came into his eyes. Then he grinned broadly. "For my part, I admire a woman of spirit, so I promise not to hold your impertinence 'gainst you."

"You are too good," she said.

Her sarcasm was lost on him. He jabbed his whip at Jonathan. "As for you, fellow, I am a Justice of the Peace in my own county and have sat in judgment on several of your kind. I shall have a word with Sir Vinson Britewell. You belong in Bedlam, where you can't turn on some helpless woman or child!"

It wouldn't take much, Jennifer knew, for the villagers to speak out against "Crazy Jack," and Howland would be glad enough to see him condemned to that ghastly asylum. She said with icy contempt, "I cannot believe that any gentleman would repay gallantry in so shabby a way!"

"Gallantry, is it?" Green picked up the knapsack and the broken length of leather. "Lunacy, more like. No man in his right mind would have entrusted our lives to this makeshift rope. Lucky it lasted till the mare was dragging us on the turf, else I might have been killed!"

Jennifer assisted Jack to a group of boulders and said

over her shoulder, "I take it you'd have preferred that he let you fall."

She expected an impassioned response, but Green was silent, frowning down at the knapsack. "Sit here, Jack," she said kindly. "You must be quite exhausted, poor soul. And only look at your hands! Much thanks you got for your bravery!"

Lord Green wound the leather around the knapsack and said, "Don't set all those scrapes to my account, Miss Jennifer. He was well marked before he climbed down. Likely got into a brawl with some public spirited Roselley folk." He strolled closer. "Tell the lady the truth, fellow. That's it, ain't it?"

Breathing hard, and clutching his left arm, to which feeling was returning with a vengeance, Jonathan muttered, "No."

"Leave him alone, for mercy's sake," exclaimed Jennifer.

"Why, so I will. When he answers me politely. Explain why you look as if you'd swum through a bramble bush, looby, or my lady will be blaming me! And address me properly, unless you enjoy the feel of this whip."

Jonathan said wearily, "I had climbed . . . up the cliff. My lord."

Jennifer gave a start and stared at him, her eyes wide.

Green's jaw fell. "You—had—climbed up—the cliff?" He threw back his head and bellowed with laughter. "What a rasper! Oho, but you've chose a fine liar to pity, Miss Jennifer! Climbed up the cliff, indeed! No one could make that climb—save maybe a monkey!" Laughing still, he marched to the bay horse, which grazed nearby, and mounted up. "I offer you my escort, ma'am."

"And I decline it," she said disdainfully.

To her surprise, he voiced no argument, but turned his mount and rode away. Watching that erratic departure, she said through her teeth, "Horrid, *horrid* creature!"

She was very sure of the tale that would be poured into her brother's ears. For her own protection she should go home at once, and yet . . . She glanced at the man who sat on the boulder, head downbent and eyes closed. The boorish baron had taunted her with having "taken a fancy" to him. How typical of Green to have uttered such a vulgarity. She was interested in Jack because ... because he was a puzzle. And because she had never been able to see anyone suffer and not want to help.

She touched his shoulder, and said gently, "I am truly sorry that Lord Green treated you so badly. You were magnificent, and I shall see to it that you are rewarded for ..." She faltered to a halt as she felt him stiffen.

Not looking up, he said, "Thank you. You had best go, ma'am."

She had offended and had been politely set down. Torn between astonishment and vexation, she said, "Yes," and took a step towards Chanteuse, who was cropping the turf contentedly. But she could not bring herself to leave him in such a way. She thought, 'I suppose I was clumsy, and should have known the poor man still has some pride.' She turned back. "Are you all right?"

"Perfectly. I thank you."

But his voice was less sure and he hadn't once looked at her. She crossed to take his chin in her hand and tilt his head up.

My lord's whip had left a long crimson welt from his left temple to the corner of his mouth, and another blow had reopened the cut on his brow. "Oh, my!" she gasped, and in an attempt to hide her rage and the sense of being partly responsible because one of her father's guests had done this, she said with a tremulous smile, "I see I must sacrifice another kerchief. I seem to spend a good deal of my time tending your hurts."

Although he had allowed her to raise his head, his lashes were lowered and he still would not meet her eyes. He said expressionlessly, "You are very kind. But—but I can manage now. There is no need for—for you to stay."

"Oh, none," she responded, his humility only adding to her mortification. "I am very sure you would be happy to bleed all the way home. Dear me, this will not do. Perhaps I must form the habit of carrying one of my papa's handkerchiefs with me if you will persist in your show of humble martyrdom!"

At that his eyes opened wide, and a flood of colour lit his scratched and dirty face. "Show!" he exclaimed. "What could I have—"

"Oh, I know. I know." Amazed that she should have made such a waspish remark, she flashed a repentant smile at him. " 'Tis the very thing I said to Lord Green, is it not? That you dare not resist a peer of the realm. And, do you know, for a moment I was sure you meant to give him back his own."

A twinkle came into his eyes. "So was I."

"Thank heaven you did not! Though I cannot help but marvel you were able to restrain yourself."

The twinkle faded. He muttered, "I have not the right to—to raise my hand 'gainst any man."

"Of course you have! 'Twould be folly were you to strike an aristocrat, of course, but—" She bit her lip, and knowing that had sounded patronising, she added hastily, "Though I'd not be surprised to find that you're as well born as Lord Green."

"A dubious distinction, madam." The dry response was out before he could check it.

Again, Jennifer had caught a glimpse of another man. She burst into laughter, her merriment warming his captive heart and bringing his slow smile into being.

"Oh, Jack," she said breathlessly. "How he would rage if he'd heard us! Here," she gave him the gory handkerchief, "this will help a little. Now— What are you about, sir?"

He stood. "I must gather—gather my—"

"Your wits!" She tugged at his sleeve pulling him back down again and sitting beside hm. "You are scarce able to stand straight, and white as any sheet, and small wonder! When you have rested a little you shall ride Chanteuse as far as Triad, and—" Relieved to see his lips twitch at this prospect, she said laughingly, "Ah, you can still smile, thank goodness!"

"I think 'twould make a quaint picture, ma'am, for me to ride sidesaddle, while you walked! A few minutes rest and

I will be very well, I promise you. If you would be so—so very kind as to send someone here with my knapsack, I—"

"I will be so very kind as to tell you to stop trying to be rid of me."

Be *rid* of her? He stared at her speechlessly. He ached from head to foot, his arm throbbed miserably, and he was crushingly tired, but to be near her, to be able to talk with her alone without shocked or disapproving glances, was joy beyond measure.

He had, decided Jennifer, what Caro Morris would term "speaking eyes." She said firmly, "Oh, you may stare, but I know very well that the instant I go away you will start bustling about, pretending to be some mythical being, above such mortal things as pain and exhaustion."

"Lord Green was evidently able to overcome such weaknesses."

"Lord Green is twice your size and has never known what it is to go hungry, much less practically starve for—for heaven only knows how long! Besides which, all he had to do was hang onto a rock until he was rescued. A far cry from what you very bravely achieved. Now, sir, although I am very willing to sit and make sure you do as you are bid, I'm not willing to discuss that—nobleman, so we will talk of something else, if you please."

Briefly, the quirkish grin touched his mouth. He sketched a bow, and said meekly, "As you wish, Miss Jennifer. Would you like to comment upon my—building materials?"

Slight as it had been, the bow was rendered with unconscious grace, and reinforced her belief that he was of gentle birth. She said, "Aha! You took my advice, I see. Then that is for your little bird? How is he? Have you given him a name?"

"Yes, ma'am. Duster will go along better when I've made him a proper cage. And so shall I."

Her eyebrows lifted in a silent question, and he explained, "I fashioned him a makeshift swing, which I think he likes, for he becomes agitated if I take it out. But he has a withered claw, you know, and now and then—usually in the middle of the night—he seems to lose his grip on the

71

swing and goes crashing down, and then rushes about creating a great deal of noise and confusion."

Jennifer laughed. "Whereby your sleep is interrupted, is it?"

"So much so that the next swing will be far more sturdy, *and* lower!"

"I cannot credit that so small a creature could cause such a fuss, Jack. Do you not—" Interrupting herself, she asked, "Were you christened Jack? Or is it just a nickname?"

He said slowly, "My name is Jonathan, ma'am. And I seem to recall someone . . . calling me 'Johnny.' "

"Someone? A man? A lady?"

"A lady."

'A woman—and likely he is wed,' she thought, and wondered why that possibility had not occurred to her before.

Jonathan stared blankly at his scattered driftwood, and Jennifer frowned at Chanteuse.

After a brief silence, she asked rather brusquely, "Why did you tell Lord Green that you had climbed up the cliff?"

"Because I had, ma'am."

She shook her head. "Come now, Ja—Jonathan. My brother Royce has climbed in Italy and is considered most skilled, yet he told me there is no way up the cliff face north of Devil's Ladder, without a man uses climbing equipment."

His lips tightened, but he said nothing.

"Won't you tell me what really happened?" she persisted, thinking that the children would be punished if they were responsible.

"I told you what happened, Miss Jennifer."

Taken aback by the touch of hauteur in his voice, she demanded, "Look at me."

He met her eyes with a cool and steady gaze. It went against common sense for her to believe this ever more incomprehensible man, but she found she could no longer doubt him. Awed, she murmured, "You must be a superb climber. Even so, the risk was dreadful. Why ever would you do so mad a thing?"

His eyes fell.

"It is as I thought!" she exclaimed. "Those boys were tormenting you again."

"No. But—please, do not ask, Miss Jennifer. See, I am better. Allow me to throw you up. You will be missed by now."

She really was being dismissed! The effrontery of the man! Irked, she said, "Oh, very well," and as she settled herself into the saddle, added, "if you must be so surly, I will—"

His hand closed on her boot. A pair of ardent grey eyes gazed up at her, and he declared with passionate intensity, "Never that! 'Fore heaven, I would die sooner than—" He broke off with a gasp, then drew back, and stammered, " 'Tis only that— It is something I try not to— I do not like to—to speak of."

But he had betrayed himself. More moved than she would have thought possible, she felt her face flame, which was ridiculous. Confused by her reaction, and not a little embarrassed, she turned away and gazed out to sea. "Oh, look!" she exclaimed, admiringly. "What a great ship! Such a lovely sight!"

He watched her slim figure, the feather that curled down beside her smooth cheek, the little boot that peeped from under her habit, and he said quietly, "Very lovely," then lowered his eyes quickly as she turned to him.

"You're not looking!" she said accusingly. "Johnny, you must! She is under full sail!"

"Yes, for the breeze has come up."

"She is a ship of the line, do you agree?"

He stared fixedly at the ground. "More likely she is just a—a merchantman."

"Never! I demand that you inspect her and admit I am right! She carries that new sail they call the—oh, what is it? Off the bowsprit, I mean." Finding that he still had not turned his head, she tugged his hair gently. "Why must you be so stubborn, wretched creature? You will know what 'tis called. See there."

His glance was very brief, and his voice sharp with strain when he answered, "It is called the jib."

Having dwelt always on this wild coast, the sea and ships were so much a part of her life that it had never occurred to her that anyone might view them in a different light. With sudden intuitive comprehension she murmured, "My heavens! So *that* is why you waited for a thick fog before you would go down to the beach for your driftwood! You fear the sea! Did the tide come in while you were on the beach? Is that why you made that frightful climb? Johnny—*is* that why?"

With a muffled exclamation he met her eyes, and said as if the words were torn from him, "Very likely. I don't remember. I was on the beach one moment and—and next thing I knew, I was halfway up the cliff. My—my mind, you see, so often plays me false. Your brother was right, Miss Britewell. You should ... steer clear of this—this shadow of a man!"

And he turned and left a lady who was alternately indignant and sympathetic, and more perplexed than ever.

Howland Britewell stared at Lord Green in mystification. "A spy?" he echoed. "You jest, I think. The man has not two brains to rub together. He don't even know who he is!"

"Does he not?" Green threw a quick glance to the door of the large apartment that was Howland's bedchamber and private parlour, then thrust a knapsack and a length of frayed leather at the younger man. "See here!"

Howland inspected the items curiously. "Is this what he used to haul you up? It does but confirm what I said. None but a lunatic would trust the lives of two men to such a botch!"

"The knots, you fool! The *knots!*"

To be addressed in such a way did not please Mr. Britewell. He said sardonically, "They appear to have held. Of itself, remarkable."

"Stap and spit me! Are you blind? They are *nautical* knots, or I'm a confounded Dutchman!" Green stamped to the window and back again. "Your precious village idiot is—or was—a *seafaring* man!"

Beginning to be very bored, Howland pointed out, "This, being a coastal region, is home to all manner of sailors, ex-sailors, smugglers, pirates—"

"Do not patronise me, damn your eyes!"

"My apologies, sir." A muscle rippled in Howland's jaw, but he was in no position to antagonise this uncouth individual, and he contrived to keep his temper. "If you're right, I'd judge him a deserter off some navy frigate, or an East Indiaman perchance. Why you should see a threat in that possibility is beyond me."

"I see a threat because he ain't what he seems! He may cringe and creep about like a looby, but when he come down after me he was mighty sure of himself. Ordered me about as though I were a blasted servant!"

Inwardly amused, Howland said gravely, "Still, he got you to safety. For which you must be grateful, my lord."

Green's response was as crude as it was explicit. He thrust his inflamed face at Howland, and hissed, "Shall I be grateful if he is come to undo our plans?"

Leaning forward in his chair and speaking as softly, Howland said, "If aught has leaked out it has not come from me! I've told no one of your discovery. Not even my father. If you think the Horse Guards suspect—"

At once Green's fierce little eyes became guarded. Drawing back, he said irritably, "Did I say he was from Whitehall? How if he is an *Excise* spy, would you *then* be as nonchalant?"

Howland shook his head. "You really must not take me for a complete fool, sir. I'm fully aware that whatever he has come to, there's no doubt Crazy Jack has known better days. Nor could there have been any doubt but that he was in desperate straits when our witch rescued him. The clod near died. His body carries numerous scars to attest to the rough treatment he was given, and they ain't painted on, you may be assured. Certainly, had he been a Riding Officer his comrades would have come to his aid sooner than stand by and see him expire. Perchance he's a poltroon who ran from the enemy. Or a rake who ran off with his colonel's mistress. Whatever the case, he's a derelict now; broken in mind and spirit. Not worth a pauper's grave."

Unconvinced, Green tossed his bulk onto a groaning sofa and tugged at his pouting lower lip. "What more do you know of him? He's been here only a short while, by what I hear."

"Six months, about. He was judged possessed of the evil eye in St. Just, and whipped from town at the cart tail. He

76

fared no better at Zenor, where they suspected him of being a wrecker, and stoned him from the area. That was a year or so back. More recently, he found work in Garrison Pen—the hamlet is gone now, buried under blowing sands. Some miners objected when one of their women took a fancy to him, and nigh beat him to death. That's when he dragged himself here, and the widow took him in."

Green, who had listened intently to this unhappy history, said a triumphant, "So you mistrusted him sufficiently to put out an enquiry!"

"And found him to be no more than he claims. May I hope your mind is at rest, my lord?"

"You may not! I mislike the way your sister smiles on him."

Whatever Howland might think privately, he permitted no member of his family to be criticised by an outsider. He said coldly, "Miss Britewell pities him, besides which she is pleased by the work the block has done for her. If you suppose she would for one instant look with favour on a mindless vagrant—"

"I'm not so daft. But he plays on her sympathies, and the lady has a tender heart. Is one of the reasons I want her for my bride."

Watching his companion's leer with revulsion, Howland leaned back in his chair and asked smoothly, "How does your courtship progress, my lord?"

"She delights to tease me." Green chuckled. "Saucy chit. She plays her cards exceeding well, affecting to be disinterested. Oh, never fear, I'm not deceived. You haven't seen my castle, m'boy, but I promise you 'tis one of the showplaces of Hampshire. I hold my court there, y'know. Put the fear of God into the miscreants who come before me. I fancy I could show you a hundred ladies who have dropped the handkerchief, for my fortune is large, and I've a way with the fair sex, besides. The women like a forceful man." He winked into Howland's rather set smile, and went on expansively, "No, no. The female don't draw breath who wouldn't give her soul to be Lady Hibbard Green, and mistress of Buckler Castle. Your pretty sister likes to play coquette, and I've no objection, for I enjoy a good chase, so you've nothing to fear on that head."

Howland was reminded of some of the rumours he'd heard about his lordship's treatment of the hapless prisoners who were haled before him. For just an instant he could not command his voice. Then he said, "I'm glad you are a patient man, sir."

"To a point!" Green's good humour vanished, and he said coldly, "But I want that dock, Britewell. And I want your father's signature on my deed. I've no doubt the old man delays, thinking to run up the price, but—"

"He delays because he don't like the prospect of an ugly dock on our beach, and ships unloading supplies at all hours!"

"Well, he'd best make up his mind. Everyone believes the Blue Rose Mine to be played out and worthless. He's getting a generous price for such a property."

Britewell said with soft emphasis, "Yes, if it *was* such a property. But if he knew what you and your alchemist have found in there . . . !"

"Then he would run up the price and likely bring in a flood of other bidders. And you and I, my dear fellow, would stand to lose a fortune! Besides which"—his lordship's smile was unpleasant—"I would have to demand immediate settlement on the very considerable sum you owe me."

Britewell's handsome features flushed with anger. "Oh, all right! All right!" he said sulkily. "I'll go down and have a word with my father."

Standing also, Green accompanied him to the door. "Choose your words carefully, friend," he advised. "Sir Vinson has *such* a prejudice 'gainst gaming. What a pity if I were obliged to shatter his faith in you."

Approaching her father's study, Jennifer heard irate voices and she paused for a moment, listening. Howland was there, but she could not detect my lord Green's harsh accents. She scratched at the door and went inside.

Both men stood at once, and Sir Vinson came around his

big desk to take her hand and scan her anxiously. "You have had a frightening experience, child. I wonder you can look so composed."

"And why you did not come home with Lord Green," murmured Howland, all innocence.

"Yes indeed. We worried about you." Sir Vinson guided Jennifer to a chair and pulled another close to her. "His lordship should not have left you alone after such a shock."

Howland's eyebrows went up. "Were you alone then, Jennifer?"

Ignoring him, she said to her father, "I stayed to help poor Jack. I expect his lordship will have told you, sir, that he fell from the cliff and that Jack climbed down and—"

"And also claims to have first climbed all the way up." Howland laughed. "What a farradiddle!"

Sir Vinson's fine eyes widened. "He never said such a thing? Oh, well. I suppose the poor fellow can scarce be held accountable."

"Or be thanked for a courageous rescue?" Angry, Jennifer flared, "He risked his life for that horrid man. And a fine reward he was given!"

"Guard your tongue, if you please, miss," said Sir Vinson, sternly. "Lord Green is my guest and I'll not have him insulted whilst he is under my roof."

Howland drawled, "If the looby expects to be paid for his services, I'll give him a guinea or two."

Jennifer sprang to her feet. "He asked *nothing* in return! And if to risk one's life can be dismissed with contempt as having rendered a 'service,' you've an odd notion of gallantry, brother!"

Sir Vinson waved his indignant heir to silence. "Your sister is overwrought, which is not to be wondered at. I feel sure Lord Green was more than grateful for Jack's intervention, Jennifer. Likely, he was too overset to be able properly to express himself."

"Oh, he expressed himself, sir! With his whip!"

Howland stared at her. Incredulous, Sir Vinson said, "Do you say he horse-whipped the man who had saved his neck? In the name of— Why?"

Jennifer sat down again and smoothed her windblown hair with quick angry movements. "Jack found something his lordship had evidently dropped. He made no attempt to conceal it, and was looking at it quite openly, but Lord Green flew into a passion and accused him of trying to steal it."

"What was it?" asked Howland curiously. "Did you see?"

"I only caught a glimpse. It was an odd little stone carving. I think there was an opal inset, but—"

"An 'twas bejewelled, he very likely *was* of a mind to pocket it. I doubt he earns enough at his carpentering to keep body and soul together."

"He did *not* try to steal it, I tell you! He gave it up at once, but Green was like a man gone berserk, and kept beating at him till he fell! Oh, I was *never* so disgusted!"

"I should think not, indeed!" Much shocked, Sir Vinson exclaimed, "A pretty way for a gentleman to conduct himself! And especially in front of a lady."

"Nor the kind of behaviour I could tolerate in a husband," said Jennifer, fixing Howland with a challenging stare.

Sir Vinson broke into whoops of laughter. "Jupiter, I should hope not! Have you set your heart on becoming a baroness, m'dear? You shall have to find another baron, for I've no wish to name Hibbard Green my son-in-law!"

Howland's lips set into a thin, tight line.

Jennifer said, "You cannot know how you relieve my mind, dear Papa."

Sir Vinson looked from her grateful smile to his son's look of chagrin, and his amusement faded. He said sharply, "What's this? Howland? Has that rogue been abusing my hospitality?"

"Lord Green admires my sister, sir. Is it a crime that he should do so? Jennifer's not beseiged with suitors—especially one of high rank and a great fortune."

"The devil you say! She is admired throughout the county! Has she not suffered that damnable accident in the mine, she'd have been wed long since! And a good match she'd have made. Young Merwin Morris was forever mooning about here till Lord Kenneth packed him off on the Grand Tour. He'd have wed her, despite—er, all, had his sire allowed it. And there was Kingsley and Lancen, and any number I'd have welcomed to the family. But—*Green*? No, by the powers! Jennifer, has he dared pay you his addresses behind my back?"

Jennifer saw the appeal in her brother's eyes, and hesitated. "His lordship has made it clear he considers himself a great catch," she evaded. "And that, as Howland said, he admires me."

Howland put in, "He *is* a great catch, sir! Jen would have a magnificent home, everything money can buy, and a—"

"Have done!" snapped Sir Vinson. "I'd sooner see my daughter in a nunnery than wed to that rascal! Damme, but he's almost as old as me! If I discover that he has caused Jennifer one instant of embarrassment, you may escort him from our lands! Or I will! That he should whip one of our people after the very same man saved his unlovely hide should tell you what manner of crudity he is, if nothing else does!"

"Crazy Jack is not one of our people, sir," protested Howland. "He's no more than a vagrant, and short of a sheet, into the bargain!"

"Perhaps, but your friend Green could learn a lot from observing his manners!" Sir Vinson rose, and took Jennifer's hand. "You must be worn out, my dear. You'd do well to lie down upon your bed for a while." He ushered her to the door where he smiled down at her and said softly, "Have no fear, child. I'll spike my lord's guns. He'll treat you with respect, or take himself off, mine or no mine!"

"Dear Papa, you are so good," she murmured, reaching up to kiss his chin. "But I feel dreadfully that Jack was treated so badly by our guest. Could we find him some work here at the castle, do you think? He's honest and conscientious, and a hard worker."

He chuckled indulgently. "Another of your charities?

You've a heart of gold, like your Mama. Very well, I'll see what can be done for the poor fellow. But take care to keep him at a distance, Jennifer. He's a different article to his lordship, but you must not let kindness blind you. However courteous he may appear, his mind is not as it should be. And"—he grinned broadly—"we cannot have even the village idiot developing a *tendre* for you, now can we?"

"Men!" Mrs. Newlyn whisked her cloth vigorously at Jonathan's small chest-of-drawers, routing dust, and also the candlestick, which flew off causing the candle to break in half and sag forlornly. "Well, that was foolish of you," she scolded, replacing it and straightening it up again. "Had you been wax instead of tallow, you'd not behave in such a common way. But there . . ."—she turned her attention to the table—"we cannot change what we are." Her flying cloth sent a dog-eared but cherished book hurtling across the shed, and knocked over a small pot, which scattered bird seed in all directions. Disregarding these minor annoyances, she held to her train of thought. "And that's not entirely true, for owls and hares *can* change their shapes." She sang in a quavery soprano voice,

> " 'Ware the hare all clad in white,
> a daemon dwells within.
> He can change, before your sight,
> into a witch or cruel goblin . . .
> An evil, cruel goblin, goblin.
> A wicked cruel goblin!"

Duster, who had been peering at her uneasily, gave a little gobbling sound, and she laughed and bent to look in the cage.

"That's right, my dearie. Be ye going to talk, then?"

She decided to offer encouragement and, drawing up the chair, she sat down in front of the cage and addressed the parakeet earnestly. "You really ought, y'know. Jack was good to you, and we must always repay a good deed. He needs someone to talk to him. But not about goblins. He's known too much of misery, poor lad. We must be cheerful, Duster! Cheerful!" She waved her cloth for emphasis, and the parakeet, enveloped in a cloud of dust, retreated to a corner of the cage and gave vent to a very tiny sneeze.

"I shall teach ye a word," declared the widow. "A happy word that will cheer him up and give him some hope. Let me see ..." She thought for a moment, then said in triumph, "I have it! One of my favourite-est words! Listen carefully, Duster. 'Lend me your ears!' Where are they, by the way? Mercy me, they don't look like much. But perhaps mine look like *too* much to you, do they?" This thought amused her so much that she laughed heartily for several seconds, before recalling her purpose.

"Now—where was I? Ah, yes—my word. Duster—are ye attending? Her 'tis then—posthumous! Pos-tume-us! Isn't that a lovely word?" She leaned nearer and confided, "I'm not altogether sure of its meaning, mind ye, but it begins with a 'pos,' like pos-sible and pos-itive, so it must be a cheery sort of word, eh? And goes with such a lovely ring. Pos-tume-us! Listen closely, small bird, and say it after me ..."

She devoted quite some time to her lesson, throughout which the parakeet tilted its head this way and that, but kept its bright eyes fixed upon her. Some might have interpreted this as denoting apprehension. The Widow Newlyn, unfailingly optimistic, was convinced she had arrived at a perfect understanding with the bird, and went out at length, telling Duster that he must practice, and blithely disregarding the havoc her "cleaning" had created in the shed.

"Turn round." Noah Holsworth eyed Jonathan critically, tugged at the back of the frieze coat and smoothed the fabric with his gleaming hook. " 'Tis not the best of fits, I'll own," he muttered. "You've a good pair of shoulders, for all you come so nigh to slipping your wind. I'd have sworn my boy was bigger'n you. It appears he isn't."

"You're very good to have loaned me his clothes," said Jonathan. "But—are you sure? When he comes home—"

"Hah! I'll believe that when I see it! Them as is pressed

don't come home for years. If at all. No, don't ye be wasting sympathy. The boy was bound for trouble here. Maybe he'll do better on the high seas. And I don't want thanks," he added in his brusque way. "Nor no more work tonight. The sun's going down, and ye look fair gut-foundered."

"I'll just finish this," argued Jonathan, taking up the hammer fumblingly and turning to the ark.

"Get ye gone, I say! Ye cannot hardly hold the hammer. I wonder ye did any work today at all. Be off with ye, and tell the widow to pour some spirits on those hands. I'll wager," he added, "she'll keep at ye till she's been told what left that stripe 'cross your face, and why you can scarce use your left arm. Which is more'n I got outta ye!"

"I told you—"

"You told me you fell. You didn't say you fell down the cliff. I'm not a clacketing female and I don't stick me nose where 'tis not wanted. But rumours is thick in the village, so if ye don't care to be badgered, ye'd do well to take the long way home."

Embarrassed, Jonathan tried to thank him, but the big man only waved him away, and turned back to his task once more.

The long way home would mean following the gully northeast to the high moor and commencing a wide loop around and above Roselley. A tiresome detour, but infinitely preferable to the taunts that doubtless awaited him in the village. He set off at a steady pace, but he was much more tired than he'd realised. By the time he reached the high moor he ached from head to foot, the bruises around his left arm being especially troublesome. His steps wavered and became ever more slow until at last he succumbed to fatigue and sat down to rest for a minute, propping his back against an obliging boulder and stretching his legs out gratefully.

Concern for Jennifer crowded out his discomfort. He had heard Lord Green growling something about her "missish airs," and when he'd looked up after finding that odd little piece of quartz, he'd had the impression that she had just wrenched free of an embrace. If that brutish lout was forcing his attentions on her, he'd— He gritted his teeth. He'd do—what? Warn the fellow off? He gave a snort of bitter laughter. Much chance that Hibbard Green would be checked by the warning of "the village idiot." He'd be more apt to laugh for a week! 'Besides,' he acknowledged wearily, 'what right have I to interfere? It is the duty of the men of her house to protect her. . . .'

The wind woke him. He must have slept for half an hour at least, for the sun was gone now, and the light was failing. He started up, and swore as his stiff muscles protested. His oath seemed to find an echo. Curious, he peered around the boulder. Two riders came slowly down the rise, on the other side of which the land sloped down again to the old mine. Recognising the first voice, he moved back quickly, waiting for them to pass. My lord, it would seem, had made a fast recovery.

". . . damned arrogant pup," observed Green harshly. "But he'll do as he's bid."

"Your arrogant one, 'e does not to me seem a—er, biddable fellow." The accent was French, and the voice unfamiliar. "You are sure of this pup?"

Green gave a cynical snort. "Very sure. He is in my book for ten thousand, and his self-righteous papa regards gaming as one of the deadlier sins. Oh, he'll obey me, never fear."

"*Mon cher*, fear I do not. It is you must the fear 'ave, I think. When our Squire learn of the visitor to Breton Ridge, 'e will say, '*Hein!* What 'ave my so loyal friend do to bring such a one 'ere?' "

They were level with the boulders now. Hoping they would move on quickly, Jonathan gave a mental groan as his lordship reined up abruptly.

"What the hell d'you dare imply? I had nought to do with the bastard coming! There's a perfectly logical reason he would visit—".

"*Mais oui!*"—with heavy irony—" 'e 'ave visit so often. What is it? Once before in 'is entire span? Cast back your mind, milor'. Is not the thing possible that you were followed to this place?"

Green's voice rose. "You mean by Rossiter, or one of his miserable cronies, eh? Nonsense! They've no cause to suspect me. Besides, had I been followed I'd have discovered it soon enough, I promise you."

"Me, I need not your promise." The Frenchman sounded amused as he started off once more. "The Squire it is who will demand the account from you. I am told 'e allow failure but one time, eh?"

His lordship snarled, "I warn you, monsieur. If you go back to Town and fill his ear with your stupid suspicions, you'll rue . . ."

Their voices had faded and Jonathan didn't hear the end of that threat, but the Frenchman's contemptuous laugh drifted to him. He stood, and watched frowningly until the dusk enfolded them. If Howland Britewell was the "arrogant pup" who was so deep in debt to Green, then Miss Jennifer would get scant support from her eldest brother in keeping the amorous baron at bay. Noah Holsworth, outspoken in his criticisms, had said that Fleming Britewell was "an intellectual, strong on brain and weak in the backbone," while Royce Britewell was "harum-scarum" and probably too young to wield any influence over his sire. The thought of Jennifer's gentle loveliness in Green's arms made Jonathan seethe with rage. It must not happen! She belonged to some worthy gentleman who would care for and—

A gust of wind sent his hair flying. Jove, but it had turned cold! He'd evidently been too lost in thought to pay heed to the lowering temperature. Shivering, he turned towards the village, took one long stride, then jerked to a halt. A lady wrapped in a long blue cloak stood just behind him. He had all but collided with her. He could not glimpse her face in the shadow of her hood, but he gained an impression of youth and beauty before he stepped back, murmuring his apologies.

She said nothing, but came straight towards him. He bowed humbly as she passed, then looked after her curiously. She moved with fluid grace, her cloak swirling about her, and her head held high. She was very proud, he thought, but he was not surprised that she had disdained to speak to him. The wonder was that she had come anywhere near him. He was sure she was a well-bred lady, and it was surprising that her menfolk should allow her to walk out alone on the moor at dusk. She was going up the rise, in the direction from which Green and the Frenchman had come. Perhaps she had intended to meet them, or perhaps she was a guest at Castle Triad and had felt the need for a brisk walk before dinner. But—alone? There were gullies and unexpected fissures on the moor that could be treacherous. Troubled, he hurried after her. It was risky to warn her that the gentlemen had already passed, even if he said he'd only seen his lordship from a distance. She would surely tell Green, who might fear to have been overheard. Still, it was getting darker, and a fellow could not stand by while a lady lost herself out here. He began to run, his stiff muscles not helping his speed.

Reaching the top of the rise, he peered about. The light was almost gone, but he should be able to distinguish her. He could not. Strain his eyes as he would, there was no sign of the blue cloak. She'd been walking swiftly, but not so swiftly as to have passed completely from sight. Perhaps she'd fallen. He went on, scanning the thick turf and occasional furze bushes anxiously. And then he heard hoofbeats once more; a male voice, and a woman's low laugh. That must be the answer: the lady had been met and was likely safely on her way to the castle. Relieved, he turned back toward Roselley.

There was more now to concern him. Green and the Frenchman had spoken of an expected and evidently much disliked visitor to Breton Ridge. They'd also mentioned a squire, whom they both feared. Lord Kenneth Morris was the local squire. He was known to be a proud man, but scarcely the type, thought Jonathan, to inspire anxiety in a bully like Green. Nor was Lord Kenneth in London at present, as Green had indicated the "squire" was, so they had likely referred to another squire. The Frenchman had implied that someone had followed his lordship "to this place." A man named Roberts—or was it Robson . . . ?

Rossiter! That was it! His frown deepened. Might this Rossiter be the man the lady in the blue cloak had gone to meet? Was "this place" Breton Ridge or Castle Triad? Or could the Frenchman have been referring to the Blue Rose Mine? He and Green had come from the direction of the old mine, and the lady had gone that way, and had been met.

Puzzling at it, Jonathan went slowly through the gathering darkness. Why a'plague should anyone have the least interest in following his lordship anywhere? And why all this interest in a mine that hadn't been worked for several years?

A cold drizzle was falling when Jennifer dismissed the children, and their exuberance turned to squeals as they scuttled for home. She held Isaac Blary back, and picked up the sketch that lay atop a pile of others on her desk. "This is very good, Isaac. Why have I never seen any more of your drawings?"

His broad features had flushed with pleasure, but he lied, " 'Cause I hasn't never done any. Me pa do not hold with such fool stuff." Jennifer looked up at him steadily, and his flush deepened to scarlet. Abandoning bravado, he mumbled, "If ye please, Miss Jennifer."

"That's better," she said quietly. "You're big for your age, and will soon be a man. Big men, Isaac, have an extra obli—duty to others. Because the Lord has given them a healthy body and more strength than many, they should repay Him by being kind to the weak and the less fortunate."

He hung his head. "I never pulled Lily's hair. But her brother's allus punching me 'cause I were took on at the castle, and he weren't."

"That should be 'was not,' " she pointed out with a smile. "Do you like working for my father?"

"I'd like it better if Crazy Jack didn't work there now. Me pa don't like it neither. He says as it's meaning."

A little frown creased her brow. "I think he must have said 'demeaning.' But Jack is a fine worker and a good man. He was very ill, and can't quite remember things, that's all." She saw his lips parting, and went on hurriedly, "This is King Arthur, no? And the knight on horseback—what a fine horse, Isaac!—would be . . ."

"Sir Lancelot!"

"Yes, of course. And how beautifully you have drawn poor Guinevere. I see that you think of Camelot as having been a great city."

"I reckon as it were a better place than Tintagel. A king like Arthur wouldn't never've had a crumbly old hole like that! And I doesn't s'pose it was like Castle Triad, neither. Nor I don't mean to be a rudesby," he added with a scared look, " 'cause there's lots as does, I know."

She had noticed the resemblance to herself in young Blary's drawing, and said smilingly, "Do you mean that people believe I am descended from Queen Guinevere?"

His eyes fell away and he said with sudden bashfulness, "A queen might look like you, Miss Jennifer. Not that you're a bad lady, or nothing like that."

"Perhaps the queen wasn't, either. It was all so long ago. Nobody really knows what happened."

"No. And 'sides, she's trying to make it up, ain't she?"

Jennifer walked to the door with him. "Do you mean that business about the Spanish Armada?"

"Well, folks saw her, didn't they? And she come just 'fore the Battle of Bodmin Moor, *and* Bosworth Field," he declared, his eyes alight. "They do say so."

Jennifer opened the door, admitting a gust of wind and a spattering of rain.

"I know they do," she admitted. "But I should rather see you working at your sketches than listening to superstition, Isaac. I want to see more, if you please."

He nodded and went out, pulling up his ragged collar against the wind, and directing a low-voiced taunt at Jonathan, who stood on the steps holding an oilcloth over a large flat object balanced beside him.

"Have you been sent to bring me home, Johnny?" asked Jennifer warmly. "Good gracious, how wet you are! There was no need for you to wait out here. Come in, do!" She ushered him inside, looking at his burden curiously. "Autumn is chasing summer very fast this year, I think. Now, leave your parcel there, and use this." She handed him the towel she brought each day. "Your hair is soaked. Did you bring the coach?"

"Yes, ma'am. Young Porter is walking the horses for me."

He rubbed at his hair vigorously, reducing it to a tangled mop of elf locks that made her laugh and remark that he looked like a rumpled little boy. He grinned and retied the riband.

Returning to her chair, she said, "Now sit down for just a minute and tell me about yourself. I've not seen you for days. How is your arm? Mrs. Newlyn said it was very badly bruised, as I was sure it would be. You should not have gone straight to work for Noah Holsworth after you'd rescued Lord Green."

"But I had promised Noah," he said, sitting on a desk, and noting how charmingly the little dimple beside her lips came and went when she smiled. "My arm is very well, I thank you. And—and I've to thank you also for the work at Triad."

" 'Twas small reward compared to the hundred pounds you were promised. No," she chuckled, "do not go up into the boughs again! I meant no offence. How is it that my brothers are at loggerheads over you?"

"Are they? Mr. Royce wants me to gentle the young chestnut stallion he brought back from Newton Abbot."

"I would have thought Oliver Crane should do that."

He did not answer. The head groom was a competent individual with a thorough knowledge of horses, but he had a heavy hand for man or beast, and young Royce Britewell, aware of that trait, had decided that Jonathan's way with horses was more to his liking.

Having drawn a few conclusions of her own regarding Mr. Crane, Jennifer said shrewdly, "Royce does not want the animal's spirit broken, is that the case?"

He replied with a faint smile, "I did not say so, Miss Jennifer."

'But I fancy Mr. Crane had plenty to say,' she thought.

It was typical of her younger brother to have cared not a whit for the head groom's inevitable resentment of such a situation. Especially since she chanced to know that Crane held Jack in contempt and referred to him as the Shadow Man. Troubled, she asked, "Does that make things difficult for you?"

"It—er, keeps me busy," he said, in a massive understatement.

"It must, indeed. Besides which, you help Noah Holsworth, and work for Mrs. Newlyn! My goodness, have you no time for yourself?"

"Yes, ma'am. In fact"—he stood and began to unwrap the oilcloth from his bulky parcel—"Noah allows me to use his tools and any spare pieces of wood. So—I—er, was able to make . . . this."

"A chalk board!" She clapped her hands, and ran to admire it. "And what a nice frame you have made!"

"There is a—a stand, also." He unfolded that sturdy object eagerly. "I tried to make it the proper height for you to use comfortably, but I think your pupils will manage to reach, if the small ones stand on a box."

Her face alight, she declared, " 'Tis lovely! Oh, I have *needed* one! Sir Vinson promised and promised to have one sent from Plymouth, but he always forgets." She ran one slender finger along the top of the frame while Jonathan watched her, overjoyed because he had pleased her. "This carving is much too fine for so commonplace an object. You must have worked and worked!" She clasped his arm, her bright eyes looking up into his smiling ones. "Oh, *thank you*, Johnny!"

Instinctively, his hand rose to cover the slender beloved fingers resting on his shabby sleeve, but he restrained himself in the nick of time. His hand clenched hard and he lowered it and stepped back from her.

Jennifer gazed at his averted face and could hear her father's words: 'Keep him at a distance . . .' She had not kept him at a distance. She *must* stop behaving as though he was an old and dear friend. He was *not* of her own station in life and must never be encouraged to believe—Well, must never be encouraged.

She said with forced lightness, "Will you set it up near to my desk, please? And tell me what you've been doing for Mr. Fleming. Are you making something for him?"

Jonathan carried the stand to the spot she indicated. "He wanted a shelf for his compendium of Christian Apologetics, and whilst I was installing it we fell into a discussion of the *Octavius* of Minucius Felix, and—"

Jennifer blinked. "Which is written in Latin, surely?"

"Mmn." Concentrating on the exact adjustment of the legs of the stand, he said absently, "He says my accent is deplorable, but that I can translate quite well."

"Whereupon he commandeered you!" Hiding her astonishment, she said, "He would, of course. And has doubtless kept you poring through his dusty old tomes and writing translations, or searching out references for him!" In the same airy tone, she added, "You'll be an Oxonian, I suppose?"

"No. Eton and then Addiscombe, because all—" He bit off the words, his head jerked up and he stared at her, his eyes dilated with shock.

As triumphant as he was dismayed, she exclaimed, "You are starting to *remember*! I knew you were an educated man, I *knew* it! Oh, when I tell Papa, he'll be—"

"No! You must not!" He saw her smile die and a rare frown replace her enthusiasm, and he said distractedly, "He would want to know— I mean, he'd be sure to think—"

"What I begin to think, probably. That you know exactly who and what you are! That you are running, or hiding from someone. From the authorities, perchance!" Chilled by that possibility, she drew back slightly.

He searched her face, and stepping closer to her, demanded, "What are you thinking? Can you suppose for one instant that I could harm *you*?"

She'd never realised quite how tall he was, and he looked different somehow, and rather grim. She said, "You—you might harm my family."

"No, I tell you! I would die sooner than bring you grief!"

He was indeed different! An intense stranger who was a far cry from the shy, shrinking young man she knew. A little frightened, but intrigued, she said, "Who *are* you? Tell me the truth."

"I don't know!"

"I think you do know. Certainly, you are not what you pretend to be!"

"I do not pretend, I swear it! People judge me crazy because I can only recall snatches of my life. And because I have—lapses, even now, that cause me to do things I cannot understand. But it's not nearly as bad as it was at first."

Her imagination conjured up a trail of victims with their throats slashed, and she asked faintly, "What do you mean 'at first'?"

His eyes fell away. He muttered, "I mean—when I first came here."

"No, that is not what you meant."

He was silent.

Irked, and bewildered by a painful sense of betrayal, she accused angrily, "You still deceive! Creeping about, and pretending to be afraid to stand up to others! Hiding the fact that you have had a fine education, and making me believe all that fustian about being afraid of the sea! Oh, how gullible I was! 'Tis all a shield for something. You have some secret reason to stay here! Admit that you are a Riding Officer, come to spy on us all!"

"No! Why must you think so ill of me?"

"Because you hide the truth. And since you continue to do so, you leave me no choice. I must warn my Papa 'gainst you." She started to the door, but he was very fast and ran to block her way.

"I beg you, do not! He'll send me packing, and I've done nothing. All I ask is—is to stay."

"Then tell me the truth!"

The truth . . . He flinched, and turned away.

Cautiously, she trod closer, but he did not move, standing there with his head bowed low, as if he were crushed by despair. In a sudden wave of sympathy she touched his shoulder and said with gentle compassion, "Whatever is it, Johnny? Can you not confide in me?"

"If I . . . did," he said haltingly, "you could only . . . despise me more."

She considered that, and leaning back against her desk, prompted, "You have done something bad, is that the case?"

He faced her and nodded, but did not look up.

"Very bad?"

Another convulsive nod. His hands were tightly gripped, his eyes fixed on the toe of her shoe.

Despite her earlier apprehensions, she knew somehow that he had not committed murder. He might have killed in a fair fight, but there were, in her estimation, worse things than to have duelled to the death. She said slowly, "I think there is one crime I could never forgive, and if you were involved in—in that, I would have to send you away at once. Were you—a wrecker?"

His head flew up. He said vehemently, "No! Acquit me of that, I beg you!"

"Very well. But—are you quite sure you really did—whatever it was? You say you've forgotten much of your life. Is it not possible that there is a mistake?"

His eyes fell again, and he muttered bitterly, "If you knew how I've prayed that was so. But . . . God help me—it isn't. The very thing I wish I could forget is the thing I most clearly remember. I am guilty of—of what I was accused. Even if I could be forgiven, I should never be able to forgive . . . myself."

She sighed. "Poor soul. How dreadful to carry such a burden. But why stay near the sea, if you fear it so?"

A brief silence, then he said low voiced, "I have no choice."

"If 'tis a matter of money—"

He shook his head.

"Is it perhaps that you are to meet someone here?"

"It is that—I am under oath," he said wretchedly.

"Oh, my goodness!" Her thoughts tumbled over one another. She asked, "Is that what you meant when you said you had no right to defend yourself?"

"Yes."

"For—for how long?"

"Until I can make . . . amends."

Appalled, she watched him and scarcely dared to ask, "Johnny—shall you be able to do so, do you think?"

"I can try. But . . ." He shrugged helplessly.

"I see." She tried to weigh all that she knew of this man and her undeniable interest in him, against the possible consequences, then said, "You ask me to trust you. But I ask if you will pledge me another vow." He looked at her squarely, and she went on, "Will you give me your word of honour that nothing you have done in the past, or mean to do in the future, will bring trouble upon my family?"

"Could you accept my word after what I have told you?"

"Yes," she answered, and with the word her doubts were quite gone. "Because I believe you are a good man, and despite what you say, I think you *are* mistaken about yourself."

Blinking rapidly, he seized her hand and before she could protest touched it to his lips. "God bless you!" he muttered huskily. "You have my word of honour, Miss Jennifer, that I have never meant harm to you or to your family, or ever will!"

"Good," she said, unwontedly flustered. "In that case, I—I think we must rescue Young Porter. I'll get my cloak."

What with one thing and another, she quite forgot about her new chalk board, and turning quickly, collided with it, gave a startled cry, and tripped.

She was caught and held safe and tight in arms of steel. Her embarrassed little laugh faded.

Perhaps because he had been so deeply moved, Jonathan's stern self-control slipped. He made no attempt to put her down, but held her close and gazed at her.

There was a light in his eyes that snatched Jennifer's breath away. She forgot the impossible gulf that separated them. For a timeless space she was only a girl, cradled in a man's strong arms, and without the least objection to her captivity.

Young Porter's shrill howl fragmented that enchanted moment. "The hosses be getting wet, Crazy Jack! So be I, if you please!"

"Oh—dear," said Jennifer.

Jonathan set her down, retrieved her cloak from the wall peg, and wrapped it about her. The hood was drawn tenderly over her head. She was ushered to the coach, assisted inside, and the rug tucked around her. A glowing look was slanted at her, the door slammed, and the coach jerked into the start of its journey.

Bemused, Jennifer took a deep breath, "Well!" she said.

On the box, Jonathan scarcely felt the wind-driven rain or the chill on the air. Surely, this was the most wonderful, the most incredible thing that had ever happened to him. He had told her about himself—not all, but enough to give her cause to dismiss him at once. And instead, bless her dear heart, she had doubted his guilt. Even when he admitted that guilt, she had been willing to accept his word of honour. Conscience sniggered, but he shut it out. Joy was too rare in his life, too heady to be defeated by Conscience. He had held her in his arms and she had neither struggled nor railed at him. He could still see the expression on her lovely face. For as long as he lived, he would see it. The face of a maid; innocent, wondering, and above all— trusting.

He dashed rain from his eyes as the team started up the hill. His heart was so full of gratitude. If life offered no more than this, it was more than he'd dared to hope. And he would still be able to see her sometimes. He thought an impassioned 'Praise God!' and when he dragged a hand across his eyes once more, it was not entirely because of raindrops.

❦ *Chapter 6* ❧

The wind was strong that evening. It howled off the ocean to thunder around the tower, and the air became chill so that a fire was lit in Sir Vinson's study. Jennifer had poured tea at ten o'clock, then made her escape, leaving the gentlemen to their cards. Lord Green, having indulged himself too generously at table, had dozed off at eleven, much to Royce's amusement and Fleming's disgust, and gone, yawning, to his bed. Now, Howland sprawled in the deep chair before the hearth and waited out his sire's tirade, his handsome face expressionless.

"I'll not have it, I tell you," reiterated Sir Vinson, tossing several engineers' drawings onto his littered desk. "I do not want my beaches spoiled, and I dislike the man. To say truth, I dislike everything about him. His looks, his crude talk, his table manners—or lack of 'em. And I will be *damned* if I'll have him making sheep's eyes at Jennifer!"

"I'd think you have made yourself quite plain on that suit," murmured Howland placatingly.

"So would I. But one cannot be sure a creature like that will behave as a gentleman."

"I've done my best to keep him busily occupied, sir. Besides, Jennifer would have told you had he annoyed her."

Sir Vinson grunted and came around his desk to lean back against it and frown into the flames. "She might, save that she's loyal to you. Why a'plague you like the fellow is past understanding."

"I despise the clod! But—" Howland sat straighter in his chair. "That's a right generous offer, sir. It would do my heart good to lighten his pockets."

"That smacks of chicanery. And I don't want him for a neighbour. No!"

"How can it be chicanery, Papa? We have told him the truth repeatedly. An he's fool enough to believe there's more tin to be mined, be it upon his own head. In addition to the losses we suffered when my grandfather was ensnared in that accursed South Sea Bubble, you've had a struggle to keep us solvent since the mine was closed down. D'you fancy I'm not aware of it?"

"If you were aware of it," said Sir Vinson dryly, "one might have supposed you'd have stayed here and been of help, rather than go frippering off to London and be bilked of most of your inheritance."

Howland flushed and leaned back again. After a small silence he said in a contrite tone, "I know, sir. I let you down. That was very bad." From under his long lashes he watched his father's expression and saw it soften. He was well aware that he was the favourite, but he knew also that he must tread carefully. Sir Vinson could be manoeuvred, but like many weak men, he could fly into a sudden rage and at such times could prove stubborn as a donkey. "I was trying for a solution," he went on. " 'Twas in Town that I met Green and learned of his interest in Cornwall. I thought you would be pleased when he came and made his offer. I see now that—alas, I have but failed you again."

He looked downcast, and Sir Vinson said bracingly, "No, no. I'm aware you mean well, m'boy. Lord knows, I sowed my share of wild oats when I was a green 'un. We'll come about somehow, but not at the expense of our good name, for *that* I value more than any loss of fortune!"

"I know you do, sir, and so do I. Still, we'd come about faster were that bank draft deposited to our own account. And 'tis but the first payment. When the dock is built—"

Sir Vinson's expression darkened. He interrupted sharply, "*No*, damme! I'll not bring more ugliness to desecrate our proud coast! Are those stark mine chimneys not sufficient of a blot on the landscape?"

"You're in the right of it, as usual." Howland sighed deeply. "Our people will just have to tighten their belts. Though they'll be sadly disappointed. They've been praying for your approval."

"Then they're bigger fools than I take 'em for! They know the mine is worthless."

"To their way of thinking, if an outsider with more money than sense chooses to sink a new shaft, and to construct a dock on the beach, it must mean work for them, sir. Jove, but if you could be the means of putting wages back in their pockets, even for a little while, you'd be a hero to them all!"

"If Hibbard Green yearns to put wages in my people's pockets, he don't need a dock to do it. The Blue Rose was a successful operation for years without a dock on my beach. There are several fine docks already in use on this coast."

"Very true, sir. But fees are high, the off-loading is slow and unreliable, and then the goods must be transferred into waggons and hauled for miles over impossibly bad roads, and in places no roads at all! How much simpler to—"

Sir Vinson's scowl had become more marked during this argument and now he interrupted testily, "If his lordship can afford to squander his lettuce to shore up and modernise a played-out and unsafe mine, he can afford to ship overland. By Beelzebub, I begin to think he has more cobwebs in his loft than has Crazy Jack! No, Howland! Absolutely—and—finally! *No—dock!*"

Jonathan was awakened by a gust of wind that seemed likely to topple the shed. It was still dark, but he lay snug in his blankets for a while, listening to the clamour outside, and thinking of Jennifer and that never-to-be-forgotten moment when he had held her close against his heart.

Duster's complaints roused him from his dreaming at last, and he got up, deciding to make an early start. He was feeding Sprat and preparing to leave Mrs. Newlyn's cottage when the cat darted to the parlour door.

"Only look at his fur crackle," said the widow, taking up the cat and stroking him. " 'Twill be hot today, Jack. And with this wind, very dry for a change. You're early, lad."

He had never seen the lady *en déshabillé,* and for an instant he stared, silenced by the sight of a billowing and exotically hued satin dressing gown, and hair in countless twists of paper. "Oh—er, hot," he stammered, and averted his eyes.

Mrs. Newlyn chuckled and put the cat down. "Have you never seen a lady in her nightrail before?" she asked, sitting at the table.

"I—suppose I might have. I—I don't know. I'll be getting along, ma'am."

"Put the kettle on to boil, and stay for a cup of tea. We'll toast some bread and have a little chat. I doubt ye ever saw a finer dressing gown than this, eh?" She gave a saucy wink. "A gentleman gave it to me for my birthday last year. Come all the way from France, it did. And never paid no tax, neither!"

He admired the dressing gown dutifully, and took down the toasting fork. The widow buttered the slices as he handed them to her, and told him of the village gossip, which appeared to revolve around the exciting fact that Mrs. Gundred was to journey from the village and the Hundred, and even from the county altogether. "She's been invited to visit her sister in Dorsetshire," said the widow, her eyes round. "All that way! Imagine! She's a brave woman. But—there, nothing like family, is there Johnny, lad?"

He glanced at her sharply. "Why do you call me that?"

She watched steam curl from the spout of the kettle. "I was talking to the Spirit of the Ocean yesterday," she said in a dreaming voice. "He was telling me about you. Watch you don't burn that piece!"

He rescued the endangered slice hurriedly. "What—er, was he saying of me?"

She spread butter with a sparing hand. "You don't remember your family at all? Whether there was anyone you were . . . especially fond of?"

He frowned. "No. There were some people, but they may not even have been related to me." It was all folly, no doubt, but he could not refrain from asking, "Why? What did your Spirit of the Ocean tell you?"

"It might be a mistake, of course. He does sometimes give me messages that should go to other folks. Though he's much more to be trusted than the yellow leaves!" She sighed, and put tea into the pot as the kettle began to shoot out a hissing cloud of steam. "There seems to be some question whether you will go back to your home," she went on then. "But if you do, someone you expect to meet won't be there."

He watched her curiously.

She smiled, and passed him a piece of toast. "But then again," she said, "the message might really have been for Mrs. Gundred."

The wind staggered Holsworth and he dropped the nail he'd been fitting into the small device attached to his hook. He swore under his breath and took another nail from the box.

"I got a right to speak me mind!" Mrs. Newlyn clasped the shawl tighter around her head, pursed her lips, and eyed the ark critically. "And I say again 'tis the wrong shape!"

"And what brings you out on this fine breezy morning, marm?" he snarled.

"Gundred. He never did pay me the penny he owed since his sign blew down."

"But that were weeks since!"

"True. Thought he could wait me out and I'd forget. But I don't forget a penny so easy. Nor did I come into your garden to hear strong language, Noah Holsworth! Never go for to deny it, as if me ears was on holiday. Powerful ears I got! Which is more than I can say for Jack's bird!"

Somewhat flushed, he apologised, then asked curiously. "Deaf, is it? How did you find that out?"

"Why, I been trying to teach it a word or two. I thought it might surprise him some day, when he needed cheering up. But the silly creature just looks and cocks its head and don't do anything but gobble at me."

"It's a foreign bird," he pointed out. "Likely don't understand English. Jack wasted his money. Ye cannot make a silk purse out of a sow's ear."

"He didn't buy it to make it into any purse," she argued, "but to save it from being put to the cliff. A good heart has Jack."

"He's a good hard worker, I'll own." He added resentfully, "When he's allowed to come to me."

"After the hours he puts in up at the castle, I wonder he has a minute to spare to work on an ark what looks like an overgrowed rowing boat. The Bible says plain as day as it should be flat bottomed. Like a box."

Despite the fact that they invariably argued, Holsworth thought Mrs. Newlyn a comely little woman, and had paused in his work while he chatted with her. At this, however, he snapped, "Thankee, I'm sure!" and hammered the nail home. "Next, you'll be burning to remind me as how my ark should be three hundred cubits long. And if Mr. John Wesley was right in what he said last Sabbath, that would be from where you're standing—without invitation!—half way to Gundred's. Which, even if I had the lumber and I don't nor ever will, would take me several lifetimes to build."

"At the rate you're going, sure enough," she agreed, then laughed in her merry fashion as he dropped another nail. "Never take umbrage, Mr. Noah, I were only teasing. You go along nice and steady, and 'tis a fine boat, flat bottomed or no. What is the little tool you're using? I thought you wasn't able to hammer nails without someone to get 'em started for ye."

He showed her the device. "Jack made it for me. I can put the nail in—so, get it set, then slip the tool free and hammer the nail all the way. 'Tis tedious, but at least I can work. Still, I'd go along faster was he here to help, rather than being forever up at the castle."

"It puts him out of reach of Ben Blary and Pughill, at least."

"I doubt he's better off with Mr. Crane. I'd not want that one for a master. I'll wager Jack has felt his fist more'n once."

The widow looked worried, and muttered, "There's worse things than blows, and whatever else Oliver Crane be, he's not a vindictive man. Noah, has Blary been speaking out against Jack?"

"Aye. Pughill as well. Some silly tale about a dark stranger Jack was whispering with in the early morning before most folk were about. And how this stranger had the eyes of . . . of a daemon. Just like Ben Blary to make up such a cockaleery tale, and for Pughill to back him on it. I'd pay 'em no heed, save that—well, young Isaac told me the same, and seemed proper scared."

They looked at each other uneasily.

The widow, who had been born in Plymouth and was still regarded by some as a foreigner, muttered, "That's Roselley for ye. Ignorance, cheek by jowl with superstition."

At once defensive, Holsworth argued, "They're not really bad folk. Being out of work takes the heart from a man as sure as poverty sharpens the tongue of a woman. They've tolerated Jack so far. But if they should start to think . . ." He paused, looking grim.

Clinging to his arm for support as a powerful gust whipped around the cottage, she shouted, "I don't like it, Noah! That's why—"

"What don't you like, Mrs. Newlyn?" Laughing breathlessly, Jennifer also caught at Holsworth's mighty arm. "Oh, this dreadful wind!"

"Strong enough to pull the hair from your head today, ma'am," he agreed, holding her steady.

"Which would be a disaster for some on us," observed the widow pertly. "On top, 'specially."

Holsworth grabbed at his knitted cap, then grumbled, "I'll thank ye to keep your unkindnesses for my ark, Widder."

"No, have you been teasing him again?" Amused by their bickering, Jennifer inspected the ark and said she thought it very fine. "It looks quite seaworthy already. If we have a second Flood, I shall know to whom to run, Mr. Holsworth. I wish you had built it closer to the beach, so that we could try it out."

He was pleased. "Too late for that, Miss Jennifer. My ark will be ready when the water gets up here."

"Then we'll all pray it never floats," said the widow. "Speaking of floating, you look ready to do just that, Miss Jennifer. All aglow you be, and your step so light one might think you walked on air."

" 'Tis the wind carries her," said Holsworth with a twinkle.

"It has carried off the glass from one of my schoolhouse windows," said Jennifer. "But you are perfectly right, Mrs. Newlyn. I have had some lovely news. Lord Morris is to play host to the son of his cousin. A Kentish gentleman, I believe, who is bringing a friend to see Cornwall. Miss Caroline Morris is prodigious excited, because 'tis years and years since she saw this particular cousin, and—"

"And he is a soldier," murmured the widow, a far-away look in her dark eyes.

Curious, Jennifer said, "Why—yes. How did you know?"

"The trees told me . . . It starts, then."

Over the years, the widow had fashioned many of Jennifer's gowns, and she had come to know the little woman quite well. She was fond of her, and did not really believe her to be a witch. Her "conversations" with trees or the Spirit of the Ocean usually proved to have no significance and were soon forgotten. Now and then, however, the information gleaned from these odd "chats" had proven to be rather uncannily accurate. The remark she had just made sounded ominous, and not wanting this happy day to be spoiled, Jennifer glanced questioningly at Holsworth.

The big man was busied with the selection of a nail, but he directed a surreptitious wink at her, and her spirits lifted.

"Is this Kent Morris coming to the castle, ma'am?" he asked.

"No. But Lord Kenneth is to give a party next week in

honour of his guests, and Miss Caroline writ to invite me! I shall take the blue gown you made in the spring, Mrs. Newlyn, and—" She laughed gaily. "Only listen to me rattle on! I must go, or the wind will have blown everything from my cottage. I came because I thought Jo—Jack might be here and could fasten something over the window for me. Is he gone to Triad?"

"Aye. They sent for him to go up to the stables," said Mrs. Newlyn, over-riding Holsworth's attempt to offer assistance. "We was speaking of him when you came. There's a silly tale going round. Likely you've heard it, Miss Jennifer. As if Jack would have done such a tomfool thing as to try and climb up the cliff north of Bridget Bay! He couldn't do it, if he wanted to!"

"But he did climb up!" Jennifer saw their astonished expressions, and added quickly, " 'Twas a sudden—er, impulse, I believe. And a foolish one, for he was badly scratched. But he went down again to help Lord Green. It was the very bravest thing!" They were both staring at her. Afraid that she might have spoken too glowingly, she blushed, said her farewells, and hurried off.

Holsworth muttered, "Then 'tis truth what Blary said. Jack must be a remarkable fine climber."

"There's a'many men 'twixt the schoolhouse and here would have been glad to board up her window," mused the widow, her thoughts having taken another direction.

"I'd not have dreamed he could bring it off," said Holsworth, equally, if differently, preoccupied.

"Then you're a blind fool," she declared, firing up. "For whatever folks say of him, Jack's a fine-looking young fellow. Though," she added, suddenly plunged into gloom, "I hope I'm wrong, or 'twill be a proper tragedy."

"What a'plague are ye babbling at, woman?" demanded the bewildered Holsworth. "What have looks to do with climbing cliffs? The point is that 'twas a proper daft thing to do, and gives the likes of Blary and Pughill more grist for saying he's bewitched."

The widow smiled and said with a stifled sigh, "Perchance he is ... "

* * *

Oliver Crane was a very tall man with regular if somewhat coarse features, and a fine pair of bold black eyes that had won him the admiration of more than one among the female staff at Castle Triad. He had kept a trim figure, and although he was now past forty, saw himself as quite the local Don Juan. Regrettably, he had flaws; small, but of which he was extremely conscious. One, was that his hands were large and red, an embarrassment that no amount of the Widow Newlyn's salves, simples, elixirs, or even an occasional and very alarming spell, had improved. They were strong hands, and when the head groom was in a bad humour, his underlings felt them.

Crane knew he had a quick temper, but he prided himself on being fair-minded. When his younger brother was denied employment at the castle, Crane admitted to himself that there was some justification for that decision, because the boy had got himself a reputation for shiftlessness. He could not be so magnanimous when Crazy Jack was hired. To be saddled with the village idiot was bad enough, but that he should put on the airs of an educated gentleman was an insult to all honest men. His resentment deepened to dislike when Mr. Royce Britewell made a point of assigning the training of the fine new stallion to Jack, rather than to himself. He knew the grooms and stableboys were smiling behind their hands, and waiting for him to practise some of his harsh discipline on the new man. He allowed himself this gratification, though not as often as he could have wished. This was partly because Jack was annoyingly adept at anticipating and eluding the sudden swipes of his powerful hands, and partly because the Shadow Man, as he scornfully named him, also worked for Mr. Fleming and Mr. Royce, and it might not be wise for him to appear with a new bruise daily.

Crane compensated for this unfair restriction by finding fault. Crazy Jack over-fed the horses one day, and under-fed them the next. He exercised Sir Vinson's favourite mare too rigorously so that she might very well have taken a fatal chill. He was "slow" when cleaning out stalls, and "clumsy" when applying a poultice. It soon became clear, in fact, that he could do nothing right. The other men followed Crane's lead, so that Jonathan began to dread the hours he spent in the stables.

They had their value, however. He seldom saw his love, but had plenty of opportunity to observe Lord Green's comings and goings, and his eyes, keen under their long lashes, missed nothing. His lordship rode out every morning. Alone. But sooner or later Howland Britewell also rode out. They returned separately, allowing it to be known that they had not met, but Jonathan noticed that the hooves of their mounts were often encrusted with slightly reddish mud, and he was sure they had gone to the old mine. He noticed also that Silas, Green's manservant, a watchful individual small of stature, voice, and eyes, would often loiter about the stables until Howland rode in, and then slink over to address him with the fawning and whispering servility that made him universally despised.

It was common knowledge now that Sir Vinson had agreed to lease the Blue Rose to his lordship, and that the mine was to undergo major renovations. There was jubilation among the local people, but also a deal of quiet hilarity because his lordship had been "properly duped" by Mr. Howland. Jonathan took no share in the joke. Hibbard Green was a crudity, as vicious as he was amoral, but he was no fool. If he wanted the Blue Rose, it was not in the mistaken belief that it could be made to yield up more tin. Nor was such a wealthy peer likely to be interested in using the mine as a headquarters for smuggling. The conversation Jonathan had overheard between Green and the Frenchman had implied a more widespread conspiracy. He thought it all too likely that Howland Britewell was involved, and the fear that the lovely Jennifer might be caught in a web of danger strengthened his determination to learn what his lordship was about.

To that end, however weary he might be, or however late the hour, he took to walking home by way of the high moors. After several nights of seeing no sign of life, he decided that tonight he would venture inside the mine. The weather had been hot and dry, and he was dismayed when at about four o'clock, the temperature dropped and fog began to roll in. It was easy to become lost on the high moor after dark, and the fog was likely to—

A sudden outbreak of shouts, a frantic neighing, and the tattoo of rapid hoofbeats cut off his train of thought, and he dropped the harness he'd been polishing, and ran.

Isaac Blary had been currying Bravo, Royce Britewell's fine new stallion. Something had caused the horse to take fright, and he was rearing up, his front hoofs flailing wildly, and his eyes rolling with fear. Terrified, Isaac was belabouring the big animal with a riding crop, while half-screaming demands that the "black imp of Satan" get down, his shrill voice adding to the stallion's fear. Bravo kicked out with his powerful back legs, splintering the rail of the stall, then pranced sideways, trapping the boy.

No coward, Oliver Crane snatched up a whip and raced to the stall. His whip whistled down and the stallion spun with a shrill neigh of pain, his strong teeth snapping within inches of Crane's face.

Tearing off his coat, Jonathan shouted, "He knows me!"

Two grooms ran to help, but Crane waved them back. "Let the Shadow Man handle him."

Maddened by fear and the pain of the whip, Bravo reared again.

Jonathan darted under the flying hooves, snatched desperately for the halter, and hung on. Bravo's eyes started from their sockets. His scream of fury all but deafened Jonathan. "It's all . . . right," he said, dodging those lethal forelegs, and twisting the halter tighter about his hand.

The stallion's head jerked up. Jonathan's merciless grip forced it down. "Easy . . . Bravo," he said, hanging on for dear life. "Down, old fellow . . . You know I . . . won't hurt you. Gently, now."

With his left hand, he managed somehow to toss his coat over Bravo's head. It was not a procedure the stallion liked. He tried to rear up, which hurt his tender mouth. That iron hand was still there. He whirled blindly, and crashed against a post. He was frightened, but the voice was still talking steadily, and it came to him that this was a familiar voice, and one he had learned to trust. The whip wasn't cutting him now. One of the iron hands was stroking his neck. His sides heaving, he decided not to buck again for a minute or two ...

Out of breath, but still talking softly, Jonathan said, "Don't move, Isaac." He continued to stroke the stallion's sweating neck, and Bravo stood still, trembling violently. With slow caution, Jonathan removed the coat, and Bravo followed meekly as he led him out.

All work had stopped. A murmur of approval sounded. Crane started toward the shaken Isaac. His eyes met Jonathan's. He nodded grudgingly, but said, "Your brainbox is empty, all right, else you'd never have tried such a stupid trick."

"I'd say jolly well done, rather!" Sir Vinson came in at the open door, and crossed to give Jonathan a slap on the back. "You took a chance there, my lad. Good thing the horse knows you."

"Bravo's in a sweat, sir," said Crane, hiding his chagrin that the master should have come in at just that moment. He jerked his head at Jonathan. "Cool him down, and—"

"Someone else can do that," said Sir Vinson. "Let the man catch his breath. How's young Blary?"

Isaac came up looking pale and sheepish, and said that he was all right.

"Aye, well you've Crazy Jack to thank," said Sir Vinson. "Never allow a horse to trap you like that! You came precious close to being killed."

Isaac nodded, mumbled his thanks to Jonathan without looking at him, and slunk away.

Sir Vinson turned to Crane, who watched enigmatically. "Change of plans for tomorrow, Crane. I'll need you here. Lord Green has two teams of draft horses coming down from Barnstaple. Had 'em shipped from Ireland. There seems to have been some trouble in the harbour—that damned silt again, I fancy—and his lordship wants you to check the animals over to be sure they're not ruined."

Briefly, Crane looked stunned. "But I'm driving Miss Britewell down to Breton Ridge tomorrow, sir. Worden's a good man. He can check his lordship's animals."

"Very likely." The edge of annoyance in the head groom's voice had not escaped Sir Vinson, who did not tolerate opposition from his servants. He said coldly, "However, I have told Lord Green he can have the benefit of your knowledge, so we must find someone else to drive my daughter."

Greatly daring, Crane persisted, "But that would mean he'd be away several days, sir, and I can't spare—"

"Jupiter, what a bobbery you make, man! I wonder *you* could be spared if we're so pinched for grooms!"

"It's not that, sir! But it's a tricky road. Biddle's the only man I trust with a coach and four, and he let one of the hacks step on his foot, so he can't work. There's only me, sir."

"Nonsense! Why, I'll warrant any of 'em—even Crazy Jack here, could do the thing!"

Crane's jaw dropped. "Sir! You'd never trust *him* to drive Miss Jennifer? Besides, he's to work for Mr. Fleming tomorrow!"

He had overplayed his hand. Sir Vinson, who'd really had no intention of allowing Jonathan to serve as coachman, lost his temper. "Then, dammit, he can work for Mr. Fleming when he gets back! What about it, Jack? Have you ever driven a coach?"

Jonathan answered eagerly, "I've driven a four-in-hand, sir!"

"Have you, by Jove! Couldn't be better, and I know Miss Britewell thinks well of you. Come on up to the house, and we'll find you some livery. Can't have you driving in to Breton Ridge wearing those—er, garments. Lord Kenneth would think we were properly in the basket!" He laughed at this witticism, and the small crowd laughed dutifully, with many a sly grin being directed at the glowering head groom.

Well aware that Crane could have strangled him, and not giving a button, Jonathan followed Sir Vinson out.

It took half an hour for the housekeeper to find livery of an approximately suitable size, and another twenty minutes involving measurements and pins, before Jonathan was dismissed. The alterations would be made this evening, she said, and he could collect the livery in the morning.

His hope for a glimpse of Jennifer was not gratified. A vastly superior footman conducted him to the servants' entrance and said in a far from superior accent, " 'Op orf, *Mister Coachman*! Coachman, h'indeed!" and with a derisive snort, slammed the ponderous door.

Dusk was deepening to darkness, and the courtyard was clammy, the light from two flambeaux creating diffused haloes in the foggy air. Determined to have a look at the Blue Rose Mine, Jonathan turned eastward, and strode along, his steps as light as his heart, envisioning the joys of being close to his adored lady on a beautiful estate free from un-'ovely barons and heavy-handed grooms. So lost was he in this bright dream that he was startled when a boulder suddenly hove up directly in front of him. The light was gone, and the fog was now a dark wall.

"Jupiter!" he muttered, and peered about for the rough track that led from Triad to the mine. He'd have thought he could follow it blindfold, but in his happy preoccupation he had evidently strayed from it. He stood still, and could hear the faint crash of breakers off to the right, which meant he'd been heading southward. He turned to the east, and kept on cautiously, his narrowed eyes searching for gullies. He had progressed some distance when he heard a muttering behind him and checked at once.

A familiar voice with a strong French accent said argumentatively, "There was not such a thing, 'ave I not say it? Me, I 'ave ze ears *par excellence*, and I should, if any man pass by, know it."

"Like yourself, don'tcha, Frenchy?"

A London voice, this, and it triggered a flood of French invective that brought a grin to Jonathan's lips and also enabled him to move on without fear of being heard. So although the Frenchman had never appeared at Castle Triad, he was still loitering about the area, and it sounded as though he was guarding—

Only his early training in the high rigging enabled him to catch his balance as the earth seemed to fall out from under him. His next step was no less steep. He was on a downward slope. It had to be the approach to the mine! He moved ahead very slowly, groping his way. All sound was muffled now, but he was soon conscious of a change. There was the faint smell of burning wood, and he sensed that something hung over him. He reached up and touched cold stone. Triumphant, he thought, 'By heaven, I'm inside!'

Soon, the fog began to thin, and he found that he was in a narrow down-sloping corridor. It was still very dark, but occasionally through the eddies he could discern a faint glow. Someone was here, all right! Everyone knew of the plans to reopen the Blue Rose, but nothing was certain as yet; no supplies had been brought in, no hiring started. So, why the guards outside? And if his lordship wanted to do some preliminary explorations, why all the secrecy?

He heard a murmur of many voices interspersed with laughter, and a moment later, froze, his fists clenching as there came a faint rattling sound, as of pebbles displaced just ahead.

Without warning a hand clamped onto his arm. A voice hissed, "Damn you for a clumsy fool, Jamie! Now we'll have to—"

He said softly, "I'm not Jamie."

"Well, why the devil ain't you?" The voice was indignant and the grip on his arm tightened.

Amused, he whispered, "My apologies, sir. But—"

"That you, Lord Haughty-Snort?" This voice was breathless. " 'Fraid I stumbled a trifle."

"If you're Jamie," said the first man, "who the deuce is this fellow?"

"Be dashed if I know. One of them, I suppose."

Someone yelled, *"Wer da?"*

"It's a blasted Hanoverian!" exclaimed the first man.

"I'll leave you to pay our respects." 'Jamie,' a dim outline, came up and rushed past. "Sorry, my pippin. Must trot."

Running feet were approaching. Jonathan's arm was released and the man beside him murmured an unruffled, "He has execrable manners. My apologies, but I can't seem to find my card case. Is yours handy?"

"I don't have one about me at the moment."

"Hey!" roared another voice. "Speak up, DeVries, or I fire!"

"In that case," said Jonathan's companion, "since we ain't been introduced . . ." He melted into the darkness.

Jonathan raced after him, unable to see where he was going, but made reckless by a brightening light behind him, and a babble of angry voices. He came to an abrupt halt. Someone was running towards him! "Treed!" he muttered, flung himself to the side, and collided hard with a stone wall. A deafening shot, a stab of flame, and the oncoming man cried out and fell.

Jonathan whispered, "Sorry, Father," and neglected his obligation to help those in need.

"Blasted fool!" a man howled. "You went and shot the Frenchy!"

The air was colder now, the sense of confined space was gone. Jonathan had no complaints, and he sprinted in what he hoped was the direction of the village.

❧ *Chapter 7* ❧

The early morning sunlight bestowed a faint but welcome warmth on the little donkey's shaggy back, and the two men in the cart were so deep in conversation that when his trot slowed to a walk, it went unnoticed. He ambled along, snatching up a dandelion now and then, at peace with his world.

"How d'ye know he was a Frenchy?" asked Noah Holsworth, eyeing his companion furtively. "Does ye speak it?"

Jonathan replied evasively, "I—er, they called him 'the Frenchy' when he was shot down. Besides, there was no mistaking his accent."

"Hmm. And you was chased out by a great lot o' foreigners."

"Yes. I'd likely not have got away save that it was thick fog, and night."

"And not no one else saw any of these carryings on?"

Jonathan hesitated, and for no reason he could have put into words, did not speak of "Jamie" and his companion, saying only, "Between the fog and the darkness I very much doubt it."

"Ah," muttered Holsworth, and with another oblique glance, asked, "and were it foggy the night you saw—er, that there lady what lost herself?"

"No. Have you any notion of who she was, Mr. Noah?"

"Never saw such a creature. Just—er, disappeared into thin air, did she?"

Jonathan laughed. "No, sir! She was met, and rode off with someone. Though I couldn't see him," he added reflectively.

"Someone you . . . couldn't see . . ." Holsworth blinked. "Then how—ah, how d'you know he met the lady?"

"I heard her laugh, and a man was talking quietly. I thought then that she must have been a guest at Triad, but I heard nothing of any overnight company."

"There's female servants at the castle," Holsworth pointed out. "Mr. Crane's got his eye on one of 'em, and meets her on the sly when she gets her day off."

"Likely that's the case, then. Although I had the impression—well, I mean her manner was more that of—of a lady of Quality. Still, it was almost dark, and you're doubtless in the right of it. And 'tis of no importance and has nothing to say to what all those men are about in the Blue Rose. None of the supplies have arrived for the work to begin, so why do you think Lord Green should find it necessary to put guards on the place?"

"No reason I can see, but then a lord don't have to have reasons for foolishness. I'd like fine to know where all these foreigners come from. And how they got to the mine with nobody ever seeing hide nor hair of 'em."

"At night, I should think. 'Tis sufficiently isolated. Unless . . ." Jonathan paused, and muttered half to himself, "There were all those marks in the sands . . ."

Peering at him uneasily, Holsworth suddenly became aware that the cart had come to a complete halt. "Marmaduke!" he shouted, slapping the reins sharply on the donkey's back. "You're going to make Jack late, and that'll be a fine bobbery! Hoist your hoofs!"

Marmaduke broke into a trot again, and the cart rattled up the hill towards the castle.

Remorseful, Holsworth said, "A fine help I was to ye. I'd have done better to let you walk."

"No, no. It was good of you to pick me up. Besides"—Jonathan squinted at the sun—"I doubt 'tis much after eight."

"And you wanted to be there 'fore Crane was up, so as

to hide that." Holsworth jerked his head to the new cage, which resided in the back of the cart. "You'll not do it now. I cannot think why you wanted to take him in the first place. The Widder'll feed the creature for ye."

This was perfectly true. The trouble was that Mrs. Newlyn had some odd notions as to what birds liked to eat. She had several times brought "tidbits" of salt pork or haddock for Duster, who had drawn away from them in revulsion. More alarmingly, the lady tended to be absent-minded and there was no knowing what might happen if she brought Sprat along. But her nature was generous and she meant so well that not for the world would he put his reservations into words. He therefore replied untruthfully that Duster refused to touch any food while he was away. "If I can just hide him on the box of the carriage, I'm sure Miss Jennifer won't object."

"Oliver Crane will!" said Holsworth. "Best give it up, lad."

Jonathan refused to be defeated, however, and as it turned out, the transfer was easier than they had anticipated. When they reached the castle, Holsworth stopped the cart behind the stables, where grooms were already busily at work. A light travelling coach had been pulled out and stood in the yard. There was no sign of Oliver Crane. Jonathan slipped out of the donkey cart, ran along the far side of the coach, and succeeded in depositing Duster under the box seat without being seen. He waved triumphantly to Holsworth, and the big man grinned and flourished his hook.

Watching Jonathan cross the yard accompanied by an immediate chorus of taunts from the grooms, Holsworth's smile faded. He muttered, "D'ye notice that he's not quite so timid o'late, Marmaduke? Giddap, now!" He turned the cart and started the donkey back down the hill. "I'd begun to have hopes for him," he went on regretfully. "But 'tis clear to see that he's in a sorry state. What with vanishing ladies, and men he can't see, and marks in the sands . . . to say nought of hundreds o' furriners chasing him about the moors at night." He shook his head. "Poor fellow. Fate has dealt him a bitter hand, Marmaduke. A bitter hand."

An hour later, the object of these mournful thoughts viewed Fate in a very different light. Thanks to the housekeeper, the livery now fit him quite well, and to be clad in decent garments again was a delight. Duster's cage was under the seat, partially concealed by the small bundle of his own belongings, and Oliver Crane had been unable to find fault with his handling of the four spirited bays when he'd driven around to the front of the castle.

Crane had followed the coach, and now sauntered over to remark dourly that he wondered the master had not required his "fine new coachman" to powder his hair, since he would be mixing with the hoity-toity Morris servants.

Coming up in time to hear this remark, Jennifer said, "I am sure Lord Morris knows we do not aspire to the standards set at Breton Ridge, Crane." Her warm smile rested on the disconcerted head groom for an instant, then she turned her attention to the box. The sight of Jonathan with a snowy jabot at his throat and a well-cut dark blue coat hugging his broad shoulders caused her eyes to widen, and for several seconds she could not command her voice.

Jonathan looked down on a radiant vision clad in a pearl grey travelling gown, with scarlet ribands threading through the wide low collar and repeated in the lacy ruffle of her cap. And for him, all else faded into a hazy insignificance.

Aware in a befuddled way that Crane was looking at her curiously, Jennifer pulled her wits together and said in a rush of words, "What a glorious day. Please do not travel at a great rate, Jack. I want to—"

Lord Green, dressed for riding, stamped to join them and put in rudely, "What's this? Crane, are you gone quite daft? I'll not have Miss Britewell entrusted to the care of that half-wit!"

"Weren't my doing, milord," said Crane. "If I'd had my way—"

"Yes, but I think my father did not ask your advice, Crane. And 'tis not our business to question Sir Vinson's orders," said Jennifer coolly.

" 'Tis very much my business," blustered his lordship. "Britewell! I say, Britewell!" He flourished his riding crop at Sir Vinson, who was walking over to say his farewells to Jennifer. "I think you must rectify this bumblebroth, Britewell," said Green loudly. "Some clod has been so dense as to put that looney on the box!"

Amused, Jennifer thought that my lord could scarcely have chosen words more calculated to make her father dig in his heels.

Sir Vinson's pleasant smile vanished. He said coldly, "You may be assured, sir, that I would most certainly not entrust my daughter's safety to anyone I felt unreliable."

"Unreliable? Damme, the fellow's got maggots in his loft! I'd not trust him to—"

"It was my understanding, my lord, that you entrusted him with your life." Noting how his lordship's teeth snapped together at this distasteful reminder, Sir Vinson was pleased with himself, and twisted the knife. " 'Tis because Jack was so valiant on that occasion," he purred, "that I feel he should be rewarded. Especially since he has a splendid way with horses."

Flushed with chagrin, Lord Green grumbled, "One can but hope you will not regret your—trust. I suppose, so long as you send a guard and outriders—"

Sir Vinson laughed. "Come now, my lord, we are not in your lawless London Town! My name is known and respected throughout the county. Furthermore, my people are quite aware that did a well-born gentleman insult Miss Britewell, he would answer to me. And did any commoner dare to so much as touch her, I would shoot him out of hand without a moment's hesitation. If I neglected to perform my duty, you may rest assured my sons would not! We have no need for guards and outriders here, my lord, so do not fret. My daughter goes in complete safety."

Green's jaws worked as though he ground his teeth, but he returned his host's faint smile with a nod and said nothing.

Sir Vinson embraced Jennifer and told her she must "have a lovely time."

"Do you come, sir?" she asked.

"Assuredly. Howland and I expect to be able to arrive well before the ball on Friday. You will give my compliments to Lord and Lady Morris, of course."

Howland called to him from the front door, and he kissed her, and hurried away.

Jennifer turned to the coach, and murmured, "If I may have your hand, Crane ..."

It was Green however, who rushed to hand her into the coach, and Crane drew back, his lips pursed, his eyes darting to Tilly Mays' equally annoyed face.

"How dreary we shall be without your lovely self," mourned his lordship, retaining Jennifer's hand and following her up one step. "You will miss me too, m'dear. But never grieve, I follow you at the week-end, so you will not be bereft of my company for too long."

She had hoped to be free from the wretch, and this was unwelcome news. Pulling her hand away, she seated herself on the red velvet cushions and murmured, "Indeed? I'd fancied you too busied with your plans to be able to accept Lord Kenneth's invitation."

"Were his gracious majesty, King George, coming to consult me, 'twould not keep me from your side a day past Friday, Miss Jennifer. This I promise."

She stared at him, but he met her cold eyes with an egoism that would not be abashed. 'He is quite unable to credit that I do not want him,' she thought, and called pointedly, "Pray hurry, Tilly. We must be off."

His lordship, sighing dejectedly, was obliged to give way, and within seconds Tilly was ensconced opposite her mistress. With a lurch, a clatter of hooves and a creak of leather, the carriage started across the courtyard. Jennifer leaned from the window to flutter her handkerchief to Sir Vinson and Howland, who waved from the top of the front steps.

Lord Green sprang to snatch the scrap of cambric and lace. "Thank you, fairest," he bellowed. "Though I need no token to keep your beauty fresh in my heart!"

"Oh!" exclaimed Jennifer, jerking back from the window in a rage. "That—that *insufferable* . . . !"

They were out of the yard then, and rolling along at a steady pace. It was silly to be thinking that his lordship seemed bolder these past few days, as if more sure he had won her. Just as silly to imagine that her father was brooding over some secret trouble. Likely he regretted having given Green permission to lease the mine, that was all. And there was still time to withdraw his permission, for nothing had been done as yet. She shrugged away her misgivings. My lord Green's connivings would *not* spoil this day! Nor the party, if he should come, which heaven forbid! She gave an impatient shrug of her shoulders, and dismissed the odious baron from her mind.

"How fortunate that the fog left us this bright sunshine," she exclaimed. "Only look, Tilly. Is it not beautiful?"

It was indeed beautiful. Renowned as it is for ferocious gales and sudden dense fogs, the northern coast of Cornwall can be a bleak and forbidding place. But when the western wind breathes warm, and sky and sea are matching cerulean bowls, it is a sight to touch the soul. So it was on this bright morning. The waves, ending their long journey from the Americas, foamed like white lace against the offshore rocks, then met the shore with a caress; the sunshine danced on tidal pools and streams; ever on guard, the cliffs strode strong and proud above golden beach, quiet cove, and secluded bay. The air was pure and sweet, and so clear that the ancient and mysterious standing stones that soared on the headland fourteen miles distant seemed but half a mile away.

The glories of Nature did not impress Tilly, however. She was not a good traveller, and remarked in a die-away voice that she only hoped it didn't "come over hot" for she couldn't abide heat and would likely be sick.

"Of course you won't, foolish creature," scolded Jennifer lightly. "How can you be so dismal? You should be happy to be out driving on such a morning."

"With a looby on the box," sniffed Tilly. "I only pray we will arrive safely!"

And so it went. However Jennifer strove to keep her good humour, Tilly remained obstinately miserable. Exasperated when her martyred handmaiden moaned that she knew she was a trial and unwanted, Jennifer said at her most stern, "Your whining is unwanted, certainly. Since you are determined to be a misery you may get out and wait here. Jack can come back for you later, and take you home."

Horrified, Tilly demanded, "And who would take care of you, and—and dress your hair so pretty as what I do, miss? *That* I would like to know!"

"I am very sure Lady Kenneth's housekeeper will find a woman to serve me with competence. And with none of your complaining." Jennifer reached for the check string.

Tilly gave a shriek, swore she would utter not another word, and appeared to fall into a coma.

With a furtive smile, Jennifer settled back and admired the scenery while anticipating the coming party and a happy reunion with her friend Caroline. The miles slipped away and her thoughts drifted to Johnny. He was driving very well. There was little of the swaying that really did tend to make Tilly unwell. How charmingly he looked in the livery, and how light-hearted he had seemed, the shy smile in his eyes banishing the hunted look she often glimpsed there.

She found that she was smiling, and slanted a glance at Tilly. The woman was dabbing a handkerchief at her face, which was not surprising, for it had become quite warm. "Why did you not open the window as you were uncomfortable?" said Jennifer, standing to do so.

"I didn't want to disturb you, miss," sighed Tilly. "You looked like you was having such wonderful happy thoughts."

Jennifer was obliged to apply her handkerchief to her own cheeks, which had become suddenly heated.

Soon, the breeze died away altogether. Tilly was pale and silent. Watching her uneasily, Jennifer feared the worst, and pulled the check string.

The carriage slowed and stopped, and when Jonathan

opened the trap she told him to find a shady spot. "We must rest for a little while. My maid cannot tolerate this heat."

In very short order the horses were splashing through a shallow stream towards a copse of trees. They were small trees, bowing inevitably to the east, but they offered a welcome shade, and Jonathan drew the team to a halt.

"There," said Jennifer, patting Tilly's listless hand kindly. "You'll feel better after you have a rest. Can you get up?"

Tilly wailed, and one hand flew to her mouth.

Jennifer supported her to the steps where Jonathan waited to lift her down.

With her cheek against his shoulder, Tilly revived sufficiently to scan their oasis, then shrieked, "Oh—Gawd! Oh, *Gawd*!"

A large and alarmed hare shot under the noses of the team. With ringing neighs, the high-bread animals reared and plunged. In another second, they would bolt, and Jennifer was still in the coach. Jonathan dropped Tilly unceremoniously and sprang for the heads of the leaders. He was barely in time, and was dragged a short way before he was able to pull them to a halt. He secured the reins to one of the trees and rushed to whip open the carriage door, which had swung shut.

Jennifer had been flung back on the seat, and was trying to pull her cap from over her eyes. Her gown was in disarray, revealing a very nicely turned leg, but she was unhurt, and said with a shaken smile, "That was an excitement I did not really need, Johnny Coachman."

Able to breathe again, his relieved glance took in the pretty limb and rested there appreciatively.

Jennifer's hand whipped her skirts into place, then was extended. He took it, and handed her down the steps feeling his face redden. But when he slanted a look at her, the dimple flickered beside her mouth.

Tilly was on her hands and knees, weeping loudly.

Running to console her, Jennifer said anxiously, "My poor dear. Whatever happened?"

"I knowed it . . . I *knowed* it!" wailed Tilly. "Evil's come amongst us!" Her accusing and tearful eyes fixed upon Jonathan. "To be throwed down. . . ! Like I was—was so much *dirt!*"

"I am truly sorry, miss," he said apologetically. "But I had to get to the leaders fast, or there'd have been no stopping them."

"And I am very glad you did," said Jennifer, coaxing her abigail to stand. "Had you not screamed so, Tilly, the horses would not have taken fright. Whatever made you behave in such a way?"

The only response was a renewed flood of tears and some disjointed mumblings about being blamed, "as usual!"

Jennifer looked to Jonathan in silent questioning.

He said, "She saw a hare, ma'am."

Jennifer paled. "Oh, no! Are you quite sure?"

He nodded. "It ran under the team."

Tilly clung to Jennifer's hand. "We must go b-back, Miss J-Jennifer! We daren't go on! 'Twas how I knowed it would be!" Another scared glance shot at Jonathan. She whispered, "Evil's come . . . among us!"

Jennifer stared at her, wide-eyed.

Jonathan went to soothe the still-nervous horses. It was happening again. As it had in St. Just and Zenor, and, worst of all, in Garrison Pen, where they'd almost managed to put a period to him. Yet it was that merciless beating which had brought him here, to find the lady he worshipped. He frowned, and led the horses into another patch of shade. The lady he had no right to worship. Yet in the schoolroom on that most wondrous of rainy afternoons, he had almost dared to kiss her. And today, because he no longer wore ragged garments, he had started to feel fully alive and able to hold his head up again. What utter folly! As though clothes could change what he was; or anything in the entire world have the power to wipe the slate clean and allow him to dream—

"Why do you look so grim, Johnny? Are you wishing you had let the team run away with me?"

His unruly heart gave a leap and began to pound erratically. He jerked his head up. Jennifer stood watching him, her face shaded by a dainty parasol. He said, "No. Of course not. But—but I had no thought to have thrown your maid down so roughly."

"Is that why you were looking so miserable?"

His eyes fell away. "She was very shaken, ma'am."

"Yes, but she is resting now, and will be much better for a short nap."

He looked past her. Tilly lay on a blanket spread under the trees. "You will wish to rest also, Miss Jennifer."

"Thank you, but there is not the need. If I am tired, 'tis from sitting in the coach. I shall walk for a little while."

The offer she anticipated was not forthcoming. Jonathan became deeply engrossed in loosening harness straps, and then took up a handful of grass and concentrated on a rather restricted rubbing down of the animals, not once glancing at her.

She watched him speculatively, and pointed out, "You have already tended the off-leader. Are you going to water them?"

"When they've cooled down, ma'am."

"They'll be cool in this shade. Give me your escort, if you please."

If he pleased! But he loved her too much, and to be alone with her was such a bittersweet temptation. Avoiding her candid gaze, he muttered, "If I leave them, they'll graze, and I don't want them eating while they're still warm."

"Exactly right. So we will all walk, and your horses can cool down while you keep them from devouring the scenery."

Perforce, he took the reins, and man, team, and coach, followed Jennifer obediently.

"I suppose," she murmured, at the head of this small procession, "being from London, you find our superstitions so much nonsense?"

"I'm not sure I am from London, ma'am."

"Oh, a pretty evasion! And how may I talk when you are

lagging back there? Am I to be burdened with a stiff neck in addition to my—other injuries?"

He all but sprang to her side, and said anxiously, "I'd not known you were hurt. Can I help?"

Her eyes danced. "Now that would really drive Tilly into the boughs! I fear I have bruised my— Er, I have sustained a bruise."

The dimple that must assuredly be the most kissable such article in the history of mankind was quivering beside her lips. He had to choke back a teasing response. She was lonely, poor darling girl, and she had begun, perhaps unconsciously, to reach out to him, to speak to him as an equal. But how appalled she would be to realise that such a one as he presumed to love her . . . And so it was that he did not return her smile, but said gravely, "Indeed? I am very sorry, ma'am."

To Jennifer, it was as if her rather naughty remark had been too vulgar to be acknowledged. How dare he be so aloof! How dare he presume to give her a set-down? Angry and mortified, she thought, 'You invited it, Jennifer Britewell! A fine pass have you come to, that you must play the coquette with a common groom!' It was a sobering admission. She said with rare hauteur, "And I owe you another vote of thanks. Had the team succeeded in bolting I would have had more than a bruise to complain of, but I suppose I dare not try to reward you."

Just to be near her was the greatest reward she could offer him. But it was clear that his reserve had annoyed her. He must not spoil that dismal success. He said woodenly, "You are in my care, ma'am. 'Tis the duty of all your servants to—"

"Oh, hush!" she exclaimed, stamping her foot at him with pretty ferocity. "Do not throw your humble servitude in my face!"

He blinked at this rather muddled admonition. "But—I *am* in your father's service, and—"

"And had you not been, you would have let me be carried to my death, I collect!"

"No—of course not. I only meant—"

"To act the part of a servant. And I am obliged to tell you that 'tis a role you play very poorly!"

He tensed, then, still striving, admitted, "I expect I do. It is—a big step up from being a penniless wanderer, ma'am."

She uttered a small snort of impatience. "Very well, since servants must obey their mistr—"—she corrected hurriedly—"their employers, answer my question. I asked your opinion of our superstitions."

She looked so adorably conscious of that near slip of the tongue. He kept his countenance somehow, and replied, "Cornwall does seem rather rife with it, Miss Jennifer. I cannot but—er, pity the poor hares."

She stopped walking and with an instant change of mood put a hand on his arm. "Johnny, you must *never* say such a thing to others! Not to another soul! Promise me."

Her eyes were full of anxiety that was, he knew, for his sake. Deeply moved, he could not refrain from smiling as he answered, "I promise. But I cannot think you share the belief that hares contain the spirits of the dead, or can change their form."

She walked on again. "I am Cornish born and bred. In some ways this lovely county is far more steeped in ancient beliefs and fables than is any other part of England. The legend of my own house is part of our history." She glanced at his intent face. "Do you know why the castle is named Triad?"

"I fancy it goes back to Arthurian legend. The triangle: Arthur, Guinevere, Lancelot. But was there not another such triangle? King—Marcus, I believe, who sent Tristan to fetch his bride, the Princess Iseult?"

She turned her head and looked at him steadily. "Your memory is not always elusive, is it, Johnny?"

He bit his lip. "Then you will be wishing to turn back? As Tilly asked."

"I make my own decisions. Even if I am as silly and superstitious as you think."

"I could not ever believe you to be silly!"

"Only superstitious."

He said nothing. Jennifer hummed as she walked,

twirling her parasol, and gazing out across the sparkling ocean as though Jonathan had ceased to exist. And perfectly aware that from time to time he stole a glance at her.

Yet when she looked his way it was to find that he had fallen behind and was following her at a respectful distance. "I did not require that you walk behind me again," she said, waiting for him to draw level.

"No, ma'am. But I fear that—you find me irksome."

"If I do, 'tis because you draw the curtains over your thoughts. I wish you will not."

"What did you wish . . . to know, ma'am?"

"Oh, so many things. But for the moment, what you are thinking will do."

He thought grimly, 'Oh, no it won't!' and lied, "I was thinking what a pity it will be for you to miss the party. You have so looked forward to it."

"I have. But—how did you know that?"

"Because you were so radiant this morning. I mean no offence, Miss Jennifer, but you seldom set out covers for guests. And your friend seemed not to stay for very long."

"If you mean Hibbard Green," she said, frowning, "he is no friend of mine!"

He could have kissed her for that denial. "I meant the lady who was here last week. I chanced to see her out walking."

Puzzled, Jennifer said, "I entertained no visitors last week. Unless, perhaps . . ." She thought of Howland and wondered if he had been dallying with some new light of love. "Perhaps, the lady was a friend of my brother."

That was logical enough, but still— She was looking at him curiously, and he said, "I did not mean to—to pry, ma'am. I'm only glad to know that she came to no harm."

"Harm?" Stiffening, she asked. "Why should you suppose that a friend of my brother would be harmed in my father's house?"

"No—she would not, of course! Only, it seemed rather—er, unwise. To walk on the moor, I mean. I tried to warn her about being up there alone at night, but—"

Jennifer halted and stared at him. "What on earth are you

talking about? If the lady was on the moor at night, I am very sure my brother escorted her."

"So I would have thought, but she was quite alone, and—"

"A *lady*? Alone at night? On the moor? If ever I heard of such a thing! Where was this, pray?"

"Near the old mine. Perhaps she was acquainted with one of the men up there."

"What men? There is no work going forward at the mine yet."

"I know. But there are men there. Many rough fellows. I saw them."

She was frightened suddenly. In his livery he looked every inch the aristocrat. *Could* he be playing a part, after all? Had she been a silly, trusting fool? Everyone knew that Excise officers were sly and devious. He very obviously had been prowling about the Blue Rose after dark. Her suspicions rushed back tenfold. She said in a breathless accusation, "You are trying to trap me with all this talk of a lady, and of men working at the mine!"

"Trap you?" Taken aback, he said, "How could you be trapped? I went to the mine because—"

Admired for her ability to meet emergencies with calmness and common sense, Jennifer was far from being calm now. Her common sense told her she had been stupid, and the thought that this man had cleverly deceived her awoke a hurt and a rage such as she'd never before experienced. She was thrown into a panic by the depth of her distress, and she interrupted wildly, "Because you *are* a Riding Officer! You *have* been searching for free-traders, just as I thought! It was all carefully planned to insinuate yourself among us, and—"

"Are you at that again?" Anger overwhelmed him. He seized her arm as she drew away from him. "You know how ill I was when Mrs. Newlyn found me. Do you really think I would go to such lengths only to hoodwink—"

"Yes! I do! If truth was told, you were—were likely beaten by free-traders and decided to turn it to—to good account!"

"If ever I heard such silly twaddle!"

"Oh! How dare you!"

But in his desperate need to convince her, he would have dared anything, and said fiercely, "I gave you my oath! Have you forgot?"

"You told me you were under a vow, and that because of it you had to stay here. I was so stupid as to think—you were so cunning as to *make* me think you had taken a *holy* vow because of some—some terrible crime! The truth is that your oath was to the King!" Once more she tried to pull away, but his grip was like iron. She half-sobbed, "Let me go!"

"Not until you listen! I am *not*—"

"I won't listen! I don't believe a word you say! You have lied since first you came! Deceiving us all with your loathesome play-acting! I knew you were no—no tramp, but I thought perhaps—"

He dropped the reins and took her by the shoulders. "If you will just—"

On a note of hysteria she cried, "Do not *dare* put your filthy hands on me! Open the door at once, and drive me back!"

His filthy hands . . . Shocked back to sanity, he released her abruptly, and stood very still, as white as she now was flushed. Then he turned to swing the carriage door open.

Disdaining the hand he offered, Jennifer stumbled past. Blinded with tears, confused and frightened by conflicting emotions, she tripped on the step. Jonathan leapt to steady her, but in her overwrought state she thought she was being attacked, and with a choked cry whirled and struck out frenziedly. Her flying fist caught him in the eye, and he reeled back, still holding the door. The coach rocked. From the box came a scrambling sound, followed by a strange, high-pitched gobbling. It was not a birdsong the horses knew and they were still nervous. They sidled and stamped about, causing the coach to rock violently. Caught off balance, Jennifer staggered and uttered a faint cry. Jonathan grabbed her outflung arm, jerked her to him, and sprang clear as the team lunged against the traces.

It was the last straw. Jennifer burst into tears.

"Oh, God!" groaned Jonathan. "Do not! Oh—pray, ma'am, do not!"

"I . . . cannot . . . help it," she wailed.

Frantic, he set her down, and began to dab at her wet cheeks with his handkerchief, finding it necessary to keep one arm about her, pleading with her not to cry, while she clung to his cravat and sobbed ever more unrestrainedly.

"Jennifer, please stop! My beautiful . . . dearest girl . . . I cannot bear to see you cry."

At this, her eyes opened very wide. She pulled back, peering up into his anguished face with tears gemming her lashes. "You—you're weeping, too . . ." she gulped.

"I know," he said. And lost to everything but her grief, added with a tender smile, "You hit me in the eye."

"Oh." One hand lifted to caress his cheek. "My . . . poor dear . . ."

He could no more have stopped from turning his head than have stopped the sun in its journey; no more have refrained from kissing that soft white hand, than have ceased to love her.

Gazing into his eyes, reading the adoration there, Jennifer was as enchanted as he. She lifted her face.

The village idiot bowed his head and kissed the lady of Castle Triad, and, for a heavenly stolen moment, the world and its problems ceased to be.

❧ *Chapter 8* ❧

Jennifer stirred, sighed, and opened her eyes to gaze dream-ily at a rather rumpled jabot and a dark blue coat.

Ecstatic, Jonathan bent to kiss the smooth brow of this girl he adored. And with devastating suddenness another face was before him. The face of a middle-aged gentleman with a lot of white hair and a strong, stern face, who wore the black robe and plain white stock of a clergyman.

The world of grey reality rushed back. Fate had offered him a challenge, and again, he had failed! He was a social outcast, not fit to touch the shoe of this peerless angel. His hope had been to protect and guard her from any danger. Well, *he* was the danger! And far from protecting her, he had been so lost in love that he'd dared to kiss her. Worse; he'd felt her sweetly passionate response. The Code of Honour demanded that an offer of marriage follow such an act. A bitter laugh racked him. How could a penniless out-cast such as he offer her marriage? Unconsciously, his hands tightened on her shoulders. His head began to pound, as it did sometimes, even now, but it was as nothing com-pared to the self-disgust that scourged him.

Confronted with her own awakening, Jennifer still clung to him, blinking in bewilderment into a convulsed face she scarcely recognised; flinching to that harsh embittered laugh.

He thrust her from him. "I am so sorry! Can you ever—" His voice broke. He spun on his heel and stalked toward the horses, who had wandered off and were grazing beside a group of the ancient standing stones.

Jennifer stood motionless, impressions crowding her dazed mind. Her first kiss ... An ache in her shoulders where his strong hands had held her ... *"We cannot have even the village idiot developing a* tendre *for you ..."* Papa had thought that was a fine joke. If he should find out ... If Howland knew ... They would kill him! How could this have happened to her? She'd given up hope of marriage, but she had dreamed of that magical experience called falling in love. And, dreaming, she had conjured up a dashing and handsome gentleman, well endowed with kindness and good humour. She had not considered title to be a requirement, nor great wealth, but he would be comfortably circumstanced, with a London house and a pleasant country estate somewhere. A far cry from Crazy Jack, a penniless and nameless vagrant, haunted by disgrace and the shadow of some terrible tragedy. A man so utterly ineligible that to suggest him as a possible suitor would either result in hilarity, or give rise to anxiety about her sanity. She thought, 'I must have suffered a brief attack of madness, that's what it is!'

He had come up with the horses and tethered them to a tree. She watched him wander to the tall stones, and lean there, with his shoulders bowed, and his head downbent.

The madness was upon her again, because she was running to him. "You were going to ask," she said breathlessly, "if I could forgive you."

"It was ... past forgiveness," he acknowledged, in a low, dull voice. "Even the ... wish, was inexcusable. I deserve ..."

"To be flogged."

He nodded.

"I think," she pointed out, "that would be the least of what my menfolk would do."

"Yes."

She sat on one of the fallen stones. "And I will not forgive you," she declared.

"No. Of course." He turned away, as if ineffably weary.

"Where are you going?"

"To get the team. I'll ... drive you back to the castle."

"To surrender yourself for execution, when if you had any brains you would instead run away. Very far, and fast. But you will not run. You never do run, do you? You will instead do the honourable thing."

He stood half turned from her, one slim hand on the cold granite, and he muttered in the halting timid voice of Crazy Jack, "I have no—honour."

"So! My first kiss has been taken by a dishonourable gentleman! A pretty performance!"

"Don't ... please. Do you think I ... am not ashamed? That I don't know how I have—insulted you?"

"I cannot hear you. Come and sit down."

He hesitated, then sat on a boulder some distance from her.

"No, not over there." She indicated the stone beside her. "I do not care to shout for everyone to hear."

Hesitating, he glanced at the expanse of open countryside, but then obeyed.

"So," she said, "you love me, and are ashamed of it."

His head jerked up. "No!"

"Do you say that you dared to kiss me—not even liking—"

"I worship you! And— Oh, Lord!" He gestured helplessly.

"You were born a gentleman. If you were still a gentleman, would you offer for me?"

"You know I would."

"And—would my menfolk consider you an eligible parti?"

"Yes— No—" A hand was pressed to his temple. "I don't know! I think I was well born, but not of great fortune. And—what difference can it make? It is all lost now. I have made a horrible disaster of my life. I am no longer a gentleman. I shall never ... be able to approach you."

"*Approach* me! You did more than that, Jack, or Johnny, or Jonathan! I am shamed, and quite ruined. And ..."—her voice shook slightly—"I am at my last prayers, you know."

An angry frown came her way. "Do not talk such rubbish!"

"Ah. That was Jonathan speaking, I think. But—truth is truth, sir." She leaned to him, her eyes very tender. "Johnny, Johnny, you are such a fool. Such a gloriously honourable fool."

He looked once into the dearest face in all the world, into the eyes that held a glow promising everything he daren't dream of. His breath was snatched away and it took all his resolution to turn his head.

"No." Jennifer put her hands on each side of his face, and turned his head back again. "Oh, my dear—do not take all the blame to yourself. Does it not occur to you that, far from being the fragile, dainty wisp of a creature you obviously fancy me to be, I am tall and strong? If I could keep so crude an animal as Hibbard Green at bay, should I not have easily been capable of defending my—my good name from so gentle and high principled a man as you?"

He took her hands away, and when they turned to close around his, he shut his eyes for an instant, not trusting himself to look at her. But he could not keep his voice from shaking when he said, "You are sorry for me, is—is all. You took pity on me, and you have allowed your warm heart to mistake pity for—for—"

"For—love?" She felt him tremble, and guessing how he longed to hold her in his arms, respecting him the more for his struggle against allowing her to love him, she said gently, "And what if my heart is not mistaken, Johnny?"

"You mustn't even think such a thing!" He sprang up, to stand with his back turned, and a hand again pressed to his temple, and whispered a despairing, "Dear God—help me! Make her understand, for her own precious sake!"

The intensity of his anguish deepened her fear. She bit her lip, then said, " 'Tis you must make me understand, Johnny. If I am to be denied the man who should—by rights—offer for my hand, I beg—no, I demand—to know—why?"

"Can you ask?" He swung around and said harshly, "You know what *you* are! You know what *I* am! Are you blinded to what the world would say? Do you know what I can offer you? *Nothing!* Do you want to share my lot? My God in heaven! Do you fancy me so lost to decency as to *allow* you to share a life that is a hell on earth? I have sunk beneath the scorn of the lowest criminal—is *that* what you wish to share? Shall you sleep in the rain and mud with me? Shall you beg for food as—as I have done, until you are so hungry you snatch eagerly for scraps thrown out to the dogs? Would you watch proudly while I was flogged or stoned or beaten because I am suspected of witchcraft, or, because of my speech and manner I am judged to be 'different'? And if—may the good Lord forbid!—if you should be at my side when someone from my past recognised me ..." His voice broke. He sank onto the stone once more, bowed his face into his hands, and said a muffled, "Ah—I could not ... bear it! Do you see now ... why I am so ashamed of having kissed you?"

She had listened, appalled and scarcely breathing, to his wild tirade. For a moment, torn between pity and horror, she was speechless. The voice of reason acknowledged that he spoke truly and that by any measure of common sense she should climb at once into the carriage, collect Tilly, and the instant they reached Breton Ridge send this man away forever. But she was a woman, and the voice of reason does not always speak as strongly to women as the voice of the heart. So it was that she touched his disordered hair gently, and said, "Everything you say is very well, Johnny. Except for one thing. You said I know what you are. And that is not so. I know what you have become. I do not know why."

He said dully, "I ... told you."

"You told me a thimbleful. I want to know—everything."

"I cannot tell you what—what I don't know myself."

"Then tell me what you do know. Your name, for instance."

"I told you. It is Jonathan. If I could remember my family name, I'd not further dishonour it by claiming it as my own."

"You were a sailor, I think? An officer? Navy? Merchantman?"

"East Indiaman. But—I don't even remember her name. I was—was her captain."

She was startled. So he'd captained an East Indiaman! A fine accomplishment for so young a man! She persevered, "And on your last voyage there was some trouble on board? Perchance you had to discipline a member of the crew—with—with tragic results . . . ?"

He shook his head, and staring blindly before him, began to speak, brokenly at first, then with more assurance. "We were bound for . . . Plymouth—out of Calcutta. She was a fine ship, and I had . . . a good crew. We were—lucky with wind and weather. Along with the cargo . . . we had taken on passengers. A family going home from long service; a gentleman and his wife and their three grown children and—and their . . . grandchildren; an army officer and his wife and mother. There were several merchants with their wives. And a gentleman escorting his two nieces . . . one of whom—" He paused, and touched his temple again. "One was young and very beautiful. And, she and . . . I . . ." He paused, while Jennifer listened, tense, and dreading what he would say, yet knowing she must hear it all.

"The night after we left St. Helena," he went on, "it was very hot and we were becalmed. Not a breeze for hours. I was on the quarter-deck when the—the lady brought an invitation from her uncle to join him in the roundhouse for a birthday toast." He stopped, as if reluctant to go on.

Jennifer prompted, "And you went and—er—"

"I should have guessed. But her uncle had paid extreme handsomely for their accommodations, and I hesitated to offend him." Noting Jennifer's uncertain expression, he said, "A commander is permitted to sell space to passengers, you know, and to get the best price he may."

"Yes, I did know that was the captain's right, but—I'm not sure where the roundhouse is situated."

" 'Tis at the stern, the full width of the quarter-deck, adjacent to the captain's stateroom and the dining room. On most voyages the roundhouse is partitioned off into several private spaces, each with a port, but Mr. Phillips had purchased the entire area just for the three of them. When we went inside there was—there was no one else." His eyes fell. He said, "I should have left at once . . . but she flirted charmingly, and—and she was lovely. And . . . that's all I remember clearly. Until the storm. I woke up in my cabin, alone and—and very drunk." He heard her gasp, and smiled bitterly. "You wanted to know. So now you do. I must have been drunk for most of the voyage, for it is all a blur. But I remember—her face . . . her teasing and her laughter and—and the brandy. And some hideous headaches as a result. I think, by the time we encountered the storm, I must have been ill. I was thrown from my bunk with . . . with the brandy bottle. I reeked of it. The ship was being tossed like a straw, the waves were mountainous, the wind . . . shrieking. It was night. Pitch black." The words trailed off again, and he sat still and silent, staring always at the ground.

Jennifer said incredulously, "And you were alone? What of your servants? Where was the woman?"

"My clerk and steward probably had all they could do to save themselves. There was nobody near me. We were sinking fast. My ship, and . . ." He shrank lower but made himself say it. "I discovered later—much later—that there were nine and twenty lives lost. Nine and twenty human beings. The family . . . the little children . . . Many of my crew. People with loved ones—dependent upon them, mourning them. I . . . destroyed them all. But—I can still see their faces. Heaven help me, I shall never forget them! Nor the survivors ever forget my shameful betrayal of my sworn duty. My sacred trust. Their fine young . . . drunken captain!"

There was a long silence. Stunned, Jennifer asked, "What then? How did you come ashore?"

"I—don't know. I was drowning at one minute, and on the beach the next, as it seemed. But I couldn't move. Some men came and they went and fetched a priest. He took me in, and cared for me. Though I think—I know he despised me."

"Was he the one who made you take the vow?"

"Yes. He knew of the wreck and of the—the loss of life."

"Then he must have known the name of your ship. And who you are!"

"Yes. He told me . . . but . . ." He drew a hand across his eyes. "I forget things, you see." His shoulders slumped. "I suppose . . . 'tis how I shield myself because I cannot bear to remember my shameful conduct."

She demanded, "Why do you keep touching your temple? Have you the headache now?"

He'd not been conscious of the action, and lowered his hand at once. "I am very well, I thank you."

Jennifer stood, frowning down at him. She looked stern, which was to be expected. He started up, but drew back instinctively when she suddenly sprang at him.

"What's this?" she demanded, grasping his rumpled hair and spreading it apart. "My heaven! What a frightful scar! When did this happen?"

"I'm not . . . sure."

"Was it when your ship sank? Was your head bandaged when the priest was caring for you?"

"No."

"Did it happen during the voyage?"

"I would have . . . known, I think, if—"

"You said you remember very little. Can you remember when your headaches began? I wonder they would have given you command of a great ship if you had suffered such an injury."

He said wryly, "Are you trying to find an excuse for my conduct? There is none."

"There is none, indeed!"

He winced and lowered his eyes, but he saw her hands clench into small fists and nerved himself to receive her scorn and contempt.

"If ever," she said fiercely, "if *ever* I heard such a farrago of fustian!"

His head jerked up. "But—"

"Do not 'but' me, sirrah! Small wonder they call you

Crazy Jack! You *must* be crazy to have believed all that—stuff!"

He started to his feet, but she thrust him down again, bending her flushed face over him and saying through her small white teeth, "Oh, had you been my gracious lord Hibbard Green, I'd believe it! Or one or two others I could name! But—*you*? Never! I believe not—one—word! Not *one*!"

"But you cannot think I would have invented—"

"Silence!" She raised one hand, and looked down at him, her eyes flashing with anger. "Only answer me this riddle, Jonathan. If the captain of one of their great ships had done—what you think you did, would not so mighty a power as the East India Company send investigators? Would they not have sought out and punished such a villain?"

"Not if they believed me drowned. And the sea does not always give up her victims."

"But you were not drowned. Any investigating officer worth his salt would have questioned the local people, and they'd have found the men who went after the priest to help you."

He said with a mirthless smile, "Cornish folk are notoriously averse to answering the questions of those they view as 'foreigners.' You know that. Besides, the fellows who found me were seafaring men; they might very well have sailed again by the time any investigators arrived."

"Hum." She tightened her lips, but refusing to be beaten, said, "You once told me you recollected a lady from your past life. Oh—and a gentleman, you said. What more?"

"There were—children, I think." He frowned and said slowly, "Two small boys. And . . . I remember a deep sorrow, and . . . a grave. But whether it held the older gentleman . . . I cannot say."

She nerved herself, and suggested, "Is it possible that the—the children were your own, Johnny? You said you recalled a lady—might she have been your wife?"

His brow wrinkled painfully. "I—I don't think so. But I feel that the children were—were related to me."

"Then these people were likely all part of your family. You cared for them."

"I know it was a happy part of my life."

"They must have been very proud of you." He flinched at that, but she went on ruthlessly, "Is it likely then, that you would so carelessly have brought disgrace down upon them?"

Looking up into her earnest face, his eyes misted. He said huskily, "How very kind of you, to try to defend me. But—oh, my dear, 'tis a doomed effort. I've gone over and over it all till I wonder I did not run mad. Do you fancy I've not prayed 'twas all a plot? That Miss Phillips was some evil adventuress, luring me to my doom?" Jennifer looked startled, but he stood, put a hand over her lips, and said sadly, "It makes no sense. 'Twould have taken a full-scale mutiny to keep me locked up and in a drunken stupor for such a length of time."

She pulled his hand away. "You might not have been drunk at all! You could have been drugged, or brandy poured down your throat to make it appear that you were intoxicated. Or that dreadful scar on your head might have been—"

"Inflicted by the lady? Why? To what purpose? My chief mate was a good man, but he was new to the Company and had not my training. Their *lives* depended on my abilities!"

Desperate, she argued, "You said you carried a rich cargo. They might have been after that!"

"In which case, dear defender, they'd have waited till we were close to wherever they hoped to off-load, rather than putting me out of commission when we had not yet crossed the Equator. As it is, the cargo was lost—with the ship. And—the most damning strike against me—the survivors testified that I was—was drunk in my cabin when my ship foundered!"

Jennifer's eyes filled with tears, and her lips trembled. Suddenly, she flung herself into his arms and, clinging to him, sobbed, "I d-don't care! You are *not* a weakling, else you'd n-never have held to your vow and—and endured all the misery you've suffered these past two years! It takes great courage and str-strength of will for that, Johnny!"

"Or guilt." He stroked her hair lovingly. "Conscience and remorse are terrible forces, my dear."

"Was it conscience that made you risk your life to help that—that horrid baron? Was it remorse that drove you to defend poor Mrs. Blary when her brutish husband was abusing her so? Or when you saved Isaac from that—that rampaging stallion?" She sniffed, and sat down again, taking out her handkerchief to dry her eyes. "Rubbish!" she declared scratchily. "You acted instinctively because you are a brave gentleman."

Jonathan knelt before her, and taking her hands, kissed each. "Can you even begin to imagine what it means to me that you have such faith? 'Tis far more than ever I hoped for, and I shall cherish the memory of it for as long as I live. But I must leave you. And you must not waste your dear life in worrying for my sake."

"Don't say such things," she begged, caressing his cheek even as she blinked away fresh tears. "Do not leave me, Johnny, I cannot bear the thought. I have never given my heart till now. Hold me—please."

"I—I dare not."

She pressed his hand to her cheek. "Why will you not have the faith in yourself that I have in you? Beyond doubting, you were bred up to the Code of Honour. Can you really convince yourself that a—a sudden passion for this Miss Phillips—"

"Good heavens! How did you know her name?"

"You remembered it just now when you were assuring me how evil you are. I didn't interrupt to tell you so, because I hoped you might recall more of the wicked jade. And I know she *was* a wicked jade, Johnny. Though I must confess 'Miss Phillips' doesn't sound very—alluring," she added thoughtfully. "And certainly not worth destroying your whole life for!"

He moved to sit beside her again, and said tenderly, "Tell me what you think happened. Was I to be put out of the way so that we could be boarded and claimed by some enterprising privateer?"

"I don't know. 'Tis not beyond the realm of possibility. You said she was a great ship."

"Six hundred and fifty tons."

Her eyes opened wide. "Good gracious! And you so very young! Why ever—" She paused. "Johnny, is it truth that a captain has to buy his command?"

"Yes. It cost me in excess of five thousand pounds. But a commander must have experience also. I was second mate on a smaller ship, and chief mate on my first voyage to India."

"But surely you had to be sponsored by someone? Might your family have had influence with the company?"

He smiled. "Even if they had, the owners have final approval of a commander. Now what is that pretty head conjuring up?"

"So many possibilities. And, alas, none we can really prove."

"Or ever will, I doubt. Because, after all the hopes and dreams, there comes again reality, my dearest girl. No—please don't touch me, or I'll never have the courage to go. And I must go. I only wish that—that I could leave you something you might . . . remember me by. Just—now and then, you know. But—" He paused, then groped in his pocket and took out a small and clumsily wrapped bundle. "It is such a—a pitiable gift, Jennifer. I am ashamed to offer it. But—it was shaped by the hands of the greatest of Artisans, and when I found it I hoped someday to dare give it to you." He held out the little bundle, and as she took it, he added shyly, "It reminded me of—you."

She unwound the wrappings with care, and at length held a small and unusually beautifully hued shell in the palm of her hand. Looking down at it through a blur of tears, she murmured, "It—reminded you . . . of me?"

" 'Tis so dainty. And—so perfect."

"I shall . . . cherish it for—for so long as—" She raised a tear-stained face and flung herself into his arms, sobbing, "Oh, Johnny! Don't go! I beg you!"

He hugged her tight just one last time, and longing to tell her how much he loved her and that he would never love anyone else, bit the words back and put her from him. "Whatever you think now, you will marry someday, and—I hope move away from here. Don't fly out at me, but the castle is too lonely, and you are denied friends of your own age. I would like to think of you going to parties often, not just once in a great while. I want to imagine you surrounded by light-hearted friends with whom to chatter and giggle and talk of fashions, and gossip as you ladies love to do. At Triad, the one lady I thought was visiting you, turned out to be your brother's light o' love."

"Or Crane's," she murmured with a sad smile.

"Do you mean Tilly? No, it was not she. The lady with the blue cloak was almost regally graceful and— Lord! What is it?"

She gripped his hand and gazing up at him with wide eyes, whispered, "You did not say she wore a—a blue cloak!"

"What difference does it make? My heavens!" Alarmed, he slipped his arm about her. "You're white as a sheet! What have I said?"

"This—this lady," she said, moistening suddenly dry lips. "Was she—tall . . . ? Taller than—than me?"

"I suppose she was, but—"

"And—did it seem to you—at the time—to be exceeding . . . cold?"

He frowned. "Why—yes. It did grow cold, but I was lost in thought, and— Oh, no! You're not saying—"

"Oh dear, oh dear!" She clung to his hand and said in a hushed voice, "Johnny, I am very much afraid that—that your lady in the blue cloak was . . . Queen Guinevere!"

It was a legend that had been handed down from antiquity, and Jennifer told him of it while they walked back to where they'd left Tilly. The beautiful queen, so the story went, had been deeply grieved by the tragedy that had resulted from her love for Sir Lancelot. In an attempt to make amends, down through the centuries she returned to Cornwall whenever danger threatened the realm.

"She walked on Lizard Point, looking eastward when William the Conqueror invaded," said Jennifer solemnly, "and was seen again at the time of the Plague. Cornwall was ravaged by the Black Death, you know. She is said to have appeared at the start of the Wars of the Roses, and on Bodmin Moor a week before the great battle. A nun walking with a group of orphans saw her gazing across Plymouth Sound just before the Spanish Armada came. And—and now *you* have seen her! I wonder what threatens this time!"

" 'Twould seem," he said thoughtfully, "that the lady does not appear unless there is a major threat, so I doubt Crazy Jack could be judged worthy of a visit."

"No, of course not. But—oh, I wish you'd not seen her!"

"I find it difficult to believe that I did. Most likely you'll discover your guess was the right one, and that your brother entertained some lovely inamorata."

"But suppose you really *did* see the queen? Suppose there really *is* danger coming? What then?"

He considered for a moment. He should, of course, calm her fears and assure her that there was no danger—that the legend was no more than a fairy tale. But there could be no doubt that something decidedly havey-cavey was going on out at the Blue Rose. And he couldn't deny there *had* been a strangeness to his encounter with the lady on the moors. Whatever else, *nothing* must endanger his beloved, and she, bless her dear heart, obviously believed he had seen the legendary Lady. The voice of conscience gibbered, 'You're grasping at straws! 'Tis but an excuse because you cannot bear to leave her! Go—fool! Go! The longer you stay, the harder will be your parting!' His jaw set. To the devil with conscience! He said firmly, "Why, then I cannot leave you. Not until I'm sure any danger is past."

Jennifer sent up a silent but very grateful prayer.

" 'Twere such a dangerous thing to do, miss," said Tilly, indignation written large on her countenance. She glanced out of the carriage windows and said with an all-embracing gesture, "All alone out here, miles from anyone who could help!"

Tired of this litany of reproach, Jennifer tried to be patient. "I am sure you were perfectly safe, and you needed to rest. I was glad you were able to sleep for a little while."

"The shock of it!" exclaimed Tilly. "To wake up and find meself abandoned. Not as I were fearful for meself, miss. 'Twas *your* safety as had me in a state. Faithful I've ever been, and ever will, and to know you were off somewhere at the mercy of—"

"Good gracious, Tilly! Do use a little sense. I wanted you to rest, but I was unwilling to sit in the shade and wait for half an hour. Since Jack wished to cool the horses, I persuaded him to escort me. I am sure he would have protected me did any monster suddenly appear."

"Ah, then, and what about hisself, that's what I want to know? Why your dear papa should have kept a reliable man like Oliver Coachman at the castle, and left us to the mercies of—of that looby, is what I cannot come at!"

"If you feel that my father's trust is misplaced," said Jennifer, irritated, "by all means take it up with him when we return."

Tilly gave a tight smile. "As if I'd ever do such a thing, when I hope I know me place. Sir Vinson's been took in," she added darkly. "Like some others."

Jennifer turned her head and stared at her. "In what way?"

Usually quick to sense the moods of her young mistress, Tilly was too preoccupied with the sense of her own ill-usage to notice the rare hauteur in Jennifer's tone. "Proper sly, he is, for a crazy man," she declared. "Mr. Crane says he wasn't too crazy to have got round Mr. Fleming, so now he don't hardly never work in the stables, where he's needed. Same thing with Cook," she went on, warming to her theme. "A stern woman she's allus been, you knows that, miss. Never been one to carry treats out to them as has worked at the castle all their lives. Not she! But along comes Crazy Jack with his slippery smiles and fancy ways, and she's giving him pieces of pie and biscuits and—and I dunno what, to take home! Crazy? Huh! Artful, I calls it. If not worse . . ."

"And exactly what do you mean by that, pray?"

Surely, now Tilly should have noted the dangerous sparkle in Jennifer's eyes, the heightened flush in her cheeks. But Tilly's natural kindliness did not extend to strangers, especially "strange" strangers, and she went on grinding her axe, oblivious of the pit that yawned before her. Lowering her voice, she declared dramatically, "Been seen with creatures of darkness he has, Miss Jennifer! A evil man with a great black beard and funny shaped eyes what glow like black coals in his head! Jack puts on to be a looby, but he's got *Powers*, mark my words! Only look how he drug Lord Green up the cliff! He ain't a brawny fella. How'd he do it, lest he had Powers? Him and the Widow Newlyn's cut from the same cloth. Likely he wove a spell round Mr. Fleming, to get outta doing his fair share of the work. He's wove another round Sir Vinson, so as to—"

"That—will—do!"

Tilly gave a gasp, her frightened eyes at last taking note of the wrath in Jennifer's face.

"You wicked, vindictive creature!" cried Jennifer. "To fabricate and repeat such tales of another human being, only because he has a faulty memory and a different way of speech! No, I do not wish to hear a spate of excuses! You have been walking out with Oliver Crane. Oh yes, I know of it! I fancy you both were prodigious put out when my father sent Jack with us, rather than Crane, so you have whipped up this ridiculous mumbo jumbo 'gainst him!"

"How—how can you talk to me so-so unkind?" wailed Tilly, beginning to cry again. "After all the—the years I looked after, and ch-cherished, and—"

"And hid this ugly side of your nature from me! A little gossip is one thing, but you must know that the accusations you have made go far beyond gossip and could cause real mischief! I am most disappointed in you."

"Oh, miss . . . Oh . . . miss!" sobbed Tilly, really terrified that she would lose her situation and might well have ruined her admired Oliver Crane into the bargain. "I didn't mean no—no harm! Not for the world would I . . . speak 'gainst no one as you think—think well of!"

"You may not have meant harm. But to say such things 'gainst anyone—*ever* is sinful. I will not tolerate rumour-mongering in anyone who works for me. Do you understand?"

Tilly nodded, and declared in broken accents and with floods of tears that she did understand, that she would ask forgiveness at evening prayers, and that so long as she lived, she would never do such a thing again.

For the rest of the journey there was no more talk in the carriage.

Inevitably, Jennifer's loving thoughts were on Jonathan.

Tilly's thoughts also dwelt upon Jonathan. But not with love.

❦ *Chapter* 9 ❧

Breton Ridge was not situated, as one might suppose, upon a prominence, but rather, below one. At this point of the coast the land rose gradually from the cliff edge to level out about half a mile inland, where it fell away abruptly, for all the world as though some giant hoe had cut it down. The mansion had been erected at the foot of this long plateau, perhaps with an eye to shutting out the Atlantic gales. It was a large and imposing three-storied residence, built of pale native stone in the Gothic style, with high roofs and thin unornamented chimneys; clusters of tall narrow small-paned windows topped by brick arches; and many interesting gables. Despite the lack of formal gardens, the grounds were relieved from monotony by the rolling terrain, and by the very large lake that sparkled at the foot of the slope, some two hundred yards from the house.

On this hot late morning several people were in a rowing boat making its way from one of the three small islands in the lake, and others wandered about the lawns enjoying the sunshine. At the appearance of the Britewell carriage, a young lady in a great-hooped primrose muslin gown detached herself from her companions, and ran to meet the coach, holding up her skirts to reveal layers of lace-trimmed petticoats, and calling eager greetings. Unpowdered auburn ringlets bounced about her heart-shaped face. A pair of bright hazel eyes flashed to Jonathan as he pulled the team to a halt at the foot of the steps, then footmen had hurried from the house to swing open the carriage door, and Jennifer was handed down.

"I fear I am very late, dearest," she said, holding out both hands to her friend. "My humble apologies."

Miss Caroline Morris hugged her. "I thought you would never get here! I am only glad that you could come!"

Returning the embrace wholeheartedly, Jennifer was none the less aware that one of the footmen had directed Jonathan to the side entrance, and he was driving off with Tilly and the luggage. She was drawn into the cool interior of the mansion amid a rapid-fire series of questions, mostly having to do with "dear Howland" and culminating in, "Wherever did you find your new coachman? My, such a fine creature!"

"Caroline, Caroline! I wish you will learn to control your exuberance! I saw you *running*!" Lady Georgina Morris was a small, bird-like woman with the same bright eyes and pointed chin as her daughter. In a studiedly serene fashion she drifted across the gold and white hall to receive Jennifer's curtsy and present her thin cheek to be kissed. "You will think her a proper hurly-burly, my dear," she said, with just a shade of sympathy in the glance she rested upon this unfortunate young woman. "But she is sincerely glad you are come, I need not tell you."

There could be no doubt of this, because Jennifer's attempt to thank Lady Morris for her kind invitation was cut short by her impatient friend. Dimpling mischievously at her indignant but doting parent, Caroline whisked Jennifer across the hall and up the winding staircase.

"You are in the family wing," she announced, her panniers swinging as she danced around a corner. "I persuaded Mrs. Drebbins to give you my sister Lucille's bedchamber. She won't be coming to the party, for she is in—" She paused, her eyes on the footman who followed, carrying Jennifer's dressing case and hat boxes. "Increasing," she whispered, then revealed that confidence by saying merrily, "So I shall be an aunt once more! Isn't that jolly?"

The amused footman hurried past to swing open the door

to a charming and very feminine bedchamber at the south side of the house.

When the man had taken himself off, the two girls embraced again, and Caroline said, "Now let me look at you." She drew back, scanning her friend critically. "I vow you are lovelier than ever! And yet you look . . . different, somehow." Her gaze sharpened. "Why do you blush? I declare, if I didn't know better, I'd think—"

Interrupted as the door opened again, she said, "Oh, hello, Tilly. I was just telling your mistress she is prettier each time I see her. I vow she fairly glows today! Do you not . . . er . . ."

Her words trailed off as Tilly bobbed a curtsy and applied a sodden handkerchief to her red nose. "Oh—my," said Caroline uneasily. "Were you overcome by the heat again, poor creature?"

"I w-was, Miss," gulped Tilly. "By that and . . . other things . . ."

Caroline met Jennifer's meaningful glance and said, "Well, you will be wanting us out of your way while you unpack, I am sure." Turning, she made a wry face and took Jennifer to her own apartments. "Whatever is amiss?" she demanded, when they were seated in her spacious pink and white private parlour. "What did she mean—'other things'?"

Jennifer decided to try and forestall possible complications. "Oh, you know how Tilly loves to enlarge upon gossip. She has taken my coachman in dislike."

"She is mad," declared Caroline unequivocally.

Jennifer laughed. "The thing is, he was injured some time ago, as a result of which his memory is impaired. People tend to mock him. Tilly said some very cruel things and I had to scold her."

Despite her carefree manner, Caroline had a shrewd streak. She pursed her lips and advised, "She will hate him forever. You'd as well turn her off, dearest. Better yet, turn them both off. It might be wise, you know, if he is wits to let."

"He is not!" Caroline's eyes opened wide, and regretting

her vehemence Jennifer added hurriedly, "He most gallantly saved the life of one of my father's guests. I can scarce reward him with dismissal."

"Especially since he is prodigious good to look at, eh?"

Jennifer met those roguish eyes, hesitated, then said with a smile, "Caro, if you are not a sad romp! Here I have but now stepped across your threshold after a hot and tiresome journey, and instead of allowing me to wash and—"

"Well, I would have." Caroline ran into her adjoining bedchamber and returned with a wet face cloth and a towel. "Only Tilly seemed so in the boughs I thought it best to leave her alone for a moment. One has to humour them, you know." She sat beside Jennifer on the small sofa and watched her dab the cold cloth at her face. "Now I want to know all about you and your family. It has been so long since last I saw you, and I've a strong suspicion that lots of deliciousnesses have happened, and—"

"How can you harbour such notions?" Jennifer set aside the towels and tidied her hair. "My life is dull compared with your own, and you are the one with stories to tell. Are you pleased with your Kentish cousin?"

Caroline nodded, setting her ringlets bobbing. "Yes indeed. He is young—much younger than I had supposed. And so droll, and quite nice looking besides. *But*"—her eyes sparkled with mischief—"he has brought a friend with him. Oh la, la! Wait till you see *him*! So handsome 'tis criminal! But very haughty, for all he's a half-caste of some kind. And a tongue? Faith, 'tis an asp! I wonder my poor cousin can endure him."

"He does not sound very pleasant," said Jennifer cautiously. "Do you like him, Caro?"

"If you mean am I going to fall into a decline when he leaves? No. But he is wickedly exciting to flirt with—or try to. He can administer a crushing set-down, but all the ladies are in alt just to watch him."

"And—the gentlemen?"

"Oh, they despise him, of course. But very quietly, for he is said to be deadly dangerous and has killed dozens and dozens of good men in duels."

Jennifer laughed at this, and Caroline acknowledged gaily that she may have exaggerated "just a trifle," but swept on, "Papa does not like him at all, and was vexed with James, my cousin, for having brought him. I heard Papa say"—she drew herself up, imitating her father's high-pitched voice and solemn manner—"he is not the thing, you know. And not received anywhere that *is* anywhere."

Amused, Jennifer said that it was as well Caroline's heart was already given. "Dare I ask—is Lord Kenneth to make an interesting announcement during this party?"

Caroline stared at her. "About me, do you mean?"

"Why, yes. You writ that you were hopelessly in love with Edmund Sturtevant, and I think 'twill be a wonderful match, for he is such . . . a nice . . . Oh, Lud! Have I spoke out of turn? I made sure he meant to offer."

"Well, he did, of course, but—Dearest Jennifer, what a ninny you are! As if I would *marry* him! Mama and I have settled that I will accept Pettigrew."

"*Sherwin Pettigrew?* But—but, Caro—I never *dreamed*—I didn't even think you liked him! And—forgive, but he is so . . . foolish!"

"Oh, yes. I shall likely end up strangling him! But much as I adore my Edmund, his family is *nouveau riche* at best, and his mama—for all she is sweetly natured—is sometimes rather gauche, whereas Sherwin's lineage is impeccable, and his parents are the most starched-up and proud creatures. Poor Edmund is quite heartbroken, which is prodigious affecting. Still, it does not do, Mama says, to marry beneath one. Now why do you look at me like that? One has to choose sensibly, after all. I suppose 'tis different with you, poor thing, but if you *could* choose, dearest, whom would you pick?"

'One has to choose sensibly, after all . . . ' Jennifer smiled faintly. "I should choose the man I would love above all others, and whom I could honour and respect, even though all the world rejected him."

"It sounds very romantical," said Caroline dubiously. "But he would have to be of good prospects, for it would be dreadful if you were poor and had to live among the unwashed." Her nose wrinkled. "Commoners so often . . . smell!"

Her friend surprised her by uttering a merry peal of laughter.

"What is it?" asked Caroline. "Have I said something clever?"

"I was only thinking that you are acquainted, I believe, with Hibbard Green . . ."

"Who will be here again this week-end!" Caroline giggled. "How outrageous in you to make such a remark! A dreadfully vulgar creature, is he not? But he is, after all, above criticism."

"Good gracious! Why?"

"Because he is one of *us*, you ninny! And is besides, excessive wealthy. And you are staring at me again. Are you fancying me to be an avaricious female? I promise you I do not covet the fortune of *that* one!"

Troubled, Jennifer said, "You used not to think that rank and wealth were the only qualities to be valued in a gentleman."

"No more I do. My poor Edmund has all the valued qualities, but there comes a time to discard childish dreams. I have grown up, do you see?" With sudden gravity, Caroline leaned to press her friend's hand and say, "You must do so also, dearest. My parents are concerned lest you forget your place and permit too much familiarity from commoners."

Jennifer asked in a rather faint voice, "In what . . . connection?"

"Why, your school, of course. 'Tis very well in you to visit the sick among your people, and set them an example. But to be instructing their children can only be lowering for you. Besides, to be able to read and write is of no use to simple folk, and Papa fears may inspire them to revolutionary tendencies. I told him that you, being of so kind and generous a nature, had likely not considered such things. Admit I am right, dear."

Reprieved by the mellow resonance of a gong, Jennifer exclaimed, "Oh! There is the luncheon call. And we have chattered so much I've not yet changed my gown! I *must* do so before I meet your papa! I shall have to fly!"

Fly she did. With her garrulous friend chattering along behind her.

The head groom at Breton Ridge was a plump and supercilious man of late middle age. Impressed with his own consequence, and irked to be required to find space for the team from Castle Triad when his stables were already crowded with the hacks of guests, he did little more than tell Jonathan where to put the coach and horses, and stamp off grumbling about the stupidity of sending a four-in-hand on so short a journey.

Jonathan had feared that he would face another ordeal of recognition and mockery. Relieved because he was spared that humiliation, he made no attempt to ask for the help that should have been offered, but set about the business of unharnessing the team, rubbing them down, and turning them out into the large paddock. He was in the midst of this endeavour and lost in dreams of his beloved, when an indignant protest was raised. He glanced around. The barn was a busy place, and none of the grooms and stableboys appeared to have heard that small voice. He went to where the coach stood, poles up, in a corner, and removed the cover from Duster's cage. The occupant tilted its head and gobbled at him throatily.

"Yes, I know, and I apologise," he murmured. "But I wish you will not start speaking now. We must not attract attention to ourselves, Duster."

"Wotcher got there, my cove?" A large, squarely built man, resplendent in the garb of a superior personal servant, but with features more likely to be associated with a pugilist, stood watching him.

" 'Tis just a small bird, sir," answered Jonathan uneasily. "It will cause no trouble, I promise you."

The bushy brows went up, and the shrewd brown eyes narrowed. "And 'oo might you be?" he demanded, stepping closer. "Your gab ain't like no coachman's gab wot I ever met. Wot's yer monicker?"

Jonathan hesitated. "They call me Jack, Mr. . . ."

"They call me Tummet, on account of me name's Tummet. Enoch Tummet. Wot they call you when you ain't being a coachman, eh?"

"I have no other name, Mr. Tummet." Jonathan went back to his horses, wondering why a valet, since that was what Tummet appeared to be, loitered about the stables. For the next half hour he worked very hard, and contrived to avoid Tummet's eyes, but he knew they were on him. When the last animal had been turned out into the paddock, he found that Mr. Tummet was standing beside the coach, ostensibly talking to Duster. Taking up the bundle of his personal effects, Jonathan thought that it had been disturbed. He glanced at the big man sharply.

Tummet picked up the cage and said, "I'll extend a whelping ramble."

Jonathan stared at him.

Tummet translated, "A 'helping famble." This bringing about no lessening of Jonathan's mystified expression, he exclaimed aggrievedly, "Cor! Don't none of you talk the King's English?" He waved one muscular fist in the air.

"Oh," said Jonathan, smiling as the light dawned. "A helping hand. Thank you, but I'll leave him here for a while. Rhyming slang, is it?"

" 'Sright, sir," said Tummet, and waited, but his new acquaintance betrayed no surprise at a form of address that would have astonished most coachmen. His eyes very round, he volunteered, "Quarters fer outside servants is this way."

The two men walked out together, each wondering why the other was pretending to be something he so obviously was not.

Lord Kenneth had the fair complexion and reddish hair that appeared very frequently among those born into the house of Morris. Not above average height, he was fastidious to the point of being dandified in the matter of dress, which combined with his somewhat condescending manner to conceal two obsessions. One of these had to do with his health. Although he had never suffered a major illness, ate sparingly, and was as slim at sixty as he had been at thirty, he had a deep-rooted fear of disease. He was a source of great satisfaction to the physician who enjoyed his patronage, of whom it was said that he was summoned to Breton Ridge for everything from a hangnail to a hiccup. Despite this idiosyncrasy, Lord Kenneth was devoted to his family and kind to his servants, and was generally well liked though there were those who judged that he held himself "too much up." Sir Vinson Britewell shared this opinion, and Jennifer could not dispute her father's view that his lordship considered the Britewells to be somewhat inferior to the Morrises.

There was no height in his manner, however, when he welcomed her in the charming red and white saloon where the guests had gathered preparatory to going in to luncheon. He bowed over her hand, teased her with apparent fondness because she was late, and was pleased to hear that Sir Vinson and Howland would arrive shortly. She knew most of those present, but he proceeded to introduce her to those guests with whom she was not acquainted.

Lieutenant James Morris, the guest of honour, had just sold out of the military, and wore civilian dress. He was about her own age, with a shy but engaging grin and a cherubic freckled countenance. His relationship to his host was clear to see, for he had the same fair complexion, and a hint of light red showed here and there in his rather carelessly powdered hair. He put her in mind of a friendly puppy, and she liked him at once.

Lord Kenneth's tone changed subtly as he presented the lieutenant's friend, Mr. August Falcon. Jennifer turned to meet a tall man, perhaps a year or two older than James Morris. Blessed with a splendid physique, he carried himself with proud, almost defiant, arrogance. His jet black hair was worn unpowdered and tied back. His flaring brows were heavy, and his complexion had a sallow cast, but his features were so fine that she could appreciate Caroline's admiration—until she saw the bored cynicism in the eyes that were of a deep midnight blue. Those beautiful eyes had a suggestion of the Orient in their shape. Tilly's malicious words seemed to thunder in her ears: 'Been seen with creatures of darkness he has, Miss. A evil man with a great black beard and funny shaped eyes what glow like black coals in his head.'

Jennifer's smile did not waver, but she was barely able to conceal her excitement. Mr. Falcon wore no beard, but his hair was very black. His eyes could certainly be described as having an unusual shape, and the blue was so dark that it would be easy to mistake them for black. Surely 'twas unlikely that there could be two men in the neighbourhood with such eyes and such colouring? But why on earth would a wealthy gentleman like Falcon have gone about bearded and in rags?

When she learned that he was to be her partner at luncheon, it seemed a heaven-sent opportunity to learn more of him. To that end, she went out of her way to be pleasant and attentive; agreed with his remarks, which were often outrageous; looked suitably awed by his withering appraisal of the House of Lords; and generally pandered to his vanity. In return, he was cold and faintly contemptuous. Irritated, she took up her goblet too quickly and the water splashed. She glanced at Falcon. His eyes were fixed upon her with an expression of knowing amusement. She thought, 'The wretch! He thinks I am enamoured of him! What *preposterous* conceit!' Overcoming her indignation she persisted with her efforts, and whatever his faults Mr. Falcon was not entirely lacking in the social graces, and made an effort to answer her artless questions.

She learned that his father was "a rascally fellow" whom he was constantly obliged to extricate from this or that tricky situation. His sly wink apprised her of the nature of the "tricky situations." Shocked that a gentleman would speak so of his parent, she asked hurriedly if he had no brothers or sisters.

He said, "Oh, I have a sister, ma'am." His eyes flickered to Lieutenant Morris, seated opposite, and he added deliberately, "Whom I have to guard 'gainst the attentions of every gazetted fortune hunter in Town."

The lieutenant leaned forward to say with a smile, "He numbers me among 'em, ma'am. Miss Katrina Falcon is a diamond of the first water, and 'tis my dearest ambition to make her my wife."

"What a pity it is, that the dearest ambitions of so many men are never realised." Falcon spoke in what appeared to be his customary bored drawl, but Jennifer saw a steely flash in his eyes, and Lieutenant Morris's smile was rather fixed. Theirs, she decided, was an exceedingly odd friendship.

She was bound by good manners to share her attention with the stout gentleman on her left. An extremely wealthy Irish peer, he was a lifelong bosom bow of Lord Kenneth, and the type who judged the opinions of females to be valueless. His remarks were delivered as statements of fact, rather than as topics for discussion. He offered her a chance to comment at last, by saying in his harsh accents that he was familiar with the legend surrounding the Britewells and asking with a smirk if she really believed herself descended from Queen Guinevere. Clearly, he did not, and she replied lightly that the legends were so lost in antiquity that it was difficult to say where fact ended and fable began.

Falcon had been chatting with Mrs. Dunbar, a flirtatious matron with a splendid bosom, but he evidently possessed excellent hearing. Turning to Jennifer, he said, "Now what is this, pray? Am I in the company of royalty?" He inspected her through his quizzing glass, and drawled with a slight curl of the lip, "Faith, but you must be a *rara avis*, Miss Britewell. Most ladies having the very faintest claim to a royal ancestor fairly trumpet their lineage."

She found herself wishing she had a trumpet so that she might bend it over his supercilious head, but she said with a smile, "Had I any proof, sir, I likely would be as gauche. Alas, the truth is that you are probably far more acquaint with royals than am I. You spend most of your time in the Metropolis, mingling with the mighty, no?"

He fixed her with a cold stare. "Alas for your expectations. I have better things to do with my time than spend it in so foolish a way. I am as often in the country as in Town."

"Ah, but you do not spend much of your time in Sussex, dear Mr. Falcon," trilled Mrs. Dunbar, giving his wrist a playful rap with her fan. "We *all* know you do not care for the country, even though Ashleigh is such a *beautiful* estate."

He said baldly, "You surprise me, ma'am. I'd not thought you had deigned to visit us there."

The matron's face became crimson, and she retreated in simpering disorder.

Turning back to Jennifer, he asked, "Do *you* often visit Town, Miss Britewell?"

She thought he must be the rudest man she had ever met, and said a rather terse, "No, seldom."

"And do not care for it, I see. Why?"

"I suppose because it is so very big and crowded, and I feel all at sea there."

"You would," he nodded.

She was rendered speechless. Lieutenant Morris again leaned toward her and said an amused but apologetic, "You will not believe me, Miss Britewell, but August is on his best behaviour today."

'Heaven forfend,' she thought, 'that I should see him at his worst!'

Falcon's grin was unrepentant, unexpected, and dazzling. He bent to her ear and murmured, "Morris thinks I am being rude."

"Why?" she asked, sufficiently irked to take up the gauntlet. "Because you quite obviously think me a country bumpkin? I have no doubt but that, by your lights, I am."

"Oh, yes," he acknowledged outrageously, and allowed himself to be drawn into conversation with the coy Mrs. Dunbar once more.

He scarcely spoke to Jennifer again, but when the meal ended, he drew out her chair, and offering his arm, threw her completely offstride by murmuring, "But you see, I like country bumpkins."

Jonathan had known that inevitably someone would recognise him. His unmasking occurred during the ample luncheon provided in the servants hall, and the revelation provoked first a disbelieving silence, then roars of mirth. He bore their taunts in silence for the most part, but when he did speak his accent caused another outburst of abuse. Enjoying this diversion, they demanded to see the "creature" he was said to have brought with him, and the head groom agreed that the bird should be displayed.

The small, grinning group accompanied him back to the stables and the Britewell carriage in which the cage had thus far escaped notice. They crowded around with genuine curiosity, most never having seen such a bird.

Duster made small nervous squawks and warblings as so many human faces pressed in around him.

A burly stablehand jeered, "He painted it! Let's give it a wash!" He made a grab for the cage, and when Jonathan promptly swung it aside, sent a knotted fist whizzing at his jaw. Duster, reasoned Jonathan, was a living being and had a right to be protected from this young bully. He ducked the flying fist and set down the cage. His left deflected a following punch, and his right struck home hard and true. The stablehand found himself flat on his back, and the momentarily silenced onlookers confronted a man whose eyes flashed menace, and who crouched in a manner that said he knew how to fight. Still, they were many, and he was an outsider who "gave himself airs of the gentry" while everyone knew he was touched in the head. They surged forward.

"That'll do," decreed the head groom, authoritatively. "The looby had a right. 'Sides, ten to one ain't fair odds and the master's a great one for fair play. Back to work!"

They dispersed with reluctance.

Jonathan gave his levelled opponent a hand up. The stablehand fingered his reddening jaw and muttered with grudging respect, "Looby or no, you got a right, all right, mate!"

The head groom waited till they'd gone, then said sternly, "I don't want no trouble while you're here, my cove. His lordship likes things nice and quiet like. Get yourself cleaned up, and take your cage up to the house. Miss Britewell wants to show that bird to Miss Caroline."

The afternoon heat was oppressive as Jonathan crossed the turf. Only a few guests were outside, most probably being laid down upon their beds for a peaceful nap. He proceeded to the servants entrance, and asked a formidably elegant footman for Miss Britewell. The footman gave him a brief glance, and extended one gloved hand. "Give it here."

Jonathan said, "Miss Britewell particularly asked that I bring the bird to her. She wants me to tell her friend about it."

The footman's eyes rested on him briefly. "You'll be the coachman what I have heard tell of. Well, you may put on your fancy airs among the grooms, me good man, but you need not think as to gull me! Hanson!" He waved to a hovering parlourmaid. "Take this here person to the conservatory. And see as you comes back by the servants' stairs, Coachman. You need to learn your place. Which in a great house like what this is—is low. Very low *in*deed!"

Hanson was thin, wispy, and timid, and looked not much older than fourteen. She conducted Jonathan up a narrow flight of stairs, along a corridor redolent with the smells of cooking, and through a baize door into the main part of the house. She then scurried along a wide and very different corridor, the gleaming oak floors spread with colourful rugs, and the walls hung with fine paintings. At the far end was an open glass-roofed extension which was, she advised in a nervous whisper, "The conservy-tory!" With a quick look at Duster, she hissed, "Oh, my! Fancy that!" then jerked her head to a closed glass door, and scurried away in apparent terror as Jonathan knocked and entered.

The air inside was close and damp. Plants of all shapes and sizes crowded wooden benches, overflowed on to the stone floor, or were in pots suspended from wooden beams. It was very neat and clean, and there were ample walkways through this miniature jungle, but there was no sign of Jennifer.

Jonathan called, "Miss Britewell?"

She materialised from behind a large fern, and gestured urgently. His pulse quickened as it always did when he saw her. She wore a gown of cream silk embroidered in pink, and a cream cap with pink ribands was set on her powdered curls. He hurried to her, resolutely ignoring her outstretched hands, but unable to refrain from murmuring, "How very lovely you look."

She seized his arm, and drew him deeper into the "jungle." "Thank heaven there is no one else in here!'

He detached himself from that dear but dangerous contact. "Did you really want Duster?"

"No, no. 'Twas a ruse." Searching his face, she asked wistfully, "Are you not glad to see me again?"

"I— How could any man not be glad to see you?"

She sighed. "And how well you evade, my Jonathan. I am glad to see you, and always will be. But I'll not tease you, for we could be interrupted at any second, and I've something to tell you! First, this bearded man, the one who—er, helped you when Blary smashed the cage. Did he give you any name?"

"He said his name was September."

She gave a little squeal of excitement. "Yes! I'd think that is just the sort of thing he would do! To hide his identity, yet give so blatant a clue that might betray him!"

Jonathan asked eagerly, "You've met him here?"

"If I'm right, he sat beside me at luncheon! His name is not September, but *August*! August Falcon. And—" She checked, "What is it? Do you recall the name?"

"I thought—for a moment— Never mind that. Please go on."

She told him of her encounter with Falcon. "What do you think? Why would he be here? Why did he disguise himself at first, and then come back as himself?"

Jonathan shook his head frowningly. "There's a reason somewhere. Would that I knew it. You say he cries friends with this cousin of Lord Kenneth's. What like is he?"

"A very pleasant man, some two or three years Falcon's junior, I would guess, and not at all like him. Indeed, 'tis a peculiar sort of friendship, Johnny. Were I James Morris, I—"

"James?" he interrupted sharply.

"Yes. Lieutenant James Morris. Why?"

"One of the men I encountered at the mine mistook me for his companion, and called me Jamie."

She exclaimed, "Then it must have been Falcon and the lieutenant! Only Mr. Falcon came to Cornwall first, disguised as a tramp. And whatever they are about is in some fashion connected to the Blue Rose!"

"And," he said grimly, "to Lord Hibbard Green! Where are their rooms?"

"On the third floor. But—my heavens! You never mean to go up there? No, no! I will keep watch on them for you, and—"

"You would have to watch night and day to discover what they're about. I can learn more from searching their rooms, and learn it sooner."

"Yes, and be caught! Besides, you cannot get up there without being seen."

"I'll find a way. Somehow."

She clung to his arm. "How? By deciding to climb up the outside of the building tonight? Never look so innocent! 'Tis just the kind of—" She bit her lip.

He said with a twisted smile, "The kind of crazy thing I might do? Is that what you were going to say? Sometimes, the only sensible answer is a crazy one."

"Don't you care that if you should fall, it would break my poor heart?"

Between that wistful question and the poignancy in her beloved face, he was sorely tried, and it was all he could do to declare gruffly, "Your heart will mend for—for a better man than me, Jennifer."

He tried to remove her hand, but she tightened her grip and said with fierce desperation, "There is no better man than you! And you are a much better man than you realise, my dear one! Now listen to you future wife. No, 'twill avail you nothing to flinch and try to escape me! You had as well accustom yourself to the notion. If you will persist in going up there, I've an idea of how we can manage. You must follow me to their rooms carrying the cage, and—"

"A single lady to go to a gentleman's bedchamber? Certainly not! Your reputation would be—"

"Oh, pish! If we're questioned, I shall simply explain that Mr. Falcon desires to see the little bird."

He said through his teeth, "You—will—do—no—such—thing!"

She sighed blissfully. "Do you see? Already you are ordering me about as though I belonged to you . . ."

❧ *Chapter* 10 ❧

There was no response to his knock. Jonathan eased the door open and slipped into a luxurious and fortunately unoccupied bedchamber.

With some revisions, Jennifer's scheme had worked perfectly. She'd told him the exact locations of the rooms assigned to Falcon and Morris and had reluctantly agreed to wait for him in the conservatory. At this hour on a hot afternoon the halls were deserted, and much to his relief, he'd not once been challenged.

He set Duster's cage on a small table and made a quick scan of the room. It was large, and furnished throughout in red and gold. The curtains drifted lazily in the warm breeze from the open windows, and sunlight slanted across the pegged oak floor to illumine a vase of roses on an elegant mahogany secretary. Red velvet hangings were tied back on the canopied bed. A book lay open on the adjacent table. Toilet articles were neatly arranged on the dressing table. He went first to the desk, but found only the Standish, some sheets of writing paper, a well-trimmed pen, and a wax jack. He decided on luggage next, and dragged two valises from under the bed. Both were empty. Replacing them, he started to the chest of drawers, then sprang behind the door, breath held in check, as he heard footsteps in the hall.

A woman's voice trilled, " . . . very strangest people.

Londoners, you know. What can one expect . . . ?" A man laughed softly, and the voices faded.

He could breathe again, and hurried back to his search.

The book beside the bed was entitled *Mysterious China*. A folded paper used to mark the reader's place was a note directed simply to "August," written in a firm feminine hand, and signed with a flourishing "G." It read: "You will find an interesting history of the Kung family herein. Not that I expect you to own 'tis of interest." Jonathan replaced it quickly and moved on.

The drawers in the pair of exquisite inlaid chests that he was very sure had been imported from India, yielded only the evidence of a fine valet, but in the third drawer of a matching tallboy he found a powerful spyglass, and a list that intrigued him.

> *Squire—?*
> *Collington*
> ~~*Derrydene*~~
> ~~*Norberly*~~
> *Bracksby*
> *Buttershaw*
> *Underhill—?*
> ~~*Trethaway*~~
> *Green—?*
> *?*
> *?*
> *?*

The last name caused him to whisper a shocked, "Jupiter!"

On the back of the sheet was a neat sketch that so astounded him that he failed to note the sudden inward billow of the window curtains.

An instant later, he sensed that someone was behind him. His reaction was instinctive and very fast, but even as he started to whip around something sharp bit into the back of his neck, and a deep voice drawled, "Do not."

He stood perfectly still.

A face appeared in the small oval mirror atop the highboy; a very dark and extremely handsome face with a pair of cold eyes whose shape confirmed their owner's identity.

"Mr. September," said Jonathan mockingly. "Do I mistake the month, or are you in the wrong room, sir?"

August Falcon said softly, "The point of my sword is at your back. Put that down, and turn around. Carefully."

Jonathan replaced the sketch in the open drawer. The spyglass looked solid and he snatched for it. The sword bit deeper, and his hand checked.

"I could spit you where you stand," purred Falcon. "And no one would question my word that you tried to rob me."

The door was flung open.

"What the devil—?" began a surprised male voice.

Without an instant's hesitation, Jonathan threw himself to the side. The swordpoint scratched him, but the spyglass was in his hand, and he flailed it hard at the sword sending it spinning across the room.

"You—unmitigated *clod*!" howled Falcon, turning on the newcomer in a fury, and ignoring Jonathan who had leapt to snatch up the fine Colichemarde.

"Well, well," said this pleasant-faced young man, looking with interest from one to the other. "Called me up here to watch you butcher a groom, did you, Lord Haughty-Snort?"

This would be Lieutenant James Morris, thought Jonathan. The "Jamie" of the two he had encountered during his flight from the mine. "Close the door," he said curtly.

Morris directed a curious look at him, then obeyed.

Falcon said, "We are graced by a visit from the fellow who goes about pretending to be a looby."

"What, the one they call the shadow of a man? You're slipping, poor fellow, to let a shadow disarm you." Morris glanced at Duster's cage. "What the deuce is that? Trying to turn some cat up sweet? I doubt you'll—"

Jonathan interrupted, "I want to know why you slink about in disguise, Falcon. And what the pair of you were doing at the Blue Rose Mine."

Morris regarded Jonathan curiously. "I say! Are you the fella—"

Falcon's hand blurred to his pocket and emerged with a pistol held steady as a rock.

"You'd not dare fire that thing in here," said Jonathan scornfully.

"I really think you should not place too much reliance on that," said Morris. "Logical enough, I grant you. But August ain't. Logical, I mean. Devilish reckless, in fact. His motto is 'a duel a day keeps the doctor away.' Not that this is a duel exact—"

Falcon's eyes glinted. "Have done, confound you! When this is all over, I'll give you a duel!" He turned to Jonathan. "You may take your choice. Tell me your real name, and why you were searching my room, or I'll hand you over to the authorities. I fancy they'll be glad to bring you to book!"

Morris saw Jonathan whiten. "That hit went home fairly!" he exclaimed. "D'you know him, August?"

"I know he is not what he pretends to be. Is obvious he was born a gentleman, and no gentleman would live as I gather he has done, unless there was some compelling reason. Ergo: he has something to hide. And it must be a something so shameful as to have put him beyond the pale. I fancy he has been disowned, to say the least of it."

Jonathan's eyes fell and he was silent.

Vastly intrigued, Morris said, "D'you know, I've the feeling we've met somewhere."

"Oddly enough, I've the same impression. I've an excellent memory, but be damned if I can call to mind what I know of him. Well, Mr. Coachman? Make up your mind. Do you lurk about to hide your guilty self, or is there more to it?"

Jonathan put the sword aside and pressed his handkerchief to the cut on his back. "My name is Jonathan. My family name I cannot recall. You are perfectly right, Mr. Falcon. I am disgraced and—and dishonoured. I was destitute when I arrived at Roselley, and with no other reason for being there than an attempt to survive. But now, I think something damnably havey-cavey is going on out at the mine. Miss— The Britewells have been kind to me. I'll not stand by and see them hurt."

Falcon and Morris exchanged a sober glance. Falcon walked over to close the window, then pocketed the pistol and propped his shoulders against the mantel.

"Don't know that you should've put up your pistol, August," said Morris, crossing to peer into the birdcage once more. "Our remarkable coachman has brought a most odd creature with him. Could be what they call a 'familiar,' y'know."

The notion of poor Duster being the daemoniac companion to a witch drew a shout of laughter from Jonathan.

Always ready to be amused, Morris grinned at him, and asked, "What is it?"

" 'Tis called a parakeet. A sailor brought it back from India."

Falcon said dryly, "How fortunate that it survived the journey. 'Tis become curst chancy to sail the high seas these days."

The smile died from Jonathan's eyes. Watching him, Falcon asked, "What makes you think something is amiss at the mine?"

"I'll tell you nothing more till I know what your game is," said Jonathan. "Turn me in to the authorities by all means. I'll let them handle the matter."

Morris grunted derisively. "Much good it may do you! They won't believe *us*! Small heed they'd pay to a man said to be all about in his head!"

"Keep your voice down," snapped Falcon.

Stung, Morris said, "I fancy I am safe from traitors in my kinsman's house."

"Traitors!" exclaimed Jonathan. "My God! Is that it, then?"

Falcon said, "What the deuce did you think it was?"

"Why, I—I fancied free-traders, perhaps. Though it seemed unlikely that a man like Hibbard Green would find rum running worth his while."

"You think Green is involved?" asked Morris eagerly.

Jonathan looked at each of them, and took the chance.

He retrieved the sketch from the drawer, and held it out. "Would the fact that he owns this have any—"

His words were cut off as Morris gave a whoop and tossed his tricorne into the air.

Less demonstrative, Falcon's deep eyes none the less blazed with excitement. He stood straight. "By God, but it would! Does he? How d'you know?"

"He does! I know because he—er, dropped it, and—"

Falcon's lip curled. "Never. You shall have to do better than that, friend."

"Well, he had—fallen." Jonathan saw suspicion returning, and said reluctantly, "Oh, very well. The clumsy fellow tripped over the cliff, and I was obliged to hoist him up again."

"So it was you!" Morris shook his head chidingly. "Showed a sad lack of discrimination there, m'boy."

"And that is how he came to drop the icon?" asked Falcon.

Jonathan nodded. "I picked it up. He was—not pleased."

"Rumour has it that the hound turned his whip on the man who saved his dirty hide!" Morris said. "Now I see why!"

"He evidently thought I meant to steal the stupid object."

"Stuff!" said Morris. "He knew you'd *seen* it! You're damned lucky he thinks you're short of a sheet, else you'd likely be dead by now!"

"One can but hope you levelled the bastard," murmured Falcon ironically.

Jonathan flushed scarlet. "He is—is a peer of the realm, and I—"

"You are a gentleman," said Morris indignantly.

"Or—were," qualified Falcon.

"Pay him no heed," said Morris. "He 'flutters in many directions and flies in none.' "

Falcon closed his eyes and swore blisteringly. "Why, oh *why*, must I be forever saddled with you and your putrid homilies?"

"Because you needed an observation point," said Morris,

grinning. "And I am the only one among us with connections in Cornwall."

Sighing, Falcon sat on the bed. "Tell us about Green's figure."

"He's very tall, shockingly obese, and foul-mouthed," said Morris, looking angelically innocent. "I'd have thought even you would've noticed—"

Falcon hurled a pillow at him, and Morris staggered and sat on the floor laughing.

"The icon, Mr. Jonathan," snarled Falcon. "The jewelled figurine you were so ill-advised as to take up."

Hugging the pillow to him, Morris said, "You may be seated, Jack. Lord Haughty-Snort allows us peasants some privileges."

Jonathan smiled and sat on the bench at the foot of the bed. "It was a small piece, much like your sketch, and fashioned from a clear rock—quartz I'd guess. The face was as shown, and two fine opals formed the eyes. If 'tis as old as it looks, I'd guess it to be of considerable value. Has it some significance in all this?"

Falcon evaded, "Tell us how you came to suspect something was afoot at the castle."

"Not at the castle," corrected Jonathan swiftly. "At the Blue Rose Mine. There were several things, though I didn't connect them at first. I saw a great many footprints in the sand very early one morning. The tide was out, and the prints came from the sea and went northward across the beach. I could learn nothing of a large party at the castle, or of guests having arrived overnight. Later, I overheard Lord Green having a most odd conversation with a Frenchman on the high moor, near the mine. The Frenchman was roasting Green because an unwanted visitor was coming. He said the Squire would be vexed, and would blame Green for having allowed himself to be followed."

Morris drove a fist into his palm. "Hi!" he exclaimed. "There can be no more doubt, then! Ross was right as usual. Green's a member of the League and he found out I was coming here!"

Intrigued, Jonathan echoed, "League?"

"Go on, if you please," said Falcon. "We'll explain when you've done, I promise. What else?"

Jonathan frowned, but added, "It seemed odd that a man like Green would want to reopen and restore the mine. He's a disgusting creature, but he's no fool, and to be willing to pour all that lettuce into building docks and—"

Morris sat up straight.

Falcon leaned forward, and interrupted harshly, "*Docks?* Devil you say! Where? Why?"

"On the beach, below the castle. So that ships can unload supplies for the mine renovations. Sir Vinson Britewell will have no part of it, but Green keeps at him."

"I'll wager he does," muttered Falcon grimly.

"They kept it damnably close," said Morris. "We've heard not a whisper of docks."

"It's not generally known," said Jonathan. "I've been doing some work for one of his sons, and he told me of it. I only hope that if something comes of it all, that unlovely lot in the mine are not to be employed rather than local people."

"You may be *à l'aise*," grunted Falcon.

Morris nodded soberly. "They've not been brought in for that kind of labour!"

Jonathan said firmly, "Gentlemen, I've done as you asked. Now I want to know what is going forward."

Morris said, " 'Tis a desperate business, Jack, and not for a man who is, er—"

"You mean not for the village idiot. I think I am not that, sir. I—was ill, and—"

"That's one word for it," interposed Falcon with brutal candour. "When first we met you told me you could not remember much of your past. In other words, your mind plays you tricks."

"Well, yes, but—"

"Furthermore, when you were attacked by a slimy toad of a fellow, you hadn't the gumption to defend yourself."

"I—I do not see what that has—"

"We risk our lives in this game," said Falcon. "And

sometimes our lives depend on those who play on our side. We've no use for either half-wits, or poltroons."

Jonathan's fists clenched and he said in a voice that shook with anger, "Damn you, I'm not a poltroon!"

"S'right, Guv." Enoch Tummet came into the room and closed the door. "This 'ere Johnny Coachman can fight. 'E levelled a groom neat and proper, when the cove made a grab fer that there unnatural bird."

Jonathan was mildly surprised when neither man objected to a valet entering their conversation. Tummet grinned at him as though he'd read his thoughts, and began to lay out Falcon's evening clothes.

"And to haul Hibbard Green up the cliff," said Morris, "must've been a touch chancy. Sooner hoist an elephant, m'self. If there were any about, that is. Rather scarce in England. Pity. Elephants are—"

Falcon looked at Jonathan speculatively, and over-rode, "Yet when you are attacked yourself . . ." His eyes narrowed. He snapped his fingers, and said, "Jove, but I have it! You said you were disgraced. Have you by chance taken a vow of non-violence, or some such thing?"

"Burn me, but that's it!" exclaimed Morris, regarding Jonathan in awe. "What a devilish fix! You must really have wallowed in the mire!"

Jonathan flushed. "Which is not to say I am of no use. I'm—I'm allowed to act in protection of others, you see."

"And 'e's knowed at the castle, Guv," put in Tummet, selecting a pair of lilac silk stockings from a drawer. "Might be useful. 'Specially if they all take 'im fer a looney."

Falcon glanced at Morris, who said, "I'm for it. Risky, though. If they rumble him, I mean. You'll have to let him know what he's up against, dear boy. Only fair."

Jonathan said, "I can hazard a guess. The Stuarts again?"

Falcon scowled, hesitating. "That's possible. But if Bonnie Prince Charlie is up to mischief, he's using very different tactics this time."

"Well, he'd have to," said Morris reasonably. "Made

mice feet of it last time. 'If at first you don't succeed, try—' "

"So far as we can judge," resumed Falcon, cutting off the maxim with grim determination, "a group of six gentlemen have formed a secret society that has created a most damnable lot of mischief. We mean to stop them. You'd as well know there's only a handful of us, and Lord only knows how many of them. We call them the League of Jewelled Men, because they each carry a small jewelled token, or figurine, similar to the one Hibbard Green dropped."

"Why?" asked Jonathan. "Surely, if they were caught with such a figure, 'twould be an instant indictment."

Morris said solemnly, " 'You can't catch water with a fork.' "

"Oh, *Zounds!*" howled Falcon.

Tummet interposed soothingly, "Now, now, Guv. Fur down, fur down!" Falcon's rageful glare shot to him, and he went on hurriedly, "What the lieutenant means, Mr. Jack, is that the folk what oughta be catching the varmints—ain't."

"And they carry the figurines," put in Morris, "because they don't know who they are."

Falcon said sourly, "And any man who can make sense of that bumblebroth, is most *certainly* not a dimwit!"

Jonathan asked frowningly, "Do you say that this—er society, is so secret the members don't know each others' identities?"

Morris shrugged. "Can't blame 'em for being careful. It very likely is treason, do you see? Apt to turn a man's head. Right off."

"Is this—Squire fellow the leader? Do you know what they plan?"

Falcon said, "Yes, to the first question. We have learned that much. Would that we knew *who* he is. As to what they plan—at the moment they concoct fiendishly devious schemes to dishonour and ruin public figures, and then acquire their estates. They choose aristocrats of power and prestige, and they stop at nothing to achieve their ends. Forgery, robbery, blackmail, even murder. They've been responsible for several tragedies we know of, and heaven knows how many we don't. Apparently, they're selective in the properties they want."

"Always estates?" asked Jonathan. "Country homes?"

"Almost always," said Morris. "And, thus far at least, all located in the southland."

"Around London?"

Falcon said, "Not necessarily. They damn near got their hands on Lac Brillant, near Dover, and Glendenning Abbey, which is outside Windsor."

"But—surely both those properties are entailed and cannot be sold."

"Exactly so. Luckily, we were able to put a spoke in their wheel on those occasions, but the intent was most certainly to send both families to the block for high treason."

"Which would break the entails, you see," said Morris. "For the estates would then be seized by the Crown and sold at auction, and the League could buy 'em."

"Good God!" said Jonathan, appalled. "It scarce seems possible that anyone would destroy an entire family only so as to purchase an estate!"

Morris said, "Only way they could snabble it, if it's entailed. Besides which, if high-ranking aristocrats keep getting themselves packed off to Newgate or the Tower, public confidence in the government starts to totter."

Jonathan whistled softly. "So *that's* what you think they're up to! Undermining the status quo so as to sway the public in favour of the Jacobites!"

" 'Twould be one explanation." Falcon pursed his lips. "But it might be a little flurry inspired by Pitt, who is so eager for more war 'gainst France."

"Or some scheme of Prince Frederick's," said Morris. "He'd purely delight to overthrow his father."

Jonathan pointed out, "But both Pitt and Prince Frederick are themselves aristocrats."

"As are the members of the League of Jewelled Men," agreed Falcon.

Trying to comprehend it all, Jonathan asked, "How are you able to act against so secret a group?"

"You saw the list of those we know about, or suspect," said Falcon. "The names crossed out are former members—now dead. The Squire don't condone failure. As for the rest, we keep watch on them, and try to circumvent their ploys wherever we can."

Morris put in brightly, "Been lucky here and there. I think they don't love us."

"Then they know who you are?" Jonathan exclaimed. "Jove! I wonder they haven't had you all killed!"

"I think they dare not—at least not too obviously," said Falcon. "Gideon Rossiter, he's our leader, has lodged some accusations at Whitehall. We've been laughed at, but a number of people know of our beliefs. If we were to be murdered, the authorities might really start to see the light."

"Trouble is," Morris observed with a sigh, " 'to a mole there's no such thing as a rainbow.' "

Falcon moaned at the ceiling, and said bitterly, "If you decide to join us, John Coachman, you shall have to endure his rubbishing homilies."

"What Lord Haughty-Snort didn't tell you," said Morris, suddenly very serious, "is that they *have* tried for us. Been a close-run thing now and then."

"So there you have it," said Falcon. "Are you with us?"

Jonathan said eagerly, "If you'll have me, you may believe I am!"

Wandering among the rather stifling greenery, Jennifer tried not to allow imagination to get the best of her. Jonathan should have been able to search the rooms of Mr. Falcon and Lieutenant Morris by this time. In fact, he should have been able to search every room on the third floor! It was silly to be so apprehensive. If he'd been caught there would have been an uproar, and she'd heard nothing untoward. Oh dear, oh dear, how dreadful was this waiting! If only—

The door opened. With a gasp of relief she hurried around the end of the narrow pathway.

Looking cool and pretty in a lime green brocade gown

with a train of sweeping Watteau pleats, Caroline Morris exclaimed, "So here you are! I have been searching forever! One of the footmen said you had something to show me." She peered about curiously, "Is it in here?"

Jennifer faltered, "Er—no. That is—I had told my coachman to bring his pet so I might show it to you, but I think someone must have commandeered him." She saw the puzzlement in her friend's eyes and added, "I have wanted to see the conservatory, so I—" From the corner of her eye she saw the door swing open once again, and said a relieved, "Ah, here he is! Whatever became of you, Coachman?"

Jonathan answered respectfully, "Mr. Falcon was admiring Duster, ma'am. My apologies an I kept you waiting."

"Fetch it here," said Caroline. "Oh, what a funny little creature. I never saw the like. Is it true they can talk?" She bent to peer in the cage. "Pre-tty bir-die. Say 'pre-tty bir—' " She uttered a small scream as Duster, leaning to look up at her, lost his balance and toppled from his perch. "It is *deformed*!" she wailed. "Ugh, how horrid!"

Jennifer apologised, and said, "Coachman, take it away. And do not forget that I wish to ride in the morning and shall require your escort. Pray have the horses ready by seven o'clock."

He bowed and drew back as they swept past. Caroline held a dainty kerchief to shield her eyes from the terrible sight of Duster, allowing Jennifer to meet Jonathan's gaze with one of anxious questioning. He smiled and winked reassuringly.

Lady Morris came towards them, already dressed for dinner in a charming rose satin gown with very wide panniers. Looking past the two girls, she said, "Is that not your coachman, Jennifer? Why is he inside the house? Oh—is this the bird I've heard of? You may fetch it here, Coachman."

"No, no, Mama," said Caroline, shuddering. "It has a twisted foot. Perfectly horrid!"

"What a ninny you are, child! Of course 'tis spoilt. How else should a servant afford to buy such a rare creature?"

Her ladyship stooped to view Duster. "Why does it rush about so? Can it talk, Coachman?"

Jonathan said quietly, "I've not been able to coax a word out of it, my lady."

Surprised by his cultured accent, she straightened and fixed him with a keen stare. "Your voice is likely too deep for it to hear. Hold the cage higher." He did as she asked, and she called in a high-pitched cooing tone, "Hel-lo, bird. Say 'hel-lo . . . Hel-lo . . .'" Caroline, standing at a safe distance, began to giggle. My lady dismissed her, advised Jonathan that he had a stupid pet, and sent him off. "A word with you, Jennifer," she added.

Obediently, Jennifer walked slowly beside her hostess. Maids and footmen were beginning to bustle about now, and voices could be heard as preparations went forward for the dinner ceremony.

Lady Morris asked about Sir Vinson and his sons, and expressed an interest in Lord Green's plans to reopen the Blue Rose. "Such a generous creature," she said. "It will be a great thing for the tinners, you know. I fancy you must be prodigious grateful to him."

Jennifer hesitated.

"Oh, how clumsy of me to speak of the mine! I had quite forgot that dreadful accident. Poor child." Lady Morris squeezed Jennifer's arm and added coyly, "But perchance there is a Prince Charming waiting around the bend, after all. And from all I hear, an exceeding wealthy one, eh?"

'Prince Charming?' thought Jennifer. 'That revolting baron?' She felt affronted, and said, "Not that I am aware, ma'am."

"Yet you blush, you sly minx! Well, I'll not tease you. We shall turn the subject. This coachman of yours. He is an educated man, no?"

'Eton, and Addiscombe College,' thought Jennifer proudly. But that was Johnny's business, and she said, "He speaks like one, certainly. But we know very little of him. An injury of some kind robbed him of his memory."

"Good gracious! An afflicted man with an afflicted bird.

How very odd. Surely Sir Vinson must know something of the fellow, else he'd never have allowed him to drive you."

Her eyes seemed very piercing. Jennifer wondered angrily if Tilly had been sharing confidences in the servants' hall. "All we know, ma'am, is that he is an honest worker and a fine craftsman. In fact, he built the furniture for my school." She could have bitten her tongue for having mentioned her "lowering" interest in the village children, and hurried on, "And he has besides done some translating for Fleming, which has pleased him, so—"

"*Translating?* Is he proficient in a foreign language?"

"My brother says his pronunciation is not good, but—yes, he can read Latin."

"Well, well. Fancy that . . ." Lady Morris looked thoughtful, then said as if recollecting herself, "Er, there is something odd there, my dear. Be on your guard. Faith, but I cannot think where your father has stored his wits! Lord Kenneth would *never* permit that such a misfit be employed! Of course, all great houses are not run in the same way, but . . ."

She rambled on and on.

Keeping meekly silent, Jennifer sent up a small prayer concerning tomorrow's weather.

❧ *Chapter 11* ❧

When she reached the cluster of standing stones near the edge of the cliff, Jennifer drew her rather somnolent gelding to a halt, and slid from the saddle. Jonathan rode up and looked down at her gravely.

Gathering the reins, she said, "Oh, do get down and come and talk to me! I have worried and worried. Why you must persist in keeping behind me all the way here, I do not know! Lots of grooms ride beside their ladies."

"But many would not consider me to be a groom. It were wiser for me to stay mounted. If anyone should see us—"

"Who is to see us? There is not another soul for miles, I dare swear. Johnny—please . . ."

He sighed and swung down with easy grace. Tethering the horses to a shrub, he said, "But you must not come near to me, because—" And turning, he found her breast to breast with him, her eyes tender with love.

"Because—what, my very dear?" she murmured, her hands sliding up his shoulders.

He gave a gasp and wrenched away. "You know—why."

She was beside him again at once. "Dearest, I—"

"Jennifer—do not." Stern and unbending he gazed at the far horizon. "Don't make me add to my shame."

"I am a selfish woman." She caressed his averted cheek. "I refuse to marry my only suitor, so I shall never marry. If this is—is to be my only time for happiness, Johnny, do not deny me." And when he still refused her attempt to turn his head towards her, she said wistfully, "Never be afraid, my dear. When you have cleared your name, I won't really demand that you wed me."

At that he did turn, to face her with blazing angry eyes, and to grip her arms hard. "How *dare* you think such things! If ever my name could be cleared the greatest joy of my life would be ... to ..."

She leaned to him, but though every fibre of his being longed to hold her close, he held her away. Surely, this was the cruellest part of his punishment. For so long he had dreamed of such a moment, without the faintest hope that it would ever come to be. But the miracle had happened; against all reason this pure and lovely girl offered him the wonder of her love. And Fate decreed that he must leave her. Surely everyone had a right to some happy moments? And if those moments were to be brief and few, had they not the right to gather them as though they were the jewels of life, to be marvelled at and cherished, and called back to warm the heart through all the empty years ahead? He gazed down at her and she smiled up at him. His heart ached with love for her. Involuntarily, his fingers were tracing the beautiful curves of her lips. He whispered her name and her arms slid up around his neck. She was soft and warm and yielding against him. Her hands were pulling his head down ... Her eyes closed, her rosy lips lightly parted, she lifted her bewitching face. And he was lost. With a muffled cry he wrapped his arms around her and restraint was swept away. All his long repressed adoration went into that kiss so that when at last their crushing embrace ended, she was weak and breathless, and clung to him feebly, while he kissed her brow and her eyelids and her throat.

"Johnny," she gasped. "Oh, my Johnny ..."

As shaken as she, he thrust her from him, and after a moment said harshly, "You must be stark raving mad. You've not a hope in hell to bring it off ... !"

"Thank heaven! How you frightened me!"

Jennifer's face was blurred and deathly pale. Inexplicably, she was bending over him, pressing a wet handkerchief to his forehead. Equally inexplicably, he lay on the turf. Awareness came, and with it mortification. He groaned and sat up. The cliffs and the sanding stones swung sickeningly. Jennifer's arm was about him. Resting his head on her shoulder, he said wretchedly, "I did it again, didn't I?"

She pressed a kiss on his temple, and said with a quivering attempt at a laugh, "I'd not dreamed my kiss would have such an effect on you, love."

Dreading her answer, he asked, "Was I—very bad?"

"Fortunately I have brothers who often fail to guard their tongues before me. You—you've a remarkable store of oaths, Johnny."

"Oh, my dear! I am so sorry. Was . . . was I cursing anyone in particular?" He sat up straighter, and daring to glance at her gave a cry of horror. "Dear God! I *struck* you!"

She touched the burning ache on her cheekbone. "Never look so stricken. 'Twas not me you attacked, but another lady. My goodness, how I had to fight you! I hope your Mimi knew how to defend herself."

His eyes dilated, he stared at her. "Please—tell me what I said."

"You informed me that I must be raving mad, and said I would never be able to bring something off. Then, while I was wondering whatever you meant, you went down. I ran to find some water, and when I came back and tried to tend you, you were raving."

He touched her cheek remorsefully. "My poor girl. What did I rave about?"

"It was . . ."—she knit her brows—"all jumbled up. Something to do with reefing the sails, and mumbles about the hold and the cargo, and that *they* would know. You kept shouting that. 'They'll know! They'll know.' You were clutching your head, as though it pained you terribly, and then you were whispering about changing course, and saying 'No more, Mimi.' That's when you began to fight."

"Is that—all?"

"Yes, I think so. It was—er, rather hectic now and then."

"So I see. Do you understand now what a—a menace I am?"

"What stuff!" She touched his head lovingly. "I understand that this dear article was damaged and is, I think, trying to tell you something. Have you said the same things in your other attacks?"

"I'm not sure. Father Mason said I used shocking language. The people in Garrison Pen said I was—possessed. I . . . can scarce blame them."

"I can blame them! They almost killed you, and only because you were ill! Poor darling, when I think what you've suffered," her hand clenched, she said fiercely, "I could strangle them!"

He took that small fist and pressed it to his lips. "How very good you are, not to be disgusted by—by such a stupid performance. I can only be grateful that it was a mild attack compared to some. At least, I didn't start climbing, or go rushing off."

"Thank heaven! With the cliff so close you'd not have rushed far." He was not quite so terrifyingly white now, and she probed cautiously, "Dearest, it sounded very much as though you had been held 'gainst your will!"

"Why? Because I said 'They'll know'? That could have been a fear of being found out."

"But why should you fight this Mimi lady, and beg for 'No more'?"

"Perhaps I was ill, and poor Miss Phillips was trying to give me medicine."

"But you said, 'You'll never bring it off,' which must mean you were warning her against—something. Suppose I'm right, and she *was* an adventuress? You might have caught her in someone's cabin, perhaps stealing their valuables. She could have had an accomplice, Johnny, who came in and struck you down from behind."

"And then kept me bound and gagged for weeks while none of my crew, nor my servants, or the surgeon, or anyone on board noticed that their captain had disappeared?" He shook his head and said with a wry smile, "A lovely drama, but unlikely at best, I'm afraid. And we malign the dead. Mimi Phillips was among those lost, poor soul." He sighed, then asked, "For how long was I senseless?"

"It seemed an eternity, but I suppose 'twas actually about five minutes. And I begrudge each one, Johnny, for we have so few."

He said quietly, "And have already used too many. We must go—"

She put her hand over his lips. "Not yet, please! We must plan for our future."

Taking her hand, he kissed the warm soft palm and said, "This is our past, our present, and our future. There is nothing else. We must face that, dearest love."

"No! I won't accept that! There *must* be a way for us— what we have to do is to find it. Johnny—help me!"

He looked into her anxious face and said, "I must help you back to Breton Ridge before the gabble-mongers start their tongues wagging about you and the village idiot."

"But we've scarcely had time to talk, and 'tis so hard for me to see you!"

"We have several days yet. We'll talk again, my dearest. Come—we must get on."

She searched his face, but it was unyielding, and with a sigh she abandoned her struggle. For the moment. "Are you able to ride now?"

"Quite able, I thank you." He got to his feet and helped her up, then touched her cheek with one gentle finger and said shamefacedly, "That is going to bruise, I fear. Faith, but I'm a villain!"

"You are," she said, smiling at him. "Never worry so. We'll say I rode into a branch or took a spill or something of the sort. Now if you will be so good as to throw me up, dear villain, we'll go on, and you can tell me what happened with Falcon and Lieutenant Morris. I've been fairly frantic to know."

His head swam again when he mounted up, but the weakness soon passed, and as they rode slowly through the bright early morning he told her of his meeting with the two men. He had begun to fear that her brother Howland must be deeply involved in the business, so although he described the League of Jewelled Men, he did so only in a very sketchy fashion, implying that it was probably a group of gentlemen enjoying the practice of free-trading. Lord Hibbard Green, he said, was one of them, and had evidently wanted to expand their operations by building a dock so that the illicit cargoes could be delivered directly to the beach.

Despite his careful censorship, Jennifer's eyes were very wide when he finished. She said a hushed, "Good gracious! What a dreadful thing! Johnny, they plan to use our mine as a storage area! With a dock, they could off-load in broad daylight, pretending their cargoes were supplies for the mine restoration. I must warn Papa!"

"Yes, of course. But not until we can present him with some proof. Falcon has not a scrap of evidence to back up his claim, and you may be sure that Lord Green would deny such a scheme if he was accused."

"Yes, but—" Jennifer stopped abruptly, it having dawned on her also that Howland was very probably a part of that scheme. She said lamely, "Oh. Is that what Falcon and Lieutenant Morris were about that night you were shot at? Trying to find proof?"

"Yes. I've no doubt they mean to try again, and—"

She clutched at his arm. "And you will help them! Johnny—no! Hibbard Green is a vicious creature. I do believe that if he wanted something, human life would mean not a button to him!"

"Whereas your life and well-being mean a great deal more than a button to me." He covered her fingers with his hand, and said with grim earnestness, "You may be sure I mean to prevent that scoundrel from endangering either."

"I think every lady longs for such dear protection, and I thank you for it, love. But I beg you to remember that when you risk your life, you risk mine also. No, do not tell me I must not say such things. 'Tis said, and you are not the only one, my Jonathan, who can set his chin and be immovable."

He smiled, and touching her chin, said, "What—this dimpled terror?"

"Only look." She stuck out the "dimpled terror" and summoned her fiercest scowl.

Jonathan threw up his hands in pseudo-alarm. "Pray do not! I am quite unmanned!"

"Good. Keep it in mind, sirrah!" It was time for the next move in her campaign. She asked, "Now tell me, are you able to row a boat?" She saw his suddenly fixed look and added quickly, "On the lake, I mean. I won't be able to see you again today, I know. And tomorrow there is to be a breakfast cruise aboard Lord Kenneth's yacht."

His brows lifted. "I wasn't aware he owned one. The weather should be perfect. You will like that."

"Usually, I do, for the *Deliverance* is a beautiful boat. But—how can I like to go when I shall miss you so, and 'twill steal our precious hours?"

He said teasingly, "Are you suggesting that I row out and carry you off, buccaneer style?"

"Would that you could. My plan is not so grand, but you know, Johnny, it has been so very hot, and in mid-afternoon everyone takes a nap, so I thought . . ."

The breakfast cruise was a great success. August Falcon declined the chance for a brief sea voyage, but most guests thoroughly enjoyed themselves. Lieutenant Morris devoted himself to Jennifer and proved an amusing and light-hearted companion. By noon however, the calm surface of the ocean was less calm, and the increasing swells resulted in a sudden flutter among the guests so that the *Deliverance* turned for home, and was soon anchored in her quiet and sheltered cove once more.

At half-past three o'clock, Jennifer sent Tilly away, saying she meant to take a nap. As soon as her handmaiden's sharp eyes were gone, however, she slipped into a gown of blue muslin embroidered in white and worn over many fluffy petticoats. A blue satin riband threaded her frilled cap, and carrying a parasol of pale blue silk fringed with white lace she crept from her room.

No one was about. Elated, she hurried down the stairs, and turning onto the first-floor landing, all but collided with

August Falcon, impeccable in leaf green and cream. He put up his quizzing glass and scanned her critically.

"You look the veritable spirit of summer, Miss Britewell, despite the rigours of your ocean voyage. Dare I ask where you are off to in such haste?"

Feeling ridiculously guilty, she stammered, "Oh, er—I thought I might stroll in the—er, gardens." She smiled and walked on, but to her dismay he turned to accompany her.

"Most of the guests are restoring their strength in preparation for the ball tonight. Are you always so energetic?"

"Do you admire energetic ladies, Mr. Falcon?"

"Oh, no." Her irked glance brought mischief glinting into his eyes. He drawled, "Am I *de trop*? You are perhaps en route to meet some lucky fellow."

Her heart skipped a beat. "I was hoping to meet Caroline—Miss Morris."

"What a shocking waste. And doomed, dear ma'am. Miss Morris is not so—ah, energetic as the lovely Miss Britewell. I heard her tell poor Sturtevant she meant to rest before dinner. Never despair. I shall escort you about the lawns—if one could call them that."

They were almost to the foot of the stairs. The wide hall was deserted, save for a drowsy footman who sat by the front door and sprang to attention at their approach.

Lord Morris left the book room at the end of the south corridor, and started towards them.

Desperate, Jennifer halted on the bottom step, and said, "You are too good, Mr. Falcon. But I—rather fancy to be rowed out to one of the islands."

He bowed and declared with a graceful wave of his quizzing glass, "Your wish, ma'am is my—Is . . . my—" He checked. His eyes opened wide. He snatched out a handkerchief, and gave a sudden gigantic sneeze, followed by another almost as violent.

Lord Morris jerked to a halt, and with a look of terror, fled.

Stepping back, Jennifer watched Falcon uneasily.

Over the top of the handkerchief his dark blue eyes, bright with tears, searched about frantically. A large ginger and white cat minced down the banister rail and paused beside him, tail waving in the air, and a feline smile fixed on the afflicted gentleman.

"I due it," gasped Falcon, retreating in horror. "Curst place is ... A-SHOO ... fairly crawlig with ... A-SHOO!" He abandoned Jennifer and ran up the stairs, calling something incoherent over his shoulder, apparently having to do with Lieutenant Morris.

With the perversion of its kind the ginger cat bounded in eager pursuit of the reluctant object of its affections.

"Nice kitty," murmured Jennifer, watching it fondly. The footman grinned at her as he flung the door open, and she gave him what he later described in the servants' hall as "a proper captivacious smile."

Despite the heat of the afternoon, there was a slight breeze, and several guests were not so devoid of energy as to be resting. The grounds presented a charming picture. The buxom matron who had flirted with Falcon at luncheon the previous day sat in the shade of a small tree, her deep pink skirts spread about her, while an elderly admirer clad in purple and silver plied her with sections of sliced peach. Several of the younger gentlemen had shed their coats and were playing pale-maille, their elaborate waistcoats bright in the sunshine. Three damsels in great skirted pastel gowns sat in the shade fanning themselves, and forming an appreciative audience. Recognising Lieutenant Morris among the players, Jennifer smiled and he paused to wave his mallet at her.

"Come and inspire us to drive through the hoop, lovely lady," invited another player.

Jennifer shook her head laughingly, and went on towards the narrow dock where a tall coachman waited beside a moored rowing boat.

She had to control the urge to run to his arms, but saw the white gleam of his smile fade abruptly.

"Surprise, my dear lady!" Her heart sank and she had a strong compulsion to moan aloud as that blustering voice rang out. "Here's a treat for you! I am come just as I promised. Say how pleased you are to see me."

With the sensation that a shadow had fallen over this lovely afternoon, Jennifer forced her eyes from Jonathan's expressionless face. She had no choice but to extend her hand as Lord Green bowed, and he pressed a wet kiss on her fingers.

While he had been a guest under her father's roof, she'd been obliged to treat him with at least a modicum of good manners. Even so, her rejection of his advances would have daunted most gentlemen. Such tactics had not so much as made a dint in the thick shield of his lordship's ego, however. Well, he was not her father's guest now and perchance rudeness would succeed where courtesy had failed. She said, "I will say rather that I am surprised to see you, my lord."

Ice hung on the words, and Jonathan's lips twitched with amused appreciation.

Green was impervious to insult. He chuckled, as usual refusing to relinquish her hand. "I'll warrant you are. Came through the bushes yonder. Saw a gel I thought was your luscious self, but 'twas some filly sporting in private with her beau." He bellowed a laugh. "Jolly way to pass an afternoon. But 'tis curst hot out here, m'dear. Come up to the house. Lord Morris has some fine claret I'd not be averse to sluicing down."

Jennifer wrenched her hand free. "Thank you—no. I've a wish to—"

"Hey!" His moist paw turned her face. "What's this?" he demanded, inspecting the bruise on her cheekbone.

She jerked away from his touch. "A small mishap." She had thought to have covered the bruise with paint and powder, but since Tilly had already exclaimed over it, she had no choice but to repeat her explanation. "My horse shied at a shadow and I collided with a branch. 'Tis nothing."

" 'Tis criminal," he growled, darting a glare at Jonathan. "I knew no good would come of letting this stupid clod escort you. Why does he wait? Get back to work, looby!"

Jonathan said, "I am working, my lord. Miss Britewell sent for me—"

"To do—what?" Green's small eyes rested on the boat.

"Ah, so that's your wish is it, my sweeting? How timely is my arrival! I shall row you!"

Jennifer said indignantly. "I did not ask you, sir! Jonathan will—"

"*Jonathan?* Don't dignify him, love. Crazy Jack's the name for that one! Hold the boat steady, dolt, whilst I lift the lady down!"

Jonathan looked from Green's bulk to the small boat. "My lord, I do not think—"

"How could you, when you have no brain? Damn you!" Green fetched him a hard swipe across the shoulder and boomed, "I gave you an order. Do as you're bid!"

Jennifer's indignation ended in a gasp as she was picked up in two massive arms and deposited in the stern. Unable to keep her balance she sat down of necessity as Jonathan strove to hold the rocking boat steady.

Green barked, "Help me down," clutched Jonathan's arm, and lowered himself.

The boat was sturdy, but under his lordship's weight it tilted and dipped. "Keep it still, imbecile!" howled Green.

Unhappily conscious that an amused group was gathering to witness this debacle, Jennifer said, "I did not invite you to—"

"Don't be a marplot, my pretty!" Green settled himself in the bow, seized an oar, and thrust it at the dock, knocking Jonathan's restraining hand away and propelling the boat into the lake.

Jonathan rubbed his wrist and watched tensely, schooling his mind to the fact that this was not the ocean and his dread of water must be ignored if his beloved was at risk.

Others viewed the proceedings through different eyes. A girl said clearly, "This is *so* much more diverting than pale-maille, but I do hope poor Miss Britewell can swim!"

A laugh went up.

The elderly beau with the peach said, "Some of you young Bucks will be obliged to rescue the lady, I think."

Wandering to join the merry crowd, August Falcon enquired, "Why does he wave the oar about?"

Lieutenant Morris explained, "Looking for a breeze, poor

fellow. Hi! Green! That's not for a sail. You have to stick it in the water."

His lordship glared at the hilarious onlookers and succeeded in fitting the oar into the rowlock. He had been conveyed about in a boat from time to time, and although he had never actually taken the oars, he judged rowing to be a simple task requiring nothing more than strength. "No need to be uneasy, m'dear," he bellowed at his decidedly uneasy shipmate. "And pay no heed to those blasted baboons on the dock. We'll show 'em what it means to make a boat move, eh?"

Show them, he did. One oar dipped too deep, and the other with his considerable strength behind it, sent the rowboat spinning at dizzying speed back whence it had come.

Jennifer dropped her parasol and grasped the sides with both hands.

Shrieks of mirth came from the onlookers. One young Corinthian who delighted to row with the Thames watermen collapsed on the grass and laughed till he cried. Falcon so far forgot himself as to cling, overcome, to James Morris.

Any delight Jonathan may have felt at witnessing the baron's embarrassment was lost in his concern for Jennifer. "Ship your oars!" he shouted.

Seeing the dock whizzing at him, his lordship fortunately had the presence of mind to obey this good advice, and seizing a boathook Jonathan was able to prevent a violent collision. One glance at Jennifer's alarmed face and outstretched arms was sufficient for him to swing down into the boat and reach out for her.

"What the *devil* d'you think you're about?" roared Green, starting up, but sitting down again hurriedly, his fury heightened by the continuing hilarity of the watching crowd. "Get the hell out of this!"

"You will first help me out, Jonathan," said Jennifer.

Her voice trembled slightly, but the words were cold and authoritative, and in front of so many, even the baron could not dispute her right to give orders to her own coachman.

Holding with one hand to the mooring post, Jonathan

steadied the boat and handed Jennifer up to James Morris, who waited, grinning broadly, to assist her. Jonathan turned to Green and enquired, "Are you finished, my lord?"

"Not with you," muttered his lordship vengefully. Turning his angry gaze to Jennifer, who was being consoled by the giggling ladies, he shouted, "Think I cannot row this tub, do you? Watch!"

Standing amidships, Jonathan knew what he should say, but he succumbed to the gleeful voice of temptation, sprang nimbly onto the dock then gave the boat an obliging shove.

Green leaned into his oars. On this try he performed more creditably, but with Jennifer gone and all the weight in the bow, the result was inevitable. Momentarily unaware of the cause for the renewed shrieks of laughter, his lordship was nothing if not determined. He pulled mightily, but instead of slicing through the water, the boat appeared about to leave it. Before his goggling eyes, the stern lifted high and higher. Correspondingly, the bow dipped. With a yowl of rage, the baron jumped to his feet, the violent jolt doing nothing to help matters.

It could not really be said that he went down with his ship, but he was an indifferent swimmer. His temper was not improved when some uproarious gentlemen fished him out with the aid of the boathook.

Long before the guests sat down to a light early supper, word of the afternoon boat show had swept the mansion. My lord Green was not popular, and the recounting of his predicament aroused more amusement than sympathy. Hurrying to Jennifer's bedchamber with the white silk underdress that had required some last minute pressing, Tilly relayed many of the jokes that were being bruited about regarding the "big fish" that had been pulled from the lake. One young gentleman, she advised with many giggles, had sent his friends into whoops by remarking that whatever 'twas, it "had the tail of a whale!"

Standing while Tilly threw the under-dress over her panniers, Jennifer smiled, but she was apprehensive. Hibbard Green's nature was vindictive. He'd not dare take out his rage on her, but it would be very like him to turn on Jonathan. She asked, "Have Sir Vinson and Mr. Howland arrived as yet?"

Tilly slipped the peach silk gown over the under-dress and stood back. "It do look that pretty with the silver 'broidery, miss," she said admiringly. "Oh dear, if I didn't go and forget to tell you! Sir Vinson and Mr. Howland sent their regrets. They can't come."

Supper was a glittering occasion. With the possible exception of the host, who looked rather solemn, the guests were in a merry humour. Elaborate ball gowns and richly hued coats created a rainbow of colour around the long table; jewels sparkled, heads were elegantly powdered or bewigged in the very latest fashion. Lord Kenneth's slightly pompous speech, formally honouring his young cousin, was met by applause. When asked for a few words, Lieutenant Morris, wearing regimental evening dress that added considerably to his dignity, spoke with shy brevity and won even more applause. Pleased with themselves and with their company, and further pleased by the achievements of Lord Kenneth's excellent chef, the cream of county society smiled and chattered amiably.

Jennifer was seated between an unassuming middle-aged gentleman and the omnipresent Lord Green. His lordship had recovered his equanimity and appeared not in the least offended when several pointed remarks concerning boating came his way. He joined in the laughter at his expense, and enlightened his companions with a long-winded discourse on boating on the River Thames. Jennifer was sure this was a pose to hide his inner rage, but she was glad to be spared the necessity of conversing with him, and experienced no difficulty in relegating his loud voice and booming laugh to the back of her mind.

She was very sure that no one had expected the reclusive Fleming to come to the ball, but his regrets had been conveyed with proper courtesy. Sir Vinson and Howland, on the other hand, had accepted the invitation and only at the last moment sent their apologies. If any explanation had been offered for this breach of manners, she did not know of it. In answer to her enquiry, Lady Kenneth explained that Sir Vinson had sent a note to the effect that neither he nor Howland was able to come. That so proud a lady would resent such cavalier behaviour was inevitable, and her faint shrug and elevated eyebrows had expressed her feelings.

Embarrassed, Jennifer was under no illusions about her parent. Sir Vinson's good looks and charming manners masked a strong tendency to selfishness. He would be the kindest and most affectionate of fathers until some problem arose, whereupon he was suddenly not to be found, neither knowing or caring upon whose shoulders the problem fell, so long as his were not the ones so burdened. If backed into a corner and forced to make a decision he had hoped to avoid, he would simply choose the easiest course, regardless of its merits. Should it later became obvious that his judgment had been poor, he would fly into one of his violent rages so that no one dare make any further allusion to the matter. But, whatever his faults, she had never known him to be deliberately rude. Nor would she have believed he would abandon her in so embarrassing a situation as being isolated in the home of friends he had all but insulted. He must know she would be worried, and the fact that he'd not deigned to send her even a brief note of explanation made her fear that something was very wrong.

When the meal ended, the diners drifted into the ballroom, where a small orchestra was already performing some traditional airs. More guests began to arrive. Lord Green wrote down his name on Jennifer's dance card, then made a determined effort to keep it. She twitched it away, remarking airily that her papa did not permit that she dance more than once with any gentleman. His small eyes glittered with annoyance. He said softly, "But I assure you he will not object from now on, m'dear."

Both look and tone added to her unease. Lieutenant Morris begged a dance, and she gladly surrendered her card. Green's further attempts to monopolise her were thwarted at every turn. As more and more guests swelled the crowd, she was surrounded by eager gentlemen. August Falcon secured a country dance, and when Green glared at him, he eyed the baron up and down using his quizzing glass with devastating effect. "Do I offend, sir?" he drawled. "Ah, no. I see you are already writ in for the Gavotte. Such a lively dance. Of itself . . . surprising."

"I think I do not follow you," growled his lordship menacingly.

"One can but hope," sighed Falcon, and sauntered off leaving Green so incensed that he lost his place and the merry crowd closed once more around the lady he considered his own.

"The thing is," explained James Morris, walking with Jonathan beside the lake, "it's dashed fortunate you brought him with you. Gives us an excuse to summon you, as it were." He held up Duster's cage and peered inside. The gaily coloured lanterns that brightened the grounds around the mansion had not been extended this far, the lake being too exposed to the wind. "Dashed dark," said Morris. "He *is* in here, ain't he?"

"Yes, I promise you. He doesn't make much noise, and I think the strange surroundings have confused him, rather."

"D'you think he'll ever talk?"

"I try to teach him, but . . . , Lieutenant, had you something to say to me?"

"Eh? Oh, Gad, what a clunch I am! The thing is you see, that your mistr—er, your— That is to say, Miss Britewell wants a word with you. No, don't fly into the boughs. Falcon will bring her down when he claims his dance. Have to be careful, though. Old Hibbard's hot after her, and might not take it kindly if he knew she'd come here to meet you."

"Very true. Has something happened?"

"We're not sure. Green has a habit of losing himself. Disappears y'know. Done it several times, and when he does, be dashed if we can run him to earth. Falcon thinks he's hob-nobbing with another member of the League, so he don't want to leave here for another day or so. And I can't go jauntering off. Guest of honour, y'see."

"Yes, of course. But—"

"And there's the cousin. M'father's cousin, to be exact. But there you are. Family. And I can't have my family besmirched by anything havey-cavey. Have to make a push to find out who Green's meeting on the sly, and warn the old coz."

"Yes. But—er, I don't quite see—"

"What all this has to do with you? Well, your lady has taken it into her pretty head to leave, and Falcon wants you to let us know what's to do at the Blue Rose. Try if you can get inside. If you catch a whiff of what they're about, come to us at once. Bring Duster, and we'll say we asked you to fetch him. Oh, almost forgot! August warns you to have a care." He gave a snort of mirth. "Just like him to send you into the fiery furnace with no shoes and tell you not to burn your feet!"

Jonathan grinned. "I'll do my best to—" The words trailed off and were forgotten, and his heart began to thunder.

Peering at him, the lieutenant shook his head, then proceeded to offer Duster some instruction as he went to join Falcon. "You must talk for your supper, birdwit. Here's a good quotation for you: 'Drink not the third glass.' Got that? 'Drink not . . .' "

Jonathan neither heard him nor saw him go. Jennifer was running to him, arms outstretched. He caught her up, and for a blissful moment held her tight, then began to walk with her along the shore.

"My dear, what is it? With Green lumping about you should not take the chance of meeting me."

"I know, I know! But—I just had to see you! Johnny, I am so worried! Did Lieutenant Morris tell you that my father and Howland have not come?"

"No. But I heard. Is that what has alarmed you?"

"Yes. Partly. Papa may not always see eye to eye with Lord Kenneth, but to accept an invitation and then refuse to attend is not his way!"

"Nor the way of any gentleman. But I fancy there is some compelling reason for his absence."

"Yes," she said anxiously, "that is just what I fear! And

that he didn't write to me of it, because he was reluctant to spoil the party for me. You will think me foolish, I know, but I—I dread that he or one of my brothers may have become ill. I know how fanciful that must sound, but— I have such a presentiment of trouble. I must leave at once."

"Not tonight. 'Tis too dark for safe driving." He heard her muffled sob, and halted, turning to face her. "What is it that you're not telling me? Has that ruffian been forcing his attentions on you?"

For answer, she clung to him, burying her face against his chest. "He is loathsome. He watches me. And—and he smiles . . . Oh, it makes my flesh creep!"

Inwardly enraged, he said in a controlled voice, "The man who would not smile at the sight of you, Miss Britewell, must have solid rock between his ears, and granite for a heart!"

"But—it is not that kind of smile, you see. 'Tis a horrible sort of—of *gloating*. Oh, I do so dislike the man!"

He tried to comfort her, pointing out reasonably that she must tell her father if Green became a real nuisance. "You know Sir Vinson would send him packing. The great oaf cannot harm you, Jennifer."

But his jaw set, and he thought, 'Heaven help him if he tries!'

❧ *Chapter 12* ❧

The morning had dawned hot but the sky was overcast and the air heavy and oppressive. Haunted by the persistent sense that all was not well at home, Jennifer gazed through the open window of the carriage, and fanned herself absently. She had said her farewells to Lady Morris last evening. Caroline had been disappointed, at first protesting and then becoming petulant. My lady had been regally polite while making not the slightest attempt to detain her. It was worrying to think there might be a real rift between the two families. From earliest childhood Caroline had been one of her few friends, and she was fond of all the Morrises. If Lord Kenneth had approved of her, she might have been his daughter-in-law by now, but he had not approved, and dashing young Merwin Morris, her most ardent suitor, had been hurried off on the Grand Tour, with scarcely a chance to bid her goodbye. At the time, she had been hurt, but not really surprised. Now, she could only be grateful. She'd been fond of the handsome red-head, but she had never loved him, as she loved Jonathan . . .

Tilly was quick to note the softened expression on the lovely face opposite, and her lips pursed knowingly. She could not have been more pleased that their stay at Breton Ridge had been cut short. So superior did his lordship's staff fancy themselves, and so pleased they'd been to make fun because Miss Jennifer had brought a lunatic to act as her coachman. They'd changed their tune a bit when the looby had knocked down one of the stablehands, and there'd been less name calling after the boat business had given them something they could laugh about for months. Some of the maids even had the flutters over Crazy Jack, which just went to show what a silly lot they were, for all their high and mightiness. She would have plenty to tell dear Mr. Oliver Crane! The prospect brought a glow, but it was a brief glow, because her attempts to ingratiate herself with her mistress had met with a cold reserve. Miss Jennifer was in a huff, thought Tilly, because she likely guessed that her little trysts with the looby had been seen. Well, they'd been seen, all right, and it would be doing the poor dear no disservice were a careful hint dropped in the right ears at the right time. Crazy Jack's days in Roselley would be done then! Oliver Crane would be glad to see the back of him, and so would she. The very *idea* of the looby! As if it wasn't enough that he gave hisself such airs and graces, he'd dared to make sheep's eyes at Miss Jennifer! Bewitched her, is what he'd done, and got her sighing over one what wasn't fit to touch her little shoes!

On the box, Jonathan's thoughts followed a different course. Hibbard Green's pursuit of Jennifer was as relentless as it was crude. There could be no doubt but that he was a member of the sinister League of Jewelled Men, nor that his determination to acquire the Blue Rose Tin Mine was in some fashion connected with the activities of the League. Surely, in the furtherance of those interests it would have been logical for him to escort his chosen lady back to Castle Triad. That he had not done so was a blessing for Jennifer, but *why* he had not done so was a puzzle. Stable gossip had it that Lord Morris could barely tolerate Green, and that while his lady could always find a smile for the possessor of both rank *and* fortune, in the privacy of her own apartments she had once been heard to remark that Lord Hibbard Green had the charm, wit, and address of a maggot. Green also had the hide of an elephant, but his acquaintanceship with his host was too brief for him to regard Lord Morris as a friend. And if it was not affection for the Morrises that kept him at Breton Ridge, it followed there must be another reason, a very compelling reason, for him to cool his heels there while his lovely quarry rode away.

August Falcon was convinced that Green stayed to meet someone; perhaps another member of the League of Jewelled Men, or even its mysterious leader, the deadly "Squire." By watching Green, he and Lieutenant Morris could, he hoped, learn the Squire's identity.

The hole in that plan, of course, was that the members of the League knew the identities of the men who opposed them. If Green were a member of the League, then he would be aware that Falcon and Morris were his enemies and was unlikely to take any chances while they were present.

He had pointed this out to Morris, who had admitted, "True, to an extent, dear boy. But I doubt if our Hibbard knows we've rumbled him. Fact is, we weren't sure at the start that he *was* a member of their slithery club."

"Then—why did you follow him?"

"Didn't. Old August did, because Green had visited the home of a lady we know to be involved with the League."

"A—*lady*? Jupiter!"

"No. Name's Buttershaw, actually. We'd been keeping an eye on her, and when Green kept trotting in, Rossiter set August to see what the fellow was up to. August followed Hibbard all the way to Cornwall, then lost him. Poor lad was probably biting those standing stones with frustration— dreadful temper has my future brother-in-law. He disguised himself and went about like a fugitive from a hermitage, trying to winkle out where he'd mislaid the dear peer. When he learned Hibbard was at Castle Triad, he sent word back to Rossiter. Since I have family here and might quite logically visit them, Ross sent me down. I collected August and tidied him up a bit, then brought him here, so that we could have a local—er, base, as it were. Last thing in the world we expected was that Green would pop up at my kinsman's home."

"I see. Then when I told you about Green's figurine . . ."

"It did the trick, dear boy. Proof positive. With luck, Green thinks it pure coincidence that I should be visiting my family while he's here. If so, he might feel perfectly safe to go on with—whatever he's about." Looking disturbed, Morris had muttered, "To say truth, I'm a shade uneasy. Don't much relish the notion the League might be after Breton Ridge . . ."

If the League of Jewelled Men had set their sights on the Morris estate, Jonathan thought they'd have their work cut out for them. One could scarce find a more proper and upright gentleman than Lord Kenneth, and if there were any skeletons in the Morris closets—

His introspection ceased abruptly as Roselley came into view. There seemed an unusual number of people about. He slowed the team. Heads were turned to them. Some of the men he didn't recognise, but those he did know were changed: the look of hopelessness was gone. Several people shouted a greeting to "Miss Jennifer" as the carriage passed. Mrs. Blary, known for her slovenly ways, was industriously sweeping her doorstep, and the prevailing air of optimism was unmistakeable.

They had passed Noah Holsworth's cottage and were splashing through the stream atop Devil's Ladder when Jonathan glanced eastward and muttered an astonished, "Be dashed!"

A small army of men toiled at clearing and levelling the ground for what appeared to be a new road leading from the cliffs to the Blue Rose Mine. Looking westward, he stared in disbelief. The long clean stretch of beach had been transformed. Some quarter-mile out, a large partially completed dock rose from the sands, several men hammering busily on the platform. The incoming tide lapped around the pilings. More pilings stretched in a long line from the dock to the beach, supporting a walkway that was under construction. A two-masted schooner, sails reefed, lay at anchor about a mile offshore.

The check string jerked imperatively. He opened the trap. Jennifer called, "Stop, if you please. I wish to get out."

He secured the reins, climbed down to swing open the door, and handed both ladies down.

Jennifer walked to the brink of the cliff, Tilly following.

Standing at the heads of his leaders, Jonathan thought that Green's engineers had chosen well. Clearly, they meant to link a new mine road to another flight of steps going down to the beach.

While he took in the practical aspects of the construction and wondered how it had all been done so fast, Jennifer saw only the destruction of the previously unspoiled coastline. Heartsick, she exclaimed. "But—Papa said he'd not allow it! Johnny, 'tis so ugly!"

Tilly's annoyed glance darted to him, and he answered woodenly, "Yes, ma'am."

The enigmatic response was of itself a warning. Jennifer gathered her wits and returned to the carriage.

The horses leaned into their collars and soon they were winding up the rutted road to the castle.

Jennifer could only be glad she had come home. Her apprehensions had been justified. Whatever his reasons for having agreed to the erection of that atrocity on the beach, poor Papa must be miserable now that he saw the result. Perhaps it was still not too late to prevail upon him to tear it down.

"Tear it down?" Sir Vinson Britewell mopped a handkerchief at his heated countenance and scowled at his daughter. Sultry weather always tried his temper, and his irritation was increased because here she was, looking cool and pretty in her full-skirted morning gown of fawn muslin with lace trimming the snowy fichu and edging the frill of her dainty cap. She had no business to have come so soon and to look so very like her dear mama. He didn't want her. He wasn't prepared. He sat down at his desk and grumbled, "Of all the cockaleery notions! But I suppose, being a female, you cannot even guess at the cost of such a structure."

"I apprehend it must be costly, Papa, but I also know that it is far from what you like. You have always loved our beautiful beaches, and you told me how vehemently opposed you were to the very idea of such an eyesore being—"

All too aware that he had indeed made such a statement, he waved his handkerchief and interrupted irritably, "Must a remark made early in business negotiations be regarded as being chiselled in stone? Especially in the case of an extreme complex matter touching the lives of many. You must take me for a proper fool if you think I am above revising my opinions when it appears—er, wise to do so."

"No, no, Papa! I was only surprised that— Well, when I left you were set 'gainst the scheme, and now I come home to find so much of the work has been done, and so swiftly. I could scarce believe my eyes when we drove through the village. Everything seemed changed and there were so many new faces."

"Change is the path to the future. And they were happy faces, I'll warrant! The common folk have prayed for the mine to re-open. 'Twas to please them I gave way, and *they* find no fault with my actions, I can tell you!"

He was whipping himself up, which meant he was worrying about the decisions he'd made. She leaned forward in her chair and said cajolingly, "I do not find fault, dear Papa, if 'tis what you really want, but—"

"You cannot know how you relieve my mind. 'Faith, but a man is beset from every side! If you came rushing home from Breton Ridge only to take me to task for having reached a decision in a matter that is none of your affair, you had as well have stayed!"

He was all but shouting at her. Shaken, she drew back. "I would have stayed, sir, but when you did not come and sent me no word, I was afraid you might be ill."

"I most certainly *did* send word! I despatched a groom to Lady Kenneth with my apologies. Was that not to your liking?" He stood, his chair scraping noisily across the floorboards as he thrust it back, his voice loud and shrill as he demanded, "Or is it that his high and mightiness has taken offence because I did not run to kiss his hand? Sent you packing, did he?"

"Of course not!" Coming to her feet also, Jennifer said anxiously, "Neither Lord Morris nor his lady was anything but courteous. I think they were perhaps a little surprised that you offered no word of explanation."

"I fail to see why that should discompose you." Sir Vinson marched to the window and stood glaring outside, his hands tightly clasped behind his back. After a moment, he said in a calmer, but rather odd kind of voice, "But perhaps 'tis as well you should have come home now, for we have something to discuss." He turned and regarded her almost furtively, then walked to the fireplace. "The thing is . . ." He thrust both his hands deep into his pockets, cleared his throat, and stared at the rug.

"Yes, Papa?"

"The thing is— You ain't getting any younger. No, I don't say that out of unkindness. We—er, we none of us can help that, can we?" He laughed too heartily but did not look at her.

She waited, saying nothing.

"The thing is," he said for the third time, "you should be wed. Should have been wed long since. If anything should happen to me—" He coughed, and tugged at his cravat as though it strangled him.

Dreading what was coming, she argued. "You are a fine healthy man, Papa. I think you will be here to take care of me for many years yet."

"One never knows, child, what may lurk just around the corner." He looked stricken, suddenly, then went on, his words alternately halting then tumbling over one another, so that she found it difficult to follow them. "You should be in the care of a loving and—and comfortably circumstanced husband. I have told you so for years, but you paid no heed."

"But—Papa, I—"

"Be silent, miss! I have therefore—er, come to a decision, and— In short, I have—I have accepted an offer for your hand."

It seemed to Jennifer as if that terrifying pronouncement echoed and re-echoed around the room. Her mouth was dry as dust, and her knees shook so that she sank into the chair again. She said in a thread of a voice, "I—cannot believe you would ... would do so without discovering my feelings in the matter."

He barked, "You know I have your welfare at heart. The gentleman I have approved for you is of—sufficient fortune that you will never know want, and—and he is—titled besides."

She half-whispered, "Papa—in heaven's name—not—"

"He is—Lord Hibbard Green."

She closed her eyes for a moment. 'Johnny,' she thought in anguish. 'Oh, my Johnny!' The image of his clean-cut face came into her mind. She realised in a remote way that her father was stamping up and down the room informing her at length of how fortunate she was and how happy she would be in her new home. " 'Tis a great castle, you know," he said rapidly, "so it will be not so much of a—"

Jennifer had stood. She said quietly, "No, Papa."

He stopped in his pacing, and whipped around, his face a thundercloud. "What d'you mean—no?" he roared. "Do you dare defy me? God knows I've been patient these many years, but if you think I'll brook you setting up your will 'gainst mine, you're vastly mistaken, my girl!"

Her nerves were tied in knots and she felt a little sick, but she said with determined calm, "I believe you love me, sir. You laughed when first Howland suggested Lord Green for my husband. You said you did not want him. Why you would now seek to bring such misery upon me, I cannot guess. But we live in a modern age, thank God, and you cannot force me. Of all the men I ever have met, Lord Hibbard Green is the most repugnant to me. I will not marry him, Papa. Sooner would I be dead."

Sir Vinson had lost all his colour, but at this a sudden flush darkened his face. "How *dare* you question my judgment?" he raged. "I have every right to choose you a mate, and by God, I have chosen! You *will* marry Hibbard Green, you ungrateful chit! And count yourself fortunate that any man would have you!"

Tears stung her eyes, but she winked them away and did not falter, though this man she had always loved and honoured stood before her like some demented stranger, his chin outthrust, his eyes blazing. Her voice sounded very far away in her own ears, but she managed to say, "You had the right to select my mate whilst I was under age, sir. I am five and twenty now, and my own mistress. I will leave your house, if you desire it, but you cannot by law compel me to—"

"Little *fool!*" He took her by the shoulders and shook her fiercely. "Of course I can force you! What *law* would you call upon to help you defy your own father? Scholars write out our laws, and the poor are obliged to observe them, but do you think they're given more than lip service by people of our class? We live by our own law! And even if that were not so, to whom could you turn for aid? There are a hundred ways I—I might . . . compel . . ."

Her beautiful face was so white, so stricken, and tears trembled on her lashes. Releasing her, he turned away, and cried wildly, "And if I did not choose to—to resort to such means, d'you think *he* would hesitate? One night alone with him and—and you'd have no choice but to—" His face convulsed suddenly, and he sank into a chair, his head bowed into his hands. "Oh . . . my dear God!" he moaned. "I cannot . . . I cannot!"

With a smothered cry, Jennifer flew to kneel beside him and seize one of those clutching hands. "Papa!" she sobbed. "Dear, dear, Papa! I knew you could not speak to me so. I knew it! What has happened? Has Green managed to convince you I really care for him? If you knew—"

The words were cut off as he snatched her to him and hugged her close. She was appalled to know that he was weeping, and she clung to him, patting his shoulder, trying to comfort him.

Abruptly, he broke away and walked hurriedly to stand with his back to her, busied with his handkerchief. Jennifer dried her own tears, then went to the credenza and the decanter on the silver tray.

"Here, sir," she said gently, offering him a glass of cognac.

He glanced at her through reddened eyes, took the glass and muttered his thanks, then noted with a broken laugh that she had poured herself a glass also. "Rascal," he croaked.

When he returned to his chair, she knelt on the floor at his knee, as she had done so often as a child. "Can you tell me what he said to you, dear sir?"

He sighed deeply and leaned his head back for a moment. Then, he said, "You lay the blame at the wrong door, my dear. 'Tis not Hibbard Green drove me to—to that disgraceful display, but—but my heir."

"Howland? But—surely, Papa, you can deny him?"

He nodded, and said slowly, "Yes, child. I can deny him. And so can you, for I have done as much of bullying as I can bear. The decision now, must be your own . . ."

"And you need not think as Mr. Fleming's going to whistle you away so you can laze about with a lot of wormy old books," said Oliver Crane irritably. "Wasted enough time, you has, gallivanting about pretending to be a coachman. I'm that short handed I need every man I can get. Even the shadow of a man!"

After returning Jennifer and Tilly to the castle and driving the coach into the stableyard, Jonathan had gone at once to change clothes. He'd hoped to be assigned to Fleming Britewell, but when he'd returned his livery to the housekeeper, he had been told to report to the stables. It was clear that the head groom's animosity had not diminished during his absence, but Crane's complaint was to an extent justified; there were only half as many men to be seen as had been employed here last week, and twice as many horses.

Ordered to care for the team then wash and polish the coach, Jonathan worked busily, but kept his ears open. Whenever Crane was out of earshot, the grumbles were many and bitter. Mr. Howland and the foreman in charge of erecting the dock had between them hired every able-bodied man in the area. Overnight, it seemed, the pendulum had swung from widespread unemployment to more jobs than there were men to fill them. The crews working on the dock were better paid than those building the new road from the mine and cutting the steps in the cliff face. On the lowest rung of the pay scale were the grooms and stablehands, whose hours were longest, with the result that tempers were short and resentment was high.

With new shared grievances to occupy them, the stablehands appeared to have mellowed somewhat towards Jonathan; he was less frequently ridiculed, and by inserting a quiet word into their conversation now and then, was able to learn a good deal.

The dock foreman had been brought in by Lord Green. He was a big Welshman named Bronwys; a dour, brooding individual with a sharp tongue and a fine knowledge of his craft. So far as Jonathan could learn, all the workers, with the exception of Bronwys, were from this area. There was no mention of any other "foreigner" who haled from farther away than Devonshire, and he was very sure that if a man had been hired who was so beyond the pale as to have been born outside the British Isles, it would have been a prime topic of conversation.

So Falcon had been right; for whatever purpose the unsavoury lot at the mine had been brought in, it was not to build the dock. As far as he could tell, the presence of those men was still unsuspected, and he was mildly surprised that it had not occurred to anyone to have a look round the Blue Rose. He mentioned this to Isaac Blary, who had become quite friendly toward him in a guarded fashion, and was startled when the boy said that gates now closed off the entrance, and KEEP OUT notices were posted warning that the mine was unsafe. This was unsettling, but did not deter him. Somehow, and with the least possible delay, he meant to get inside.

It was dark before he finished the long list of tasks Crane had set him. He collected Duster and went home. Mrs. Newlyn had left a thick piece of bread and dripping, and a pickle on his small table. He was touched to find that she had been so kind as to wash and mend his torn shirt and breeches. He discovered later, that she had mislaid her needle, but although his sudden leap and following comments alarmed Duster, he was able to remove the needle without major damage to his person.

When he went, yawning, to the cottage at dawn next morning, Sprat was waiting, and rushed inside to jump onto the table and knock down a note that had been left there. Jonathan put the cat down and took the note up. It informed him that Noah wanted to see him—"wenever yu kan manidge." That would have to be this evening, since Noah would still be sleeping when he went to work.

Sprat escorted him back to his shed, then went racing off. Inside, he was faced by a small rebellion. Duster hopped and fluttered and gobbled furiously each time Jonathan tried to catch him, and eventually, and with much whirring of wings, took up residence on his shoulder.

"So that's it," said Jonathan, amused. "You've become used to company, and don't want to be left alone all day."

It had occurred to him that the shed must be lonely and dim during the hours he was away. "I'm sorry for that," he said. "Mrs. Newlyn offered to take you in while I'm at work, but for all her kind heart, she's just a shade absent-minded. She has a friend named Sprat, who is of the tortoise-shell persuasion. He's a nice little fellow, but was his mistress to leave the cage door open for only a minute, I fear that Sprat would be very glad of a Duster *à la carte.*"

Duster heard him out with few comments, but resisted all attempts to dislodge him, emitting piercing squawks and hooking his claws so firmly into the shoulder of the new frieze coat that Jonathan at length surrendered. He took the cage along for later use, and Duster entertained him by chirping happily all the way to the castle. Surprisingly, Oliver Crane made no objections beyond remarking that if the stupid bird fell off and got stepped on by one of the horses, it would serve him right. The men were variously amused or contemptuous, but at least there was no open hostility, and Duster enjoyed an hour of strenuous shoulder balancing before he tired and Jonathan put him back in his cage.

The press of work was even heavier than the previous day. Word of the new dock had spread, and a steady stream of callers descended upon Castle Triad, so that the overworked grooms were obliged to care for the various vehicles and hacks of the visitors. At noon, Howland Britewell came to the stableyard in a black temper and ordered that one of the new teams be driven towards Redruth to collect a load of goods from a waggon that had lost a wheel and broken its axle along the way.

Crane stared at him, and repeated stupidly, "Load of—goods, sir?"

"Ah! You can hear! You encourage me to think you can also obey! *Goods*—fool. Supplies Lord Green wants stored in the mine. Now d'you see why the dock will be a boon to us? Get a couple of men out there at once. I want the goods delivered to the Blue Rose before nightfall."

"But—Mr. Howland, sir, I can't spare two men, nor even one! We're so short-handed now we can hardly—"

"Oh, stop your whining. There must be someone who can be spared." Howland's angry eyes flashed around the barn and rested on Jonathan, who was forking hay from the loft. "Send the half-wit. You can't tell me *he's* irreplaceable." He gave Crane a few brusque instructions, and advised harshly that he wanted to hear no excuses for failure.

"Nor you won't get none, sir. But if Jack's to drive a far piece on *them* cart tracks, unload the broke waggon, then get back and off-load—why he'll be all night, sir! Can't be—"

"Nonsense! There'll be fellows with the other waggon to help, and Lord Green has a caretaker out at the Blue Rose who'll give him a hand at this end."

The silence in the barn was sudden and complete. Every head turned to the two men.

Crane echoed, "A caretaker? I didn't know there was—"

"Well, you know now. Dammitall! *Will* you move your lazy arse and do as you're bid!" Glowering, Britewell stamped from the barn.

The silence continued and the men exchanged grim glances.

Crane muttered, "Why in hell couldn't they simply have hired another waggon in Redruth?" Then, as if recollecting himself, he barked, "Is ye all froze? Get back to work!

Isaac—help Crazy Jack drag out one of the new waggons and pole up a pair of his lordship's dray horses. Take that damned bird with you, Jack," he added sourly. "He can help you load!"

The dray horses were fine strengthy beasts, but the big chestnut gelding was of a quarrelsome temperament and difficult to handle. When Crane stamped over to grumble about "all this danged commotion" the chestnut made a teeth snapping lunge at him. The head groom had to jump back and fell over a bucket, which did not brighten his mood.

Ten minutes later, Jonathan was guiding the team out of the yard, Duster's cage on the seat beside him, and his mind full of speculation. Howland Britewell's mention of a caretaker had been a proper bomb blast. One could almost hear the men wondering who he might be, and why a caretaker was needed. More importantly, thought Jonathan, Howland had given him a perfect excuse for getting inside the mine. With luck, by tonight he might have the answers to many questions.

His thoughts turned to Jennifer. He had caught not so much as a glimpse of her since they came back from Breton Ridge. She must know he was working in the stables. She could have ordered a mount for one of her early rides, and even if he was not allowed to escort her, he could at least have seen her sweet face, and she might have found a way to slip a note to him. She might, of course, be tired, after the hectic days at Breton Ridge. Or perhaps she simply had no news for him. He was a fool to start imagining that something was wrong only because he missed her so. That was a feeling to which he must become accustomed.

Crane had warned him to keep with the rough track that led inland. "And take care ye're home before dark, else ye'll likely never get home at all." To this ominous direction, Isaac had added in a whisper, " 'Ware low, smooth ground, Jack. 'Tis likely swamp or marsh." With these cautions in mind, Jonathan kept the horses to a steady pace. They were good goers. The chestnut, encountering no creature to attack, tended to business, and the miles rolled away.

Very soon Jonathan had lost sight of any human habitation, but even on this cloudy afternoon the scenery was spectacular. He was on the high moor now, and could see for miles: the blue glitter of the Atlantic to the south and west, rocky knolls and outcroppings dotted about, a distant cluster of the ancient standing stones, and far to the north the loom of frowning tors and crags. The only sounds were the calls of birds, the clip clop of hooves, and Duster's occasional remarks. Jonathan relaxed and dreamed dreams of his beloved.

The respite was all too brief. The track became harder to follow, at times almost vanishing in the thick turf. The terrain was ever more hilly and broken, and Jonathan had no difficulty understanding why the other waggon should have broken down. Surmounting a rise, the track plunged into a small valley and wandered through a belt of low trees. Without warning the horses were knee-deep in a rushing stream that bisected the track, unseen in the deep shadows. Emerging on the far side, the track became ever more rutted and pot-holed, making it necessary to proceed with caution. Jonathan was uneasily aware that too much time was passing. If he didn't come upon the wrecked waggon soon, he could never hope to be back in Roselley while the light held, and his chances of finding the way home after dark were slim indeed.

Moments later he gave a sigh of relief when a waggon came into view, squatting ignominiously at the side of the track, the front end high in the air. There was no sign of horses or men, but when he shouted an enquiry an untidy scratch wig hove over the side. A bell-mouthed blunderbuss was levelled at him. Narrow dark eyes in a narrow face scanned him suspiciously, and a high-pitched London voice demanded his identity.

His reply appeared to satisfy because the waggoner clambered down, grumbling, "Took yer perishing time!"

"And I've precious little left to get back before the sun goes down. Where's your mate?"

"Rid the horses off, but he'll be back soon. If he don't go boozing. Which wouldn't be the first time."

"I can't wait. We'd best get started." He loosened girths and let the team graze. The waggoner began to haul boxes down while airing his grievances about heavy loads, lazy animals, and terrible roads. Listening with half an ear, Jonathan was dismayed by the number of crates, barrels, and boxes to be transferred. "What the devil is all this?" he asked.

"Vittles, they said." The waggoner spat into the road. "By the weight of some of these big 'uns, they must be cast iron 'taters!"

It took an hour's back-breaking labour to load the supplies, and the task wouldn't have been accomplished as rapidly had not the other waggoner returned driving a donkey cart. He was a stout man who sang merrily while he worked, and when they finished and Jonathan was readying his team for the return journey, he chatted with Duster and offered to buy him for sixpence. He looked genuinely disappointed when his offer was refused, but waved and called a good-natured farewell, and for quite some distance Jonathan could hear him singing.

Clouds were building to the east, but luckily the dry weather held. Because of the heavy load, Jonathan had expected the return journey to take more time, but the team proved their worth and moved along steadily. The only difficulty arose when the track led through a patch of low ground that was soggy from the rains. It had presented no difficulty on the eastward journey, but the added weight caused the waggon wheels to sink into the mud and the team was unable to haul it clear. For a time Jonathan thought he was beaten, but fortunately there was a thicket nearby, and by levering deadwood under the wheels he was able at last to get them turning once more.

The battlements of Castle Triad came into view as the sun was setting. Jonathan was tired and hungry, but he turned off the track, drew the team to a halt, and climbed into the back of the cart. He used a sharp rock and his pocket knife to pry up the lid on a long crate. Expecting to find muskets or swords, he stared, baffled, at coats, breeches, shirts, and shoes of all shapes and sizes. Two barrels were chained and padlocked. A third emitted sloshing sounds when he moved it. 'Rum,' he thought, and turned his attention to another long box. This one he was able to open without causing too much damage, and his expectations were fulfilled. Far from mining machinery, the crate held at least a score fine pistols and as many knives and clubs. He pounded the lid down again, and advised Duster that he'd be willing to wager the two padlocked barrels held shot and powder, and that there'd be very little mine restoring done with these goods.

It was dusk when he reached the Blue Rose. Just as Isaac had said, wide iron gates were closed across the entrance. In response to his hail, a tall man carrying a musket came out.

Jonathan thought that "guard" would have been a better word than "caretaker." The musket was not set aside, even while the padlock was removed, and the tall man glanced about suspiciously as he waved Jonathan through the gates, then ordered him to stop and get down.

Obeying, Jonathan asked, "Do we off-load out here?"

The caretaker ignored him and climbed into the waggon to inspect the cargo.

Jonathan made a quick survey of the ramshackle wooden building at one side, with beyond it the tunnel-like opening in the hillside that he knew sloped down into the mine.

"Some of these is busted," accused the caretaker.

"I'm surprised they all weren't. The other waggon lost both back wheels and its axle broke. Came down hard. The waggoners looked like honest men. I doubt anything's been taken."

"Better not've been!" The caretaker climbed out again, keeping his eyes fixed on Jonathan. "A'right. Get on yer way," he said with a wave of the musket.

"I was told to help—"

"Don't matter what you was told to. Get on yer way."

"But—the team. I'm supposed to take them back to Triad."

Grinning unpleasantly, the man slouched nearer and said through his brown teeth, "The team'll be brung back. *G'night*, Sam."

"My name is not Sam. And I'll get my property first." With a lithe swing Jonathan was on the box seat of the waggon and lifting Duster's cage.

"Hey!" The caretaker aimed his musket. "You stop! Whatcha got there?"

Jonathan jumped down. "This is Duster, and why you should wish to shoot him I cannot guess. He ate none of your supplies, I promise you."

The hard eyes darted to the cage. "Let's have a look. Cor! What kinda—" The words ended in a shriek. He had trod within reach of the big chestnut.

The mine seemed to explode people. The light was almost gone now, but among those who came at the run was someone holding a lantern. Jonathan caught glimpses of savage eager faces; the flash of steel; long-barrelled pistols gripped in practiced hands. There was little outcry.

A harsh voice demanded "¿*Quien es?*"

The caretaker swore furiously. "Accursed nag bit me! If it didn't belong to his lord—"

Another man snapped, "You—with the birdcage. Get out!"

Jonathan needed no urging. Amid a sudden hush, he strode up the path and over the rise, half expecting to hear a shot, and with an uneasy feeling between his shoulder blades.

He slowed as soon as he was out of range. It had begun to rain and the wind was blowing up, but weariness, hunger, and the weather were scarcely noted. In his mind's eye was the armed and hostile crowd lit by the beams of that high-held lantern; the fierce glares that had come his way; and one face that stood out from all the others. The square ruddy face of a man for whose death he had held himself directly responsible: Joe Taylor, who had won the coveted post of ship's carpenter on the proud East Indiaman called the *Silken Princess*.

ᴤ *Chapter 13* ᴥ

"Wait! Jack—will ye cease your gallop, man?"

A strong hand caught at his arm. A large shape loomed through the darkness, and Holsworth panted, "Lucky I was . . . on the look-out for ye, else you'd have run yourself into a fine bog! Let's get out of this wind."

Jonathan followed resistlessly, marvelling that he hadn't noticed the wind was rising, or that he'd walked all this way. Inside Holsworth's snug but cluttered kitchen, the big man peered at him anxiously and pushed him into a chair. "Been off on one of your forgetting times?"

It had been more a "remembering time" and there was no end to the possible ramifications. He said, "Not exactly. The widow said you wanted to talk to me, but I thought I'd go home and get something to eat first."

Holsworth opened a cupboard and set out a tankard of ale, some dark bread, and a generous slice of cold meat. "Aye, ye look fair famished," he said. "Eat up."

Not until that instant had Jonathan realised just how hungry he was, and he ate gratefully. Holsworth used two books to brace his long clay pipe and filled it while recounting the progress he'd made on the ark. "She's ready hull and keel," he concluded with enthusiasm. "Ah, Johnny, I begin to wish I'd built her down on the beach so we could launch her and then work on fitting her out."

Jonathan said with a faint smile, "We might haul her to Devil's Ladder. It could serve you as a slipway."

"Perish the thought! She'd reach the sea as splinters! But I didn't bring you here to talk of my ark." The big man removed the pipe from between his teeth and sat staring down at it, then said, "I've no wish to see ye leave, but—'tis time you was least in sight." He met Jonathan's eyes, adding reluctantly, "There's rumours abroad. A parcel of 'em. And none to your good."

"That's nothing new." Finishing his small meal, Jonathan said, "Actually, people have been kinder of late. Even young Blary doesn't mock me as he used to do."

"*Young* Blary, maybe not. *Ben* Blary and Wally Pughill and their like, is another matter. And worse'n Ben Blary"—Holsworth leaned forward, waving his pipe for emphasis—"that ferret-faced man of Lord Green's has been hanging about the tavern and Gundred's place, stirring up trouble. Folks was talking against ye afore, ye knows that. All the business about a dark stranger what you was seen whispering with on the cliffs at dawn—the one Ben Blary says had eyes like live coals in his head. Ah, you may laugh, man. But take it along o' the fact that—well, no offence meant, but ye don't always know what you been a'doing of five minutes ago—own it, now."

"Yes, but—"

"There y'are, then. And you is said to have climbed up the cliff past Bridget Bay, which everyone knows cannot be done. And—much as I hates to say it, Jack, ye're not like the rest of us. Them eyes o'yourn can be meek as a saint one minute, and strike through a man like a spear the next." He paused, then muttered, "What really troubles me is that you're staying at the widder's. If folks should think that you and her . . ."

"Have been doing—what? Conjuring up evil spells to plague the children? If ever I heard such stuff! Why not add the fact that I saw the lady with the blue cloak? Then they'll—"

Holsworth dropped his pipe. Paling, his eyes wide with alarm, he gasped, "Ye never said 'twas a *blue* cloak! Oh—Gawd! You see the *Lady*!"

"So I'm told. But I promise you I had nought to do with

her appearance, and she seemed to notice me not at all. Besides, from what Je— Miss Jennifer said—"

"Ah! And that's the worst of the lot!" Recovering himself, but still looking unnerved, Holsworth took up his broken pipe. "There's a tale that you—er, been putting spells on Miss Jennifer." He darted a look at Jonathan from under his bushy eyebrows. "And if all the rest wasn't enough to turn folk agin ye, *that* would do it—proper!"

His face bleak, Jonathan stood and started to the door.

Holsworth ran to intercept him. "Hold up! I didn't say as *I* believed it of ye, Jack. But—oh, man! If ye could but see your eyes when you look at her! Or the—the glow that comes on her sweet face at the sight o' you! 'Tis plain as the nose on your fact that—"

"That I have dared—presumed—to love her?" The anger in Jonathan faded. Sitting down again, he said slowly. "Well, 'tis quite true. But can you think I don't know how far beneath her I am? I told her I'm going away, and I mean to. Only—she has it in her mind that because I saw the lady in the blue cloak something awful is going to happen. I know 'tis foolish superstition, but—if she really should be threatened by danger, I don't want to leave her."

"I think our dear Miss Jennifer would not like to see you put to the cliff for being in league with the devil, Jack. Nor the widow burned at the stake for a witch what has conspired with you! Nay, hear me out! You're not a Cornishman. You don't understand our ways. I tell ye, true as true, call it superstition if you will, but we've the lore of the ancient folk. We've the old Powers. And once they're set loose, there's no stopping 'em. I've seen things you wouldn't believe. And I know!"

He was a commanding figure, standing there straight and tall, the light from the candles gleaming on his hook and throwing dark shadows under his eyes. Watching him, Jonathan had the uncanny feeling that there were, indeed, "more things in heaven and earth than—"

The door flew open and crashed against the sideboard. A gust of rain-laden wind howled in, its damp breath extinguishing the candles, plunging the room into darkness, and blowing over Duster's cage. Holsworth gave a startled yell. Duster squawked frantically. His heart thumping, Jonathan leapt for the door. He collided with a dark and yielding form. A feminine shriek added to the uproar, and a wet cloak flapped about him. Groping for the door, he encountered a second arrival, and another shriek rang out.

He found the door, and shut out the ravening night. The first lady was far from slender, but the second . . . He held his breath.

Mrs. Newlyn gasped, "Let us have some light, Noah, for mercy's sake!"

Holsworth succeeded in waking a flame, and as the candles added their glow to the room, Jonathan's heartbeat eased back to normal.

The second visitor was Tilly Mays. Both women were very wet and wind-blown, and he took their cloaks and drew up chairs for them.

Holsworth righted Duster's cage and asked, "What's to do now?"

"We—we hoped to find Jack here," panted the widow, sinking onto the chair and pressing a hand to her heart. "Oh, what a wild night!"

Holsworth poured two glasses of wine. "This'll warm ye."

The widow sipped gratefully, but Tilly waved the glass away and clutched at Jonathan's arm. "It's—it's Miss Jennifer!" she cried. "I didn't know who else to turn to!" She peered up into his face, then burst into tears.

Suddenly very cold, Jonathan remembered Jennifer's presentiment of trouble. He managed to sound calm. "Please don't cry, Miss Mays. Try and tell us. Is Miss Britewell ill?"

She sobbed out something incoherent.

He looked beseechingly to the widow.

"I might have knowed she'd turn into a watering pot," said Mrs. Newlyn in disgust. "Of course, the seagull told me of it, so I had a notion. Seagulls are more to be heeded than"—she caught Holsworth's glare and said hurriedly— "Lord Green's come back, Johnny. And—"

"And my poor m-mistress," gulped Tilly, "is to—to *wed* him!"

Jonathan stood very still through a quivering stillness in which he could hear nothing but his own heartbeat.

Watching his face, the widow had to look away, and Holsworth swore softly.

In a croak of a voice Jonathan said, "But—she loathes the reptile!"

"Aye," said Tilly. "That she do, sir! Oh, Mr. Jack, I—I'll own I never liked you, nor thought you'd any right to look at my dear lady. And—and I were jealous, 'cause you driv us when my—when Mr. Crane oughta have done. But—oh, sir! She's so changed. So—sort of—froze. I be that scared of what—of what she might . . . do."

Pulling himself together somehow, he said harshly, "She'll refuse, of course! She's past one and twenty. She doesn't have to agree to such a marriage!"

"But—but she *has* agreed, sir!"

At those words a knife of ice seemed to pierce him. Jennifer? And *Green*? He turned away to hide his anguish, and heard himself say, "Then . . . they've forced her! Who? Sir Vinson? Howland?"

"Both, I think, sir. If—if you *knowed* how shocked I was! And her, the dear soul, looking like she'd died, but was still walking!"

Rage came then. Blazing; uncontrollable. *"Damn them!"* he snarled, pounding his fist at the wall. *"Damn them!* That they could *dare!"*

He turned back to face Tilly, and she retreated, frightened by this fierce stranger. "How did Green manage it?" he demanded. She gaped at him, and he seized her by the shoulders. "Tell me, woman! What does he hold over Sir Vinson? First, he gave way on the dock he was so set against! Now, his precious daughter! Why? *Answer me!"*

Tilly gulped, "I—I—"

Holsworth forced Jonathan's hands away. "Stop shouting at the wench! You're scaring her witless!"

Jonathan drew back, staring at her terrified face. He bowed his head and, shoulders hunched over, battling his own terror, he mumbled, "My apologies, Miss Mays. Did she—did she say anything to you? Give you any hint of why she—she agreed?"

"I asked her. Straight out, I did! I said—'*Why*, miss?' And she says, 'I've got no choice, Tilly. And I've give me word.' But her poor heart's broke, I think. She weeps at night, I know that. And Mr. Royce and Mr. Howland got into a terrible fight, sir. Oh, 'twas dreadful! Mr. Howland, he knocked Mr. Royce right down! And Mr. Royce called him—awful words they was, sir, as me poor ears ne'er heard the like of. Then Sir Vinson come, and he takes Mr. Howland's part and quarrels with Mr. Royce something fierce! And the end of it is that Mr. Royce says he's done with the lot of 'em, and takes his horses and his man, and goes riding out!"

"Much good that did!" exclaimed the widow. "Just like a man to run from a sticky sittyation!"

Jonathan asked tersely, "What about Fleming? Didn't he try to help her?"

"Went into the master's study, he did. I dunno what happened there, but he come out so sulky as any bear, and slammed the door of his room and ain't hardly stuck his nose out since."

"Another retreat," growled Jonathan. "She must not be—" He cut the bitter words off, then asked the question he scarcely dared to utter. "Does he ... does Green ... m-maul her? Does he dare to—to—"

Tilly sighed. "He's always touching her, sir. Holding of her hand, and putting his arm around her." A strangled sound escaped Jonathan and he closed his eyes. Tilly said earnestly, "She don't like it, Mr. Jack. Goes so pale, she do. And when he tries to kiss her, she turns her head away, but—"

Mrs. Newlyn nudged her warningly, and Tilly was silent.

Staring blindly at Duster's cage, Jonathan saw instead the delicate features of his love; the great eyes so full of tenderness, the sweet mouth smiling at him, the soft lips parting as she offered her face for his kiss ... And he whispered brokenly, "I cannot bear to think of that . . . lovely, gentle lady . . . in the hands of a crude satyr like Hibbard Green."

Holsworth asked, "What d'you know of the man?"

"I've heard the men talk of the way he treated his first wife. Of his behaviour—with women. Of the horrors that go on in the cells of his damned prison. Jennifer is—is so sweetly innocent and—" His voice was briefly suspended, then he went on, "My dear God! They'd as well have murdered her! She'd know poverty with me, but—with *him* . . . ! She'll be dead inside a year, or—or run mad! How *can* they do so—vile a thing?"

Tormented, he wandered across the room and stood gripping the mantel with both hands, his head bowed between them, while the rest watched in helpless silence.

It was only a minute, but it seemed a very long minute, before he drew a deep shuddering breath. His shoulders squared, and he turned back to them. His eyes glittered in his haggard face. He said with a hushed ferocity, "No! Hibbard Green is without kindness or conscience. They'll not give that pure angel into his hands! Not whilst I'm alive to prevent it!"

Alarmed, Holsworth said, "Now, Jack! Don't talk so silly. How can you prevent it? I know how you feel, lad, nor I don't like it neither. None of us do. But Lord Green's a nobleman, rich and powerful, and with all the force of the law behind him. *And* his hirelings! Sir Vinson and Howland would have your heart out did they suspect you'd dared to so much as look at Miss Jennifer! You haven't got a chance! And even if you had—how could you possibly get away? The village folk are already halfway to thinking you in league with the Evil One, and much as they love Miss Jennifer, there's not a one of 'em as would dare go up agin a baron! The odds are too great, I tell ye! Give over!"

"So I will," said Jonathan between his teeth. "On the day they bury me!"

Prayers were not easy now, but she could pray that when her love heard of her forthcoming marriage he not be driven to some wild attempt to rescue her. Johnny would know this wedding was repugnant to her. He would be frantic with grief, and long to come to her. Kneeling beside her bed, hands reverently clasped, Jennifer smiled sadly. How very dear to be rescued by him. To be snatched up to his saddle bow and carried away to happiness, just as she had dreamed in her girlhood. But that dream could only become a nightmare. Even if he could come near her, which was impossible, there was nothing to be done. If she should escape, Hibbard Green would take his revenge on her family. Yet the prospect of life with him— She shivered convulsively and drove away such dark imaginings, then sent up a passionate prayer for Jonathan and added a humble one that her life as Lady Hibbard Green would be mercifully short.

Standing wearily, she turned and saw him.

He stood just inside the window. Soaked. His hair straggling about his face, his clothes clinging to him as he watched her with a look of mingled love and desperation. It was such a blessed relief to see him. She was in his arms, weeping, laughing, kissing and being kissed; sure that her bones must snap under the wonderful pressure of his arms, but unable to stop kissing him, holding him, sobbing out little broken phrases of love and joy, even as he did. Until, as always it must, came reason to add its sober note to ecstasy.

She drew back from his arms, and in a belated panic demanded, "How did you get in here? Never say you climbed up, and in this storm?"

"Not all the way, my heart. Tilly smuggled me in, but there were men lounging about the halls, and I couldn't get past the first floor, so I climbed from there."

"Good heavens!" She hugged him again. "If you had fallen ... ! But—dearest, you must go. If you were found here, Green would have you killed without a second thought!"

"He'll not find me here. I'm taking you away, my love." His mouth twitched into a sketch of a smile. "Prepare yourself for a life of poverty! Now dress quickly, and—"

"No! You don't understand. I cannot leave, Johnny. Unless I wed him, he'll destroy my family."

He swore under his breath. "I knew that must be the way of it. How?"

"Howland held the bank at his club. He was deep in debt to Green, and he—he used funds that . . ."

"That were not his to use. So now his noble lordship resorts to blackmail to win your beautiful self. That cur! But better Howland should languish in Newgate than—"

"I wish that were all. Howland was desperate to make things right. He—he turned to smuggling. But not tubs, Johnny. Men. He has been carrying fugitive Jacobites over to France. If only it had been done out of compassion, I would be proud, but—it wasn't. And it is treason. He could be hanged."

"And your father dispossessed and ruined—if not hanged with him. I see. That miserable swine has his claws in tight. Even so, lovely one, you'll not pay such a price! Now, I'll own your nightdress is adorable, but I'd rather you were dressed for riding. Hurry and put on your habit."

In the stress of these moments she'd forgotten she wore only the revealing nightdress. Glancing down, she blushed rosily, but when Jonathan strode to fling open the doors of the press, she ran after him. "Dearest, I *cannot* abandon my father! Surely you see that—"

He caught her by the arms and said with low-voiced intensity, "I see that there is no castle, no fortune ever amassed, worth such a sacrifice as your precious self. Your father and brothers can get to France and start again." He saw the glitter of tears in her eyes, and knew what she would say, so he added quickly, "Besides, my beloved, I need your help."

Blinking away tears, she searched his face. "How?"

He tore a riding habit from the press, took up a pair of riding boots, and carried them to the bed while she trotted after him. "I was at the mine this afternoon," he said, turning his back. "And I chanced to see some of the men I'd told you about. And one of them was—even now I can scarce believe it!—he was ship's carpenter of the *Silken*

Princess! Joe Taylor. A man said to have drowned when she foundered!"

"Oh!" Shedding her nightdress, she exclaimed, "How splendid! And you want to talk to him, of course."

"I do indeed! If Taylor's alive, then others may be, also. And even if 'twas a simple error that he was listed among the lost, he can tell me what really happened."

She ran to a drawer and took out a clean camisole. "He will clear you, dearest! I know it! But how can I help?"

"I must get into the mine. They'd never let me in, but the widow told me once that there's another entrance. You likely know of it, and can guide me there."

She was silent. Risking a glance over his shoulder, he saw that she had donned her skirt, but was standing motionless, holding her blouse, and staring at it wide-eyed. The soft lacy lines of her bodice revealed her snowy shoulders and the rich smooth curves of her breasts. He thought she had never looked more beautiful. Somehow, he recollected what he'd been saying, and asked huskily, "Is—is there another way in, love?"

She whispered, "Yes." And then said in a firmer voice, "Yes, of course I'll show you. But—how can we get out of the castle?"

"I'll go back the way I came, and wait for you behind the stables. Do you think you can get downstairs without being seen?"

Putting on her blouse and buttoning her jacket, she said, "I can try. If anyone should stop me, I'll say that one of the villagers is ill, and I must go to help."

"Yes, they'd believe that, you've done it so often." He went to her and touched her cheek tenderly. "My gentle lady."

"Darling Johnny." She turned her cheek against his hand, and as the curtains suddenly billowed inwards, said in swift anxiety, "Please, *please* take care!"

He had every intention of doing so, but the driving wind and rain and the slippery surface of the ancient wall almost proved his undoing. He was halfway to the outward jut of the bastion roof when a great gust slammed against him so that his right hand-hold was lost. His left arm was still weakened from his struggle to haul Lord Green up the cliff, and for a heart-stopping moment it seemed that he was doomed to fall. Then, his clawing fingers caught hold again, and he was reprieved. It was still a dangerous descent, but he reached the bastion roof safely. He could see no sign of guards, the weather having probably driven them inside. He lowered himself over the edge and recovered the lantern he'd hidden in the recess of one of the gun ports.

"Like a confounded fly," drawled a voice behind him.

He could have screamed with frustration. Refusing to be beaten at this stage of the game, he whipped around, crouching, prepared for battle.

"Looks more of a wasp to me," said a second voice. "Ready to sting you, Lord Haughty-Snort, which ain't to be wondered at."

"Confound you!" gasped Jonathan, straightening up. "If I'd held a pistol in my hand . . ."

"The world would be rid of me." August Falcon was a dim shape in the darkness. "But having survived your murderous impulses, I'd as soon not drown. Could we get in out of the rain?"

Jonathan led them to the stables, keeping well clear of the faint light from inside the barn. He saw now that Morris carried the birdcage, and when they were safely under the eaves and in deep shadow, he whispered, "Why did you bring Duster?"

"Hoped to use him as an excuse to see Miss Britewell," said Falcon.

"We found your friend Holsworth," Morris explained. "He told us what had happened. Deuced sorry about your lady."

"With luck, she'll be here at any second." Jonathan's eyes searched the night. "I've got to get her away. You realise."

"I realise you're a fool," said Falcon. "Have you anything sensible to offer?"

Suddenly enraged by this man's perpetual cynicism, Jonathan growled, "I collect that if you'd a lady you cared for, you would deliver her willingly into that bastard's bed!"

"Since there is no lady I care for, the question is pointless." Morris uttered a mocking snort, and Falcon added, "Except for my sister, of course. And if Green looked her way I'd blow his head off. Now, if we must stand here gossiping, at least tell us what you've learned; if anything."

There was still no sign of Jennifer. His nerves tight as he peered fixedly in the direction of the castle, Jonathan gave a brief account of what had happened since he left Breton Ridge.

"By Jove!" exclaimed Morris softly. "So you mean to go into the mine tonight, do you? I'll trot along. Be dashed good sport, eh, Falcon? You've learned a sight more than we did, Jack. We drew a confounded blank at Breton Ridge."

Falcon said thoughtfully, "Oh, I'd not say that, exactly. I wonder why the deuce they're hauling in loads of clothing. You say one of 'em spoke Spanish, Captain?"

Jonathan stiffened.

"Captain?" Intrigued, Morris asked, "What's this?"

"Lieutenant Gudgeon," drawled Falcon. "You're the only man I know who can walk about with his eyes open and see nothing at all! What the devil are you doing with that poor bird?"

"Seems to have fallen off his perch," said Morris, fumbling with the cage. "*Are* you a captain, Jack? What was your regiment?"

Falcon sighed. "If you would cast your decrepit mind back a month or two, you'd know he was a captain for the East India Company. And—no, I'll not tell you what you should have guessed by now. If Jack wanted you to— Damme! *Now* what have you done?"

Morris had opened the door. There was much squawking and a whirr of wings, and Duster was securely attached to Jonathan's shoulder.

"Clumsy clod," grunted Falcon. "I wouldn't—"

Morris interrupted sharply, "Someone's coming!"

Jonathan stepped out from under the eaves. He felt rather

than saw Jennifer's approach, and reached out to her eagerly. "Here, love." Her cold hand slipped into his. He pressed a kiss on it, and murmured a heartfelt, "Thank heaven!"

Breathless, she whispered, "I nigh got caught, and had to hide. Is that Duster?"

"Morris brought him."

"We're both here, ma'am," said Falcon. "Wet, but willing."

"You mean to help Johnny, then? Oh, how splendid of you!"

Jonathan squeezed her hand. "You're all splendid. We'd best get started. I'm glad you wore a cloak, love."

"And I'm glad you brought a lantern. We'll need it. Come—it's this way . . ."

The rain and mud made the four miles seem more like a dozen. They were all breathless and tired by the time Jennifer halted amid a cluster of boulders on the hillside north of the mine, and pointed out the narrow opening between two boulders. " 'Tis a difficult tunnel, and we'll need your lantern now."

Jonathan slipped inside and began to scrape at the tinder box he'd borrowed from Holsworth. "Are we safe in showing a light?"

"Yes. We'll not come to the main workings for a way. This—this was a side tunnel and has long been—abandoned." She shrank back as the lantern sent out a bright beam.

Jonathan brushed away cobwebs, but even with her hand tight clasped in his, it took all Jennifer's resolution to enter the passage. The familiar smell of dank, chill air was in her nostrils, and memory blew its cold breath on her spirit so that she longed to run outside.

Jonathan could feel her trembling. Tilly had said she'd not been sleeping well, and he guessed she must be very tired. He suggested that they rest for a few minutes before going on, and they all sat on the ground, glad of the chance to catch their breath, amused by Duster's antics as he scolded and flapped his wings, sending a shower of rain-water down Jonathan's neck.

They soon went on again, picking their way along the narrow passage. It was littered with rocks and boulders, the roof so low in places that they had to stoop. Jonathan held the lantern in one hand, and kept the other at Jennifer's elbow. After a while they came to a wider passage leading off to the left, and he turned into it. Jennifer pulled him back. "We must stay on the narrow path. That way leads to the sea. Listen."

They halted and, muted by distance, came a deep rhythmic booming.

Morris asked, "Is it another way out, Miss Jennifer?"

She said threadily, "I'd not recommend you take it, Lieutenant. I believe it runs far under ground."

"But how charming," said Falcon. "Why not give it a try, dear dolt?"

Morris chuckled. "He's trying to be rid of me, ma'am. But he'll not succeed. 'Foolish the frog who whips the fog.' "

Falcon mumbled something that appeared to be an impassioned plea for patience in his hour of tribulation.

A moment later they were faced with a real tribulation in the form of a great fall of rock that so blocked the way there was no choice but to climb over.

Jonathan said, "You had best—" He broke off, to catch Jennifer's swaying form and steady her. "How tired you are," he said remorsefully. "Small wonder! Wait here for us."

She gave a little embarrassed laugh. "I'm afraid you've . . . found me out, Johnny. I—I'm quite a coward, and this place— I'd hoped I would be over it by this time."

In belated comprehension, he said, "I knew you'd been hurt in an accident. Never say this is where it happened?"

"We were playing here, which Papa had straitly forbidden. The boys liked to prove how brave they were, and I would not be left at home. I think this is the—the very spot where the roof came down . . ."

He held her close. "Yet you come in here, to help me. My love, how brave you are."

"Pluck to the backbone," agreed Morris. "You're a Trojan, ma'am. Er, if you know what I mean."

Falcon said dryly, "Clumsy as it is, I agree. But Jack's right, ma'am. We'll leave you the lantern and you can rest here."

"You'd never find the way." Pale but determined, she said, "The path divides several times between here and the main entrance, and there are places where the ground drops away into deep crevices. I am very well now."

Nothing would deter her, and at length Jonathan helped her over the pile of boulders while Duster clung to his shoulder and offered a stream of throaty comments.

As she had warned, they had to negotiate a narrow ledge beside a yawning chasm. Here, they were obliged to proceed in single file, Morris holding one of Jennifer's hands and Jonathan the other as they inched along until the danger was past and the passage widened again. After that it twisted and turned and was intersected by other passages leading off to right or left, so that without her sure guidance they would certainly have become lost. Gradually, the tunnel began to slope upwards, and soon they could detect a difference in the air—the smell of cooking and of wood burning.

Morris halted abruptly. "Hold up!"

Falcon muttered, "His sole attribute. Ears like a hawk."

Jonathan felt a quickening excitement. At first it was a distant hum, but gradually, as they crept on, he could hear the mumble of voices and then a louder outburst of jeers and laughter.

He said, "Not one step farther, Miss Britewell! No, I'll hear no arguments. Morris, I daren't leave her alone. Will you guard her for me?"

"Well, I will of course, dear boy," said Morris, clearly disappointed. "But it seems to me that you should be the one to keep at her side."

"The man who can tell me the truth of my past is in

there," said Jonathan grimly. "If 'tis humanly possible, I mean to find him."

Jennifer protested staunchly, but Jonathan pointed out that she was the only one who knew the way out, and they could take no chance she might be hurt. She agreed reluctantly to that wisdom, and he pressed a quick kiss on her hand and left the lantern with Morris before going on with Falcon. The tunnel continued its upward slope. There was a flickering glow on the walls ahead, and the voices became ever clearer. They rounded a bend and were abruptly at the top of a downward slope in full view of a wide open area just inside the main entrance to the mine.

Falcon gasped, " 'Zounds!" and they both leapt back into the shadows.

The glare thrown out by several wall braziers was dazzling. Blinking, as his eyes adjusted to the brightness, Jonathan saw that this central area was very neat and orderly. Rows of blankets and bedding were arranged along one wall. Far across the chamber a larger tunnel yawned, and he could glimpse a stove and shelves crowded with provisions and pots and pans. 'The galley,' he thought. To the right, near the entrance, were racks holding row upon row of muskets, blunderbusses, swords, and other weapons. In the centre, about forty men were gathered at long tables and benches. He was taken aback by their appearance, for here, rather than the fierce soldiers of fortune he had expected to find, were men from all walks of life. Some were clad in rags, some in the humble smocks and gaiters of farm labourers, others wearing the simple dark coats and breeches of clerks and city dwellers. There were several members of the clergy, and a smattering of uniforms, both military and naval.

A well-dressed gentleman of means stood before them, watching a street vendor, who was striding up and down, waving his arms about, apparently harranguing the onlookers.

"We need Morris's ears," whispered Falcon. "Can you make out what they're saying?"

Jonathan shook his head, and they ventured closer, staying close to the wall and trying to keep in the shadows until, gradually, words could be distinguished.

". . . asks yer. One after another of 'em. Plain as the nose on yer face. How long is we to go grinded into the—"

"No, no, *no!*" The well-dressed man began to cuff the performer, while screaming that his stupidity was unsurpassed and that he spoke either too well, or incorrectly. "Will you *never* learn?"

Falcon whispered, "Is a play, then. Though why they'd put on a dress rehearsal in—"

Jonathan's heart gave a painful leap. He gasped, *"Taylor!"* his narrowed eyes fixed on a man dressed as a merchant seaman, with a square, ruddy face, his greying hair pulled back into a short pigtail.

"Hey!" Falcon clutched Jonathan's arm. "Where the deuce are you—"

"I'm going to join the cast. If aught goes amiss, get my lady clear."

"You really are mad! You can't hope to—"

But Jonathan was gone, sauntering down the slope towards the gathering. As he approached the benches, a lean tinker grunted, "Where'd you get that there bird?"

He'd forgotten Duster. He shrugged. "Mr. Bronwys thought it a good touch."

A violent altercation had broken out between the well-dressed man who appeared to direct the "play," and an aggressive individual who declared at the top of his lungs that he couldn't be expected to remember what he was to say when his instructions were changed every day. Others joined in, and under cover of the ensuing uproar Jonathan edged closer to his quarry.

Coming up very close behind him, he gripped his shoulder, and murmured, "You're wanted over here, Joe."

The pigtail jerked around. Taylor's pale eyes bulged, his jaw dropped, and his ruddy face faded to the shade of pastry dough. "C-Cap—" he croaked.

"Quiet!" Jonathan grinned at him while adding grimly, "I've a pistol 'gainst your liver, friend. Move!"

"They said . . . you was . . . dead," stammered the erstwhile ship's carpenter, allowing himself to be propelled along. "Lor', sir. You can't never—"

"Just keep on," said Jonathan, moving steadily away from the brightly lit area. "If you want to live a while longer."

A beefy hand closed on his arm. A red suspicious face thrust at him, and a large baker with a heavy French accent growled, "Who gave you the leave to escape this practice?"

His own hand tightening on Taylor's shoulder, Jonathan replied, "My friend has eaten too much. His stomach protests. Stand clear."

With an apprehensive glance at Taylor's stricken countenance, the baker moved back hurriedly. "You are the fine friend, I think," he said, and lurched off.

Taylor whispered, "Sir, I dunno what you're about. But I want no part of this lot, if you can bring me off."

"Come, then. Up there, out of the light. Not so fast, man. Easy."

They were almost to the slope leading up to the passage where Falcon waited, when the uproar quieted abruptly. A man who looked more like a pirate than the farmer his clothes proclaimed him to be, strolled out of another tunnel offshoot and blocked their way.

"Well, if it ain't his lordship," he muttered.

Glancing around Jonathan saw Hibbard Green coming in at the main entrance, shaking water from his tricorne, and followed by Howland Britewell and the dock foreman, Bronwys. At once all the men were on their feet, crowding around.

Bronwys roared an order for quiet, and his lordship's voice boomed out. "Miss Britewell has been abducted by a sneaking spy who calls himself Crazy Jack! They can't have gone far. A hundred guineas to the man who brings him down!"

Taylor was as if rooted to the spot.

Jonathan shoved him urgently. "Get on, man!"

And in that same instant, Britewell pointed up at them, and shouted. "There he is!"

The piratical farmer jerked his head around, and pulled a

horse pistol from under his smock. Jonathan leapt at him and levelled him with an uppercut, but two more men ran from the same tunnel and joined the attack. Dodging a flying cudgel, Jonathan struck home hard to a midriff, and whirled in time to see Taylor knock down a "clergyman." An almost animal howl rang out. From the corner of his eye he saw men racing at them, pistols clutched in eager hands, knives gleaming, cudgels flourished.

He shouted, "Run for it!" and snatched up the farmer's pistol.

Taylor ran.

"Come *on!*" yelled Falcon.

The staccato roar of a shot sliced through the uproar. Duster emitted an alarmed squawk. Taylor lurched, and staggered. Jonathan came up with them, pulled the man's arm across his shoulder and half-carried him into the tunnel.

Falcon drawled, "A sorry reinforcement, Captain. He'll slow us."

Jonathan thought, 'They're too many, and too close.' He said, "Take him, and get my lady out. I'll hold 'em here!"

"You're well named, Crazy Jack!" Falcon grabbed Taylor's arm. "Come on, then. Whoever you are!"

Jonathan followed them for a short way, and turned to face the attack.

They came at him in a clamouring mass, the flickering light of the braziers shining on faces that reflected the greed inspired by his lordship's "hundred guineas." Jonathan's sole advantage was that they wouldn't be able to crowd into the narrow confines of the tunnel all at once, and they were already jostling one another to be first.

The big fellow wearing a butcher's apron took the lead, pistol aimed. Jonathan fired, the deafening explosion awakening a barrage of echoes from the other tunnels. The butcher howled and went down, causing an instant melée as his comrades rushed, not to help him, but to get past. A muscular chimney sweep was also aiming a pistol, and a tongue of flame stabbed from the muzzle. Jonathan ducked and the ball hummed past his ear, but his boot slipped on the dank floor, and he staggered.

"Got him!" howled the chimney sweep exultantly. "He's mine!"

At this disappointing news the uproar quieted into a brief hush.

Perhaps the reverberations of the gunfire inspired Duster, or perhaps he had some desire to perform also. Whatever the case, he spoke at last, uttering a shrill "Bobby!" that was magnified by the tunnels into a weirdly echoing and re-echoing, "Bobby! . . . Bobby! . . . Bobby!"

The chimney sweep halted abruptly. "Ma?" he cried, peering about in scared bewilderment. "Be that you . . . ? Ma?"

"You're daft," declared another clergyman, trying to shove past.

The chimney sweep threw out his arms, halting the advance. " 'Tis what she allus called me," he declared, quite pale with fright. " 'Twas her voice, I tell ye. Me dear old Mum, and her dead and gone these ten years! She's come back to haunt me fer me wicked ways!"

"Bobby! Bobby!" shrilled Duster, and pleased perhaps by the effect of his debut, he began to flutter about excitedly.

Morris ran up, lantern in hand, the light throwing an elongated shadow of those small wings onto the wall.

The sight finished the chimney sweep. With a sobbing howl he turned back and fought to escape, only to encounter oncoming bounty hunters with less troubled consciences. Tempers flared and confusion reigned.

Morris said, "My tulip, shall we trot?"

❧ *Chapter 14* ☙

There were no longer any sounds of pursuit when they reached the hidden entrance to the mine. Taylor was barely conscious, and Morris, who had half-carried him most of the way, lowered him to the ground. Falcon held the lantern close while Jonathan took off Taylor's bloodied shirt and inspected the injury. He was relieved to find that although the ball appeared to have made a deep score across the man's side, the wound did not look to be of a deadly nature. He fashioned the arm of the shirt into a pad and found Jennifer beside him with a tired, dirty face, but willing hands that were tearing the shirt into strips. Smiling his thanks, he was quick to see the troubled expression in her eyes, and said understandingly, "My dear, this has been very hard on you."

"I'm quite all right. Only . . ."—her hand closed over his—"Johnny, I am so sorry. I'm afraid you have lost Duster."

He darted a glance at his shoulder, realising that he'd not heard the bird's throaty remarks since they'd begun their mad dash to escape. The widow's conversation with the Spirit of the Ocean came into his mind, and he wondered if this was what she'd meant. He felt saddened to have lost his small pet, and muttered, "The poor little fellow must have fallen."

Jennifer leaned to kiss his cheek unashamedly. "Someone will take him up, dear. He is so pretty."

"Aye. If he don't get trampled." Morris looked aghast as Jennifer frowned at him, and he changed the subject hurriedly. "I wonder what our peerless peer is about."

Busied with his first aid, Jonathan said, "They likely all took different branches of the tunnels and have lost themselves. Hold the pad for me, will you Morris? Can you lean 'gainst me, Taylor?"

The injured man propped his head on Jonathan's shoulder as the bandage was wound about him. "Very . . . good 'f you, sir," he mumbled.

"I'm only sorry you were hit. I'm afraid we'll have to move on in a few minutes."

"If this is the price for getting clear o'that lot, it'll be worth it a—a . . . a hundred times over! Captain, I can't tell you how . . . glad I am to—to find you're alive, after all!"

They eased him down again. Holding an obliging finger on the knot of the bandage, Morris asked, "Acquainted with this gentleman, are you?"

Taylor's answer was faint and halting. "That I am, sir. I was ship's carpenter o' the *Silken Princess* when . . . Captain Armitage took her out o' Calcutta, and a finer . . ."

Jonathan had thought he was prepared, but to hear his name after all this time was like a knife slicing through his brain. He groped blindly for the support of the wall. As from a great distance he heard Jennifer's frightened cry, and Morris's voice raised in anxiety, but the past was rushing back, obliterating the here and now.

He was Jonathan Greville Armitage, of London and Hampshire. His father was the world-renowned artist Greville Armitage. His family— He thought, 'My God!'

Falcon said an irritated, "What the devil's wrong with him?"

"Seems to have just found out who he is," explained Morris. "Bit of a shock, I collect. Can't blame him, August. Suppose you'd lost your memory and suddenly found out who you were. Gad! What a blow!"

Jonathan became aware that someone was clinging to his arm. He blinked into Jennifer's concerned eyes, and she said, "My poor dear. Are you better?"

"Heaven be praised, but I am!" He pushed himself away from the wall and bent over Taylor. "We must get on, but I'll have a quick answer. *Was* I drunk throughout that voyage?"

Morris gave a shocked gasp.

Taylor said feebly, "That's what . . ."

"This is no time for post-mortems," said Falcon. "We should—"

Jonathan whirled on him. "Damn you, will you keep quiet! I'll know the truth—*now*! Taylor, *was* I responsible?"

His voice a thread, Taylor whispered, "Not only . . . powerful gents . . . One of 'em . . . Squire, but . . ." He sagged, his voice fading into silence.

"The Squire!" cried Jennifer clasping her hands excitedly. "Isn't that what they call the leader of that horrid League of Jewelled Men?"

"It is, indeed!" exclaimed Morris.

Falcon said, "So the League had their sticky fingers in the pie!"

His question still unanswered, Jonathan muttered, "Then Hibbard Green's part of it! I'll wring his filthy neck."

"Excellent notion," said Falcon. "When we're safe away."

Jonathan said, "Yes. Jennifer, I hate to ask it of you, but you know the area so well. Could you creep around a little outside and see if there are any torches on the moor?"

Morris started to speak, caught Jonathan's look of warning and said nothing. Glad to be of some use, Jennifer went out at once.

Low voiced, Jonathan said, "I'd not told you of it, but she is being forced into marriage with Hibbard Green."

"Good God!" cried Morris. "They ought to be shot!"

Falcon said, "If she has agreed—"

"She has," said Jonathan. "Under the pressure of blackmail. It seems that Green has the power to destroy her family, and she is prepared to sacrifice herself to save them."

"One trusts," drawled Falcon, "you mean to put a stop to such heroic nonsense."

"You may believe I do. They must fend for themselves.

I'm taking her away with me tonight. I'm far from a worthy suitor, but—"

"A blasted cockroach would be a better suitor than that overstuffed atrocity," said Morris.

Falcon said dryly, "You're never likely to receive a finer compliment than that, Captain!"

"Oh, he knows what I mean," said Morris. "Never fear, dear boy. Tummet is waiting for us, and we'll take you both in the coach, with us. Go straight to Breton Ridge. The poor lady will be safe there, for tonight, at least."

Falcon gave a derisive snort. "Safe, my aunt's corset!"

Aiding Taylor to stand, Morris was suddenly very still. In a voice seldom heard, he said, "I'll have an explanation of that remark, sir."

"Why? Are you blind? Your lordly cousin is in this up to his *ton*-ish eyebrows! And I'd not be surprised if that starchy wife of his—"

Morris hissed, "You—*lie!*"

Falcon said silkily, "We'll discuss that remark later."

Jennifer hurried back in to report that there was no sign of searchers on the moor. "The rain has stopped," she said, "but 'tis a sea of mud, and the wind is coming up." She sensed a tension among them, and glanced curiously from the imperturbable Falcon to Morris's unwontedly grim expression.

Jonathan said, "Thank you, m'dear. Then we place ourselves in your capable hands once more. Let's get on!"

Two hours later, Falcon massaged his foot and groaned, "Where in the deuce is Tummet?"

Straining his eyes through the windy darkness, Jonathan answered, "The only lights I see are far off, near the mine."

"Aye," said Morris, yawning. "They're torches. The hunt's up."

They had reached this clump of small trees just south of Castle Triad, and had taken shelter while they waited for Tummet and the carriage. The journey across the moors had been tiring, the wind buffeting them as they'd trudged and slid through waterlogged turf and clinging hampering mud.

Once again, it had been Jennifer's knowledge of the area that had brought them safely through, for several times she'd warned of gullies or bogs hidden by the darkness. Even so, Falcon had drifted too far from the group, and found himself sinking inexorably. It had taken both Morris and Jonathan to drag him clear, and he'd sworn in frustration because both his shoes had been sucked off by the bog. He'd been limping noticeably by the time they reached this spot, but in response to Jennifer's sympathetic enquiry had declared blithely that he was ready to dance the quadrille did she feel so inclined. She had declined the offer and was now cradled in Jonathan's arms, half asleep.

Taylor also was asleep. Morris said, "At least he don't have a ball lodged in him. If we can get him out of this accursed wind, he'll go along well enough, I fancy."

"If Tummet ever comes for us, that is," qualified Falcon.

"We can't wait long," said Jonathan. "They'll surely hunt us down within an hour or so, and I'd not give much for our chances."

Falcon nodded. "Very true. They'll not dare let us live. You realise what they're about, Captain Jack?"

"Mercenaries, I'd guess. Brought here to be trained and equipped, then sent out to mingle with the populace."

Morris asked, "For what purpose? Robbery? Spying?"

"Probably," said Falcon. "But more, I'd guess. You've not been in Town of late, Armitage. There's unrest everywhere. Malcontents playing on the public mind, losing no opportunity to cast slurs on the aristocracy and those in power. I'd not be surprised was the League behind most of it."

"Be dashed if you ain't in the right of it," agreed Morris, forgetting he was not speaking to Falcon. "Only a week or two since, I was set upon by a mob of varmints, who nigh—"

Jonathan interrupted, "Your pardon, Jamie. But we cannot wait any longer. I've got to get Miss Britewell away."

"If you mean to appropriate some of her father's ponies, I'm with you, dear boy."

Falcon said dryly, "And you'd be with him when they

rode you down. You're not in Kent now. It's a hell of a ride before you'd reach anyone willing to help. Chances are they'd come up with you miles from anywhere. I doubt you'd ever be seen again."

"I agree. Our best escape route is by sea." The idea had been hovering on the fringes of Jonathan's mind since they'd left the mine. But even now, the thought of venturing on the ocean again brought a chilling fear, and he was grateful that his voice hadn't betrayed him.

Morris said dubiously, "Could we find a boat?"

"There's one ready and waiting, can we but get to it."

Falcon gave a sudden snort of laughter. "You villain! You mean to steal Green's schooner!"

Jonathan smiled grimly and touched Jennifer's cold cheek. "Wake up, brave one. We've to be on our way again."

She blinked up at him, then sat straight and said apologetically, "Oh! I have delayed you!"

"No such thing. But we need our infallible guide to tell us how we may get down to the beach without being stopped."

"There is no other way than those you know of. But—why the beach? If you need horses, I will get you mounts."

"Horses won't serve, I'm afraid. And you go with us."

Distressed, she said, "But I must go home first! I cannot leave my family without a word of farewell!"

"Hibbard Green has put out the word that I've abducted you. We believe that the men he's gathered at the Blue Rose are trained to go about London promoting uprisings and sedition. He very likely thinks that you are aware of what is going on. And—I'm sorry, my love, but I think your father is also aware."

Horrified, she exclaimed, "No, no! Papa would never act 'gainst England! Howland might have sold passage to some unfortunate Jacobite gentlemen, but he wouldn't—"

"Howland was in the mine with Green tonight," he interposed. "If you go home, Jennifer, you'll be trapped and never know another free moment for so long as you live. I won't have that. If you've relations you can stay with, we'll take you there. If not, I've friends and family who will care for you." She gave a muffled sob, and he hugged her briefly as he assisted her to her feet. "It's hard, I know, but you must leave with me. Now."

Morris helped Taylor up. "Off we go! From treason to piracy on the high seas! Faith, but 'tis a busy life we lead!"

It was very late now, and there was no one about. As they approached the cliffs, they could discern the running lights of a vessel far out across the sands, and the loom of the new dock, dim seen when the moon threw occasional shafts of silver through the scurrying clouds.

Morris said sharply, "Someone's creeping about! See there!"

A faint London voice called, "That you . . . Guv?"

"Tummet!" Falcon hobbled to bend over the kneeling figure of his unorthodox valet, and say anxiously, "If you mean to expire, pray do not. Rossiter is sure to blame me!"

"I ain't meaning to . . . turn up me toes," gasped Tummet. "Just run . . . coupla 'undred miles . . . is all. Don't think as I can get on me stampers fer a bit, mate."

Reassured, Falcon grumbled, "I collect you've lost the coach."

"Not the way you think. When you didn't come, I left the team in the bushes, and—and I crept round the stables wiv me ear 'oles on the stretch. Two coves rid in . . . all of a garden-gate—Er, I mean—"

"Yes, I know what you mean, and we don't need your rhyming cant just now so try to speak plain English. What were they in a state about?"

"They said as the gent wiv the evil eyes"—there was a breathy laugh—"meaning you, guv—and Crazy Jack, 'ad stole Miss Britewell, and that 'is lordship Green 'ad yer trapped in the mine. Proper uproar there was. So I gets the coach and drives 'ell fer leather to that there new mine road. Only in the dark I lost me bearings a bit, and finished up by that big fella's 'ouse."

"Holsworth?" asked Jonathan.

"Ar, one arm 'e got. Some of the cliff's fallen dahn where that little stream goes over the edge. I didn't see it till the nags starts rearing up. I got throwed out, and the team bolted, and there I was—wallering in mud like any 'og!"

Falcon said, "So you ran all the way back to tell me you lost the team, did you?"

"In—in a manner o' speaking, Guv. They've all gorn daft in that there village. Some men come outta the mine yelling that you and Crazy Jack 'ad turned yerselves into birds, and flew orf wiv Miss Jennifer!"

"Idiots!" snorted Falcon.

"True," said Morris. "They're part of 'the herd of such, who think too little and talk too much.' "

Falcon groaned.

Tummet said, "That's as may be, Lieutenant. But 'is lordship's got 'em proper stirred up, and says as that nice little widder lady's in league wiv you, and that you're *all* in league wiv Old Nick!"

"Good heavens!" cried Jennifer. "Look there! Someone's house must be on fire!"

"It ain't no 'ouse, miss," said Tummet. "It's why I run. I knowed as you'd want it stopped. They've got the little widder, Guv. They're set on burning 'er for a witch!"

Jonathan ran steadily, spurred on by the ever brightening leap of flames against the night sky and by the terrible howling voice of a mindless mob. His weariness was forgotten now, blotted out by the fear that he might already be too late. He'd left Tummet to guard Jennifer and Taylor, having first extracted a promise from his lady that she would not go to the castle, and that if he was unable to return, she would seek out his father in London. He wondered if Falcon and Morris were still following. If he was alone, so be it. The responsibility was his. He owed his life to the good-hearted little widow, who was no more a witch than his own dear mother had been. His prayer was that Noah would protect her. If he was able . . .

Thanks to Tummet, he was on the lookout for the landslide, and when he came near to Holsworth's cottage, he was able to jump the wider gap above Devil's Ladder. His boots were caked with mud however, and skidded out from under him, so that he fell and then slid for several yards. He could see the crowd now, and gave a gasp of relief because the flames were from the burning brands they flourished, and not from the pile of wood that had been gathered about a pole in front of the tavern.

He picked himself up, panting, and clutching at his side, and heard someone call his name. Holsworth was fast bound to the signpost outside Gundred's shop. Hauling out his pocket knife, Jonathan went to him and started to slash feverishly at the ropes.

Holsworth half-sobbed, "I prayed as ye'd come, Jack! I knew you'd feel ye owed the poor soul. I tried . . . I *tried* to stop 'em, but they're too many, and gone blood mad, besides! They took my hook off, and—and they said I'd be lucky if I didn't burn with her! Folks I've known all my life, Jack! Friends, I thought! Can ye not get it, man?"

"This damned knife is blunt, but I'll cut through. Is the widow harmed?"

"Not bad, I think. They stoned her when she tried to run away. You—you know what that's like, eh?"

Jonathan's lips tightened. He did indeed know. He said, "You warned me it might come to this."

"Aye, but I don't think I believed it me own self. And likely it'd have been no more'n a few rocks throwed, but Lord Green come and opened the tavern and there was free ale and rum fer every man. And him and that shifty-eyed Silas of his and a crowd of ugly customers I never saw before starts whipping folks up! And now they mean to—"

Jonathan cut through the ropes at last, and Noah gasped a fervent, "Thank the good Lord! My feet, Jack! Make haste! They're bringing her, poor little soul! She looks half dead already!"

Jonathan jerked his head around and caught a glimpse of Mrs. Newlyn. Her cap was gone, her wild hair wilder yet, and there was blood on her white terrified face. Hibbard Green's manservant, and Wally Pughill, his face flushed with drink, were dragging her along. All about her were shouting, angry men, and excited wide-eyed boys, caught up in the unthinking, inhuman lusting that is mob violence.

Jonathan groaned a curse and tore at the knotted ropes about Holsworth's ankles.

"They're binding her to the stake," groaned Holsworth. "And 'tis my wood they've stole! Using my own wood to murder that—that dear, good woman! My God in heaven, listen to them howl! What use a thousand years of civilisation?"

'Very little,' thought Jonathan. 'At best a paper-thin veneer over savagery!' And he said, "There! Can you walk?"

Holsworth took a step, then reeled and clung to him, but said, "How can we make 'em see reason?"

"They're far past reasoning with. We must fight fire with fire. Do you get in the tavern. Set it alight. That'll cause more confusion and I'll try to get her free."

Holsworth went weaving off. The crowd was gathered about the stake. Praying that the little woman would not die of fright, Jonathan circled around to the back of Gundred's shop, coming up along the far side. The shop was empty. He ran in, snatched a dagger from a rack of weapons, and raced out again as a new outcry went up.

Hibbard Green stood before the stake holding a burning brand high. "Confess your sins, witch," he boomed. "Admit that you and the evil man we called Crazy Jack were sent by your master, the devil, to capture Miss Britewell, and drag her into hell with you!"

The widow's reddened frantic eyes were fixed on the brand he held. "It's not true," she sobbed. "I'm no witch, I swear it!"

Howls and catcalls greeted her words, stones flew, and the poor woman shrank and begged piteously for mercy.

"Confess!" roared Green. "Do you wish to die with the weight of guilt on your immortal soul? Name your conspirator before we send you to meet your master!"

"I've done—nothing wrong," she wailed. "Nor has Jack, and—" Her words ended in a shrill scream as Green thrust the torch into the wood pile.

There was a sudden silence.

Jonathan edged nearer, rage in his heart. "Hurry, Noah!" he breathed. "For the love of—"

"*Fire! Fire!* The tavern's ablaze!"

That dread howl knifed through the hush, and the attention of the crowd shifted. Perhaps many were glad not to have to watch the widow's agony. Perhaps their consciences shrank from what they had done. Whatever the cause, there was a renewed hubbub as some raced for water barrels and buckets, and others ran inside the burning tavern to salvage what they might.

Jonathan ran up behind the stake. The flames were higher at the front, and he was able to slash the ropes quickly with the razor-sharp dagger he'd appropriated. "Courage, ma'am," he said softly. "It's Jack, and Noah's here to help you."

He couldn't tell if she answered, but her frenzied struggles ceased. Seizing her by the arm, he whipped her back to him. Holsworth raced up and beat at the smouldering hem of her gown.

Hibbard Green had not left the pyre however, and his great voice howled, "The looby's here! Get him! Get him!"

"Run!" shouted Jonathan.

Noah and the widow fled into the night. Jonathan saw Green bearing down on him, his fleshy face contorted into a mask of hatred. This was one of the men whose schemes had destroyed a fine ship and many lives; who had ruined him, and doomed him to a long hell of shame and suffering that had almost cost him his reason. And this beast had dared—had *dared* to lust after the peerless Jennifer! The urge for self-preservation was swept away by a primitive fury. With an inarticulate growl, he sprang forward.

Expecting Jonathan to run for his life, his lordship was startled, and drew back instinctively, then flailed the brand he held. Jonathan smashed it aside and drove his right fist savagely at the flabby jaw. Green yelled and reeled back, but he was no coward, and his ham-like left shot out. Ducking it, Jonathan bored in again, aiming one powerful blow after another so effectively that Green fell back and strove to cover his face. Exultant, Jonathan sent a right jab at the bloated midriff with all his strength behind it. Green gulped and his eyes started from his head. Leaping for the throat, Jonathan heard enraged shouts behind him. A cudgel was whipping at his head, with Silas's grinning face behind it. He flung up his arm and diverted the blow that would certainly have brained him, but the shock sent splinters of pain from wrist to shoulder, and his arm fell helplessly.

He thought, 'Blast! It's broken!' then was gasping in anguish as ruthless hands seized him, forcing him to his knees.

Blurrily, he saw Green tottering towards him, supported by Silas and another bully. Almost incoherent with rage, his lips bloodied, one eye blackened, and a tooth conspicuous by its absence, Green choked out, "You—damnable—spy! Rossiter sent you here—own it!"

Jonathan looked up at Death, and smiled. "Yes," he lied. "They know about your traitorous conniv—"

Green uttered a gobbling snort of fury, and kicked out. Jonathan doubled up and hung on the hands of his captors, blinded, deaf, sobbing for breath. They were hauling him up. Flames were very near, but he was conscious of little but pain, and voices came to him echoingly.

"Burn him!"

"Where's the witch?"

"She can burn later! We'll get her! Onto the fire with him!"

Heat, and rough hands. His left arm was most assuredly broken . . . Jennifer, my love, my own . . . God keep—

"*Stop! Stop!* I am here—do you not see? Nobody kidnapped me!"

The dearest voice in the world . . . she had come to him! . . . Why hadn't Falcon and Morris kept her away? This monster would be as like to order her death as his own! Trying to see clearly, aware that the cruel hands had eased somewhat, Jonathan peered about. She stood facing that angry mob, straight and tall and proud, her face smeared with mud, her garments torn, her hair hanging in wet clumps, yet beautiful still in the flickering glow of the flames.

The crowd had quieted. Someone exclaimed, "She's here! Miss Jennifer's safe!"

She cried ringingly, "I'm safe because Jack saved me from—"

Green bellowed, "She's bewitched!"

Wally Pughill shouted, "She's been ill-wished!"

"The woman's possessed," howled Silas.

Jennifer stretched out her hands. "Don't listen to them. Lord Green does not mean to restore the mine, but—"

"She wants to stop me restoring the mine," roared Green. "She wants to deny you all the chance for a decent life again! She's as evil as he is! To the fire with both of 'em!"

But he had reckoned without the loyalty of Cornish folk to their own. He offered hope to those who had lost all hope, but it was a hope they'd not seize at such a cost. This was the gentle lady who had brought them jellies and broths when sickness came, whose kindness was legendary, who had tried to teach their children. Muttering, they drew back.

Jonathan shouted, "Miss Jennifer speaks truth. Let me up!"

Green blustered and threatened, but Pughill was silent now, and Blary allowed Jonathan to get to his feet. He cried unevenly, "There's no . . . tin in the mine! Green has brought his own men to—"

"Enough!" boomed his lordship, and with a wave of his arm brought his own men to move eagerly towards Jonathan.

A woman screamed, "*Look!* See there! The Lady! 'Tis the *Lady!*"

All heads turned. And there, on the very edge of the cliff some half mile northward, stood a tall graceful figure lit by an eerie glow, and wearing a hooded blue cloak.

Cries of fear and dismay rang out. Cold fingers crept down Jonathan's spine as he blinked at that distant unearthly figure. Jennifer slipped to his side. He put his good arm around her and edged back from the flames as a wild confusion erupted. Everyone seemed to be shouting at once. Panicked villagers crossed themselves and sank to their knees; boys raced about wildly, suddenly discovering an urgent need for the protection of their fathers; the mercenaries, bewildered, strove to control the crowd; his lordship, momentarily stunned and having his fair share of superstition, gawked at the distant Lady, his unlovely jaw sagging.

Jonathan drew his love back and back, urging her to run. His own effort was at best a halting stagger. Her arm tight about him, she said, "My darling, you're hurt! You can't get far!"

"I've a chance now, thanks to you," he gasped. "Go on—I'll catch up."

"You waste your breath. Come, try harder!"

Green's bellow came to them. "*Find* them! A hundred guineas to the ones that catch them!"

"That stupid hundred guineas," Jonathan muttered, and he pleaded, "I'll hide here. You fetch Falcon and Morris—they're—"

Her eyes were clearer than his now. She said, "Too late, dear. He has called down more men. They're all about the village. I can see their torches far past Bridget Bay."

He groaned his helplessness, then tensed as Holsworth's voice hissed, "Jack! Over here, man!"

Together, they tottered to the door of the cottage. Holsworth ushered them inside, a blunderbuss hooked over his right arm, and his hook restored to his left. With a keen look at Jonathan, he said, "Brandy, Widder. He's far spent."

Mrs. Newlyn, white-faced and trembling, hurried to them. Despite himself a cry escaped Jonathan as she took his arm. She ran for the brandy, and said, distressed, "My poor Jack, who came so bravely to rescue me. The arm's broke, Noah."

Apprehensive, Jennifer exclaimed, "Oh, no! Are you sure?"

Holsworth pulled up a chair and pushed Jonathan into it. "Never be pitying him, Miss Jennifer. Had he not charged Green, like a fool, he might have got clean away!"

Gasping to the bite of the potent brandy, Jonathan said, "It was—worth it! I knocked out one of the brute's fangs!"

"For which ye're now more crippled than me, when your lady needs all your strength!"

"No, pray don't scold him, Mr. Holsworth," said Jennifer. "I'd not have him changed one whit."

Jonathan said fervently, "You're the bravest girl in the whole world. But—oh, my dear, how I wish you'd not come."

Mrs. Newlyn called from the window, "They're almost here, Noah!"

Jonathan dragged himself to his feet. "Have you any weapons for me?"

"Never mind that. With luck and the grace of God, ye'll not need 'em. Come!" Holsworth led them into his seldom used front parlour, pulled back the threadbare rug in front of the fireplace, inserted his hook into a decorative brass ring on the fender that edged the hearth, and tugged mightily. The entire outer area of the hearth folded back against the grate, disclosing narrow steps leading down into a cellar.

Handing a candlestick to Jennifer, Holsworth waved them down. Jonathan lifted his left arm, and sweating with pain guided the useless hand into the front of his coat, then followed the ladies. It was a spacious cellar, full of barrels and kegs that were stacked neatly around the walls.

"I should have guessed!" muttered Jonathan.

Holsworth was lowering the trap, and arranging the rug carefully as it closed. "We'll hope they think I'm a poor housekeeper," he grunted.

"What you are," Jonathan accused softly, "is a confounded free-trader! I wondered how you were able to live so well and buy all your supplies and tools."

Unrepentant, the big man said with a grin, "Aye, well the Trade has been good to—"

Jennifer gestured urgently, and blew out the candle. Scarcely daring to breathe, they waited. Jennifer stood very close to Jonathan, and his good arm went around her.

There came the crash of the front door being kicked in, much shouting and thumping about of boots, glassware and china being smashed.

"Your lovely French chiney," whispered the widow sadly.

"May they rot!" growled Holsworth.

Jonathan prayed that Green not decide to burn the cottage.

A loud voice said, *"Il n'y a personne!"*

Mrs. Newlyn whispered, "What'd he say?"

"There's nobody in," translated Jennifer.

An exultant shout announced that the bottle of brandy had been discovered. In no time they were quarrelling over it. The beleaguered little group strained their ears, and heaved a collective sigh of relief when the boots went stamping off.

After a period of quiet, Holsworth crept up the steps, and raised the trap very slowly. "They've gone!"

They climbed into the shambles left by the mercenaries. Jonathan crossed to the front door and opened it a crack. He could hear angry voices from the village. The torches were moving from house to house. Slipping into the night, he saw a line of flickering lights at regular intervals, ringing the village from north to south and blocking off the path that led down to the beach.

Borne on the rising wind came Green's familiar bellow. "Someone here is hiding them! Speak up, or we'll burn your damned village, a house at a time!"

It was the thing Jonathan had feared. He went quickly back inside. "You heard?"

Noah said, "Aye. We're fairly trapped. The cellar won't save us if they burn the house down."

The widow said in a quavering voice, "Might we not creep out the back and up to the moors?"

"I'm afraid they expect that," said Jonathan. "They've ringed the village with men and torches. We'd not get a mile. Our only hope is to make our way to the beach."

"D'ye mean to fight our way through to the path?" asked Holsworth. "Small chance, Jack, but—" He ran to the window as screams pierced the night. Peering out, he exclaimed, "Lord above! There's three cottages ablaze! All right, let's try for the steps!"

Jonathan said curtly, "Pointless. We'd never reach them. We must go down the cliff." He heard their shocked gasps and went on, " 'Tis a desperate chance, and we'll likely all be killed. But if we stay here, we'll die by fire."

Holsworth stammered, "Are ye gone d-demented? *I* couldn't climb down that stone face! How on earth can you expect the ladies to attempt such a feat?"

"We're not going to climb. We're going to ride your ark down, Noah."

Silence.

He thought, 'They think I'm really crazy,' and went on, "I know it sounds mad, but I saw it done once in India. There's mud everywhere; exceeding slippery mud. And the storm has torn away a section of the cliff under the waterfall. If we can push the ark that far, she might slide down."

Holsworth exclaimed indignantly, "And break all our necks!"

"Very well. Show me a better way."

Gripping her hands nervously, Jennifer said, "I'd sooner take the chance than die here."

"S-so would I," gulped the widow.

Holsworth argued, "But—they'll *see* us!"

"The men in Roselley may not," said Jonathan. "They'll be dazzled by their fires. The guards around the village likely will, but they'll take a few minutes to get here through the mud, and by that time, God willing . . ."

A minute later they were all out in the windy darkness. To the south, the sky pulsed red with leaping flames, the glow illumining the enraged and heartsick villagers who were held at bay by the blunderbusses and muskets of Green's hirelings.

His lordship's bellow reached them. "They're in that stupid schoolhouse, I'll wager! Fire it next!"

Jonathan murmured, "Thank heaven we put her up on the platform, Noah! Let's see if the wheels will turn in this muck."

Hampered by his injured arm, he managed to push at the platform, while Noah hauled the thick ropes at the bow, but although both men strove with all their might, the ark moved not an inch. Jennifer and Mrs. Newlyn ran to help. From the corner of his eye, Jonathan saw several distant torches begin to wave frantically. Gritting his teeth, he exerted every ounce of his strength, and heard Jennifer's gasping little grunts as she strove beside him.

And then, with a sudden lurch, the ark was moving.

"Alleluia!" gasped Jonathan, and as a gust staggered them, added, "Oh, for a sail!"

But they had no need of a sail. Once started, the wheels turned fairly easily, and the unwieldy ark bumped and swayed and moved towards the break in the cliff down which the little stream still flowed.

A howl rang out behind them, followed by the crack of a musket.

"We're seen!" panted Holsworth.

"Out—of range," gasped Jonathan. "Pull, Noah!"

And after a second, "She's sloping down," Holsworth screamed. "Get in quick, or she'll go over without us!"

Jonathan all but thrust Jennifer into the teetering ark. Holsworth ran to assist Mrs. Newlyn, and Jonathan handed her up, gave her plump derriere an unceremonious shove, then clambered in after her.

The ark lurched, tilted, and left the platform behind. Noah's hook shot over the side. Jonathan grabbed his arm and heaved, and head-first the big man tumbled in. The ark slid and bumped and skidded down the shallow track the water had worn year after year in its journey to the beach. The occupants were tossed about helplessly. Jonathan fought to protect Jennifer, and she clung to him, trying to shield him also.

It sounded as if the ark was being battered to pieces. Expecting it to turn over at any second, or to crash against some outcropping and hurl them all to their deaths, Jonathan had the sudden eerie sense that they were no longer in contact with a solid surface, but flying through the air. The next instant they crashed down again with a force that sent them all tumbling. Jennifer was torn from his grasp. He heard her scream, and then he was hurled against the side and into forgetfulness.

❧ *Chapter 15* ❧

Something was tickling Jennifer's cheek. She thought it should be removed, and heard her name spoken in a prayerful sob. It came to her that she lay with her head in Johnny's lap, and she enquired with mild indignation, "Why do you allow a little crab to walk about on my face?"

"Thank heaven!" he gulped, sending the small crab about its business. "I have never been . . . so afraid! My—Jennifer, I—I cannot lift you. Are you much hurt?"

She considered that, and replied that she was sure she must be one large bruise. Full awareness returned then, and she sat up and looked about her. They were on the beach, the ark lying on its side, battered, but far from demolished. Awed, she said, "We are alive? I cannot believe it! My poor dear—how is your arm?"

He was sure it was damaged beyond repair, but said in a steadier voice that it was not as bad as he'd expected.

Holsworth hurried to them, the widow on his arm. Peering at Jonathan, he thrust a flask at him. "Take a good swig, Jack. Ye likely have the need." His voice was muffled, and he was limping markedly. He told them he'd suffered a broken nose and a wrenched knee. Mrs. Newlyn was obviously much shaken, and said she was sore all over, but insisted she had taken no serious hurt, and was only grateful that they all were alive.

"If we hope to stay alive," said Jonathan, feeling stronger as he returned the flask, "we must get on!"

Holsworth explained as they hobbled along the beach that they'd been so fortunate as to end their journey in a tidal pool. "I think you won't recall, Johnny, but the ark ploughed through the water which eased our—er, arrival before she foundered." Glancing back at the wreckage, he laughed. "She was a good ship, Johnny man!"

"Good!" said Jonathan. "She was superb! I can scarce believe she . . . still . . ." He gave a gasp and stopped speaking, his eyes very wide as he gazed at the tall cloaked figure that was moving toward them.

Holsworth whipped his head around, yelped, and crossed himself. Jennifer uttered a faint shocked cry, and the widow started babbling muddled incantations.

A familiar voice drawled, "There's nought like an impressive entrance."

Incredulous, Jonathan exclaimed, "Falcon? How—on earth . . . ?"

Morris came up. "Who's dead?"

Falcon said, "Impossible as it seems, I think they survived their suicidal jaunt. Did you find a boat?"

"There's one tied up at the dock," Morris answered. "The tide's going out, but we'll be able to use it, if we hasten."

The battered little group hastened as best they might, and Falcon said, "I hope you can row, Armitage. Be damned if I can."

Jennifer said, "His arm's broken."

"Poor planning," sighed Falcon.

The irrepressible Morris suggested, "We could ask dear old Hibbard. D'you suppose—?"

They all laughed, and nobody mentioned the line of torches moving rapidly along the top of the cliffs towards the castle steps, or the second line to the south of them where Green's bullies were coming down the cliff path.

Later, Jonathan had no very clear recollection of their journey, save for the peculiar circumstance of the moon shining up at him. He realised after a puzzled interval that the moonlight was reflecting in the tidal pools. This seemed hilarious, and his arm wasn't so horribly painful now. 'I must,' he thought contentedly, 'be very drunk.'

They were on the dock, and then he was sitting in a large rowing boat beside Joe Taylor. Morris was at one oar, and Falcon's unorthodox valet, Tummet, had materialised from somewhere and was manning the other.

Jonathan crooned softly,

> *"Oh, when I was a sailor,*
> *a sailor, a sailor.*
> *Oh when I was a sailor*
> *A jolly life had we!*
> *What with rum at sea*
> *And gin on the shore*
> *Little cared I*
> *If I seldom had—"*

A hand was clapped over his mouth.

Morris gave a snort of mirth.

Falcon said sternly, "He's properly lushy! You were fools to fill him with brandy."

Holsworth said, "If ye'd seen his arm—"

From out of the darkness a voice hailed: *"Wie is daar?"*

Morris whispered, "Save us all! Dutch now!"

Falcon dashed an icy wet handkerchief at Jonathan's face and shouted, "Captain Jonathan Armitage of His Majesty's Royal Navy, and troops following. Prepare for boarding party!"

Jonathan shook the cobwebs from his brain and heard someone exclaim a dismayed *"Maledictions!"* followed by a flurry of agitated chatter.

Falcon hissed, "Are you sober, Armitage? You'll have to bluff this."

"I'm—almos' sober," said Jonathan, striving. "Has anyone a letter? A notice? Something written?"

They came alongside to the accompaniment of a good deal of commotion aboard the vessel.

Falcon handed him a folded paper. "I've this letter is all."

"It'll have to—serve. With luck they cannot read English."

Jennifer said softly, "They do not lower a ladder."

"And I'm not waiting," said Morris. "Row along to the anchor chain."

The boat slid along. When the anchor was reached, Holsworth took the oar, and Morris seized the chain and was up it, hand over hand.

On the ship, a man was howling for the sails officer to come and deal with "some pig of an English officer, with his men most fast coming!"

Falcon followed Morris and seconds later a rope ladder was slung over the side.

Morris grinned down at them and called cheerfully, "All aboard!"

Tummet helped Jonathan to the rungs. "You'd best go first, sir."

The climb was another challenge, but he was over the rail at last, and facing a small Frenchman who came running while pulling on a coat and with a stocking cap all askew on his mop of dark hair.

"You—off my *capitaine*'s vessel will go!" he screamed, his face red with anger. "Where your uniform is? You 'ave ze look of ze officer naval—*jamais*! Depart!"

"Silence!" Jonathan thrust Falcon's letter at him, and by the light of the lamp which a very dishevelled and unshaven sailor brought, he saw it was the note that had been in Falcon's book at Breton Ridge. "As you see," he said in the loud voice of authority, " 'Tis an order demanding instant cooperation of all ship's masters sailing British waters. You will note the royal signature—'G'."

The international crew members peered uneasily at the letter. Behind them, Morris grinned broadly. Very conscious of the torches and muffled shouts that drew ever nearer, Jonathan noted that Taylor was aboard, leaning against the rail, and that Jennifer was helping Mrs. Newlyn, with Tummet following, carrying the birdcage.

"Enough!" He snatched the letter, and said in French, "You will at once up-anchor and—"

Half a dozen men ran along the deck, brandishing weapons. A seaman crept up behind Morris, knife upraised to strike. Falcon sprang to push Morris aside. The razor sharp blade that would have plunged into Morris' back slashed through his own coat. He caught the flying wrist, pulled hard, and with a cross-buttock twist sent the would-be assassin flying over the rail.

Simultaneously, Holsworth whipped his hook about the throat of the small Frenchman and held him goggle-eyed and powerless.

Tummet levelled the birdcage as though it had been a blunderbuss and roared, "In the King's name!" and the muscular seaman running at him with cudgel upraised, halted, staring in confusion at this strange weapon.

Shots rang out from the dock. Waving recklessly at that murderous fire, Jonathan howled, "Boarding party! Advance!"

What they could have been expected to advance in, had there been a "boarding party," was debatable, but the crew of this illegal vessel did not stay to argue the point. As one man, they abandoned ship.

The victors sent up a ragged cheer.

Holsworth's captive cried, "Me, I 'ave surrender, *mon capitaine*! I am ze prisoner of ze war!"

Falcon panted, "Well, we've pirated her! Now what do we do with her?"

Exhausted, in considerable pain, but elated, Crazy Jack said, "We sail her, friend! We sail her!"

August Falcon opened the door to the *capitaine*'s cabin, then stood aside as the widow came out carrying a torn sheet and the remains of the mop handle they'd utilised for splints.

"How does he go along?" enquired Falcon.

She shrugged her plump shoulders. " 'Twas hard on the lad, but he's full of pluck."

"It looked more than a trifle ghastly. Will he lose the arm?"

"With myself tending him? He will not! Though," she

muttered limping away stiffly, "I'd have gone on better with some rhubarb and a black cat."

Falcon stared after her.

She turned and waved the sheet in his face. "Tomorrow, I'll use this to try and clean that cupboard they call a kitchen! If ever I saw such a filthy lot! And let him rest— he's worn to a shade!"

"Er—yes," said Falcon and went inside.

Jonathan lay on the bunk looking exhausted. Morris was at the low cupboards that lined one side of the cluttered cabin, pouring rum into a chipped mug. He glanced around as Falcon entered, and said, "Good thing you've come. He wouldn't take any of this till—"

Jonathan sat up. His arm ached wretchedly and he felt considerably wrung out, but he asked, "Did that fellow Armand follow my orders? Who's watching him? I'd not trust—"

"Peace, peace, *mon capitaine*." Falcon drew up one of the crude chairs and dusted it with his handkerchief before lowering his muddied person onto it. "The Frenchy seems eager to please, now he's turned cat-in-pan and decided to work for us. Tummet is watching him with the aid of a blunderbuss, for the time being. Not for long, I fancy. Already he's looking greenish about the gills, and if it blows, we'll have him at the rail all night. He's a poor sailor."

"Not the only one," said Morris, handing Jonathan the mug.

Falcon sighed. "I do not love an ocean voyage, I'll own."

Jonathan took a healthy swallow of the rum, and coughed. "What about Miss Jennifer?" he croaked.

Morris said, "She was fast asleep when I laid her on the bunk. It ain't the cleanest of cabins, but I think 'tis a bit less redolent of spirits than this hovel."

Falcon drawled, "The poor lady is properly compromised, you know."

"I do," Jonathan said. "You must know it was my intention to make her my wife, but . . ." He shrugged and didn't finish the sentence.

Morris handed a mug to Falcon, kept one for himself,

and carried over a plate of some chunks of cheese and broken biscuits. Removing Duster from Jonathan's shoulder, he sat on the end of the bunk and offered the bird a crumb of cheese.

Duster recoiled in disgust, and fluttered back to Jonathan.

Morris shook a finger at him. "Your master needs his sleep, you stubborn ingrate."

Fighting that need, Jonathan said, "First, I'll know what it is that you keep from me." They exchanged a quick glance, and he went on with a trace of impatience, "When first I met Mr.—ah, September, I'd a fleeting impression of familiarity, and you, Falcon, were sure you knew me."

Falcon inspected the contents of his mug.

"I believe," Jonathan went on, "that 'twas your name and—er, reputation I knew. I cannot recall that we ever actually met. Yet you knew me—or knew of me. The truth, if you please." He saw Morris's troubled expression and added, "I'm not a child, Jamie. If a price has been set on my head, or some such thing, I will not fall into a decline." He gave a wry smile. "I am no stranger to disgrace."

Morris said unhappily, "The fact is, we could neither of us think where we'd met you. Which was logical because—we hadn't. We recognised you—or Falcon did first, of course—by the er, strong family resemblance."

Jonathan jerked forward, then winced and cradled his arm painfully. "Do you say you are acquaint with my family? Are they well?" and still disturbed by the widow's conversation with the Spirit of the Ocean, he asked, "Is my dear father—"

Morris interposed with a look of desperation, "We—ah. That is to say, er—no, we didn't meet your papa, er—exactly. But we chanced to visit the Chandler estate, and—"

"Ye Gods and little fishes!" cried Falcon explosively. "Do you mean to take a year and a day to caper around the simple truth? Your sister is now betrothed to Gordon Chandler, Captain Jack. A most eligible match. Your father is dead. He died a year after your ship went down."

Jonathan lay back and closed his eyes, and the mug sagged in his hand. So it was truth. Papa, always loving and unfailingly proud of them all, was the person he was "specially fond of" who would not be there to meet him . . .

Springing to snatch the mug, Morris exclaimed, "Damn you, Falcon! Your tact is exceeded only by your compassion! He's in no state to weather a shock like that!"

"He'd as well hear it tonight rather than wait till next week whilst you try to get your tongue from 'twixt your teeth! It gets no easier for beating about the bush, Lieutenant Mealymouth!"

Jonathan pulled himself together. "No—I am all right now. I think I have—feared this for some time . . . Do you know how—what happened? Please do not wrap it in clean linen."

"As you wish," Falcon said. "From all I heard, your father refused to believe the charges against you. He spent a fortune trying to prove your innocence."

Jonathan smiled. "Yes, he would have done that. He is—was—the very best of—" He bit his lip, then went on, "His fortune was small, unless— Did he sell the house? The country place?"

Morris gestured sharply, but Falcon ignored him. "I believe he lost everything."

"My . . . God!" Jonathan put a trembling hand over his eyes for a minute while Morris glared at Falcon, and Falcon looked back at him enigmatically.

"My—apologies," said Jonathan trying to keep his countenance. "The last time I saw him, my father was in excellent health. He is—was a relatively young man. Did—did his health break down because—of my disgrace?"

"No, no, dear boy," said Morris kindly. "Never blame yourself. Anyone can suffer a heart seizure, you know, and—"

"A heart seizure!" Jonathan shot a narrowed glance at Falcon. "Is that truth?"

"Ask not for truth, if you want rather to be spared it."

"Yes," said Jonathan numbly. "Yes. The inference is—sufficiently obvious." He took a deep breath. "I know you are both very tired. But—would you be so kind as to tell me of—of the rest of my family . . . ?"

Jennifer climbed up the companionway stiffly, and stepped into a radiant morning, the skies dotted here and there with fluffy clouds, the sea sparkling in the sunlight, and a brisk breeze billowing the sails. The distant loom of the coastline was off the port side, which meant that Johnny had decided to go around Land's End rather than head north towards Bristol. Briefly, she wondered why, then thought, 'Plymouth! Of course! He's running for the fort and the Harbour Master!'

She was surprised to see that the fiery Frenchman they'd captured last night was manning the tiller quite cheerfully. Two sailors were swabbing down the decks. Enoch Tummet, a blunderbuss across his knees, and an expression of profound gloom on his faintly green countenance, sat on the hatch, keeping watch over the prisoners. He rose and bowed, and she called a "Good morning" to him. Towards the bow, Falcon and Morris sat on some coiled rope examining the contents of a small bag. They both stood to greet her.

"I am very ashamed," she said, extending a hand to each of them. "To think I would fall asleep at such a moment! I don't even recollect going down to my cabin."

Morris said, "You were exhausted, ma'am. Faith but I was astounded any of you could walk about at all after your wild boatride! 'Twas my very great pleasure to carry you. Falcon would have, but he has frippered about Town too long, and lacks the stamina to—"

Falcon said, "You'll find out how much stamina I have if you ever summon the gumption to face me!"

"The scowl you see on his handsome phiz"—Morris grinned and ducked the bag Falcon hurled at him—"is because he saved my life last night. Major tactical error."

For just an instant Falcon looked disconcerted, then he drawled, "I mean to ensure that when you meet your just deserts, 'twill be at the point of my Colichemarde!" He bowed to Jennifer, and sauntered away to confer with Tummet.

Looking after him curiously, she murmured, "I stand in his debt, Lieutenant. But—I cannot but wonder why you cry friends with such an acid-tongued gentleman."

"Oh, I don't," he said cheerfully. "This business of the League chances to throw us together."

"And I believe you said you hope to marry his sister. Is that why he threatens you with a duel?"

"Er—not exactly. I made a—er, small error." She looked at him questioningly, and he added with a sigh, "I chanced to shoot him. Accidentally. Took him for a highwayman, when he was actually escorting a carriage. He—ah, takes rather a dim view of the matter."

She chuckled, "I can see that he might. But—surely, if you apologised, he would forgive."

"There's rather more to it. Still—don't let him throw dust in your eyes, ma'am. In Town they dub him the Mandarin, and mock him because of his mixed blood. But if a fellow had his back to the wall, he could do worse than have Lord Haughty-Snort at his side."

Jennifer liked him the more for that generous remark. She said, "I think he could do no better than accept you for a brother-in-law. What a pity he is so proud."

"Eaten up with it," he agreed. "For instance, mark how gracefully he walks. Wouldn't dream he can scarce set one foot before the other, would you?"

"Oh, dear! I had forgot. He lost his boots when we were coming across the moor, yet walked all those miles barefoot! And he managed to help us by donning the cloak and pretending to be the Lady. How was it that he seemed to glow?"

"We couldn't keep up with Jack, but when it began to look as though he might need a diversion, we lit a small fire between two boulders and Falcon put on your cloak and climbed up so that the light shone on him."

Puzzled, she said, "It was a wonderful diversion! But—'twas not my cloak, Lieutenant. How did you come by it?"

"It was lying on the boulders, and we thought you must have dropped it." He said remorsefully, "Jupiter! We've stole some poor lady's cloak!"

'How very odd,' thought Jennifer. 'Why would a lady leave such a garment lying about on a stormy night ... ?"

There were more pressing matters on her mind, however, but before she could ask the all-important question, Morris said kindly, "Never look so worried, ma'am. The Widow Newlyn set Jack's arm last evening."

"Thank goodness! She is as good at healing as any apothecary. What did she say of it? Was it very bad for him?"

"If it was, he made no fuss. A good man is Armitage. The widow says the bone will take some weeks to knit."

"Poor soul," she murmured fondly. "And I suppose you gentlemen were obliged to stay up all night?"

"We took it in turn, ma'am. Had to keep an eye on the prisoners. Fellas like that would smile at you one minute, and slip a knife 'twixt your ribs the next."

Falcon rejoined them. "I think I am without a man." His rare grin blazed at them, and his dark eyes twinkled. "Tummet has turned me off."

"Your own fault," said Morris. "You know he cannot abide sea travel."

"With luck he won't have to abide it for long. That fellow Armand says that if the wind holds we could very well be in Plymouth Sound by afternoon, though I fancy he would very much like to steer us to Le Havre! I wish Captain Jack would wake up. We cannot afford to go off course."

Jonathan was already up, and with Holsworth's assistance had shaved. His arm ached this morning, but the ache of grief was keener. It was very clear that his beloved father's death had been brought about by his own disgrace. And if he had earned that disgrace, then he alone could bear the guilt. He had racked his brains last night in a frantic need to remember what had really happened on the *Silken Princess*. The snatches of memory that had come before he at last fell asleep had been muddled and there were the same long blank intervals, so that he was desperately anxious to talk with Joe Taylor.

Duster uttered a fair approximation of "drink" and preened his feathers, as though proud of his effort.

Staring at him, Jonathan muttered, "I'd give a deal to know how *you* came up with us!"

Holsworth helped him into his coat and draped the left side over the sling Mrs. Newlyn had insisted upon. "Blest if I can understand it, Jack," he said. "Mr. Falcon and the lieutenant were sure the bird was lost somewhere in the mine, but that man of Mr. Falcon's says he come upon the cage after Miss Jennifer had followed you to Roselley, and there was Duster sitting inside so cool as any cucumber!"

"A small miracle," said Jonathan, thinking there had been several large ones for which to give thanks. "How is Mrs. Newlyn?"

Holsworth gave him an oblique look, and reddened. "Fair aside of herself because of the filth in the galley. She's in there now, making breakfast for all on us."

"I can smell it. She's a rare woman, Noah."

"And ye're thinking I could do worse, eh?" The big man nodded. "I've been thinking the same, I've a brother living in Plymouth who's long been wanting me to go into the building trade with him. I've a mind to leave the widow with him whilst I go back and see if there's anything left of my cottage, or if all my goods burned with the rest. There's a strongbox in my cellar will provide a fresh start for us, if the widow'll have me."

The remark sent Jonathan's thoughts to another strongbox that was, hopefully, still in the care of his faithful Indian general steward. He'd been given command of the *Silken Princess* so unexpectedly that there had been no time to retrieve the box prior to leaving Calcutta. It had been a vexation then; now 'twould appear it was a blessing, for it seemed it was his entire fortune. He realised that Holsworth was looking at him expectantly, and he said quickly and honestly that he had no doubt the widow was destined to be the second Mrs. Noah Holsworth and that he wished them happy.

Holsworth thanked him and said with a knowing wink, "I'd not go far wrong in wishing you the same, I'll wager."

Jonathan smiled, took up the *capitaine*'s glass, and made his way on deck.

The vessel heeled over, and the freshening breeze dashed salt spray into his face. The flapping of sail, the hiss of the waves foaming back from the bow, the roll of the deck brought the old panic. He fought it away. He had no time for fear; but it took all his strength of will to look out over rank upon rank of waves. His hand was sweating when he raised the glass, but he triumphed, and scanned the horizon. There was no sign of a following ship. Turning about, his practiced eyes lifted to sun and sails. He greeted the unhappy Tummet, instructed the obsequious Armand to keep her on a steady northeasterly heading, and sent the two Spanish seamen scrambling to raise the topsail on the mainmast. Only then did he go forward to where Jennifer waited with Morris and Falcon.

She reached out to him, and he clasped her hand, marvelling that despite the ordeal she had endured, and the lack of such vital necessities as maids and cosmetics and curling tongs, she managed to look fresh and beautiful. Her loving eyes were searching his face also, noting the dark smudges under his eyes and the smile that did not quite reach them. She rested her fingers very lightly on the sling that supported his left arm, and asked, "Are you better today, Johnny?"

"Much better, I thank you. Are you sadly bruised?"

She said with a twinkle, "Alas, yes, and am horridly stiff. But I slept well, and feel guilty to have done so under . . . the circumstances."

"I very much doubt that Green will inform 'gainst your family. It couldn't fail to draw attention to his own activities, and you may be sure the villagers will have turned on him for burning down their homes."

Falcon said dryly, "You will pardon if I interrupt to wish you a good morning, Captain Jack."

Jonathan reddened, and mumbled an embarrassed apology.

Touched, Morris said, " 'There's precious little scrubbing done, when two fond hearts they beat as one.' "

"I rather doubt that Armitage means to ask that Miss Britewell scrub the decks," said Falcon witheringly.

Something nudged Jonathan's boot. He glanced down and bent to take up the small bag that lay there.

Jennifer said, *"Don't!"* and pushed his hand away.

Falcon snatched up the bag and tossed it over the side. "A pretty gift," he drawled.

"Nothing in it but feathers," said Morris.

Jennifer asked, "How did it—come here?"

Morris grinned. "Falcon has such charm for the fair sex. One of his admirers tossed it at him when we were driving up to Castle Triad yesterday."

"Did you pick it up, Mr. Falcon?"

He looked at her curiously. Her eyes had a scared expression. "Yes. I hoped it might contain at least a pair of bedsocks, but—" Amusement came into his dark face. "Aha! 'Tis one of your quaint Cornish spells, eh? Tell me, Miss Jennifer, have I been—what is it you say?—ill-wished? Am I doomed to be passed under the belly of a piebald horse?"

She managed a laugh. "That is the cure for whooping cough, sir, and I've heard no whoops from you."

Morris's inevitable comment was cut off as the schooner seemed to leap ahead, and they all glanced upward as the topsail billowed out against the blue sky.

Jonathan said, "I think Green's bullies cannot come up with us overland, but it's as well for us to take advantage of this breeze. I mean to drop anchor in the west inlet of Plymouth Sound and get to the fort as soon as may be. The sooner a naval frigate can be despatched to Bridget Bay, the better chance we'll have to prove our story."

Falcon said thoughtfully, "We've tried to bring the Squire and his ruffians to book several times. The authorities invariably laugh at us."

"They cannot ignore all of us," said Jonathan. "I *saw* them training their mercenaries. 'Tis past doubting that they mean sedition, and I'll back you under oath in any court in the land!"

"Well said, by Jove!" exclaimed Morris.

"Always providing your oath is—valid . . . ," murmured Falcon.

It was a harsh reminder, and Jonathan had to bite back an angry response. He said stiffly, "Very true. If I cannot clear my name, my word is worthless."

"I don't know if my word's worth much, sir," said Joe Taylor, coming painfully along the deck. "But I'll gladly tell ye what I know of the business."

Jonathan's heart turned over. He jerked around to wring the hand of this man on whom his whole future depended, but he dreaded the telling also, some of which showed in his face.

Morris saw, and said kindly, "We'll allow you your privacy, dear boy. Come August. We'll relieve poor old Tummet."

"He can wait," said Falcon. "Serve him right for turning me off. I feel no obligation towards him. None. Besides—bless her heart, here comes a charming lady bearing breakfast!"

Mrs. Newlyn and Holsworth both carried trays laden with dishes of bacon, buttered bread, eggs, and sliced beef. There were plates and mugs, and two big jugs giving off the mouth-watering aroma of coffee.

Morris ran to help as the widow tottered sideways and her precious burden tilted.

She thanked him breathlessly, and said it was so dirty below decks that it seemed best to eat in the clean fresh air. Nobody argued with this decision, and so laden plates were carried to Tummet and his charges, seats of coiled rope were formed for the ladies, the gentlemen sat cross-legged on the deck. They all (with the exception of Jonathan, who was suddenly too tense to eat) enjoyed their food in the brilliant morning, while Joe Taylor, erstwhile ship's carpenter of the East Indiaman *Silken Princess*, told the tale of Captain Armitage's disgrace.

"In a way," he began, around a mouthful of bacon, "it

started with Miss Phillips. In another way, I reckon it started a lot earlier, but—I'll tell what little I know of that later. Miss Phillips was a remarkable fine woman, no doubt about that, and it didn't take long to see as she'd set her cap for you, sir. We saw how you handled the lady, and we didn't think too much of it, at first. But in all my days, I never see such a persistent female. It come to be a joke among the crew, it being such a long voyage, who'd outlast—er." He gave a guilty glance at the two women and said lamely, "Well, you know what I mean. Then you was seen going into her cabin one night, and that were the *last* time I see you on the whole voyage, Captain!"

Jonathan asked intently, "What were people told?"

"At first, that you'd been took ill. Then, rumours began to get about that you'd been so drunk you'd fallen down the bell ladder to the poop deck and nigh killed yourself. After that, there was always some tale. You wasn't making a good recovery, or you'd had a relapse, or something of the sort. But then there was whispers that you'd taken to drink. Folks said they heard you singing like you was very well to live, or that you was laughing and chasing Miss Phillips round your stateroom, and her squealing like any wanton. The passengers was proper put out, and lodged a complaint, and Mr. Wright told the surgeon that you was a disgrace to your calling, and he meant to make a full report to the Company. It wasn't fair, he says, him being saddled with a captain's responsibilities when he'd only just been made chief mate, and that if anything happened to the *Princess* it wouldn't be him as took the blame."

He paused to drink his coffee, and nobody spoke.

Jonathan stared at the bow as it rose and fell steadily, and knew how much he had built on the fact of Taylor's still being alive, and how bitter would be the disappointment if he was about to hear a verification of his guilt.

Taylor set his mug aside. "The way I see it, they was all in on it, sir."

Jonathan's heart gave a spasmodic leap. "In . . . on it?" he echoed breathlessly.

Taylor shrugged. "Hadda be, sir. The senior merchant

and your servants certainly knew you was being kept by force. And the chief mate—he must've knowed, though he made a good show of acting like he was hardly done by."

"For the love of heaven," croaked Jonathan. "What did they hope to gain? The cargo?"

"Before we sailed, I remember thinking it a bit strange they'd have give command of the *Silken Princess* to such a young gentleman—no offence, sir. But 'twasn't till months afterwards I came at the truth. It was all planned long ago, Captain. Some very rich and powerful gents wanted a special captain for the *Silken Princess*. A brilliant man, with a fine record, but he had to be under thirty—so that when she went down everyone would be ready to blame him 'cause he was too young for his command."

Under his breath Jonathan swore savagely.

Morris said in disgust, "What a filthy trick!"

"You were selected for ritual sacrifice," murmured Falcon. "Clever." Jonathan's glare scorched at him, and he raised a languid hand and said, "Well, you must own it worked perfectly."

"Not quite, it didn't, sir," said Taylor, eyeing the depleted plate with regret. "They counted on Captain Armitage being proper bowled out by the lady. And a rare pretty lady she was, but he rumbled her, sir. So he had to be silenced, and that made it more risky. But they weren't after the cargo, Captain. 'Cause there wasn't none to be after!"

"Jamie!" exclaimed Falcon, forgetting himself in his sudden excitement.

Equally excited, Morris said, "The same ploy that was tried on Gordie Chandler!"

"Do you say your confounded League has done this before?" demanded Jonathan harshly. "To other masters?"

Falcon nodded. "To many, we now think—poor devils. The cargo is stolen *before* sailing. The vessel goes off with a hold full of weighted casks and boxes, and then is 'lost at sea' and no one the wiser. In Chandler's case it was intended that the wreck be blamed on him, and so neatly contrived it came nigh to succeeding."

"One of our victories," said Morris. "In fact, that's how we came to meet—" He stopped abruptly.

Taylor said, "We was s'posed to drop anchor in Plymouth Sound, you'll remember, Captain. But we got separated from the fleet soon after we left St. Helena. We was near home when we got blowed miles off our course—or so it seemed, and into thick fog. Two days we drifted, and the third night a wind come up. Along about midnight there was a terrible crash. The bo'sun shouted that the cargo had shifted, and I went down to have a look, but then the *Princess* started to list to starboard, and everyone was screaming that we were sinking. Mr. Wright gave the order to abandon ship. I barely got off. And it didn't come to me till later that there was boats already lowered and well away! That poor *Princess* never went down on account of damage from shifting cargo, sir. She wasn't meant to reach port. They scuttled her!"

Seething with rage, Jonathan said in a rasp of a voice, "You speak of a wind. Yet I seem to remember a great gale."

"Right you are, sir. They didn't count on that. Come up very quick it did. But not when the cargo was said to have shifted. It didn't really blow till the boats was away."

"Were there really nine and twenty drowned?"

"Counting you—yes, sir."

Jonathan stalked over to stand looking down at him, and Taylor scrambled to his feet and faced him apprehensively.

"If you knew all this," gritted Jonathan, eyes blazing in his dead white face, "why in the *devil* did you not speak up?"

Taylor backed away a step. "I—I didn't know then, sir. I swear I didn't! All of us was under a—a cloud, as you might say. I couldn't get a berth, and came nigh to starving. I was desperate and was glad enough to turn to free-trading. A comrade took me to see a man named Silas, who was paying big wages for a special kind of work. He said it was to let the common folk know how some rich men were no better than criminals, cheating the country and grinding the noses of the poor. I don't have to tell you what was really afoot."

Morris interjected, "But you believed it all?"

"At first I did, sir. But then this Lord Green came sometimes, and always with the lady. Pretty as ever she was, but I think her conscience was troubling her, and she'd turned to drink, and—"

Jonathan said, "You never mean Mimi Phillips? But I thought she was lost on the *Princess*."

"Not her, Captain! Though I thought the same till I saw her with his lordship. Proper up in the world she was one evening, laughing wild-like, and talking too loud. Lord Green hit her, and she started screeching at him that she'd have been better off to have told the captain the truth instead of helping them to ruin and murder him. I knew better than to stay in sight, sir. I hid, quick, but I heard enough, and I managed to get away without no one knowing I'd been there. Wasn't but a few days later the poor lady was found drowned. I knew I was mixed up in something very nasty indeed, sir. Only how to get out was more'n I could come at. Some of the lads had got tired of it all, and likely they'd begun to suspect, same as I had. They asked for their pay, but they never said goodbye to no one. Just never was seen again. I'll be honest, Captain, I was proper scared. I kept waiting me chance to hop off— only it never came. Likely never would have, if you hadn't come and found me."

Jonathan stared at him in brooding silence.

Mrs. Newlyn murmured, "How very dreadful! I cannot believe those wicked men would not have cared about the poor passengers—the little children! The Lady was right. England is threatened, sure as sure."

Jennifer went to slip her hand into Jonathan's. "And you are cleared, my dear. When we reach Plymouth, Mr. Taylor can tell his story to the harbour master, and you will be exonerated of all blame."

He looked down into her loving eyes and felt the terrible weight of guilt lifting from his soul. But he felt also a searing rage because powerful men had so carelessly slaughtered the innocent, destroyed a fine ship, and ruined him, thereby as good as murdering his father. He patted Jennifer's hand and muttered, "Yes, I pray God!" And stalking to the stern, stood with his back turned and his eyes closed, in silent and heartfelt communion with a very loved and lost gentleman.

Looking after him, bewildered, Jennifer said, "I thought he would be overjoyed."

"He's a man coming out of the far side of hell," said Holsworth.

Morris nodded. "I fancy anyone would find it hard to take in all of it at once. Give him time, Miss Jennifer. He'll get his bearings."

August Falcon said dryly, "Let us hope he gets 'em in time to take this tub into port!"

❧ Chapter 16 ❧

Shortly after three o'clock they dropped anchor in the west
inlet of Plymouth Harbour. The prisoners were locked into
the *capitaine*'s cabin pending the arrival of the proper authorities, and having first agreed to meet again at the home
of Holsworth's brother the fugitives split into three groups.
Tummet and Taylor went in search of an apothecary,
Holsworth took his blushing bride-to-be to meet her pro-
spective relations, and Jennifer, Falcon, Morris, and Jonathan went in search of the commodore in charge of the fort.

The afternoon was far advanced when Jennifer left the
stark and stuffy waiting room and wandered into the mellow
sunlight. Jonathan had suggested that she go with Holsworth
and the widow. She'd known he wanted to shield her from
having to be a witness against her father, but she had refused to leave him, and had spent much of the long wait in
mentally composing the answers she would give to the
questions she would probably be asked. It had not as yet
come to that, however. The three rather dishevelled young
men had been looked upon with shocked derision in the office of the commodore, and refused an audience with the
great man. The Sovereign Harbour Master had viewed them
with suspicious hostility and sent them to a supercilious
captain on the next lower rung who'd had "no time to spare
today." Jonathan was enraged, and August Falcon's cynicism had become ever more marked so that Jennifer could
almost feel sorry for the junior minion of the Navy Board

with whom they were now ensconced. Hungry and troubled, she had felt the need for some fresh air.

She wandered about the grounds, lost in thought and paying little heed to her surroundings. She had watched Johnny with pride, for all traces of Crazy Jack had disappeared now. The slump to the broad shoulders was gone. He stood straight and tall, head high and eyes grimly resolute. That he would be cleared and reinstated she had no doubt, and she rejoiced for his sake. Yet for her this moment of triumph was shadowed, partly from grief at the bitter parting from her family, and partly because it seemed that in losing the crushed and broken man to whom she had given her heart, she had lost also the sure knowledge that she was cherished and adored. He was as attentive and solicitous for her well-being as ever, but there was a subtle difference in the way he looked at her; it was as if her beloved Johnny had withdrawn behind an invisible wall, and that Captain Jonathan Armitage was a stranger she scarcely knew.

Sighing, she glanced up and met the disapproving gaze of a splendidly uniformed guard. She'd collected many such glances, and knew that her gown was creased and her shoes muddied, and she had lost her cap. Infinitely worse, she was a young lady with neither a gentleman at her side, not a servant to lend her propriety. She walked purposefully around the corner of the building the stern sailor guarded, and found herself in a narrow grassy area at the very brow of the hill. Below spread the blue waters of the Sound, where many ships lay at anchor, tossing lazily to the movement of the waves, their sails reefed, the gulls wheeling and clamouring about them. It was a beautiful sight, and, soothed by it, she sat down and leaned back against the high wall that enclosed what appeared to be a private garden.

A proud navy frigate was tacking slowly towards harbour. Jennifer watched her idly. The breeze was soft and pleasant, and the air warm. Her eyelids began to droop. The frigate was trimming her sails as she passed a small yacht and—

Jennifer's eyes shot open. She knew very few families having the means to own such a vessel, but she was sure she recognised this one. She sat up straighter, then stood, straining her eyes. There could be no doubt. The yacht was the *Deliverance*! Lord Morris was here, then! He had undoubtedly heard of his cousin's peril and had come at once in search of military help. Overjoyed, she hurried to the front of the building. Lord Kenneth was respected and powerful, and could be of invaluable assistance to them.

The guard was still on duty. She hesitated. If she told him the truth there would be a fuss, for he looked the pompous sort and would undoubtedly refer her to an endless succession of aides and attachés who would demand identification and explanations and think it very odd for an unchaperoned female to approach them.

A moment later, the guard was listening sceptically to the sad tale of a young lady who had been most distinctly told not to wander away from her uncle's party, but had become so interested in the fort she had done that very thing. "If you could please tell me where he has gone, sir," she said, smiling hopefully up at him, "I would be so very grateful."

"Ha-rumph!" said the guard. "I don't know as 'ow I can—"

"He is Lord Kenneth Morris," said Jennifer.

"Ho!" said the guard. The silly young creature had likely gone a'roving in the gardens, she looked that crumpled. But she did have the prettiest smile and such big beautiful eyes . . . "In that case," he relented, "I'll 'ave you took to 'is lor'ship at—"

"Oh, pray do not," she begged. "If I am taken to him, he'll know I got lost, and he will be cross. It would be so much better an you would kindly tell me where I may find him. I might be able to slip back with the others, and he'll not even know I was gone."

His lor'ship would know after one look at that creased dress, thought the guard, but he had daughters of his own, and they was all the same. Not two thoughts in their pretty heads! "Very well, miss," he said. "Matter o' fact, 'is lor'ship's in this very building. There's a garden in the back. If you was to go in the side gate ..."

He smiled and gave a knowing wink. Jennifer patted his arm and told him he was "a dear soul," then hurried to enlist the aid of Lord Kenneth.

The "side" gate was more at the back than the side of the wall, and the slope of the hill behind it was quite precipitous, but Jennifer was determined, and after a little tugging succeeded in swinging the gate open. She entered a charming courtyard with shrubs and trees set about in tubs, and some wooden chairs and stone benches. It would be a pleasant place, she thought, for a man to escape for a while from the burdens of a busy day. At the moment, however, she was the only occupant. Two glass doors stood open to the warm afternoon air, and she could hear voices inside. She ran forward eagerly and entered a large room having more the appearance of a study than an office. And she'd not been mistaken, for Lord Kenneth Morris sat in a deep leather chair talking with a civilian gentleman who was in the act of walking over to a credenza set against the far wall.

Lord Kenneth sounded angry, and belatedly it dawned on Jennifer that her unannounced arrival might not be welcomed.

" ... the deuce was I to know?" said his lordship. "I thought the damned fellow went down with his ship. We all did! When the Squire learns what a mull we've made of it, Pen ..."

Stupefied with astonishment, Jennifer clapped a hand over her mouth lest her horrified gasp betray her.

The man called Pen had poured two glasses of wine. When he turned, he would be looking straight at her. She gathered her wits and fled back the way she had come, holding her breath, her heart pounding so wildly she was sure they must hear it. Fortunately, Pen had a loud voice that effectively drowned the swish of her skirts as she whipped out of the door and leaned against the wall behind it.

"We've not made such a mull of it, all things considered," he argued. "We closed his mouth effectively enough.

277

He may have survived, but his mind was gone. And even if he *was* to remember what he saw in Suez—"

"*Whom* he saw!"

"Oh, very well, *whom* he saw—the chances that he'd ever have put two and two together are so remote as to be practically non-existent."

Lord Kenneth grumbled, "They'd have been *wholly* non-existent had we put a period to him then and there."

"But consider what a waste that would have been. Instead, the Squire took an awkward incident and turned it to good account. Armitage served our purposes nicely and took all the blame whilst we garnered a splendid cargo, and the owners collected the insurance. He was removed, his name was thoroughly disgraced, and his foolish sire played right into our hands. Besides, at the time, the Squire wanted no attention drawn to the meeting. You know how set he is on secrecy."

"Justifiably so. We walk a very tight rope, my friend. If our negotiations with *that* gentleman were guessed at, the fox would properly be in with the hens!"

"True. But that was three years ago, and Armitage can have had no least knowledge of our organization."

"He's a knowledge *now*! I make no doubt but that the Mandarin and that dullard of a cavalryman— Er, your pardon, my lord, but your young cousin ain't very bright, is he?"

Lord Kenneth uttered a resentful grunt, and Pen went on, "At all events, they're sure to have told him about the League— Oh, for Lord's sake, man! Why must you jib like a nervous colt? There's not a soul in sight and we cannot be overheard here! As I was about to say, I've paved the way for them, nicely. They'll be delayed for another half hour by which time our man will arrive with his—er, troop, and . . ."

Jennifer waited no longer. She would surely be seen now if she crossed the courtyard to the gate. She looked about in desperation. A stone deer was placed artistically under a small tree near the wall. It was no time for maidenly modesty, and she had grown up with three adventuresome brothers. She advanced on the deer and hoisted her skirts. A moment later, panting, she peeped over the wall. There was no one in sight. It was the work of a moment to sit on top, then turn and lower herself. She heard a ripping sound and moaned inwardly but walked on, her thoughts in turmoil, her eyes stinging with tears. This man she had known all her life, and whom she had judged pompous but very kind, was in fact a traitor! Lord Kenneth Morris, the father of Caro and of the boy she might have wed, had sat there and discussed without a trace of remorse wholesale murder and the deliberate destruction of her beloved. She felt betrayed and lost and longed to run to the comfort of Johnny's arms. But she dare not run. She dare not even hurry. She schooled herself to stroll around to the back of another building and paused there to tidy her hair and brush her skirts to which had been added a tear and a moss stain. Then, praying her guard acquaintance would not come after her, she walked across the quadrangle to the office where she had left the three men. She ran past the startled orderly, and flung open the inner door.

Jonathan was leaning aggressively over the desk of the young naval officer, and she staggered towards him. Falcon and Morris whipped around to face her. Jonathan sprang to her side. Leaning against him, she stretched out her hands to the other two and gasped out their names so that they came to her at once.

Anxious, Jonathan asked, "What is it, ma'am? Are you ill?"

She emitted a loud moan, whispered, "This is a trap!" and wailed, "I think 'tis the heat. I feel so horribly . . . sick!"

The officer jumped to his feet. "You had best take her into the open, quickly!" he advised, and ran to send his orderly for a glass of water.

Leaning on the arms of Jonathan and Morris, and with Falcon fanning a thick sheaf of papers at her, Jennifer whispered, "The Squire's people are coming for us!"

The officer hurried in again. "Is the poor lady any better?"

Jennifer gulped convincingly, and, alarmed, he moved back.

Falcon said, "Oh, bother!" and the papers he held flew in all directions.

Exasperated by this disastrous scattering of requisitions it had taken him all day to arrange and categorise, the officer swore under his breath and began to rush about retrieving them.

When he looked up, Miss Britewell and her escorts were gone.

"They'll be hot after us, if you're right, ma'am," said Falcon, leaning back in the carriage they'd hired at the gate.

Jonathan's eyes were on the west inlet from which their pirated schooner was conspicuously absent. He said, "We'll have to make a run for Town and East India House, or the Navy Board."

Following his gaze, Falcon said, "I doubt the authorities took them in charge. Our pressed crew have made off, I think."

Jonathan nodded. "Just as well. They'd likely have lied at all events, and made Green out to be an angel of light." He turned to Jennifer, "My dear, you told us about the men you overheard. I suppose you had no chance to see anything of them?"

She sighed. "One was called Pen, but I only saw his back. I knew the other gentleman, which is—which is why I went there."

Glancing at Morris obliquely, Falcon murmured, "Dare I hazard a guess?"

Turning to Morris also, and finding him pale and unwontedly grim, Jennifer touched his clenched hand and said gently, "Jamie—I am so sorry!"

He forced a smile. "You're very sure, Miss Jennifer?"

"How I wish I were not. I was so happy when I saw the *Deliverance*, for I was sure Lord Kenneth would help us. He's such an old friend. And then . . . oh, it is so dreadful!"

"He is the head of our house. My Papa will be—" Morris broke off and looked squarely at Falcon. "I owe you a most humble apology. You were right about him."

Falcon shrugged. "I am always right. But there's no cause for excesses of despair. There are dirty dishes somewhere in every family."

"In mine, certainly," sighed Jennifer. "I am only glad that Johnny can now clear his name."

Jonathan was thinking ahead. He muttered, "They'll be bound to try and stop me from telling what they think I know. We'll have to drive straight through." He looked at Jennifer worriedly. "It's likely to be grim."

"Perhaps," suggested Falcon, "we should leave Miss Jennifer with Holsworth and the widow."

"No!" cried Jennifer. "I must keep with you, Johnny! I can bear witness to so much of what's happened."

He smiled into her anxious face. "Yes, but Falcon's quite right. I want you somewhere safe. Hopefully, a place not too far from Town so that I can come for you as soon as we know where we stand. Have you any family living within a day's journey of London?"

She looked at him rebelliously, but in her heart she knew that, if only for the sake of all their reputations, she could not stay with him. And so, she ran her various relations through her mind, then said reluctantly, "I've not seen her for years, but my great-aunt is fond of me, I know. She lives near East Bourne. I'm sure she would let me stay with her. But surely you will take up Tummet and Mr. Taylor? And Noah and the widow must be warned."

"Never worry, we'll warn them. I owe my life to the future Mrs. Holsworth."

"Do not be looking to stay for the wedding," said Falcon. "We've a race to run."

Jennifer said hopefully, "I expect there will be other weddings I can attend."

Jonathan said nothing.

On a bright morning three days later, Jennifer stood on the drivepath of her great-aunt's house near the village of East Bourne, and watched the carriage rumble away

Londonward, taking with it the man she loved and her every chance of happiness.

Watching her with faded but wise eyes, Lady Lyme-Rufford gathered the shawl closer about her bony shoulders, fastened a claw-like hand upon her great-niece's arm, and said, "Well, they're gone, thank heaven. I like Neville Falcon, but that boy of his has honed the art of arrogance past common decency. I'll own he's a handsome devil and has broke half the hearts in London, so they say. Has he broke yours, my love?"

The endearing term brought a lump into Jennifer's throat, and she squeezed the thin fingers gratefully. "No, ma'am."

My lady led the way back into the great house that seemed less lonely now that this seldom-seen grand-niece had arrived. "Then I must pray 'tis that young military fellow with the kind eyes. If the fair boy with his arm in a sling has brought the lost look to your pretty face, you've chosen poorly my dear."

A footman closed the front door behind them. Accompanying her great-aunt across the wainscoted hall, Jennifer said proudly, "Jonathan Armitage is the finest, bravest, most gallant gentleman I ever met. And the only man for me, ma'am."

"Then you must resign yourself to eating black bread and wearing rags." Lady Lyme-Rufford waved to the hovering footman and ordered tea and cakes brought to the back parlour. "He is quite penniless, you know," she went on, leading the way down the long hall.

"So I had thought, ma'am," said Jennifer, as they entered a charming little room where a fire blazed brightly on the hearth. "But he has found that he is the son of Greville Armitage. You will have heard of him, I know. He is the most famous artist in all England, save for—"

"He was, certainly." Her ladyship sank with a sigh into a cushioned chair, and glanced up at Jennifer's puzzled face shrewdly. "Ah—the boy did not tell you, I see. Greville Armitage died—let me see now, it must be well over a year since. I am not acquainted with the family, but I heard he died a pauper having spent his fortune in trying to prove his son's innocence."

Jennifer gave a gasp and sat down abruptly.

Lady Lyme-Rufford asked, "Did he have the effrontery to offer for you?"

"Yes—no—I—"

"I should hope not! But you will be a fine prize for fortune hunters my dear. Now, I am more than pleased by your visit, and hope you may stay for a very long time, but you gave me the sketchiest of mangled nonsense as excuse for your descent upon me. I want the whole! And then, fair exchange, I will tell you what little I know of Greville Armitage, and how his son broke his heart. After luncheon we will drive into Lewes, for you must have a new wardrobe, and Lewes shall have to suffice till I can take you into Town. 'Pon my soul, that gown makes me shudder! I never thought to see a relation of mine in so shabby— Enough! Begin child. And don't forget—the *whole*! I want to know what that fool of a father of yours has done, to cause you to ruin yourself by rushing all over England with three young rascals!"

Half an hour and many interruptions later, Jennifer finished, "But they were too close behind us, so we turned about at Yeovil and fled down to Weymouth. August—Mr. Falcon arranged passage for us on what was, I fear, a smuggler's vessel and we reached Seaford at dawn this morning. The rest you know, ma'am."

Her eyes very bright, my lady clasped her hands and said, "What a *splendid* adventure you have had!" Recollecting herself, she added hurriedly, "But *highly* improper! And there are still little bits I do not understand. For instance, if 'twas not your cloak Falcon wore to frighten the mob— whose was it?"

Jennifer shook her head. "I cannot guess, ma'am. It was a fine garment, but I don't know any lady in the Penwith Hundred who would be tall enough to wear it."

"You . . . never think . . . ?" Lady Lyme-Rufford's eyes were very round.

"We were—in Cornwall, dear aunt," Jennifer reminded gravely.

"Fiddle-de-dee! I never believed all that hocus pocus! Am I to suppose that Fate—or the Lady—or King Arthur and all his knights aided that strange bird to come up with you after he was lost in the Blue Rose?"

Jennifer said with a faint smile, "You must own, ma'am, 'tis something incredible that Duster could have escaped from the mine at all. More incredible that he was able to find his way to his cage at night, when he cannot do much more than flutter about."

"Hmm," said my lady again. "Then he must have hooked his little claws into one of your garments, or— Well, there is *some* explanation, I am very sure, so we will not waste our time with it. What we have to think of now, is your dear self. You are quite ruined, of course. Or would be, if the word got out. You were very wise to come to me, my love, for—"

" 'Twas not my idea, ma'am. Johnny insisted."

"Yes," My lady said musingly. "From what you have told me, I see that he is the type, all right. All high ideals and gallantry. Lud, but those pompous fools at the Navy Board will crucify the boy! Unless ... I've still some friends in high places, despite my gout. Now—let me see ... Ah! My wicked admiral! The very man! And he owes me a favour. Indeed, was I to look back forty years, he owes me a great deal more than—" She coughed, and said briskly, "But that is neither here nor there. Ring the bell, child. We must have tea, and then I've letters to write."

"But—dear ma'am, we just had tea! And you promised—"

"Oh, so I did, so I did! Good gracious, if ever I enjoyed a tale more! You must tell it to me all over again this evening. But now we must have luncheon, for I cannot write a letter without I am fortified. Poor child, how deliciously heartsick you look!" Her bright eyes very steady on Jennifer's face, she asked, "Did your Jonathan think to mention his wife ... ?"

Despite London's sultry weather, all was stir and bustle at East India House. Stern directors, secure under their mantle of power and authority, sent clerks and young officers scurrying to obey their commands; anxious captains waited about the halls for news of ships or sailings or ports of call; equally anxious merchants pressed Company officials for the award of contracts, or protested the unfortunate allocation of those same contracts; and the stifling halls rang with talk, the slamming of doors, the stamp and jingle of spurred boots.

In one small office several men had gathered. A naval commodore and a Company director were seated at a long table. A slim young midshipman with dark luminous eyes and thin nervous hands hovered behind the director's chair. Jonathan Armitage stood before the table, an impressive figure in an immaculate dark blue habit, a snowy cravat at his throat, his left arm still carried in a sling. At the side of the room August Falcon, James Morris, and Joe Taylor sat on straight-backed wooden chairs. All were silent. It was an ominous silence, as though the lightning that flickered occasionally over the city on this sultry afternoon added to the tension in the room. At length, the commodore, a heavy-set florid-faced gentleman, wrenched his gaze from the sheaf of papers in his hand and said with an air of barely suppressed amusement, "I give you credit, Captain Armitage, for adhering to the adage that attack is the best means of defence. But your tale, while most—er, enlivening, has not one point in common with these statements made by the survivors of the wreck. By Gad, sir, you would have done better to have kept your attack within the realm of credibility!"

A faint flush lit Jonathan's features, and his grey eyes held a glitter of anger. He turned to the director. "If to tell the truth is to attack, Lord Hayes, then I must—"

The mighty director, gaunt, hard-eyed and thin-lipped, over-rode with slow deliberation, "You stand accused, Captain Armitage, of gross negligence in the performance of your duties as master of the *Silken Princess*. Your first mate reported you to have been in an intoxicated condition for most of the voyage. His statement was verified by the supercargo—" He glanced at Falcon and Morris and clarified, "That being the title of the senior merchant sailing with a ship. It was also sworn to by the surgeon and by your personal servants, Captain Armitage. You are held directly responsible for the subsequent wreck and tragic loss of life. You appear now, after an absence of more than two years, and hand us a flamboyant tale of having been lured to the cabin of a beautiful woman and clubbed down with a subsequent—and highly convenient—loss of memory. To substantiate your astounding claim of being held prisoner on your own ship, you offer nothing more substantial than the word of your ship's carpenter Mr. Taylor, who is known to be devoted to you. Now, if you had some proof, some names of those responsible, some reason for such dastardly conduct, I should be glad to hear it."

"As I said, sir, Mr. Taylor discovered the reason. They had stolen the cargo before we sailed, and—"

"Impossible!" snorted the commodore. "Such a feat would require widespread collusion and the cooperation of trusted gentlemen both in the employ of the East India Company, and in the service of their King. Preposterous, I say, sir! A most confoundedly irresponsible piece of nonsense!"

"Unless," murmured the director, "Captain Armitage can substantiate his claim in—er, some way."

Gritting his teeth, Jonathan said, "I have given you my sworn word, my lord. As have Mr. Taylor and these gentlemen who—"

Once more the commodore interrupted. "Who have already made themselves ridiculous in Whitehall and elsewhere with their farcical tales of a treasonable conspiracy 'gainst the British government. Poppycock, I say sir. Poppycock!"

Falcon drawled, "Do you consider treason to be ridiculous, Commodore? You are lenient."

Lord Hayes added to an impression of dyspepsia by

pening a small and beautifully enamelled box, selecting a tablet and swallowing it with the water the midshipman rushed to offer. "We consider it ridiculous, sir," he said, "to attempt to besmirch the reputations of the high-ranking aristocrats and military officers you accuse of being involved in your so-called League of Jewelled Men. You offer us nothing more than allegations lacking any shred of supporting evidence. Yet I am told that Gideon Rossiter, the leader of your foolish club, or whatever it is, had the unmitigated gall to point the finger at his own father-in-law, the Earl of Collington, who is a very fine gentleman, and chances to be a good friend of mine."

"And you emulate his disgraceful behaviour, Lieutenant Morris," said the commodore, "by having named the head of your house, Lord Kenneth Morris, another conspirator. I wonder, sir, that you would sink so low as to bring such wicked charges 'gainst your own kinsman! One can only assume there is bad blood between you, and that you choose this shabby means for revenge!"

Scarlet, Morris sprang to his feet. "One might better assume, sir, that you are an incompetent nincompoop with not the brains to see past your fat nose!"

August Falcon gave a hoot of delighted laughter.

His face an even deeper hue of scarlet than that of the incensed Morris, the commodore jumped up, and roared, "Midshipman! Show this disrespectful and ill-mannered person the door!"

The midshipman, neither as tall nor as sturdy as Morris, chose to show him the door by opening it and waiting with a grave expression and twinkling eyes for the "disrespectful and ill-mannered person" to pass through.

Shaking his head, Falcon stood also. "I warned you, Armitage. They're all cut from the same cloth. Dense material, at best."

"Good day, sir!" snorted the commodore, breathing hard as he sat down again. "Have you anything more substantial to add, Captain Armitage?"

Keeping his temper with an effort, Jonathan answered, "Gideon Rossiter and his friends have been able to learn that the League was organised, and is controlled by six men. They are identified by small jewelled tokens, and each of them also has a number. We know that they refer to their leader as the Squire. We believe that this Squire planned my ruin and disgrace because whilst I was in Suez three years ago, I evidently saw or heard something that was dangerous to his schemes."

The commodore shook his head. "What an imagination!"

With a faint smile the director murmured, "But you have not the very remotest notion of what that—er, 'something' may have been."

Humming softly, Falcon followed Morris to the door.

Jonathan said grittily, "Unfortunately, no sir. But we believe that they are training mercenaries to foment sedition throughout London. I've no doubt but that they intend to use the Blue Rose Mine in Cornwall as a storage facility for their stolen cargoes, and as a reception area and training ground for their—"

"Troops?" The commodore threw back his head and laughed heartily. The director's lips curved into a thin smile.

Jonathan's fists clenched and he took a deep steadying breath.

The director said, "It saddens me that a young gentleman who passed out of Eton and Addiscombe College with so impressive a scholastic record as you achieved, should have allowed his love of strong drink and his lust for a beautiful woman to destroy everything the future offered. You will hold yourself available, Captain Armitage, for an official investigation into your disgraceful conduct as master of the *Silken Princess*. In the event you are found guilty, you will be stripped of your rank, discharged with dishonour from the Company, and all back pay and prize monies confiscated. You will then be handed over to the High Court of the Admiralty to be punished for your crimes to the fullest extent of the law. Meanwhile, sir, you are free to leave with"—his sardonic gaze flickered to the door—"your friends. However"—he leaned forward—"do not attempt to leave England!"

Jonathan said with proud defiance, "I have told you the true facts, my lord. To the best of my ability, I shall attempt to serve England. With my friends!" He bowed and stalked from the room, the midshipman closing the door behind him.

" 'Pon my soul but they don't breed men like they did in my young days," snorted the commodore, rising and taking up a fat satchel.

"What I fail to understand," said the director, a thin hand on his thin middle, "is what in the world they hope to gain from it all."

"Notoriety, very likely." The commodore waddled to the door. "Though one might think the half-breed would have had enough of that; he's the joke of London."

"A deadly joke," said Lord Hayes thoughtfully. "I think few men laugh to his face."

"They laugh like hell behind his back," grinned the commodore. "And he knows it. He's outspoken in his contempt for the *haut ton*, and would do anything to slander as many gentlemen as was in his power. Only look at their little group, m'dear fellow. Not a man of 'em who ain't got some sticky skeleton in the family closet. And now they've added a real gem to their ranks. Jonathan Greville Armitage. What'd they call him in Cornwall? Crazy Jack?" He chuckled, nodded his thanks as the midshipman opened the door for him, and went out shaking his head and saying, "Jove, what a fine recruit!"

Once more the midshipman closed the door, walked back to stand by the table, and waited.

The director asked, "Well, nephew Joel? What sayest thou?"

The midshipman answered gravely, "I sayest, it fitteth, my lord."

"The question is," murmured the director, "is it a perfect fit? The stakes are extreme high. There can be no slips, you understand."

"I understand. About Armitage. I fancy he'll be thrown to the lions?"

"Probably."

"He's had a very nasty time of it, sir."

"Pity," said the director. "But—we have no choice, do you see?"

With slow reluctance the midshipman said, "Yes, uncle. I see. But I wish we knew what it was that Armitage saw—or heard, in Suez."

"So do we all, dear boy," sighed the director, taking out another tablet. "So do we all."

Chapter 17

The afternoon was grey and drizzly, and the three men came gratefully into the warmth of palatial Falcon House. They shed their wet cloaks and went up the stairs to August's comfortable private parlour, where a crackling fire awaited them.

A lackey hurried to light a branch of candles. When he'd drifted silently from the room, Falcon said, "Well, 'tis done. I fancy you mean to leave Town, Jack."

Morris looked sharply at Jonathan. "When? Where do you go, dear boy?" He added with a sly grin, "Sussex, perchance?"

Jonathan shook his head. "I must see my family. I'd have gone down sooner had I not been prevented by this stupid board of enquiry."

"It was a strange business," said Falcon thoughtfully. "To say truth, I'd have laid odds you would be held for Admiralty justice. They dealt lightly with you."

"Lightly!" Morris expostulated. "Despite the testimony of those navy physicians regarding his head wound, and the information Joe Taylor gave them, the best they could do was to decide against further prosecution pending a more far-reaching investigation."

Jonathan said, "Which means—an I know anything of governmental manoeuvrings—that those involved will busy themselves in finding scapegoats, or in covering up all evidence of their own wrongdoing, and prolonging their investigations till the matter has been forgot!" He smiled suddenly. "But only listen to me grumble, when I should instead be full of gratitude. I know now that I was not responsible for the loss of all those lives; I have taken back my self-respect and my wits—"

"Such as they are," inserted Falcon.

"Such as they are," agreed Jonathan with a chuckle. "And at least I am not obliged to languish in prison, which I'd thought very likely."

"Had Admiral Chetwynd not come so eloquently to your defence," said Falcon, "you'd not be sitting here now."

"Very true! He's a grand old sea dog, is he not? He told me I owe his intervention to Lady Lyme-Rufford. I gather he courted her when he was a young man."

"I wonder he didn't win the lady," said Morris. "He has a silver tongue."

Falcon said, "Even was it studded with gems, I still say Armitage was let off surprisingly easy. The League was more of a threat."

"We can't prove those varmints were aiming at Jack," argued Morris.

Falcon fixed him with an incredulous stare. "The ball that was fired at our carriage on Monday made a hole in his tricorne. The knife that came through the window yesterday missed him by a hair. I should have realised that both were intended for you! What sorry assassins the League hires to—"

He was interrupted as Tummet rushed into the room balancing a laden tray precariously. "That 'orrid 'ound, guv," he panted, kicking the door closed behind him. "Be the death o' me, 'e will! Not that you'll care," he added.

A deep bark resounded in the hall. Morris grinned and suggested that Falcon give Apollo to Jonathan.

"Certainly not," said Falcon. "Miss Rossiter would never forgive me if the League put a period to the animal. You must learn how to deal with him, Tummet."

"I shoulda brung back one o' them Cornish spells," grumbled Tummet, setting his tray on a handsome sideboard.

"I know a few," said Falcon obligingly. "If you wish someone ill, you've only to drop a toad on his doorstep, and he'll be visited by the most wretched luck."

Tummet said, "Even if that 'orrid 'ound 'ad a doorstep, which 'e don't, it wouldn't do no good. Show 'im a toad and 'e'd likely eat it. 'Course," he added, brightening, "I could give 'im a bag o' feathers! A long and painful dee-mise! That'd serve 'im right fer—" Given pause by Mor-ris's aghast stare, he looked at two other arrested expressions and said uneasily, "Cor, I don't never mean it, gents! A 'orrid 'ound 'e might be, but I wouldn't wish 'im a slow death!"

Jonathan said quickly, "Besides, 'tis all superstitious non-sense."

"And those stupid spells only work on—on native born Cornish people," said Morris.

Falcon laughed. "I collect I must be prepared to awaken some night and find a charmer or diviner waving a de-ceased fowl over my bed, or some such thing, to break the spell! Wake up, Tummet! Must you stand there with your jaw at half mast? You're here in the capacity of a valet—try behaving like one!"

Tummet blinked, and unstoppered a decanter.

Morris asked, "Given any more thought to the Suez busi-ness, Jack?"

Jonathan took the glass of Madeira Tummet offered. "My brain's numb from puzzling at it. Suez is always bus-tling, of course, but I can recall nothing outlandish occur-ring when last I was there."

"Wouldn't 'ave to be nothing outlandish, mate," said Tummet, thrusting a generous measure of cognac at Falcon. "Mighta bin some cargo being moved what shouldn't oughta bin. Or some ship wot shoulda bin somewhere else."

Jonathan sighed. "We've gone over those points a dozen times. If there was something of that nature, I know nought of it."

Morris complained, "Not going to forget me, are you Tummet?"

The valet, who had been staring at his employer in a disturbed fashion, offered another glass and declared with his broad grin, "Can't ferget you, mate. Got a good 'eart you 'as."

"There's a thought." Quite aware of his man's furtive and apprehensive scrutiny, Falcon said, "What about hearts, Armitage? Any blatant *affaires de coeur* being conducted? I fancy there were plenty of British people about?"

"Always." Jonathan blotted out the yearning of his own heart, and the memory of a certain lovely lady in East Bourne. "Government servants, employees of the Company, merchants—what have you—coming across the desert from Cairo, and waiting for East Indiamen to carry them on to Aden and India. Others, preparing to return home."

Falcon shuddered. "The desert conjures up appalling visions of heat and flies. Not the place for affairs of the heart, I'd think."

"You're out there. Suez has some fine hotels, and the air is very fresh and invigorating. Quite a number of young ladies travel that way in search of advantageous alliances, and are undismayed by the desert journey. Though I've often thought it must be hard on their chaperones, and people of more advanced years. I recall one English lady who seemed so frail, yet betrayed no sign of fatigue. I heard later that she had been badly burned in her youth, and that her health was uncertain, but she was singularly sweet natured and uncomplaining. Her sister, though! Gad, what an odious woman! A voice like a nail on slate, and—"

Falcon all but leapt from his chair. "The *Buttershaw* dragon?" he exclaimed.

Morris choked on his wine and Tummet pounded at his back until he begged for mercy.

"Was that her name, Armitage?" demanded Falcon. "Lady Clara Buttershaw?"

"I've no idea. I think I was never introduced to the lady. I assisted her sister once when she tripped on the veranda steps, is all."

"Miss Jennifer said the men she overheard in Plymouth spoke of Suez and three years ago. That would have been

'45. Was the Buttershaw woman from Town in '45, my clod?"

"How the deuce would I know?" said Morris. "I was with my regiment in the Low Countries, and—"

"Well why had you not the sense to be in England when you were needed? Oh, have done with your feeble excuses. Describe the large lady, Armitage."

"Jove ... 'tis three years. You describe her for *me*, and I may recollect."

Falcon sprang up and began to pace up and down in his excitement. "She is tall and hatchet-faced, and I think has never said a conciliating word to anyone—"

"Except you, my tulip," put in Morris with a grin.

All too aware that the usually cantankerous Lady Clara Buttershaw had a pronounced *tendre* for him, Falcon scowled at him. "Have you anything sensible to offer?"

"Her sister," Morris offered, "is the Lady Julia Yerville, and as gentle as Lady Clara is harsh. Her voice is very soft, indeed she speaks in a sort of—er, breathless whisper, and—"

"And she always wears white!" exclaimed Jonathan, his eyes glinting.

"She does!" cried Falcon exuberantly.

"We have it then!" Morris checked and added dubiously, "Or have we? Perhaps Lady Buttershaw was merely visiting relations in Calcutta or Bombay, or Karachi, or—"

"Or Timbuctoo, or Tooting!" exploded Falcon. "Have done with your geographical gibberish!"

Jonathan grinned and pointed out, "We can scarce charge the lady with treason only because she chanced to be in Suez three years ago. The worst that could be said of her conduct was that she seemed to delight in antagonising everyone she encountered. Except for the Frenchman, apparently, but—"

"Frenchman?" Falcon, who had sat down again, demanded, "What Frenchman? Did he travel with them? Do you have his name?"

Jonathan frowned, racking his brain. "He escorted them about once or twice and dined at their table, but he certainly was no courier, if that's what you mean. It struck me as rather odd, because one night I chanced to see him leaving their room in the wee hours. He was looking back and speaking very softly, but when he saw me he turned red as fire and rushed off. As to his name, I've not the remotest notion. Nor can I think that my having stumbled upon so trite an incident would constitute a danger to the League."

"Depends on the way you look at it," argued Morris. "Take a snail, for instance. It don't alarm *me* to see one, but to a cabbage it might mean death!"

"Then you'd best guard your head," snapped Falcon, "for a snail would take it for a cabbage any day! Jack, this may have been a far from trite incident. It sounds most smoky to me! You must have noticed *something* about the fellow! Cast your mind back! It may be of great importance!"

Jonathan groaned and put a hand over his eyes. He said slowly, "He was strikingly good looking, I remember that. Not above forty."

Morris asked, "Dark? Fair?"

"He wore powder ... Jupiter! I don't recall anything more. I only saw him for a brief— No—wait! There was one thing. He had an odd sort of gait. Held his right thigh when he walked—almost as if he was making it move, but—"

"My ... dear ... God!" gasped Morris.

They both stared at him.

He shook his head dazedly. "No—no, it can't be!"

Falcon said, "You're chatting with an idiot. Be so good as to include us in your conversation."

Morris blinked at him. "I saw him in the Low Countries. He's—he's a legend! The darling of France ... I can't believe—"

Falcon's eyes widened, he said in hushed incredulity, "*Barthélemy? Is that* who you mean?"

Morris gave him a half-embarrassed, half-apprehensive look. "It couldn't be! I mean—*could* it?"

"Do you speak of Marshal Jean-Jacques Barthélemy?" asked Jonathan.

Tummet whistled softly. "That's gorn and done it, that 'as! 'E's a real tartar, 'e is!"

Falcon said, "Wasn't he seriously wounded in some battle or other?"

Morris nodded. "Lauffeld. The doctors wanted to amputate his right leg, but Barthélemy wouldn't have it. Rumour says the leg's been a nuisance ever since."

"I heard he's the most ambitious man in Europe," said Jonathan slowly. "In which case—he might very well be—"

"Be involved with the League!" Falcon exclaimed, "Zounds! Rossiter must hear of this, and fast!"

Morris said uneasily, "If the League is dealing with France, the Horse Guards should be told of't."

Falcon regarded him pityingly. "My poor blockhead. Do you never learn? We suspect General Underhill of being one of 'em. If we trusted the Horse Guards with this we'd very likely be invited into a dungeon at the Tower and never live to tell another soul anything!"

"I may be a blockhead," said Morris stubbornly, "but I've not got so grand an opinion of myself as to know what to do in this case."

Jonathan said, "Nor I. Perchance your friend Rossiter will have the answer."

"Very likely." Falcon looked solemn. "But meantime I think it best that we say nothing of this to anyone. Are we agreed?"

Morris hesitated, but at length agreed, and Jonathan pledged his word also, then came to his feet. "I must get on my way if I'm to reach Dover while the light holds."

"Stay in touch with us," said Falcon. "You have opened another door for Rossiter's Resistance."

"When the time comes," Jonathan told him, "I'll go through that door with you! I've some long overdue debts to settle!"

"I think we are being foolish past permission," said Jennifer, turning with a sigh from Lady Lyme-Rufford's front gates. " 'Tis nigh three weeks, Duster, and not a word, not a line."

Duster, who never seemed quite at ease on a shoulder smaller than that to which he was accustomed, bobbed up and down and offered his latest remark, which appeared to have something to do with drinking "the third glass."

"Very true," agreed Jennifer absently. "But, I know him, you see. If things go badly, he will not come. Or is that conceit, do you fancy? Might he have long since decided 'gainst coming back at all?"

She wandered slowly up the drivepath. With the approach of evening the house was bathed in the glow of a magnificent sunset. The scent of honeysuckle hung on the warm air, and birds were making a great to-do in the trees as they hurried home. All of which was lost upon Jennifer. "If he should come," she told Duster, "I shall have to greet him with disdain, for he did not tell me that he was wed. Great Aunt said the poor lady only lived a little while, but—he should have told me, Duster. On the schooner, he had remembered her. I am certain that is why he was so . . . distant."

Duster appeared to become impatient with her topic, and with much squawking spread his wings and fluttered back towards the gate.

"No! Oh, you naughty bird! Come back here at once!" cried Jennifer running after the small creature.

She heard the pound of hooves then, and her heart gave such a lurch that she was sure it would break through her ribs. The tall rider with one arm in a sling set his mount at the hedge, cleared it in fine style, and was out of the saddle and running before his horse had come to a halt.

Jennifer uttered a small sob and, quite forgetting both disdain and propriety, picked up her skirts and ran to meet him.

A gardener trudging home with his tools stopped and gawked at her.

"*Jennifer—Britewell!*" called an indignant voice from the front steps.

Jennifer paid no heed to her aunt's disapproval and reached out yearningly.

Scant inches away, Jonathan plunged to a halt. He took up her hand and pressed it to his lips, but saying nothing, strode past.

Lady Lyme-Rufford, awesome in her outraged dignity, was suddenly just an elderly lady who stepped back, uttered a small shocked scream, and was swept up in one strong arm, whirled about, and kissed whole-heartedly.

"Oh! You wretch! How dare you?" she gasped, her bright eyes and glowing cheeks betraying her. "Put me down at once!"

"How may I ever thank you?" Jonathan set her on her little feet again, and smiled down at her. "Admiral Chetwynd told me that 'twas your letter persuaded him to intercede for me. His defence won me my freedom."

"Well you may tell me about it inside the house," said my lady. "And you shall overnight with us. Oh, my goodness, only look at that bird! Let that be a lesson to you, Jennifer! All men are fickle!" Duster had landed on Jonathan's shoulder and was scolding him fiercely. Struck by uncertainty, Lady Lyme-Rufford asked, "He *is* a gentleman bird, isn't he? Oh well, never mind about that. Heavens, how different you look! Quite the dashing Corinthian! Samuel!—Captain Armitage's hack! William!—our best guest suite for the gentleman, and hot water! At once! Mary!—tell Chef to set dinner back half an hour, and if he faints, throw a jug of water over his wig. Captain!—we shall expect you in the withdrawing room in twenty minutes exactly, for I am quite twittering with eagerness to hear your news, and Jennifer is—well, never mind."

And so, over a long and excellent dinner, Jonathan told them most of what had transpired in Town, his gaze lingering often on Jennifer's lovely face as she listened raptly, her eyes shining, and a becoming blush on her cheeks. When he finished, she asked, bewildered, "What does that mean, exactly? Are you reinstated? Will you be given another command?"

"I am neither condemned nor reinstated. But I think they

299

must acquit me, eventually. As to whether I shall be offered another command—" He shrugged. "I don't know."

She said fiercely, "Well I think they are a lot of—of muck-worms! They should have awarded you a medal, *and* your back pay, *and* your prize money! What about Lord Green and this dreadful League of Jewelled Men? Would they listen to what you had to say on that score?"

He gave a wry smile. "Falcon was right. I was reprimanded for associating with . . . now how did they word it? 'A group of bored young aristocrats having nothing better to do with their time than to circulate false and malicious accusations 'gainst gentlemen they happen to dislike.' "

"Oh, how *can* they be so stupid?" said Jennifer in exasperation.

"If they were not, they'd never rise to be government servants," snorted my lady, taking up her cane. "Now, I am tired and 'tis past time for me to get to my bed."

Jonathan stood at once to pull back her chair and usher her into the hall.

At the foot of the stairs she murmured with a twinkle, "The moon is very bright tonight, Captain. And my gardens offer a charming walk."

He lit her candle and handed it to her. "So I had noticed, ma'am."

"I thought you may have." She looked up at him. "My, how tall you are. Not above a half hour, if you please."

When he returned her smile but said nothing, she put a hand on his arm and said, "You kissed me, but I did not see you kiss my grand-niece. Am I mistaken in thinking you had something to ask me, Captain?"

He said slowly, "I can no longer claim that title, my lady. In truth, I think I shall never again be the master of a ship, even were a command offered me. I am not rolled up, but for the moment I am not able to—to ask your permission to—"

The smile faded from her eyes. She interrupted, "You are aware that Jennifer is something of an heiress?"

His chin lifted. He said, "No, ma'am. I was not aware."

"And I have put your back up, I see. Pride is a great

thing, no matter what some strait-laced humility-ridden dullard may tell you. But, I'd not see my grand-niece hurt, Jonathan. Don't let pride smother your chance for happiness."

Five minutes later, strolling in the fragrant, moonlit garden, Jennifer was beginning to think her chances for happiness were lost after all. The man to whom she had given her heart was beside her, he was safe and his arm was almost healed; the terrible weeks of waiting were over, and they were alone together in an idyllic setting for romance. Yet not once had he attempted to kiss her or to speak the words of love she so yearned to hear.

Even as she had the thought, her arm was seized and she was wrenched to face him. "Jennifer," he said huskily, gazing into her hopeful eyes.

"Yes, dearest?" she answered provocatively.

"Jennifer ..." He bit his lip, drew back and began to walk on again, then said in a strained voice, "You told me you have heard from your family?"

Offstride, she answered, "Yes—er ... Oh, yes! My great-aunt was furious when I told her how Papa had tried to make me marry Hibbard Green. She sent off what I suspect was a very fierce letter to him, and ten days later, Tilly came to us, with his reply. He asked that I go home at once, Johnny, and—"

"The devil!" Once again she was jerked to a halt while his eyes searched her face. "You will not?"

She leaned to him and murmured lovingly, "Don't you want me to, my dear one?"

He released her, but said fiercely, "I'll have a word with Lady Lyme-Rufford at once!"

"No!" She caught his hand. "Do not disturb her. She would not let me go."

"Do you say you *considered* such a foolish step?"

She sighed. "Howland is very ill, Johnny. It seems that Hibbard Green deceived him into believing he had found gold in the Blue Rose. Oh, 'tis not so outlandish as you may think. Gold has been found here in times past. Green convinced my brother that it must be kept very secret, or we would have all the world digging about the mine. Howland began to be suspicious, but he was too involved by then, and could not get clear. When his lordship decreed that we must all be killed, Howland tried to stop him, and was shot down. Papa wrote that he is getting better, but—but has not as yet the use of his legs. He wants to see me and beg my forgiveness for the way he treated me."

"I am sorry for him. Is Green still at Triad?"

"No. Tilly said he and his men went back to the mine after we sailed away, but next day there was no sign of them. Papa is helping the village people rebuild their homes, and"—she smiled sadly—"Lord and Lady Morris have evidently been exceeding generous."

"Noble of 'em," said Jonathan ironically. "Did any of the military ever put in an appearance?"

"A naval midshipman and several army officers arrived just as Tilly was leaving. She says my father told them some tale of a fight with wreckers. The village folk would say nothing, of course. Poor souls. At the end they stood by us, Johnny."

"Even so, I'll not have you going back there."

Joy and hope were reborn. Swaying to him, she asked, "What do you . . . propose, Captain Armitage?"

"Mr. Armitage," he corrected, releasing her hand so as to run his fingertips down her temple and along the delicate curve of her cheek.

Jennifer shivered, and closed her eyes.

The moonlight bathed her lovely face. Leaning to her, Jonathan had to call up all his self-control before he could manage to draw back. "I—propose," he gasped, "that we leave very early in the morning, ma'am. I have something to—to show you."

Disappointed, she opened her eyes and looked at him uneasily. "Where?"

"In Dover. My—er, sister is there. I find that in trying to clear my name, she also lost the home and inheritance her husband bequeathed her. I must—somehow—repay her. She is betrothed now to Gordon Chandler, a splendid man. Had I told you that? I forget, but—"

"You forgot to tell me one thing," she said, interrupting the nervous rush of words. "That you were married."

He had started to walk on, but at this he jerked to a halt and stood rigid and silent.

"Why did you not tell me, Johnny?"

He stared at the moonlit path, and said, low voiced, "I would have, if I'd remembered it."

"You remembered when Mr. Taylor spoke your name, I think. But still you did not tell me."

"No." Looking anywhere but into her wistful eyes, he said, "I had thought, you see, that you would be better off with me, even in poverty, than wed to Hibbard Green. That however bad it might be, we would be together. What I'd very stupidly not foreseen was that I might not even be able to offer you my—poor protection, for I could very well be sent to prison for my dereliction of duty. Perhaps even hanged. And you would be left all alone, which was not to be thought of. So I had no right to speak, and there seemed no point in—in telling you about . . . Lillian."

She thought tenderly, 'How dear that his every thought was to protect me.' And she said, "But now you are not in prison, nor condemned to death, and still, you did not tell me."

He took a deep breath. "What do you want to know?"

"What she was like. Whether you loved her very much. Whether she was a good wife."

They walked on, and after a small pause he said quietly, "She was tiny. Golden hair and blue eyes, and flawless pale skin. So very lovely, but—a fragile, almost ethereal loveliness. From the time she was in the nursery, artists would want to paint her. My father's portrait of her is quite famous. You may have heard of it."

Jennifer said in awed disbelief, "Not—not the one they call 'Lily of the Valley'?"

"Yes!" He asked eagerly, "Have you seen it? My sister tells me it was sold."

"Fleming is acquainted with the Earl of Elsingham, and I was so fortunate as to be invited to his country seat last year. It is a great castle near Falmouth, and the earl is a rather formidable gentleman, but he likes Fleming, and was very gracious. The portrait hangs in the Great Hall, and is one of his most prized possessions. I was quite in awe. Your wife was indeed exquisite. Had you been long acquainted?"

"I knew her all my life. Everyone loved her, but when we were children she used to cry because she couldn't climb trees or swim in the pond, or jump her pony over the hedges, like the rest of us, for the least injury would make her ill. It was an arranged marriage. We both were very young but we were perfectly content with the arrangement. And—yes, I loved her. Only . . . I lived with fear, because I had to be away a great deal and she was so delicate. She was devoted to me, and she had such plans . . ." He stopped talking, and then said abruptly, "She did not even live long enough to celebrate our wedding anniversary. When I look back, I see her more as—as a precious thing of beauty that shone on my life very briefly, and that I scarcely dared to touch for fear it might shatter and be gone."

She clasped his hand and tried not to be jealous of the beautiful Lillian. But she was afraid and it took all her courage to say, "Now that you remember her, Johnny, perhaps your feelings for me have—changed. I shall quite understand if—"

He jerked his hand away, and demanded harshly, "Will you come with me? We would have to overnight, but my sister has a cottage on the estate, and you could stay with her. It would give you a chance to—er, to become acquainted."

He had not responded to her question, but at least he wanted her to meet his sister. She said, "Yes, of course. I will like to meet her."

❧ *Chapter 18* ❧

It was quiet and very peaceful in the garden, and seated on a stone bench, Jennifer looked about her with delight. Jonathan had told her something of Lac Brillant as they drove through the sweeping park, but she'd not envisioned anything so breathtaking. The mansion consisted of three separate white stuccoed villas in the Italian style, set in a wide crescent. The extensive gardens were bright with flowers, and several quaint little bridges crossed the meandering stream. A great fountain sent delicate plumes high into the warm afternoon air. Fine trees provided a verdant frame behind the houses, the tower of a small chapel could be glimpsed nearby, and to the south was the rich blue sweep of the Channel. She did not quite understand why Johnny had asked her to wait here, rather than taking her up to the mansion, but she thought she had never seen such a beautiful estate, and was quite content to sit down and admire it.

She was gazing dreamily at the chapel when he spoke her name.

She stood, smiling as she turned to him.

He looked pale and anxious and somehow pleading. And with him were two small boys, about five years old, she thought, and so much alike that they could only be twins. Their fair curls were lighter than their father's, and their eyes were deep blue, rather than his cool grey, but the resemblance was strong and the relationship unmistakeable.

Stunned, she knew at last why he had been so hesitant to speak of marriage.

Her eyes flashed to meet his. He said, his voice strained, "May I make my sons known to you, Miss Britewell? Thorpe, Jacob, make your bows."

They responded obediently, but their eyes never left her, and she knew she was being appraised critically from top to toe.

"How do you do?" she said, trying to be calm. "I expect you must be very happy now that your papa has come home."

"We are," said the boy she thought was Jacob.

"Aunty Ruth takes care of us," said Thorpe.

"She's pretty, too," added Jacob.

"And we don't want to go 'way," said Thorpe with faint defiance.

"I can see why." Jennifer sat down again. "This estate is—is like fairyland. It must be lovely to live here."

A pause, through which they stared at her.

Then, "Papa says you live by the sea," said Jacob. "In a castle."

"An' he says you like boys," added Thorpe doubtfully.

She said, "I like boys, and girls. I wanted very much to have some children of my own, in fact. But, sad to say, I will never have any."

"Oh." Intrigued, Thorpe edged a step closer. "Why?"

"Because some ladies aren't able to have babies. I'm one of them."

"If you'd got some," said Jacob, coming up on the other side, "how many would you have wanted?"

"Lots and lots," she answered. "But—I'd have been so happy to have been given even one."

Another pause. The two pairs of blue eyes bored at her.

"We've got a hedgehog," said Thorpe.

"His name's Being," supplied Jacob.

Jennifer laughed, clapping her hands. "What a good name!"

They looked at each other. Thorpe asked, "Would you like to see?"

"I would, indeed."

They were away, knees pumping, heads back. One of them called cheerfully, "P'raps she won't take him away."

"She's not as pretty as Mama's picture. But she's got smiles in her eyes."

Jennifer stood and walked into Jonathan's arms. After an ecstatic moment, he drew her down beside him on the bench. "You don't mind? I was so afraid—"

"Foolish, foolish man! Didn't you think I meant it when I said I had longed to have children? Oh, my dear—they are so splendid! I shall—I shall have a family, after all! If"—she wiped away a happy tear—"if you mean to ask me."

"Ask you? I mean to implore you! But—darling, darling Jennifer, I have so little to offer you!"

"You have already given me a gift I treasure above all others." She lifted the golden locket she wore, and opened it. Inside was a seashell, small and fragile and of a rare beauty.

Looking at it, the past swept back, and Jonathan was so overcome that his eyes blurred. He said gruffly, "It is a poor gift, but—"

Her fingers touched his lips. "It was given with love. I want to have it put into a proper setting, and I shall wear it proudly. And now, you offer me the family I thought I'd never have. Only . . . your sons seem devoted to your sister, my dear. And they love this beautiful place."

He took both her hands and held them tightly. "I hope to be able to offer you a proper home in time, dearest heart. I've quite a sum set by, but it is in the care of my dubash— that is to say, my general steward, in Calcutta. He's a splendid fellow and will be wondering when I mean to return. I've written instructing him to arrange for my funds to be sent here, but in the meantime—well, it seems that the Chandlers have been long in need of a good bailiff. Sir Brian, he's Gordon's father, has offered me the position. It is a far cry from what you deserve, my love, or what I once could have laid at your feet. But—if you were willing there's a charming house that goes with the offer. The old fellow is extreme fond of the twins, and— Oh, my beautiful, brave, and most adored love—could you—would you stoop so low as to consider . . . ?"

The lady from the castle threw her arms about the neck of the village idiot, and there was no doubt as to her answer.

They were married ten days later, by special licence. The ceremony was performed in the small thirteenth-century chapel at Lac Brillant. Jennifer and Jonathan's sister, Ruth Allington, were already fast friends, and Jennifer was overjoyed when her brother Royce came to give her away. Lady Lyme-Rufford looked very spry and saucy on the arm of a distinguished gentleman named Admiral Chetwynd. Sir Brian Chandler attended, with his son Gordon, who was soon to marry Jonathan's sister, and James Morris and August Falcon arrived from Town accompanied by Falcon's sister, Katrina, who was a striking beauty, as dark as her brother and with the same intriguing slant to her midnight blue eyes. Last to arrive was Joe Taylor, shy and self-effacing, but overjoyed to commence his new duties as his Captain's manservant, and losing no time in gravitating to Tilly's side.

The weather was chilly and overcast with a tang to the air and much whirling about of falling leaves that spoke of the coming of autumn; wherefore the wedding reception was held in the building known as West House. A small orchestra played in one corner of the ballroom, a delicious supper was set out in another corner, and when the meal was done there was dancing.

Everyone agreed that the bride was radiantly lovely in her gown of white satin with tiers of lace on the skirt of the under-dress and edging the décolleté neckline. Jonathan led her out in the first country dance, his worshipful eyes bringing shy blushes to her cheeks. Very soon afterwards they slipped away and across the park to the fine house they would share with Jacob and Thorpe. Tonight, the only other occupant was Tilly, who giggled as she helped her mistress change into a nightdress that was a cloud of ivory silk and lace, and then giggled her way out of the house.

When the door closed behind her, another door opened, and Jonathan went to claim his bride.

Enchanted by the love in her eyes, he took her in his arms. His kiss left her breathless, but was more passionate than any she had known, so that in her innocence, she trembled. Smiling at her, he asked tenderly, "Don't you know yet how much I adore you, my beloved? Don't you know how I dreamed of this day—and this night, when we could be alone together?"

Shyly, she murmured, "And I also, darling, darling husband . . ."

With a blissful sigh, Jonathan blew out the single candle.

He had, however, omitted to close the door.

The sound of a small crash and a great deal of confusion and squawking drifted up the stairs.

Jennifer hid her face in her bridegroom's shoulder, but could not stifle her laughter.

Groaning, Jonathan left the warmth and promise of the four-poster, and crossed to the door. He did not slam it shut, as his bride had expected, but instead grumbled his way downstairs and into the parlour where hung a large and gilded birdcage.

"I suppose," he muttered, "you think you have every right to be rewarded."

"Bobby!" said Duster, adding a somewhat confused, "Take third glass!"

"Thank you—no." Jonathan busied himself with a package he'd left on the table. "Now . . . ," he said. "I do not want to hear from you again tonight, you feathered marplot!" And he went eagerly up the stairs to his beautiful bride and the safe harbour of her love that was so deep and true, and that had been given to him when he had abandoned all hope of happiness.

He left behind a cosy parlour that was silent now.

Perhaps Duster was appeased, who shall say? But if there was any billing and cooing in the house that night, it did not come from the small blue bird in the large gilded cage—over which was spread a cover of purple velvet.